AFTERGLOW

Then Leah's eyes found him. Richard. Standing before the fire. Broad back and long legs formally clad in black coat and matching trousers. Dark hair gleaming in the firelight.

The devil in evening clothes, backlit by the flames.

She made no sound—unless it was the soft movement of her gown that alerted him to her presence—but his back stiffened, his head swung around, and his obsidian eyes met hers through the haze. Her sudden lack of breath was anger at having to wed where she would not, or so she told herself. But as he sauntered toward her, her aching heart once again warned her that she lied.

Also by Janmarie Anello

FOREVER YOURS

Published by Zebra Books

A DANGEROUS MAN

Janmarie Anello

ZEBRA BOOKS
Kensington Publishing Corp.
www.kensingtonbooks.com

ZEBRA BOOKS are published by

Kensington Publishing Corp.
850 Third Avenue
New York, NY 10022

All Kensington titles, imprints, and distributed lines are avail-
able at special quantity discounts for bulk purchases for sales
promotion, premiums, fund-raising, educational, or institu-
tional use.

Special book excerpts or customized printings can also be created to fit specific needs. For details, write or phone the office
of the Kensington Special Sales Manager: Attn. Special Sales
Department. Kensington Publishing Corp., 850 Third Avenue,
New York, NY 10022. Phone: 1-800-221-2647.

Zebra and the Z logo Reg. U.S. Pat. & TM Off.

ISBN-13: 978-1-4201-0001-3
ISBN-10: 1-4201-0001-7

First Printing: May 2008
10 9 8 7 6 5 4 3 2 1

Printed in the United States of America

Chapter One

London, 1821

"The Duke of St. Austin to see you, sir," the butler intoned from the library door.

"Well, what are you waiting for? Show the man in."

Thaddeus Jamison stood in the center of his book room, its shelves stuffed to overflowing with leatherbound volumes he collected as a testament to his wealth. His heartbeat quickened. His chest felt tight as a surge of anticipation rushed through him. He was playing a dangerous game with a powerful man, and all of his dreams hinged on the outcome of this meeting. He had to remain calm, in control, or lose before it even began.

When the door swung open, Jamison drew a steadying breath, then turned to meet the man approaching him with a swift and forceful stride.

Richard Wexton, the sixth Duke of St. Austin, was the pinnacle of aristocratic elegance and everything Jamison longed to be. Power and authority were etched in every line of his face, from his firm, high cheekbones to his strong, square-cut chin. The raven hair that fell in reckless disarray about his face conveyed an air of negligent grace, while the haughty tilt of his head and proud, squared shoulders spoke of an arrogance ingrained through the ages.

There was no doubt about it. The man would breed fine sons, and Jamison wanted him for his daughter.

"Thank you for agreeing to meet with me on such short notice," the duke said. His baritone voice rang with the easy self-assurance one would expect from a man of his station, and Jamison couldn't help but smile.

"Not at all, Your Grace. Would you care for a refreshment? Perhaps a glass of claret?"

"No, thank you. I would like to come straight to the point, if I may."

"Certainly." Jamison gestured to the leather-padded armchair facing his mahogany pedestal desk before returning to his seat. Sunlight from the bay windows behind him glinted off the polished desktop. He moved a ledger to block the glare. "How may I help you, Your Grace?"

"I am here on behalf of my brother," he said. "I understand he lost a substantial amount of money to you at cards last night. I would like to settle his debt."

Jamison grabbed a quill from the standish. He ran his fingers up and down the feathered tip as he carefully worded his response. He eyed the duke. "He was your brother, you say?"

A flicker of amused disbelief flashed in the duke's black eyes. "Are you implying you didn't know who he was?"

"No, I did not. Truth to tell, until a few moments ago, I thought he was you. He said he was St. Austin."

Not a hint of emotion crossed the duke's face. "That is a very serious and upsetting claim. And, I might add, somewhat difficult to believe."

Jamison flung the quill to the floor and shot to his feet. "Do you dare to imply that I lie?"

"Not at all," the duke replied without hesitation. "It merely seems my brother neglected to provide me with all the details of his encounter with you. Perhaps you would care to enlighten me?"

Jamison gave a stiff nod, then settled back on his seat. "The lad claimed he was St. Austin. I thought it strange, a duke in a place like that—The Pigeon Hole ain't real popular with the titled folk, don't you know—but I saw no reason to doubt him."

"I see." The words were clipped, controlled, the slightest tightening of his jaw the duke's only visible reaction before he continued in a cool voice. "Please, allow me to apologize for any inconvenience this misunderstanding might have caused you. You may rest assured, I will deal with my brother when I get home. If you would present me with his vowels, I will settle them for you."

Jamison crushed his shaking palms against his knees, all the while praying he could keep the quiver from creeping into his voice. "I'm afraid it might be a trifle more complicated than that."

"What do you mean?"

The words, spoken with icy disdain, sliced through the air like daggers hurled at Jamison's chest. Sweat drenched his neck even though the temperature in the room seemed to have dropped twenty degrees. He yanked his handkerchief from his waistcoat pocket and swiftly mopped his brow. "Well, he was pretending to be you. So he signed his note with your name. And lest you don't believe me, I have the note to prove it! It seems what we have here, Your Grace, is a case of forgery and fraud, not to mention the insult given me by this deception."

"I see. Exactly how much did Geoffrey lose?"

"Thirty thousand pounds."

"A significant amount of money indeed." The duke flicked his hand through the air. "Although no excuse, Geoffrey is young and given to rashness as all young men are. How much would it take to rectify this situation and alleviate the pain you suffered from this deception? Would, say, sixty thousand pounds suffice?"

"You insult me again!"

"Forgive me," the duke drawled in a voice that implied he was anything but sorry. "I fail to see how an offer of sixty thousand pounds could be construed as an insult."

"I do not want your money."

"It is merely a settlement to ease the anguish you suffered from this deception."

The condescension dripping from the duke's voice made Jamison seethe. "I do not want your money," he bit out. "I do not need it. I own most of the cotton mills in Lancashire. I've no doubt I have more money than you!"

The duke relaxed in his chair and crossed a booted foot over his knee. His sun-darkened features were perfectly composed, but the eyes that studied Jamison over steepled fingers were as hard and unforgiving as the jagged cliffs that carve the northern coast of Devon where Jamison had lived as a boy. Bitter memories of gnawing hunger and ragged clothing flashed through his mind.

At that moment, he hated the duke for his privileged birth almost as much as he coveted his noble title and envied his cool composure. Good God, how could the man look and act as if they were discussing the weather rather than a criminal act that would cast shame and dishonor upon his family name?

Suddenly, the duke smiled. It was more a savage baring of teeth than an expression of amusement. "Exactly what is it you want?"

A shiver coursed over Jamison's skin. This was it, the moment for which he had waited a lifetime. He perched on the edge of his chair. "I have a daughter. A lovely girl, just eighteen. As sweet and biddable as you please."

He stabbed his finger through the air. "I want you to wed her. In return, after the birth of an heir, I will give your brother's note to you. If you refuse, I will have no choice but to go to the authorities."

The duke grinned. "What an amazing man you are. You think lying beneath you, and yet, you've managed to refine blackmail into a true work of art."

Jamison bit back his angry retort. "What will it be, Your Grace? A scandal? Or a wedding?"

The duke said nothing. He merely arched one thick, black brow. He kept his keen eyes trained on Jamison as he waited, seemingly undisturbed by the silence between them.

Jamison fought the urge to wiggle beneath the duke's unrelenting stare. He had come too far to turn back now. He clenched his fist. "I repeat: What will it be?"

The duke laughed. "Although I admire your ingenuity, I fear I must decline. A cotton miller's daughter is hardly suitable material for a duke's wife."

"There is nothing unsuitable about Leah," Jamison retorted. "She is pretty enough to look at, but her dowry is the real prize. Two hundred fifty thousand pounds, plus more at the birth of an heir. Such wealth makes her acceptable to any level of the nobility, eh, Your Grace? It's done all the time, ain't it? If you don't agree, your brother will find himself in the Fleet."

The duke shrugged. "A few months in the Fleet will not kill him. Then again . . ." A wry smile graced his lips. "Let Geoffrey wed the chit as payment for his debt. It is a supremely fitting punishment, and given the option of a wedding or gaol, even he would choose the wedding—"

"Oh, no, Your Grace, that won't do. The boy's a tosspot as well as a gamester. I have no desire to see my money lost at the tables. Besides, I'm of a mind to be grandfather to a title. It will have to be you, or no one."

"Then it will be no one."

Jamison slammed his fist on the desk. "If your brother's

treachery becomes public knowledge, the Wexton name will be synonymous with scandal and dishonor."

"Scandal is nothing new to the Wexton name, so that threat holds no weight." The duke rose from his chair. He pulled tan kid gloves from his frock coat pocket and slowly drew them on. "Better men than you have tried and failed to bring me to the altar with their 'ever so sweet and biddable daughters.' Go to the authorities, with my blessing. But remember, extortion is also a crime. You will find yourself in the Fleet right beside Geoffrey."

He pivoted on his heel and headed for the door.

"I do not think you want to do that," Jamison called after him, his voice laden with quiet confidence.

The duke swung around and fixed him with his cold, dark stare.

"Your brother was deep in his cups." Jamison shook his head in mock dismay, then heaved a heavy sigh. "Drink. Loosens the tongue, don't you know. Things get said that are better left unsaid. Things of a delicate nature. Very delicate, I'd say. And once a rumor starts, well . . . there is no calling it back, is there?"

The duke took two steps forward and flattened his palms on the desk. His eyes flashed with lethal promise as he towered over Jamison. "I am not sure what you think you know," he said in a voice gone soft and deadly. "But take caution if you dare to threaten me."

"Threaten you?" Jamison held up his hands. "No, you mistake the matter. 'Tis the truth I'm talking about. How can the truth hurt? Unless, of course, one is afraid of the truth. Tell me, St. Austin, are you afraid of the truth?"

The duke narrowed his eyes.

Confident now that he had the man right where he wanted him, Jamison smiled and leaned back in his chair. "Before you refuse my offer, you should contemplate that scandal . . . then think of Lady Alison."

Chapter Two

"Should we send for the doctor?" Leah Jamison pushed the auburn hair off the young boy's brow. His skin, slick with sweat and sticky beneath her palm, was growing hotter by the moment, and still he shivered.

Mrs. Bristoll, her cheeks ruddy from boiling a posset of milk and ale, placed the steaming cup on the sideboard by the make-shift bed. They had moved Thomas into the pantry in hopes of keeping the illness from spreading to the other children. "Do not worry yourself, miss. 'Tis only a childhood grippe. It will pass."

Leah's doubt must have shown on her face, for the stout matron patted Leah's shoulder, as if she were one of her charges. The scent of sorrel and red sage rose from her apron. "The posset will sweat the fever from him. He will be up and about by tomorrow. I promise you that."

The illness had come on so swiftly, Leah greatly feared it was much more serious than a mere childhood complaint, but Mrs. Bristoll had years of experience caring for children. Surely she must know of what she spoke.

With a sigh, Leah gathered her cloak. She did not want to leave, even though she knew she must. Her father would suffer fits if she did not appear properly dressed at their evening meal. Provided she remained the dutiful daughter, he did not seem to care how or where she spent her days, though she shuddered to think what would happen if he learned of her visits to the foundling home.

No, she could not risk it. She had to go.

She cast a last, lingering look at Thomas. Huddled beneath the blankets, he looked too small, too helpless. If only her father were a different man, she would scoop the boy into her arms and carry him home. She pulled her hood up over her hair. "You will send word if he worsens?"

"Of course," Mrs. Bristoll said. She escorted Leah to the door, waiting until she climbed into her carriage before disappearing back into the house.

As the carriage rattled its way over the cobbled streets, the crumbling, overcrowded tenements of St. Giles soon gave way to the beautiful homes of Bloomsbury Square.

The stark contrast never failed to startle Leah.

Her first warning that she had stayed away from home too long came when she climbed from the carriage and noticed that the afternoon sun had given way to dusk. The second came from her aunt's frantic greeting at the door.

"Where have you been? You are late," Emma said, her hands fluttering through the air. Tufts of gray hair had escaped from the knot at the base of her neck and now curled wildly about her cheeks. "Your father wishes to see you in his library. He is in such a state. Hurry, my dear. Hurry."

Her aunt's obvious distress was so at odds with her usual placid demeanor, Leah cringed. Papa must be furious indeed. She handed her cloak to the waiting footman before heading through the hall. "Any hint to the crisis?"

Emma shook her head as she scurried to match Leah's rapid pace. "But he set the servants to searching for you over half an hour ago. As Alexander chose that moment to call, you can well imagine your father was not pleased."

No, he would not have been, as Papa had no liking for

Alexander, though Leah could not imagine why. A kinder, more respectable young man had never existed. "I was not expecting Alex until this evening. Did he leave a message?"

"The dear boy was most apologetic," Emma said, a tender smile softening her harried expression. "He cannot escort us to the theater tomorrow, as he had hoped. An urgent summons from his grandmother has called him to Suffolk."

Oh, bad news indeed, but Leah had no time to dwell on this pronouncement, as the library door had snapped open and her father was glaring at her, his lips curling as he took in the soggy state of her frock.

When he lifted his hand, Leah stepped back, but not quickly enough to keep him from grabbing her forearm and dragging her into the room. He propelled her toward a gentleman who stood facing the bookshelf on the far wall.

The stranger did not turn or give any indication that he heard the commotion behind him. The exquisite cut of his clothing revealed a powerful frame blessed with long legs and glossy black hair curling roguishly over a pair of stunningly broad shoulders. Hands crossed behind his back, he held his head high and his spine straight in the easy, graceful stance of a man supremely confident of his worth.

A magnetic attraction about his person drew all of Leah's inner awareness and pulled her closer, her feet moving her toward him as if of their own volition, or perhaps it was her father's hand pushing on the small of her back. When the man finally turned, Leah found herself staring into the eyes of the devil himself.

Who else but Satan could possess such unrelenting black eyes, as dark as the midnight sky with no hint of light? Who else could seduce her senses so swiftly, so thoroughly, that she was unable to speak or decipher her father's words through the buzzing in her ears?

Surely there could be no other explanation for her gaping stare, as if he were the first handsome man she had ever seen, which was decidedly untrue—Alexander was quite the handsomest man she knew—but Alexander's beauty was like basking in sunlight, not drowning in the bewitching, dark, brooding visage of an underworld lord.

"Leah," her father said, his anger at her tardiness evident in his sharp tone, but it was the underlying glee lurking in his voice that swung her gaze to his face.

His wide smile and gleaming eyes did not bode well for whatever words he was about to say. "Leah, my dear. May I present to you, the Duke of St. Austin." His chest expanded as he took a deep breath. "Your betrothed."

Leah blinked. Her mind went blank, as if her wits had suddenly scattered like raindrops on the wind. After the perfidy of his past actions, she had thought nothing her father could do or say would ever surprise her again.

She had been wrong.

Her breath rushed from her lungs. She turned to the duke, but her brain had yet to start working again. She watched as his dark gaze dropped to her lips, then traveled over her face in a slow, sensual caress, before wandering back to her eyes.

Good Heavens, her skin actually tingled, as if he'd swept the back of his knuckles over her cheeks. She expected him to deny her father's outrageous announcement, but he said nothing. He simply stared at her through obsidian eyes that revealed no emotion.

She held up her hand. "This is a jest, is it not?"

"I assure you, Miss Jamison, it is not." The deep timbre of his voice sent heated shivers over her already burning skin, then he bowed. "I must bid you good day."

She could find no fault with his exquisite civility, even as he turned, leaving Leah to gape at his back as he strode from the room then moved through the hall, the sharp rap of boot heels on marble the only sound in the stillness, then even that tapping drifted off into silence.

Her words became trapped in her throat. Not that she knew

what she wanted to say. This was shock, she realized. The same choking sensation, the same swift pain in her stomach, the same swirling dizziness she had suffered on the day her father had turned her sister out of the house.

After five long years, she still felt the pain of his betrayal. Now this! "What have you done?"

Papa fairly pranced to the sideboard. "I've caught you the best fish in all England, that's what. He's a prime one, he is, and you stand there all sulky. You should be dancing circles 'round the room at your good fortune."

"Good fortune? Did you see his face? He hates me! He doesn't even know me, why would he want to marry me?"

Her father splashed liquid amber into his glass. "Your dowry, my dear." He punctuated each swallow of brandy he took with a satisfied sigh. When he finally downed the last mouthful, he swiped his hand across his wet lips. "When a man has enough money, he can buy anything he wants—even a duke—and I've got money to spare."

There was a gleam in his eyes that told her he lied.

"One day, you will thank me for this," he crowed.

"Thank you? For forcing me to wed where I would not?"

She doubted he even heard her words, so happy was he, throwing out names and dates and titles.

"Please, Papa," she said, touching her hand to his arm. "Do not do this. I beg you. I am perfectly prepared to do my duty, but I want to wed a man *I* love. A man who loves me . . . a man like Alexander Prescott."

"You would choose that piddlin' pup over a duke?"

"There is nothing wrong with Alexander. He is a fine man. And he cares for me."

"What does that have to do with this?"

"It has everything to do with it. I want to marry a man who loves me. As you loved Mama."

He turned his head so that she could not see his eyes.

"That was different," he said softly, almost gently, a glimmer of the man she remembered from her childhood, the man he used to be before her mother had died, before money and power became his only passion. Then his jaw hardened. "Think, girl. You are going to be a duchess."

The hard line of her father's chin jutting out past his teeth told Leah further discussion was futile. "You must excuse me, Father. I have duties to which I must attend."

The frantic beat of her heart brought a sticky sheen to her skin as she strode toward the door.

"I know you don't believe me," he said as he followed her from the room, "but I did this for you. I could not let you waste yourself on that ne'er do well, Prescott. He is not good enough for you."

She should keep walking. She should not let him goad her into further discussion, but she could not let him insult the one person who truly cared for her well-being. "No. He is not good enough for *you*. Alexander is a fine man and a dear friend. And were he to ask, I would deem it my *very* great honor to marry him."

"But he ain't never asked, 'as he?"

The slip in his diction would enrage him more thoroughly than any retort Leah might make. She picked up her skirts and walked with quiet dignity up the stairs.

She would not allow him to see his words hit their mark. While she had long cherished a tender regard for Alexander, they were friends, nothing more.

Yet, on more than one occasion since her arrival in Town, she had caught him staring at her with an intensity that brought a blush to her cheeks. In her foolishness, she had allowed herself to hope, to dream of a future.

Now, instead of sunshine and laughter, she was betrothed to a man with devil-dark eyes that had seemed to devour her, that had seemed to see into the deepest part of her soul. Until her father had spoken. Then his eyes had turned hard and cold and unrelenting, glimmering with fury.

Was she to marry a man who hated her?

To endure his contempt for the rest of her life?

No, it was insupportable.

She had always tried to be the dutiful daughter, but she could not do this. She could not marry a man who despised her.

Chapter Three

Richard strode up the steps of his Park Lane mansion. He threw open the door before his butler could reach it and stalked through the hall. "Where is Lady Alison?"

"In the gardens, Your Grace," the servant said, tripping along beside him. "With Mrs. Parrish. They are to dine *alfresco* this evening." The butler's tone held no hint of alarm, no indication that all was not as it should be.

The crushing weight in the center of Richard's chest gradually eased. Of course, he had known she was home. Of course, he had known she was safe. Still, there was that one moment of gut-clenching panic when that bastard, Jamison, had mentioned her name. Had Richard possessed a weapon at that moment, the man would have been dead.

Then again, he had never suspected his true enemy lived within his own home. "Inform Lord Geoffrey I wish to see him. Immediately."

Without waiting for a reply, he flung open the library door and marched straight to the sideboard, where the finest selection of whisky awaited him. He chose a potent highland brew, letting the pungent liquid roll over his tongue, but he strongly suspected it would take the entire bottle to burn away the bitter taste of this day's disgusting events.

He prowled the room, a savage anger pushing the blood through his veins. He could not help but feel a grudging admiration at the skillful maneuverings of his adversary, even as he vowed he would have his revenge.

Innumerable options presented themselves. With each came the delicious vision of seeing his enemy squashed like the repellent insect he was—but not one, short of murder, would guarantee the bastard would keep his tongue between his teeth. *Damn his eyes.* As much as it would bring him pleasure to kill the cur, Richard found he had not sunk quite so low as to shoot a man in the back, even if the bastard deserved it.

Which left only one option. Marriage to the man's daughter.

Richard stripped off his cravat, tossed it onto the desk, rubbed his hand over his throat. She was either the greatest actress ever born to Britain, or a complete innocent in her father's vile scheme. The startled, wide-eyed look on her face as her father had announced their betrothal had seemed unaffected, as had her color change from a healthy, tanned glow to the pasty hue of the sickroom.

No—startled was too mild a word to describe her face at that moment. Horrified would be more accurate, as if she had awakened in the middle of a nightmare only to discover she hadn't been dreaming after all. It was a feeling with which Richard was all too familiar. Was she a willing accomplice? Or innocent victim? Did it even matter? He had to marry her.

He had to protect Alison.

Damn Geoffrey and his recklessness!

How could he drag Alison into his schemes?

Richard paused at the grate. Hand resting on the mantel, he stared into the fire, but he didn't see the flames. All he saw was the bronzed gold of Miss Jamison's hair.

Oh, she was beautiful, Richard would grant her that.

When their eyes first met, his senses had scattered, and his mind ceased to function, and all he could see were her eyes and her lips and the sensuous shape of her breasts rising and falling in her hideous dress. In those few brief moments, unwanted—unwelcome—desire had surged through him, stronger and faster than ever before, until his body had tightened and his breathing had shallowed.

Then her father had spoken, and his senses returned, along with the memory of where he was and why he was there.

Geoffrey shuffling into the room pulled Richard from visions of wide, green eyes dusted with amber.

It was her eyes, he decided. Her eyes had bewitched him.

"You wished to see me," Geoffrey said, stopping just inside the door. His bleary-eyed gaze still bore witness to last night's debauchery, as did the stench of smoke and ale oozing from his uncombed hair.

Perhaps he should wait to confront his brother.

In his present temper, Richard greatly feared he might lay violent hands upon him.

He quickly vetoed that idea and poured another drink.

This time the fool deserved a beating.

"Yes, Geoffrey, I did." Richard grabbed the bottle of whisky before sauntering over to his desk. He sprawled in his leather-backed chair, stretched his booted legs out before him, and fixed his brother with a penetrating stare. "I just returned from a most fascinating meeting."

Geoffrey pulled his right hand down the side of his face. "And?"

"It seems you forgot to provide me with a few, oh, minor details. Would you care to enlighten me now?"

"I do not know what you mean."

Richard arched a brow, but said nothing. He was too busy grappling with the urge to wrap his fingers round his brother's neck and throttle him.

"I suppose you are referring to the vowels," Geoffrey

said as he ambled closer, his low voice dissipating into the cavernous room.

"Yes, Geoffrey. The vowels. The forgery. The fraud. The deception that could result in your hanging from a noose."

Geoffrey's lips pulled back. He rubbed his hand over his neck as he lowered himself onto the chair facing Richard. "It . . . it was not my fault," he stammered.

"It is never your fault. Tell me, please, how you could fail to remember you went to that hellhole pretending to be me!"

"It was a mistake," Geoffrey said, babbling now in a breathless rush. "I never claimed to be you. You had given me money, so I bought tankards of ale and gin for everyone round the table, and I said 'compliments of the Duke of St. Austin.' They assumed I was you! It was not my fault."

"Amazing." Richard waved his glass through the air. "Do go on, Geoffrey. You have piqued my interest."

"Well, the play got deep. Then the others left until only Jamison and I remained—and you know the rest! I lost a lot of blunt and had to give him my promise to pay."

"Except you signed your vowels with my name."

"What else could I do?" Geoffrey pushed from his chair. "I could not very well tell him, then, that I wasn't who he thought I was."

"Did you never think he would find out?" Richard exploded, rising to face his brother, hand tight on his glass. "Christ, Geoffrey, you asked me to intercede for you. The man is not an idiot. If he hadn't already determined the truth, do you not think he would have realized it today?"

Geoffrey flung his arms through the air. "What harm was done? You've paid the man, have you not?"

"I will tell you what harm was done, you stupid, irresponsible fool. You told him about Alison!" Richard rubbed his hands over his face, then glared at his brother. "I truly want to kill you. Were we not brothers, we would be meeting over pistols as we speak."

Geoffrey slumped his shoulders. Moisture gathered in his eyes. "I was so foxed, I thought I dreamt that part. I remember him asking me questions, question after question, but I was so high in the altitudes . . ."

"I assure you, it was no dream. And you can be certain that leech knew exactly what to do with the information."

"What do you mean?"

"I mean, I had to sell my soul to guarantee his silence." Richard topped off his glass and raised it in a mocking toast. "You may wish me happy, brother. I'm to wed the miller's daughter."

Geoffrey's eyes widened. "You cannot be serious?"

"What would you have me do? Allow him to announce to all and sundry every sordid detail of our family history? I swear to Christ, if it were only you, I would have let you rot in gaol."

"I am sorry," Geoffrey said. "So sorry."

"Sorry is too little too late," Richard snapped. Trying to rein in his temper, he rubbed the aching muscles at the back of his neck. A sudden weariness throbbed through his bones. "I did not even realize you knew . . . how did you learn the truth?"

Geoffrey stared at him through haunted eyes. "You forget. I lived with them. Rachel flaunted that news before Eric every chance she could. She did not care if I was in the room or not. I do not understand, if she hated him, why did she marry him?"

Richard snorted. "For the title, of course."

"She made his life miserable. I swear she drove him to his death."

"No doubt you are right," Richard said, gripping his glass. He stared into the golden liquor, mind closed to the memories and betrayals that had led to disaster. His skin was cold, despite the languid heat of the whisky in his belly. "Why did

you go to that hell? Why not go to one of your clubs with
your friends?"

Geoffrey did not respond. His face was the same bleak
gray as the marble monument marking their eldest brother's
grave. The ticking of the mantel clock was the only sound in
the room.

Richard strode to the window.

The sun was just now casting its last feeble rays before
sinking into darkness. He did not know what to do anymore.
He only knew Geoffrey was chasing disaster and seemed
determined on taking the family down with him.

An unbearable thickening at the base of his throat threatened to choke him. He had already lost one brother.

He had no intention of losing another.

"Come here, Geoffrey. Tell me, what do you see?"

His eyes rolled heavenward, but he hobbled to the window.
"Torches. Servants. A summerhouse. Roses."

"Yes, and inside that summerhouse is a young girl who
needs not only your discretion, but, more importantly, your
protection." Richard met his brother's gaze. "If you cannot
mend your ways for yourself, think of Alison. Think of me.
And remember this warning. If you ever endanger her well-
being again, by word or by deed, I will kill you myself."

Geoffrey pressed the heels of his hands to his eyes as he
nodded. His chest heaved, once, twice. "I swear to you,
Richard. I mean to change my ways."

Richard could only hope this was true, but he had heard the
words too many times before. Still, his brother had the shattered appearance of a man reaching the bottom of his own
private hell, only to realize he'd destroyed everyone he loved
on his journey down the cliff.

Perhaps this time, there was hope.

Geoffrey drew a strangled breath. "So, when do you get
yourself buckled?"

"As soon as possible. I want to silence that bastard."

Richard thought for a moment. "Rachel is hosting a ball two days hence."

"Yes. One year to the day of Eric's death."

"Not too eager to shed her black gloves, is she?" Richard murmured. He sipped his whisky. "I believe I shall procure a special license and do the deed that afternoon, then present my wife to the *ton* at Rachel's soiree."

He smiled, for the first time finding the slightest bit of humor in this sordid situation. "It should provide ample entertainment. I must admit, I rather relish the thought."

Geoffrey laughed. "It is perfect. Will you inform Rachel of your plans?"

"No." Richard stared at his reflection in the window.

"That could be dangerous for your new bride. What of Lady Montague?"

Richard grimaced. No, Margaret would not be well-pleased. "She can find out with everyone else. I do not think she could keep the secret."

"You are truly going to marry this girl? What is she like?"

Richard thought of sun-kissed hair and satin skin that flushed so prettily. "I have no notion, but I am sure to find out, more pity that."

"Why? Why must you wed? Eric never denied Alison. Even if Jamison spreads his tale, no one could prove it was true."

"But the damage would be the same, regardless," Richard said, refilling his glass before stretching out on his chair. "You know as well as I, the truth does not matter in the face of the latest *on dit*. Alison's name would be bandied about like so much garbage. And when she is old enough to make her come-out, it would all start again."

Their whispers would precede her into every room, and follow her out again when she departed. She would spend her life the object of malicious speculation and gossip, knowing her parents had betrayed her, as they had betrayed everyone around them.

Richard would not let her suffer that.

He'd rather wed the Jamison chit. Perhaps, after the deed was done, he would simply stash her away at his Cornish estate and forget he ever met her. Yet even as the thought took shape, a vision of her tumultuous green eyes rose in his mind and he strongly suspected she would not be easy to forget.

A rap on the door broke the silence.

"Enter," Richard commanded.

The butler stepped inside the room. "Pardon me, Your Grace. A Miss Jamison is here. She begs a moment of your time on a matter she says is quite urgent."

Richard told himself the sudden surge in his gut was anger. He certainly wasn't eager to see her again.

"Where is she, Harris?"

"In the gold salon, Your Grace."

"You will have to excuse me, Geoffrey. My anxious bride awaits." He drained the remaining liquid in his glass, then rose and walked on not-quite-steady legs to the door.

Damn. He was a trifle foxed. Perfect.

Chapter Four

The moment the duke strode into the room, Leah realized she'd made a dreadful mistake. The sardonic lift of his brows, the insolent curve of his lips, the raw, unleashed power as he moved, all warned her exquisite civility was gone.

His bold gaze swept over her person in a languid perusal that was as scandalous as it was shocking and made her skin burn as if she were bundled up with hot coals.

He did not stop walking until the tips of his boots touched her leather-clad toes, until she breathed the exotic scent of his skin, a sensuous, mysterious blend of jasmine and amber and spice. As much as it irked her to show any weakness, she took a step back, needing to put distance between them.

Arms crossed over his chest, he leaned on his heels and watched her retreat through his smoky black eyes.

Firelight flicking red and gold shadows over his face made him appear more than ever the underworld lord. His hair was disheveled, as if tossed about by the wind.

"Miss Jamison," he said. "I find myself . . . surprised."

This was her moment to convince him they could not possibly suit, but she only just realized he'd left off his neck cloth, and his shirt was unbuttoned, revealing a dark, intriguing shadow at the base of his throat.

She forced her gaze off to his left, to the burnished gold, damask-covered walls, to the crimson brocade draping the windows. The luxurious appointments confirmed her worst fears.

The duke did not need her money.

Her father had tricked him into the match. But how?

"And a bit puzzled," he continued, his voice coldly mocking, yet infused with a smoldering sensuality. "Your father assured me you were as 'sweet and biddable as you please.'"

This was an ill-conceived plan, she realized that now. Still she had to convince him to withdraw his proposal.

"But I fear he might have misled me," he said. He took her right hand in his, his fingertips feathering over the sensitive curve of her wrist. "For what sort of biddable miss would visit a man, alone in his lodgings, at night."

Dressed in rags, his gaze said, as he glanced down her person, though he did not speak the words.

So much had changed in the last few hours, she had not even realized she still wore the same paisley frock as she had worn this morning, wrinkled and stained from her visit to the foundling home. No doubt he was usually surrounded by elegant women with their satins and lace.

A moment of feminine vanity caught her wishing she'd donned a more flattering dress, one that highlighted the gold of her hair and the green of her eyes.

She thrust the foolish thought away. She was not here to attract his attention. She needed to convince him to withdraw his proposal, but he was talking circles around her.

Not to mention what he was doing with his hands, his thumb circling over her palm. The sensual motion set off a dull ache in her belly, a fluttering of her pulse, a rapidity of breath that left her quite dizzy.

"It is a decidedly dangerous and foolhardy action," he said, his low voice wrapping around her. "Then again, what does your reputation matter, given that we are already betrothed?"

He thought she had come here for seduction. Of course, what else would he think when she had yet to say a word?

"Come, come, Miss Jamison. Do not be shy. There is no shame in wanting to get to know your betrothed."

"For your information," she said, finally gaining control of her senses, "I have come here to tell you I cannot possibly marry you." She pulled her hand from his grasp, then linked her fingers together to keep him from reaching for her again.

"Why ever not, Miss Jamison? Is my title not high enough? Do you, perhaps, aspire to be queen? Unfortunately, our dear king is already married." He tilted his head and stroked a finger along his beard-roughened jaw. "Twice, actually, though he denies one and tries to shed himself of the other. So perhaps there is hope for you, after all. It might not be a prudent match, but I do think your dowry would tempt him."

Outrageous, as he had no doubt meant it to be. She was tempted to laugh. She wished she could think of something equally sardonic, cutting and witty, but she had no wish to bandy words with this man. "I have no desire to marry you, sir, and, I am quite convinced, you have no desire to wed with me. If you would only withdraw your offer—"

"Now there you are wrong, Miss Jamison. I do wish to wed with you."

"Why? Why could you possibly want to marry me? You do not even know me."

"For the usual reasons, Leah. I may call you Leah, may I not? As we are about to wed, we need not stand on formality. Please, call me Richard."

"What are the 'usual' reasons, Your Grace?"

Her refusal to use his given name brought forth a low chuckle. "As your father so eloquently phrased it, *Leah*, you are pretty enough to look at . . ." His sultry gaze made a languorous sweep from her eyes to her throat, to the swells of her bosom, which suddenly seemed too much exposed, though she knew the cut of her dress was modestly demure. ". . . but your dowry is the real prize."

His face betrayed not a hint of emotion, but his voice came out husky and low. His swift inhalations seemed to match the pace of her own frantic breathing.

She glanced pointedly around the room, noting the Flemish tapestries, the Persian carpets, the Roman antiquities. "Yes. I can see where you desperately need my money."

The treacherous man smiled. The rigid planes and forbidding frown of the cold and arrogant nobleman melted away, revealing a hint of the boy behind the man, a mischievous rogue with dimples and laugh lines framing his eyes. "I admit I do not have pockets to let, but one can never have too much of the ready. . . ."

His voice dropped to a whisper as he leaned toward her, bringing his mouth so close to hers, she could feel his breath upon her lips. "Leah."

She found herself unable to move as her capricious heart pulled her on toward disaster, as she realized she loved the sound of her name spoken in his rough, rumbling voice.

Suddenly, she was afraid. This man was dangerous.

She had to make him understand as quickly as possible and return to the safety of her home. "I know my father is forcing you to marry me, but if we stand together and refuse—"

"You know nothing of the sort. I am marrying you for your dowry and for no other reason."

"—but if we stand together and refuse," she persisted. "We can make him understand that we cannot possibly suit. Or perhaps I could simply cry off. Then the blame will be all mine." The words left her mouth before she thought through the implications. Her father would be furious.

Dark brows shot up. "You would jilt me? Becoming a duchess does not appeal to you? I assure you, it is a most sought-after prize."

"It has never been one of my dreams," she said, unable to

hide the disgust in her voice. "I want to wed a quiet country gentleman and live a quiet country life."

His nostrils flared as he leaned toward her, closing the little distance remaining between them. "And do you have a beau, Leah? A tender lover waiting for you at home in the country?"

"Yes, but I—"

A ruthless gleam lit in his eyes. "Do you fancy yourself in love with your swain?"

Throat constricting, Leah nodded.

"And have you given yourself to him?"

"I . . . I do not know what you mean—"

"I mean, have you given him the gift of your virtue?"

His vulgar words cut through the mists of attraction.

She longed to send her palm swinging toward his cheek, but she had degraded herself enough simply by coming here. She would not degrade herself further.

His face was scant inches from hers.

She could clearly detect the scent of strong spirits on his breath. Why hadn't she noticed this before?

Because you were too busy gaping at his good looks, she thought in disgust.

"Have you?" he snarled.

Her jaw ached from clenching her teeth. "How dare you insult me so?"

"I think, perhaps, you protest too much."

"I think, perhaps, you cannot think at all. You are disguised, Your Grace. And you are disgusting."

He lowered his head until his mouth was just a breath away. "I'm not too deep in my cups . . . Leah." Her name escaped on a whisper as he touched his lips to hers.

Oh, he was wicked to kiss her like this, his mouth moving hot and hard over her lips. Sanity warned her to push her hands against his chest and demand he release her, but she found herself unwilling, unable, to do so.

His arms slid around her, his large hands pressing into her

spine, drawing her closer until her breasts were crushed to his chest. Instead of pain, she felt a strange, tingling ache, a physical longing, a yearning unlike anything she had experienced before. The scorching heat of his kiss was like fire licking over her skin. This was more than a mere touching of lips.

This was a claiming. A branding.

A soft sound escaped from her throat, and he pulled back, staring into her eyes as if searching for answers to questions unknown, before possessing her lips once more in a kiss so demanding, the world spun away, and all she could feel were his lips on her mouth, hard, yet supple, unrelenting. Then, oh, God, dear God, his tongue was in her mouth and it was beyond anything she had ever imagined.

This was passion, this onslaught of sensation. Her hand rising, stroking his hair, finding it surprisingly soft, sensuously smooth against her fingertips. His scent, jasmine and amber, filling her senses. His breath, hot and sweet with a faint taste of honey blending with spice. An ache burning low in her belly. She clung to his shoulders.

She did not understand her pull toward this man, but there was something so right about this moment, something so powerfully moving. Then everything changed, as his kiss grew more urgent, more reverent, more moving, and his hands traced her cheeks, feathered over her jaw, until he finally thrust her away.

His breathing was ragged, his eyes dark and demanding.

She grew so afraid, not of him, but of what she was feeling. She thought she should speak, but she could not form the words. She tried to turn away, but he captured her chin in his hand.

"You will wed me," he said. "In two days."

She shook her head as she tried to push past him, but he captured her arm before she could make her escape. She couldn't bring herself to look at him. She was too ashamed, and all she could think was two days, two days . . .

His hand clamped around her arm, he led her through the antechamber to the entryway. Mere seconds passed before the butler appeared with her cloak in his outstretched hand.

Richard grabbed it and wrapped it around her shoulders.

It was useless to resist. She did not even try.

Did she look as disheveled as she felt? Did she look like a woman who had been thoroughly and repeatedly kissed?

She chanced a glance at the butler.

He stood stiff and tall, his eyes carefully averted.

"Escort Miss Jamison home and see to her safety," Richard instructed a nearby footman, then he lowered his head and whispered in her ear, "Two days."

Richard watched her fly out the door and down the steps, a half-dozen footmen racing to keep up with her. Once she was safely ensconced in the carriage, he stumbled back to the salon, slouched down on the settee, dropped his head onto the cushions.

That he had caused her trembling fear made him itch to shove his fist into the wall. She was right. He was despicable. His words had been coarse and vulgar, his actions crude.

What malicious demon had possessed him to attack her like that? Why had he felt such a blinding, raw rage at the thought of her in the arms of another man?

He did not understand his bizarre reaction.

It was not as if he loved her, or wanted to marry her. She was an inconvenience being thrust upon him by trickery and deceit. So why should he care?

Yet she had seemed so sincere as she'd told him she did not wish to marry him, that they could not possibly suit.

And again, his mind churned with the dilemma.

Was she a total innocent? Or a vicious schemer?

He did not know what had caused him to kiss her. He tried not to think of the taste of her lips, the innocent abandon with which she'd surrendered to his kiss, her eyes darkening with passion, hands running through his hair. Only the realization that he had been mere moments away from pressing her to the floor and ravishing her had given him the strength to thrust her away.

Good God, it must be the whisky.

Either that, or he was insane.

The faint scent of roses lingered in the room. He breathed deeply, letting the fragrance fill his lungs. Good God, now he was acting like a moonstruck calf.

So, she was beautiful. So what?

She was also the woman he was being forced to wed.

Evil schemer or a total innocent, he did not care. He did not want a wife. Especially one thrust upon him through trickery and deceit. So what if her hair was the color of spun gold and felt like the finest silk?

So what if her eyes were the green of sparkling emeralds, her skin smooth and pure, untouched by the rouge-pot?

Her lips . . . her lips . . .

The heavy throbbing in his groin told him exactly what he wanted her to do with those lips.

Richard jumped to his feet. He needed a woman. Any woman would do. A quick trip to his mistress would cure the fever Leah had fired in his blood.

Chapter Five

Richard flung himself onto a chair before the fire in the reading room at Brooks's. He ordered a bottle of brandy and stared into the hearth, as if he would find the answers to his dilemma in the flames. His body was hard and aching, yearning for release from the desire Leah had stirred within him.

Much to his self-disgust, not only had he *not* buried himself between Margaret's oh-so-willing thighs, he had found himself breaking off their arrangement, with no good reason other than the fact that he could not banish from his mind the image of Leah's haunting eyes.

Or the sweet, sultry taste of her lips.

Not to mention her bold assault upon her enemy, which he found himself admiring now that the whisky haze had dissipated, almost as much as he cringed when he remembered his own base behavior and his coarse words.

For Richard had no doubt she was a virgin. Even as he'd attacked her virtue, he had known she was a total innocent. He only wished he knew if she were as innocent in her father's despicable blackmail scheme as she was in the ways of the flesh. Did it even matter?

In two days, they would wed.

"Heigh-ho, Richard. You look as if you have just buried

your boon companion." Pierce Daimont flopped onto the wing-back chair flanking the fire. He ran his hands through his hair, pushing the sandy curls back from his brow. His roguish smile matched the good-natured gleam in his eyes. "Since *I* am your boon companion, I know that cannot be true. At least, I think I'm still alive, but after last night's debauchery, I might be dead and have yet to realize it."

Richard found himself smiling despite his foul mood.

"Looks as if you've drained this one already," Pierce said, grabbing the bottle from the table between them. He signaled a passing servant for another, then flashed Richard a lopsided grin. "Are you in for a night of drinking and gaming? Or drowning your sorrows?"

Richard raised his glass. "Drowning my sorrows. Care to join me?"

"Absolutely." Pierce took the decanter and glass from the servant who had appeared at his side, then waved the man away. "Truly, you look fit for the grave. What has happened?"

Richard shrugged, strangely reluctant to give voice to the tale, even to the one man he trusted with his life. They had forged a deep and abiding friendship during their schooldays at Eton. They'd shared personal triumphs and bitter tragedies, both at home and during the war. Richard knew the man buried beneath the reckless façade and was proud to call him friend. "Your news first. When did you return to Town?"

"Only just. I called at your house but Geoffrey did not know where you were. As I had no other engagements, I thought I'd make the rounds until I caught up with you."

Richard leaned forward. "Do not keep me in suspense. Tell me what happened at Greydon Hall. Why the urgent summons?"

"You will never believe it." Pierce took a long swallow of brandy. "Do you remember when Greydon's son drank himself to death? It was just before my father died? Well, last week, his grandson and heir got himself killed in a duel over some redheaded wench, or so I am told. The shock was too much for the old goat. When he heard the news, he closed his eyes and never opened them again."

Pierce stared into the glass he held cradled between his palms. "It seems sad, you know. To outlive your children, and your children's children. I never really thought about it before, but it does not seem quite right . . . anyhow," he said, swiping one hand over his face before breaking into a grin. "As I am the nearest male relation, you find yourself gazing upon the new Viscount Greydon."

"I suppose I must now address you as *my lord*," Richard drawled.

"Absolutely. And I shall expect a proper amount of respect from you, as well, now that I am among the ranks of you high-flyers. Who would ever have thought . . . "

Richard knew his friend was torturing himself with painful memories and sought to drag him back to the present. He raised his glass. "Here's to you, my lord."

"Right-o. Here's to me," Pierce said with a laugh. "Now you. What has happened?"

"I am to marry, two days hence."

Pierce choked on his drink. "You cannot be serious!"

"Oh, but I am. Quite serious."

"Forgive me, Richard, but you must admit, this is quite a shock. Before I left for Greydon Hall, you never said a word."

Richard clenched his jaw against the fury he held under tight control, but he could not mask the bitterness in his voice as he related the tawdry tale. "Ever since Eric died, I've had more outrageous schemes and proposals cast my way than I care to count—it sickens me. But this. This was a clever trick. This whoreson was the first to use my family to bait his trap."

"Egad," Pierce said. "However did he discover—"

"Geoffrey, of course. Stewed to the gills and babbling at the mouth." He rubbed his hand across his brow. "I tell you, Pierce, I do not know what to do anymore."

"Leave him alone and let him destroy himself," Pierce said,

his features grave as he gazed at Richard over the rim of his glass. "He is not going to stop, no matter what you do or say."

Richard gave his friend a hard stare. "You speak from experience, of course."

"Of course," Pierce agreed cheerfully. "Ever since you mended your wicked ways these twelve months past, haven't you tried to reform me? To lead me down the straight and narrow path of righteousness like some evangelistic minister? And have I listened to you?"

"Dammit, I cannot do it. He's my brother." Richard clenched his fist on the arm of his chair. "It is not easy to sit back and watch someone you care for try to kill himself."

Pierce had the good grace to flush.

"Tell me about your bride," Pierce said, pulling Richard from his latest fantasy of tearing his brother apart. "What is her name? Is she beautiful? Is her body? Tell me everything."

Beautiful? Yes, but not in the classical sense of fine lines and a delicate air. Leah's was a captivating beauty, sensuous and earthy with her dusky green eyes and golden blond hair. Good Lord, just thinking about the way she had felt in his arms made his body harden, made his blood surge.

This was bad. "Her name is Leah Jamison."

"Leah Jamison? I've heard that name before."

"Perhaps you know her family. They originate from Lancashire. In fact, I believe their estate is not too far from Greydon Hall."

"Possibly. But I do not think so . . ." Pierce tapped his chin. "Ah, yes, one of Randall's friends is always going on and on about a Leah Jamison and her beauty, her Christian charity, her eyes, her ears, her nose, her mouth . . . could it be the same girl?"

Richard grimaced. "Do you remember the color of her eyes?"

"How could I forget? Green. Not just any green, mind you, but a lush, leafy green, shining like a sparkling pool of shimmering water in spring. The boy is positively ears over head for the chit."

"It is the same girl," Richard muttered. Now he was going to have to deal with some lovesick puppy. He remembered Leah telling him that she wanted to marry some country bumpkin and inexplicable anger hissed through him.

Why should he care if she wanted to marry another? She would wed with Richard whether she willed it or not.

He flexed his hand. "What is this fop's name?"

"Alexander Prescott. Sir John's son. He and Randall met at Greydon Hall some years ago. Geoffrey must know him. They would have gone to school together."

"I am sure he does." Richard stared into the flames. "I am sure he does. Would you care to witness the deed?"

"Can't, old chap. Have to meet with the solicitors in the morning and set out for Greydon Hall by early afternoon at the latest. Tedious business, this. Mayhap you could postpone a week or so? I could be back by Friday next."

"No," Richard said. "I want the evil deed done as soon as possible. Stop by when you return and I will introduce you to my bride. Now hand me that bottle, and call for another. I want to forget about today, tomorrow, and yesterday. In fact, I want to be so high in the altitudes, I cannot think at all."

Her visit to the kitchens the next morning was a mistake, Leah realized, as the conflicting scents of cooking grease and roasting meat caused her stomach to lurch. Still, she could not wallow in her room, immersed in self-pity, or take to her bed with a fit of the vapors, as had her aunt. Though she was tempted.

"Are you unwell, Miss Jamison? You look a bit pale," the cook said, shuffling toward the wooden pedestal table with a dozen loaves of freshly baked bread cradled in her arms. Most of her beet-colored hair was tucked up beneath her cap.

The few strands clinging to her brow emphasized the concern in her eyes. "Shall I heat the kettle for tea? It would take but a few minutes."

Leah sent the servant a shaky smile. "No, no, Mrs. Hawkins. I am well. Just a bit tired." Which was not quite a lie, as she had spent most of the night tossing about in her bed, haunted by the devil's black eyes. And the taste of his lips. And the sensual sweep of his hands. "Though I wonder if you might spare a few jars of your famous currant jelly? And perhaps a wedge of your best cheese?"

Plump cheeks blushing with pleasure, the cook nodded. "For you, miss, anything. I'll be just a moment."

Leah stacked the warm loaves into the large wicker basket on the table. When her father had announced his plans to bring her to London, she should have suspected what he was about, but all she had thought of was Alexander. How dreadfully she had missed him since he had joined his family in Town for the season. How she had feared he would fall in love with someone else while he was away. Now she was the one on the verge of marrying another. All her childhood dreams were dying.

Tomorrow was her wedding day.

She rubbed her hands over her aching eyes, then pressed her fingertips to her cheeks, as if she could smooth away the burning heat. Tomorrow was her wedding day!

A day she had envisioned for years.

She would wear roses in her hair and the most elegant gown ever created. Her joy too great to contain, she would smile and weep as she walked down the aisle on her father's arm while her groom awaited her arrival with his love shining proudly in his eyes. Always in her dreams, Alexander was the one who stood there waiting. Now, she could not see Alexander's face, or the chapel, or the roses.

All she could see were the duke's eyes, blazing with emotion, burning with need. All she could feel was the heat of his hands holding her, touching her as no one else ever had. All she could dream of was his kiss.

A full day had passed and she could still taste his kiss.

Leah groaned as the flood of memories quickened her breathing and the beat of her heart. She was drawn to him in a way she did not understand. He consumed her thoughts. He possessed her soul. But he did not love her.

Was she wrong to want to marry for love?

Was she a fool to hope that someday he might come to love her? Did she want to marry him even without his love?

If she were truly honest with herself, Leah had to admit that she did. But not like this. If only they had met at a garden party, or at a soiree, or at any of the other places where men and women usually meet. If only he wanted to marry her for who she was, her beliefs and her dreams . . . if only he loved her.

He was so handsome with his curly black hair and his charcoal eyes, his hard, chiseled cheeks and his breathtaking smile. But it was not simply his looks that called to her.

From the moment he had taken her into his arms, from the moment they'd kissed, she had felt connected to him in a way she did not understand and could not explain. His pain was her pain, his desire, hers, and beneath it all, a quiet need that had called to her, as if she and she alone could ease his loneliness.

Or perhaps it was her own loneliness she had tasted, her own desperate need. She chided herself for her foolish notions, but she felt them all the same.

The clink of glass hitting glass pulled her from her torturous thoughts. The ache in her belly remained.

"Here we are," Mrs. Hawkins said, arranging the jam jars in the basket. She tucked a muslin cloth across the top, motioned for a footman to carry it out to the waiting carriage.

"Mrs. Hawkins, you are wonderful. Thank you," Leah said. She returned to her room to gather her gloves and her bonnet.

Wrapping her shawl around her shoulders, she headed for the door.

Her father stepped into her path. "Leah, a word if you please."

For the briefest of moments, she contemplated striding past him, but experience had long ago taught her that he would not hesitate to chastise her in front of the servants.

She moved into the library, crossed her hands at her waist, and waited for him to shut the door. Perhaps, one day she might forgive him. One day in the distant future when the pain of his betrayal had diminished.

But not today. His continued silence dragged a weary sigh from her. "Was there something you needed?"

"Just wanted a few moments with my daughter before I give her away." He heaved himself onto the window seat, his portly belly hanging over the waistband of his pantaloons. He rubbed his hands together, his grin widening. "By this time tomorrow, you will be a Wexton. A fine old name from a fine old family. I've done some research, Leah. Did you know that boy can trace his pedigree back to the days of the Conqueror?"

Truly the man had no shame. "He is hardly a boy, Papa. But never mind that. Do you think I care about his pedigree?"

"Well, you should." He jabbed his finger through the air. "Think of the bloodlines, Leah. Think of Jamison and Wexton blood mingling together. Think of the children you will have. You should be thanking me rather than moping around the house."

"I am hardly moping. I am going about my duties as I always have." She stared out the window, at the storm clouds gathering low in the sky. The air was damp and chilly. She should have ordered warm bricks for the carriage. "How did you get the duke to agree to this match? I've tried to determine the truth, but I truly haven't any notion."

"I told you. I dangled your dowry and he took it."

Had she honestly believed her father would tell her the

truth? "Papa, is there a purpose to this visit? What is it you want?"

"To see you happy."

She shook her head. "You do not care if I am happy. May I please be excused?"

"I want you to accept your fate."

"Do I have any choice?" she asked in a choked voice. "You are certainly not going to change your mind, so unless he changes his by tomorrow, I will find myself wed. What else can a daughter do? Unless, of course, I decide to flee."

"You would not dare!" He narrowed his eyes as he studied her features, then said in a tiny squeak, "Would you?"

She could hardly admit the notion had crossed her mind. Unfortunately, she was all too aware of the bleak fate a woman without protection faced, even if that protection came from a dastardly father willing to force his daughter into marriage against her will. A tiny voice in her mind told her that she lied, that she wanted to marry the duke. For she greatly feared she had fallen in love with the blasted man. Was this love at first sight? This turbulent churning? This aching need?

"By this time tomorrow, you will be a duchess—someday, my grandson will be a duke." He slapped his hand against his thigh. His laughter bounced off the stuccoed ceiling. "I never thought I would live to see this day."

The breath rushed from Leah's lungs. Her hands clenched as anger surged. "I am sick unto death of hearing you say that. You seem to forget. You already have a grandchild!"

"No, I do not!"

"Of course you do," Leah cried, weary of the secrets, weary of the lies, weary of holding her tongue as if nothing had happened. "Just because you pretend it isn't so, does not make it true! Somewhere out there is a child who has your blood running through its tiny veins, and we do not even know if the child is a boy or a girl."

She pressed her hands to her forehead and started to pace.

"Oh God, he must be four years old by now. How can you ignore that? And what of Catherine? Do you never wonder where she is? Or even if she is still alive?"

"Be silent," he shouted. "I told you never to mention her name in my house again. She is dead to me."

"But she is not dead to me. And I will not be silent. Not anymore. There is not a day that goes by that I do not think of them, and pray for them, and despise you for what you did to them." She sucked in her breath. She could not believe the words that had just left her mouth.

Her father looked equally stunned, with his cheeks fiery red, his eyes wide, his lips pushing out. "Well, despise me if you will," he said, rising to his feet, advancing on her with his arms tight, hands fisted. "But that changes nothing. Tomorrow you will wed St. Austin."

The urge to flee was strong, but she stood her ground. He would not dare strike her now. "Yes, I imagine I will. And I will pray that God forgives you your sins. Now, if you will excuse me, I am late."

The carriage ride was torturous. Every rut in the road, every surge of the wheels rattled through her bones, but a visit to the children was just what she needed to ease her anguished thoughts and emotions.

Yet even here, surrounded by a dozen young boys, all laughing and talking at the same time, their eager faces covered in jam, bread crumbs speckling their shirts, her doubts and her fears still plagued her.

Her spirits did not lift until Thomas appeared at the pantry door. The red glaze of illness still covered his eyes, but the fever had dropped and the chills were gone.

God was good, after all.

"Something has come up," Leah said to Mrs. Bristoll. "Some . . . urgent business."

She could not bring herself to mention her upcoming nuptials. She had yet to give in to her fate.

She pressed a purse into Mrs. Bristoll's hand.

The good woman tried to protest at her having done too much already, but Leah simply shook her head. "I want you to have this. For food and medicines. I do not know when I will be able to return. Not for a sennight, at the very least. Perhaps even a fortnight." If at all.

The enormity of her situation finally struck her. She had no idea what her future would bring, or even where she would make her home. A chilling numbness spread over her skin, even as the air around her was stifling hot from the burning coals in the grate. Still, she could not worry Mrs. Bristoll or the children. She pulled her shawl tight around her shoulders to hide her trembling. "You will always have my support for the good work you do here, Mrs. Bristoll. When I am settled, I shall send you my direction. Now, children," she said, forcing a cheerfulness into her voice as she rummaged through the basket for the books she had buried there. "Who would like to hear a story? I have *Sonnets for the Cradle.*"

Chapter Six

"Your betrothed does not seem anxious for her nuptials," Geoffrey said, his low voice barely audible above the long case clock tolling the hour. "I wonder why that is?"

Richard stared into the grate. All he wanted was to finish this farce, but his bride seemed determined to make him wait and his brother was chattering in his ear as if this were an ordinary wedding and not a disaster brought about by his drinking and gaming. The muscles in his shoulders clenched as he gripped the marble chimney piece. "Geoffrey, if you value your life, you will not say another word."

The coals shifted in the grate. The flurry of sparks flared as brightly as the golden flecks in Leah's eyes as she had announced she would not marry him. As the minutes ticked by, Richard was forced to consider that she had meant what she'd said. What if she'd left town to escape him?

No, she would not be so foolish, but he had to admit, she possessed the courage to give it a try. Not that she would succeed. He would track her down and haul her to the altar if he had to. He needed this marriage to buy her father's silence and to keep Alison safe from the dangers surrounding her.

Geoffrey shuffled his feet across the carpet, the sound grating on Richard's nerves like fingernails scraping through chalk dust. Even her aunt looked worried, casting furtive glances toward the door. He looked at the clock.

It was now going on the quarter hour. He would give his bride one more minute. Then he was going to search the house, and so help him, when he found her, he was going to give her a lesson in wifely obedience.

"The duke is here. It is time."

Leah ignored the treacherous lurch in her stomach brought about by her father's words. She had not yet eaten today. Naturally she suffered an indigestion. She was tired from lack of sleep. Naturally her legs felt weak. She was being forced to wed a man who surely must despise her. Naturally, her throat ached and her head was pounding and her father's pronouncement looped through her mind. *He is here. It is time.*

"You look so like your mother," Papa said, the lines around his eyes softening as he gazed at her, as if he were a fond parent and she were an eager bride.

She rubbed her hands up and down her arms, as if the friction would ease the chill spreading over her skin. The dress truly was a stunning creation, silver shot silk covered with beading and pearls, made for her mother, but never worn.

How she needed her mother, now more than ever.

The longing she felt for her sister brought the threat of tears perilously close, a longing for her strength, for her guidance, for her loving support. But more than anything, Leah wanted to know she was safe. Try as she might not to lose hope, it was growing more difficult to believe she would ever see her sister again, much less the child.

No, she pushed her treacherous thoughts away.

She would not give in to despair.

Her father cleared his throat, picked at the folds of his neck cloth, then blurted out, "As your aunt is a spinster and your mother is dead, it has fallen upon me to instruct you in your marital duties."

"Please, do not," Leah choked out, her hands flying to her cheeks, her mind rushing forth with memories that brought a flush to her neck, the bold, sensual caress of the duke's lips upon hers, the answering ache tugging low in her belly, the uncomfortable yearning that haunted her still.

Of course, her father ignored her protests, his only purpose ensuring she knew how to breed his future noble grandsons. Granddaughters were never mentioned as he stammered out a useless summation that basically told her to *lie still, do your duty, and do not protest, come what may.*

It was the "come what may" part that brought an unladylike sheen of sweat to her palms and a clenching to her stomach.

Some small part of her had truly believed this moment would never arrive, that the duke would come to his senses and withdraw his offer, but he was here. It was time.

She took a last look at her room, at the pleasing hues and harmonious blends of blues and golds. She would not miss it, she decided. All she would miss was her aunt.

She drew a deep breath and strode down the stairs, leaving her father to follow her. This marriage might not be of her choosing, but she would face it with dignity and honor.

What else could she do?

She found some comfort in the knowledge that her pin money, an annual sum settled upon her by the duke to spend at her discretion, would ensure her ability to see that the children of Mrs. Bristoll's foundling home never suffered from want again.

It seemed a coldly calculating reason to wed, but, then again, the duke was only marrying her for her money, or so he had claimed, though she did not believe him. Just as her racing heart warned her that her own faulty reasoning was a lie.

Was this love at first sight? This aching need so unlike anything she had ever felt before?

At the salon door, she paused, her legs refusing to bring her forward, her vision blurring, images floating past her like moments of awareness in a dream. Her aunt by the window, linen handkerchief pressed to her lips, the sky beyond a deathly gray from the lingering clouds and the setting sun. The vicar perched on the settee, his well-worn prayer book clutched in his hands. A younger man she did not recognize, though his features proclaimed him a relation to the duke.

Then her eyes found him. Richard. Standing before the fire. Broad back and long legs formally clad in black coat and matching trousers. Dark hair gleaming in the firelight.

The devil in evening clothes, backlit by the flames.

She made no sound—unless it was the soft movement of her gown that alerted him to her presence—but his back stiffened, his head swung around, and his obsidian eyes met hers through the haze. Her sudden lack of breath was anger at having to wed where she would not, or so she told herself, but as he sauntered toward her, as her senses filled with jasmine and amber, her aching heart once again warned her that she lied.

Self-preservation set her tongue against her teeth.

"Your Grace," she murmured, her voice amazingly steady, given the churning in her stomach and her lack of breath.

"Miss Jamison," he said as he bowed before her. His lips curled up a fraction in what some might consider a smile. He held out his arm. One dark brow arched as he waited.

Exquisite civility had returned, though the unrelenting gaze of the insolent man who had kissed her remained.

Despite the tension gripping his gut, Richard felt a smile tug at his lips as her eyes met his with a glimmering challenge, the gold buried within the green reflecting the flames.

Had he truly expected fits of female hysterics? Fluttering lashes as she fell into a faint? From the woman who had dared to storm his home and toss his marriage offer back in his face?

Not that he'd actually *offered* her marriage, his conscience nagged him. No, he had announced she would wed him in two days, as if she were an underling hired to carry out his commands.

Yet here she was with her head held high, placing her hand upon his arm without hesitation. As she walked by his side to stand before the vicar, Richard found his admiration soaring, which made his arm clench beneath her palm.

He did not want to feel anything for this woman.

Certainly not admiration, or pity.

Definitely not the desire that plagued him still, an aching awareness of her standing beside him, the faint scent of roses bathing her hair. His skin grew hot, then cold again, his emotions racing from rage to resignation.

He tried to attend to the moment, but all he could think about was the woman at his side. That she was lovely, he could not deny, yet she also appeared so young, so vulnerable, standing beside him, the slightest tremor shaking her hands, the beading on her gown glimmering in the candlelight, reflecting the burnished gold of her hair.

How could he want this woman?

By rights, he should hate her, and he probably did.

But he also wanted her, had wanted her from the first moment he'd laid eyes upon her. He should be grateful, he supposed, that he felt some lust for the woman to whom he would soon be shackled for life. After all, she would be the mother of his children, should he ever choose to bed her. Was she a party to this treachery? Or a sacrifice to her father's ambition?

The long case clock tolled the half hour. His eyes downcast, cheeks covered in sweat, Geoffrey took his position at Richard's side. Her father cast Richard a wide-lipped smile, as if they were all one happy family gathered for a feast.

He flattened his palms against his thighs to keep from strangling the bastard where he stood.

That pleasure would have to wait, at least for the moment.

The vicar was mouthing the words that would bind Richard to this woman for the rest of his life, this beautiful, brave woman who faced him boldly, unwavering eyes meeting his, and all he could think was he did not want a wife.

Then it was over, as quickly as it began.

Only moments before the room was silent, save for the vicar's monotonous voice droning on and on. Now everyone seemed to be speaking at once. His brother welcoming Richard's wife— his wife!—into the family. Her aunt, hugging her while weeping all over her shoulder. The vicar offering his congratulations.

Her father walked over to where Richard stood, slapped him on the back. "Beautiful ceremony, eh, son?"

Truly, the man did not recognize his danger.

Hands clenching, the muscles in his legs tightening with splendid tension, Richard smiled. "Geoffrey, would you please be so kind as to escort—" Good God, he had to clench his jaw to push the words past his teeth, "*my wife* out to the carriage? I would like a word with her parent in private."

"Please, call me Thaddeus," the man said, the pink in his cheeks matching his waistcoat. "Or Papa. I rather like the sound of that."

"Yes, I am sure you do," Richard said, keeping his voice soft, relishing the moment at hand and the anger pushing the blood through his veins. "Lest you forget, I married your daughter for one reason and one reason only. I have fulfilled my end of the bargain. Now let me explain yours. You are never to come near me or any member of my family ever again."

"Now see here," Jamison sputtered. "If you think to renege on our deal, I will tell the world about Alison—"

Richard grabbed him by his over-starched cravat and hauled him off his feet. "If you so much as whisper her name in your dreams, I will know it. My vengeance will be fast and furious.

I will crush you beneath my boot like the worm that you are. I will throw your daughter to the wolves like yesterday's trash. I will institute a very public, very ugly, divorce. And if you think I won't, then try me. For I would have nothing left to lose, which would make me very dangerous indeed." He leaned in toward the man. "Now, have I made myself perfectly clear?"

A blood-red flush stained the man's cheeks, but he pursed his lips and nodded his assent.

"And one other thing," Richard said, flexing his hands as he thrust the bastard away.

Jamison rubbed his fingers over his throat. "What's that, son?"

"Never call me son again or I will be forced to kill you for the insult."

Leah embraced her aunt one last time as they said their farewells at the curb. The urge to cling to Emma's shoulders and never let go was strong, but she forced herself to step back. "Please, Aunt, do not weep. I will visit you often, and you must call upon me at my new home."

"You are right, of course," Emma said, touching the back of her hand to her brow. She raised her tear-stained gaze to the duke's. "You will treat my niece with kindness, my lord?"

He did not correct her mistaken address, a small act of compassion that brought a faint smile to Leah's lips.

"I assure you, madam, she will have my utmost respect and attention," he said with a bow before handing Leah into the waiting conveyance, then hauling himself in behind her.

The door swung shut with a resounding thump.

"Your brother will not accompany us?" Leah heard the breathless catch in her voice, but with each passing second, she was finding it more difficult to control her spiraling tension.

She was alone in a dimly lit carriage with a man—not just

any man, but her husband! Heading toward his home. Where they would be alone. In the dark. In his bedchamber.

Dear heavens, what had she done?

"Geoffrey will ride ahead to ensure all is ready for our arrival." His large presence loomed heavily on her senses as he sprawled on the bench opposite hers, his too-long legs touching her knees, his booted feet resting against her slippers.

The feeble light from the single lantern cast unearthly shadows over the hard, chiseled lines of his jaw, the curve of his sensuous lips, the dark, dangerous glint in his eyes.

The coach was too small. There was not enough air. She slid along her bench until her shoulder touched the wall.

His dark brows arched up. "Leah, I assure you, there is no need to fear me."

She forced a little laugh, though it sounded more brittle than the scornful tone she had hoped to achieve. "I do not fear you, sir. Nor have I given you leave to use my Christian name."

"As we are now wed," he murmured, his dark eyes studying her face, as if he would memorize every inch, every curve. "It would seem a trifle odd to stand on formality, at least when we are private. But if you prefer, shall I address you as Your Grace?"

Your Grace? No, she was simple Miss Jamison, not the Duchess of St. Austin, but it could not be a dream.

She wore his ring on her finger. A lovely gold band.

"Yes, I would prefer it," she said, twisting her hands in her skirts. This conversation was inane, but she could think of nothing of import to say. All she could think was she had made a dreadful mistake. She would love him, she already knew it.

She was in very great danger. She had to fight her perilous attraction to this man. She had to protect her heart.

The coachman called to the horses and gave a quick snap of the reins. The sudden lurch of the vehicle as it rolled into motion stirred the queasy sensation in the pit of her stomach.

Before she could think to utter a protest, the duke closed the distance between them, captured her trembling hands between his palms. Though they both wore gloves, she was well aware of the strength of his fingers, of his powerful grip and the heat of his skin, which sparked an answering heat in her belly.

"Your Grace," he said, his lips pushing together in a tight line, as if he were fighting a grin. "We are not the first to wed out of duty and honor and family obligation. We surely will not be the last. We must find a way to move forward from here."

It was a perfectly reasonable, rational thing to say.

"I would prefer to find a way out," she grumbled, which was not quite as reasonable, nor even slightly rational, but he had hold of her hands and he was gazing at her through his intensely disturbing, devil-may-care eyes and his beguiling scent was wrapping around her. Then he did the most despicable thing yet.

He laughed, a deep, rumbling sound that sent shivers over her skin. His eyes darkened. His gaze dropped to her lips and she knew . . . he would kiss her again. She meant to lean backward, but she moved forward, her eyes drifting shut.

He was making a grave mistake.

Even though he recognized this truth, Richard could not stop himself from lowering his head and tasting her lips, lightly tracing her teeth with his tongue, waiting until she invited him in with a soft, little sigh that made his body go instantly hard.

He forced himself to keep his hands on her back, only her back, as he drew her closer, breathed her scent of roses and lotion, felt the warmth of her breath against his lips. And now he knew. It was *not* the whisky that had made him kiss her.

Chapter Seven

The carriage rolled to a stop before he could deepen the kiss, before passion swept away reason and he found himself taking his wife, his virgin wife, in a cold, dark carriage with no thought to her pleasure or his peace of mind.

His pulse marched swiftly to the beat of his heart. He lifted his hands away from her person, threw himself back against the stiff leather squabs. Uncomfortable tension clenched his legs as he watched the slow dawn of awareness creep into her eyes. As passion waned, their amber-green softness darkened with the glimmer of some strong emotion. A burgundy flush spread over her cheeks, drifting down her neck, drawing his gaze to the rapid rise and fall of her bosom as she fought to catch her breath.

"Do not kiss me again," she said, brushing her palms down her arms, as if she could wipe away the heat of his hands from her skin. "And do not touch me."

"Do you intend to deny us both the pleasures of our marriage bed?" Why he said it, he did not know, as he had no intention of ever bedding her—though the heavy ache in his groin gave truth to that lie. Now that he thought about it, why the hell not?

He might not have wanted a wife, but he had one. Should

he not reap the benefits that went along with it? Had he not paid for it with his pride? With his manhood? With his very soul?

Besides, it was time he had an heir. He couldn't chance the estates falling into Geoffrey's hands. That fool would run them into the ground, if he didn't lose them at the gaming tables first. Richard could not allow that to happen. His duty was to secure the title and property for future generations of Wextons.

But what if she were in league with her treacherous father?

"If you wanted pleasure," she said, her voice shaking, whether from fury or desire he could not tell, "you should have married for love, not for money."

He laughed when he really wanted to sneer, not at her, but at himself as the truth became stunningly clear. She was an innocent victim in her father's vicious scheme, for naught but a naïve innocent—or an untried youth—would ever believe love, if it even existed between a man and a woman, was a basis for marriage. A feeling akin to hate, or perhaps it was guilt clawed at his throat, churned in his gut. He did not want to believe it, but he did. He wanted to hate her, but he could not.

She did not deserve it. Nor did she deserve his anger and resentment. For wasn't she also trapped in a marriage she did not choose?

Good God, what a mess. What a bloody, miserable mess.

He ran his hands over his face, then through his hair.

Before he could speak, the door popped open.

A footman in full livery lowered the steps.

Richard lunged from the carriage, turned to help Leah—his wife, goddammit—to the ground.

The sound of laughter brought his gaze to the house, where every window was ablaze with hundreds of candles, the rooms filled to overflowing with lords and ladies in elegant dress.

How had he forgotten Rachel's ball?

What had seemed a good idea at the time—to waylay the

gossip regarding his hasty marriage by boldly throwing his nuptials in society's face—now seemed a horrible punishment to the proud beauty who walked by his side. Of course, when he'd first conceived the plan, more whisky than blood had flowed through his veins, not to mention his untamed, savage fury. At her father, at Geoffrey, at himself and at his situation.

He wrapped his hand around Leah's arm, intent now upon swinging around the side of the house to the gardens, where they could enter through the lower levels. From there, a short passage led to the stairs of the private apartments, enabling them to avoid the crowd. But his brother was awaiting their arrival.

Geoffrey pulled open the front door and waved his hand at the butler, who bellowed, "The Duke and Duchess of St. Austin."

"We need dance only one dance," her husband, evil, wicked man that he was, whispered so close to her ear, his lips tickled the tender skin on the curve of her neck. "Then we may retire."

All Leah wanted was to seek the privacy of her chambers, wherever those chambers might be, but she donned a bright smile as if she were the happiest of brides on the happiest day of her life as he led her into the house, then into the ballroom where three or four hundred people clustered together, all staring at her. What else could she do? Turn and run from the room?

No one spoke. No one moved. Not even the servants, their trays of champagne suspended before them, as if hanging in air.

She might have found their wide-eyed, open-mouthed expressions heartily amusing, if it weren't for the bottomless feeling in her stomach or the dizziness swirling through her head. The room was astoundingly large, with a domed ceiling three levels high. Pillars of incense burned in the corners. Light from the chandeliers shimmered off the gilding and marble, giving the room a fairy-tale glow.

Were she a young girl still in the schoolroom, she would imagine the dark, dangerous man striding along at her side was an enchanted prince sweeping her away to his kingdom.

The reality was not so pretty, nor so easily explained.

She could not even dredge up the energy to hate him for thrusting her into this awkward situation. No, she hated him for kissing her once again, for making her want him . . . need him . . . love him . . . when he felt none of these things.

A lovely woman dressed in peach gossamer silk glided across the room to greet them. Her honey blond hair gleamed in the candlelight. Delicate ringlets framed her perfect oval face.

As she moved, she motioned with her hands and the music resumed, breaking the silence that had fallen over the crowd. The ladies, at least, tried to hide their covert gazes and whispers behind their fans. The men simply gaped without care, their voices blending in with the din from the orchestra.

"St. Austin, you wretched beast," the woman said as she stood before Richard. Her skin seemed aglow with the same peach-colored hue of her sensuously flowing gown. Her smile never wavered, but there was an expression about her eyes Leah found disconcerting. "Why did you not you tell me you were bringing home a wife this evening? Are you not even going to have the good grace to introduce us?"

The woman did not pause long enough for Richard to reply before turning to Leah. "Oh, never mind him. We need not stand on formality and convention, as we are sisters, you and I. I am Rachel, Duchess of St. Austin. Oh, dear." She gave a delicate laugh. "Now *you* are the Duchess of St. Austin, which makes me the *dowager* duchess. I always think of *much older* ladies when I hear that word. I never imagined it applied to *me*. I fear this will take some getting used to."

For a terrible moment, Leah did not know what to say.

Good heavens, she did not even know how to style her own name, so much had changed.

"I am Leah," she finally said, choosing not to attach a surname or a title. She ignored the rumble emanating from the man beside her that sounded decidedly like a low-pitched growl or a burst of strangled laughter.

"Welcome to the family, dear." Rachel clasped Leah's hands in hers. She gave her fingers a firm squeeze, then released her just as swiftly. "It shall be so wonderful having a sister in the house . . ." She continued to speak, but Leah heard not a word.

She was weary, her legs were starting to shake, and the heat of the candles and the crowd rushing to meet them spreading a feverish flush over her skin. Certainly it had nothing to do with the "wretched beast" of a man hovering much too close by her side.

Despite her best efforts to remain aloof, coldly detached, her eyes sought him out again and again. He returned her gaze with his dark stare, his expression telling her nothing of what he was thinking or of his emotions. He was so proudly elegant, so beautifully noble, and she was a plain country miss. She did not belong in this world. She would never fit in. Oh, she did not doubt her own self-worth, she was confident in her abilities, but she knew nothing about moving through this level of society.

She had tried to warn him, but he had refused to listen.

To fulfill some unknown obligation to her father, he had married her. His honor was intact. Now she had to find a way to set him free. But what could she do?

A distant memory started to tease her.

Snatches of conversations overheard as a child.

She chewed on her lips as she tried to remember, the bottom of her belly aching. Her eyes stung, but she blinked back her tears. Once she had accepted that she must marry him, she had started to dream of their future together. A future filled with children, happiness, and love. Especially love.

Though she had tried to deny it, even to herself, she had dared to hope that eventually he would come to love her. She was such a dreamer, a weakness that had plagued her all of her life.

"Your Grace?" Richard said, his tone surprisingly gentle, perhaps even teasing, as he bowed before her. "Would you do me the honor of granting me this dance?"

Without waiting for a reply, the arrogant man slipped his hand around her elbow and led her onto the dance floor, his arm encircling her waist as the first trembling notes of a waltz filled the air. The sensuous melody seemed to surround her, seemed to ease her unbearable tension, at least for the moment, or perhaps it was her awareness of the man holding her close. One hand pressing low on her spine. His enticing scent of amber and jasmine conjuring memories better left in the darkness.

"You do realize," he said, his deep, rumbling voice wrapping around her. "That you are supposed to flatter me while we dance. Strictly speaking, it is proper dance floor etiquette."

His unexpected flirtation brought a startled smile to her lips, pushing anguished thoughts and painful plans into the distance, until only this moment remained. "I believe you are mistaken, sir. It is you who are supposed to flatter me."

"Agreed. I shall make an attempt at it. But mind you, I don't usually do the flattering. I receive it."

"Oh, I do not doubt that for a moment." Leah glanced around the ballroom. She could feel the burning jealousy of the women staring with unabashed longing at her husband. "I am the envy of all the girls around me."

His lips curved into a smile, infused with the same boyish charm she remembered from when she had foolishly confronted him in this very house a mere two days ago. Now she was his wife!

He was playacting, of course, for the benefit of those around them. Still, his teasing bantering felt strange, somehow comfortable, as if they could have been friends had they met under different circumstances.

"Should I compliment the cut of your coat?" She fluttered her lashes, dropped her voice to what she hoped was an enticing whisper, though she strongly suspected her strangled laughter ruined the effect. It was shockingly bold, and so contrary to her usual reserve, but it felt so fun, as if she were a carefree girl again, back before her sister went missing and her father betrayed her. "Or the fall of your neck cloth? Or the decidedly wicked way your raven hair curls rakishly over your brow?"

He laughed, and her heart raced ahead of her breathing, beating in tune to the spiraling dance. Words were lost, her thoughts drifting away, all of her senses centered on her overwhelming attraction to this man, his pleasing scent, his much larger hand wrapped around hers, the heat rising from his skin and his devilish grin that rendered her spellbound.

Until the music finally ended.

He held her a moment longer, as if he were reluctant to release her. Then he stepped back and offered his arm.

"You did not do your duty, sir," Leah tried to tease.

One brow arched up. "How so?"

"You did not pay justice to *my* vanity."

"I will attend to your vanity later," he promised as he raised her gloved hand to his lips and kissed her fingertips. "When *you* grant me leave to kiss you again."

The sensual promise of his words sent a searing heat though her veins. Unable to breathe, the tension too much to bear, Leah forced her gaze off to his left, only to notice a woman draped in shimmering primrose silk slinking toward them.

"There you are, St. Austin," the woman murmured in a

breathless whisper, running her fan down his arm. She angled her chin toward her shoulder so that her autumn red hair swept sensuously over her brow. A seductive pout curved her rouge-stained lips. "Are you not going to introduce me to your wife?"

Where moments before there had been teasing and laughter, now his jaw grew tight, his features hardening before Leah's eyes until his face was completely devoid of emotion.

This was the cold, arrogant duke who wrapped his hand around Leah's elbow and hauled her to his side. A moment passed as if he were considering the notion, then he made the introductions, choosing his words with exquisite civility to indicate Leah was the one bestowing her honor by deigning to notice Lady Margaret Montague, a woman of inferior rank. Leah would have found the stiff formality laughable, if it did not cause her so much pain.

"Your Grace," Lady Montague murmured, giving the slightest nod of her regal chin in Leah's general direction while moving so close to Richard that her skirts flowed around his ankles.

Geoffrey appeared at Leah's side. "Might I have the honor of dancing with my most beautiful new sister?"

"It would be my pleasure," Leah said quickly, the swift heat running through her veins vying with a sudden desire to rip Lady Margaret Montague's luscious red hair out of her head.

Who was this woman with her clinging hands and her palpable animosity? A sudden suspicion brought a chill to Leah's skin, a churning low in her belly. Everything had happened so swiftly. Without warning or time to get to know one another.

Was Richard in love with this woman? Would he have wed her had Leah's father not interfered with his treachery?

Leah pressed her hand to her stomach to ease the ache building beneath her ribs. Somehow she managed to keep the smile on her lips as Geoffrey led her away. She would not suc-

cumb to her shattered emotions in front of these people, all
waiting with barely restrained glee for her to blunder and fall.

"Do not worry about her," Geoffrey said, as if reading her
mind. "She is nothing to Richard."

Leah did not believe it. Were it true, Geoffrey would not
have felt compelled to remark upon it. She watched Richard as
he conversed with Margaret on the side of the ballroom. Lady
Montague was tall, slender, and coolly self-possessed. She belonged in this world, and from the way she was clinging to
Richard, she obviously thought that he belonged with her.

The sudden stinging in her eyes warned Leah she needed
to make her escape. "Would you mind very much if we did
not dance?" she said, dragging her gaze away from Richard,
only to find Geoffrey watching her, his brown eyes soft with
concern.

"Are you unwell? You do look a trifle peaked."

"Not at all." She forced a bright smile. "I simply feel the
need for a breath of air. Truly. That is all."

"These events can be tediously overwhelming," he said as
he steered her toward the French windows, through which she
could see a terrace lit by brightly colored lanterns. "But never
fear. You will get used to it. Shall I fetch you a lemonade?"

Leah nodded. She searched for a glimpse of Richard through
the blur of unfamiliar faces. Her smile never faltered, but a
heavy ache settled in her chest as she found him, still conversing with Lady Montague. She would not have to worry about
getting used to these tedious events.

After tonight, she would not be here.

With practiced ease, Richard assumed a casual indifference
to his stance that belied the rage seething inside him. He
waited for Geoffrey to lead Leah far enough away so as not
to overhear this conversation. He might not have wanted to

marry Leah, but that no longer signified. She was his wife, and he'd be damned if he let anyone treat her with disrespect.

He had not even seen the danger approaching. One moment he was drowning in clear green eyes sprinkled with gold dust, lost in the fantasy of sweeping Leah into his arms and dragging her to bed. The next, Lady Margaret Montague was sliding her fan along his arm. Were Margaret any one of the other guests, Richard might even have felt grateful for the interruption, which allowed reason and sanity to restore his mind, if not his body.

Before disappearing into the crowd, Leah cast one last glance at the woman edging closer to Richard's side. Her expressive eyes narrowed slightly, her brows drawn together, not in anger, but more a puzzled bewilderment.

"What is the meaning of this?" he demanded of Margaret, keeping his voice low, his features calm and controlled.

The lovely widow lowered her chin toward her shoulder. She titled her lips in the merest hint of a smile, a pose meant to allure and intrigue him. "Dance with me, darling."

"Do not toy with me, Margaret." Richard plucked a glass of champagne from the tray of a passing servant. "I thought you understood discretion, yet you flaunt yourself before my wife? Touching my arm? Murmuring throatily? Were I a different, less honorable man, I would be tempted to throttle you."

She fluttered her fan, then drew it down her neck, an obvious ploy to drag his gaze to her overripe breasts barely concealed by the outrageously low neckline of her dress. "I am sorry, Richard, truly, I am. It is just that I miss you."

He watched her hazel eyes fill with tears, and he gave an exasperated sigh. Over the month of their association, he had learned what a talented actress she could be when it suited her needs. Obviously now, it suited her needs.

But to what purpose? After all, he had broken off their arrangement. "I never made you any promises. Nor you, me.

Ours was an affair of convenience, a fact to which we both agreed when *you* first invited me into your bed. Not to mention, the *discretion*." Upon which he had insisted.

Though Margaret, as a widow, possessed more freedom to take lovers as she saw fit, Richard had suffered a strong aversion to finding himself suddenly trapped into marriage.

Such brutal irony. If Margaret only knew.

The tears disappeared as quickly as they arrived. "You said you would never marry anyone, yet you show up tonight with a wife on your arm. What happened, Richard? Get caught with your breeches 'round your knees?"

His hand tightened on his glass until he thought it might shatter. "Let me make something perfectly clear, Margaret. I expect you treat my wife with *all* due respect."

Her sudden loss of color showed she did not mistake the cold menace in his tone. As he swallowed the last of his champagne, he cursed his own stupidity. Given the haste of his marriage, he had known gossip would run rampant. Now it appeared speculation would run from the merely tawdry to the viciously depraved.

He would have to play the besotted fool.

Having seen Leah's earthy beauty, the wolves of the *ton* would have no difficulty believing Richard's lust had overcome his reason. As he searched for sight of her yet again through the crowd, as the heat of desire surged through his veins, he stifled a disgusted sigh. He was doing well enough with that plan already—and he wasn't even trying.

"You are despicable. You know that, don't you?"

"Yes, I do." More so lately than usual, he thought. Ever since he had met Leah, his behavior seemed better suited to a dastardly rogue than a finely bred English gentleman.

"I will try to forgive you," Margaret said, fluttering her lashes. She dropped her voice to a sultry whisper. "And if you come to me tonight, I'll endeavor to keep you amused."

And he knew from experience that she could. But to his

surprise, he wasn't even tempted. "Do not waste your tricks on me. Save them for your next conquest."

"There won't be a 'next conquest.' You're all I want, all I need. Your marriage needn't make any difference to you and me."

"You sell yourself short, madam. You should cast your lures about you for a husband."

"I did cast my lures . . . toward you. But it seems I didn't have the proper bait. Oh, for heaven's sake," Margaret said, waving her fan before her face. "Do not glare at me. I admit it. I knew you did not want to marry me. I wanted you then. I still want you now. I see no reason we cannot continue as we were."

He searched the room for Leah. She was walking beside Geoffrey, laughing at something he said, and the beauty of her smile, so unaffected and pure, called to him like a siren's song. Bewitching, beguiling . . . dangerous. "No, it is over."

"Who is she?" Margaret asked, dragging Richard's gaze from his wife. "Where did you meet? How long have you known her?"

"Why could you possibly want to know?"

"Curiosity? Jealousy? I imagine any woman would want to know about her replacement. You owe me that much, at least."

"No, I do not. We agreed." Margaret was a problem that could wait for tomorrow. Tonight, he had much more pressing issues with which to contend. Such as what to do with his lovely bride. He passed his glass off to a servant. "I bid you adieu. I must find my wife."

"You do that," Margaret snarled as he walked away. "But you will come back to me, Richard. I promise you that."

Any hope Leah had harbored for a moment of privacy while Geoffrey fetched her lemonade disappeared as soon as she stepped onto the terrace and saw the shape of a man lurking in the shadows. The torches reflecting off the tawny gold in his hair were too far away to reveal his face.

She glanced around the promenade. It was deserted. The gardens beyond covered in darkness. Before she could turn and run for the house, a rose-scented breeze swept up. The clouds pushed away from the moon. Hazy light spilled over the terrace.

"Alexander?" She reached behind her, needing the solid support of the balustrade to steady her knees. "Is that you?"

He nodded, as if he didn't trust himself to speak.

A shiver ran over her skin. She was so cold, deep inside, but not from the breeze. She knew she should speak, but she could not find any words. His features were tight. White lines digging into his brow and around his mouth ravaged his flawless skin. His sunny blue eyes were wide and brimming with the pain of betrayal. She had thought only *her* heart was in danger from her father's perfidy. Had Alex loved her after all?

"I returned mere moments ago," he finally said as he approached her, his movements stiff, tightly controlled. "I went to your father's house straightaway. He told me something I can scarcely credit. Is it true? Have you married him?"

Her heart wrenched so painfully, she was surprised it still beat, surprised her breath still moved in and out of her tightly clenched throat. She did not want to add to his pain, but he deserved the truth from her lips, rather than the lies her father would tell him. "Yes, I am married."

"I will kill him," he growled, turning for the house.

Leah grabbed his arms. "Alex, do not be a fool."

"Is that what I am to you?" He stared at her through wide eyes, his face ghostly white in the pale moonlight. "A fool?"

"Oh, that is not what I meant, and you know it," she cried, turning toward the balustrade. She gripped the wall until she could feel the cold from the stone seeping through her gloves. She would not weep. She would not add the burden of her tears to his pain. He walked up behind her, so close she could feel the warmth of his breath sweeping the back of her neck.

"What happened, Leah? Tell me."

His voice was so soft, so gentle, urging her to share her worries and fears, but she could not. It was too late for him to help her now. The truth would only hurt him more.

Besides, if Richard agreed to her plans, her reputation would be ruined, tainting any and all who sought her acquaintance, even through friendship. "There is not much to tell. My father made all the arrangements. I found myself betrothed and married so quickly my head is still spinning."

"And you . . . agreed?" He stumbled over the words. He grabbed her arms, spun her around. His grip hurt, but she bit back her cry, which would only bring the gossiping hordes down upon them.

She pushed her fists against his chest until he lifted his hands and backed away. "My father was pleased with the match."

"And you? Were you pleased with the match?"

"What choice did I have?" Leah cried, choking on the words. "A daughter's duty is to do her father's bidding."

"That is not what I asked you. Did you want to marry him?"

"I don't even know him—"

"That is not what I asked."

"You do not understand."

"You wanted to marry him, didn't you?" His chest heaved as he sucked in his breath. His gaze raked over her face. "Did you never love me, then? Was your tender regard a lark to keep me dangling on a string, waiting for a better catch to come along? A mere baronet's son wasn't good enough for you? You needed a title I couldn't give you?" He glared at her in cold, hard contempt. "What? No response?"

Leah knew his words sprang from his pain, but they cut like a dagger thrust deep in her heart. "I never kept you dangling on a string. Until this moment, I did not know you cared for me as anything more than a sister. You have ever been my dearest friend, Alex. For you to accuse me thus is cruel."

"Cruel?" he sneered, rocking back on his heels. "I'll tell you what is cruel. To discover the woman you've loved your entire life is nothing more than a lie, *that* is cruel! To discover her sweet smile and tender words were a facade to hide a calculating bitch, that is cruel!"

She did not speak. There were no words to say. She looked out over the gardens, at the shadowy plants, indistinct in the darkness. She gripped the balustrade, thankful for the solid support to steady her knees as she listened to the steady breeze rustling through the potted plants on the terrace.

A sudden burst of laughter drew her attention to the house, to the man standing before her, glaring at her as if she were Medusa, with serpents slithering out of her hair.

Her chest ached and her throat burned. She drew a ragged breath. "As you have ever been my dearest friend, I forgive you your harsh words. Now, I think you should leave, before we hurt each other more."

A long, tense moment passed before he spun on his heels and disappeared into the night. She closed her eyes, rubbed her forefingers over her brow. She couldn't remember a time when they had not been friends, introduced by their mothers when they were just small through a never-ending round of social calls. Even after her mother had died, and in the face of her father's growing animosity, his quiet support had never wavered.

Now, he hated her. She wanted to cry. She wanted to drop to the floor and weep like a babe, but her tears were locked up inside her, where they would remain.

The night sky stretched out before her, the stars barely visible in the midnight tapestry. All Leah could see was the fathomless depths of Richard's eyes, their smoky darkness haunting her now, even as they would haunt her forever.

Would he agree to her plan? Why would he not? It was not as if he had wanted to marry her. No, she had her father's treachery to thank for the agony about to befall her, and for the lines of misery now etched into Alexander's face.

"Leah, are you out here?" Lord Geoffrey trotted through the door, two glasses clutched in his hands. His smile was the easy, unaffected grin of a perfectly charming man and Leah couldn't help but like him. "I've brought your lemonade."

She laced her hands together at her waist before he drew near enough to notice their trembling. She even managed to smile, and then to laugh at his playful bantering, as if she were happy, as if her heart weren't breaking, as if her dearest friend did not hate her, as if the man she loved were not, at this moment, in the ballroom conversing with another woman, as if she were not about to set him free.

Richard found her on the terrace, her wispy golden hair shimmering in the torchlight, framed against the midnight sky, his brother standing at her side.

She tilted her face into the rose-scented breeze and closed her eyes. A mysterious smile touched her lips, as if she were lost in a pleasant dream—or planning her escape.

Geoffrey murmured something near her ear, and she laughed.

It was a simple sound that seemed to float above the musical notes sweeping out of the ballroom until it wrapped around Richard, until he didn't know whether it was guilt or need clenching his gut. He had made her shiver in fear, and then in desire, but he had never made her laugh.

He leaned one shoulder against the wall, the bricks cutting into his back keeping him sane as he crossed his arms over his chest and allowed himself to gaze at her—at his wife, dammit.

Would he never get used to the word?

This was the first time he had seen her at peace, her hair

flowing over her shoulders, lustrous gold silk he itched to feel tangled around his wrists, his fingers buried in the curls, holding her close for his kiss.

She laughed again and the sound beckoned him closer.

Good Lord, he should hate her. Truly he should. She was the daughter of his enemy, for pity's sake, but he found he could not. Nor could he deny his growing admiration. In the face of their situation, did she weep and wail? No, she held her head high and moved into her future with courage and conviction.

Faced with the *ton* did she whimper and faint? No, she marched into the ballroom and dared them to condemn her.

And every time he touched her, she responded with dawning passion, making him hard. Dammit, everything about her made him hard and aching to touch her. She was beautiful, more beautiful than any woman of his memory, but it was her eyes that slayed him with their intensity, with their expressive honesty that seemed to show all her emotions. And now she was his wife.

Whether he willed it or not, it was done.

They had to find some way to carry on from here.

Self-preservation warned him he should send her to Cornwall.

Lust told him to drag her to bed.

As if sensing his presence, her chin lowered. Her smile waned. Her face turned as pale as the stars glimmering in the night sky beyond her. She turned, slowly, meeting his gaze with her own unwavering stare, her green eyes reflecting the light from the torches, and something else, a touch of misery, or pain.

Richard pushed his gaze to his brother, saw the glasses gripped in his hands. A simmering fury leapt to life within him, set his pulse to pounding, his hands into fists.

Geoffrey, who moments before had been laughing like a

young boy without care, turned as gray as the stone balustrade upon which he was leaning. He pushed away from the wall.

"Dear sister, I must bid you goodnight," he said, sweeping Leah a courtly bow. "I shall see you at breakfast."

As he passed Richard, he paused. "It is lemonade," he said, his voice gritty and low, like sea-glass being scraped over gravel. "I have had nothing stronger than coffee, tea or this . . . putrid concoction in three days."

Only now, standing this close, could Richard see the sooty pallor to Geoffrey's skin, the thin film of sweat on his brow, his shaking hands. Still, he wasn't sure he believed him.

"I told you, I mean to change. By the way," Geoffrey added, as if only just remembering. "I do like your wife. She is perfectly charming."

With that he disappeared into the ballroom, leaving Richard alone with the woman in question. His wife.

Leah could not take one more moment of this unbearable tension, of his dark and smoky eyes returning her gaze, his expression, inscrutable. His stance, unaffected.

"I would retire," she said, not recognizing the low rasp of her own voice. After her confrontation with Alex, she was weary to her soul. Now only one more conversation remained.

The most difficult yet.

Perhaps she would wait until tomorrow. "If you would have someone show me to my rooms."

"Of course. I will escort you myself." He offered his arm. Ever the gentleman. Exquisitely polite.

He led her down the steps, into the darkness, and her heart raced faster than the rapid pace he set. Though she needn't have worried. Once they reached the bottom, he merely opened a door and led her through a private entrance, bypassing the crowd still lingering in the ballroom.

In a matter of minutes, he steered her through a maze of

passages and staircases to the family apartments. She was excruciatingly aware of every breath he drew as he walked beside her. She wished she could think of something to say, something witty and charming that would draw his attention to the person inside her, but, as always, the moment he came near her, all rational thought slipped away.

At the far end of the corridor, he stopped.

"These are your chambers," he said, his voice rumbling with an odd sort of huskiness that trembled over her skin.

Her father's words came back with a vengeance.

Lie still, do your duty, and do not protest, come what may.

Her heart seemed to leap into her throat. She could not swallow. She could not even breathe.

Surely he did not mean to claim his husbandly rights. He did not know her. He did not even like her, she was sure, although there was something in his eyes that gave her pause.

Her skin grew cold, yet shivering hot at the same moment. Time stretched out between them, coherent thought dissipating into the tension, until all she could see was this man standing before her. All she could hear was her own heart beating and the steady whir of his breath moving in and out of his chest.

His head inched lower, his lips, warm and spicy and oh-so-enticing, hovering mere inches from hers. Her hand came up, whether to push him away or to pull him near, she did not know.

He gave a muffled curse, then opened the door.

Leah walked into a nightmare. Grecian urns and Egyptian tables. Chinese paintings and Turkish carpets.

It had to be a nightmare. It was too ugly to be a dream.

Still, attending to the furnishings eased her trembling and gave her the courage to speak the words she needed to say.

She tried not to notice how handsome he was, standing with his hands tucked into his pockets, night-dark hair curling over his brow. Or the play of candlelight on the burnished bronze of his skin, or the heated look in his eyes as his gaze made a languid perusal from her eyes to her toes, then back again, leaving her breathless and aching in his wake.

"I want you to know that I did not marry you because of your charming proposal," she said as she crossed to the window, putting the length of the room between them.

"I am happy to hear it." He approached her slowly, a soft smile on his lips that made her throat tighten, made her stomach burn. Good heavens, she was about to leap out of her skin.

She wrapped her arms around her waist. "Nor did I wed you because my father . . . coerced me into the match."

His eyes grew darker still, not with desire, but with a hard, ruthless gleam. "Did he strike you?"

The cold menace in his voice brought her brows up, but she was not afraid. Did he think to protect her?

Not trusting her voice, she shook her head. Still, her course was set. She could not back away now.

"I married you because *I* wanted to."

He nodded, but his eyes said he did not believe her.

She breathed deeply. "And now, I want a divorce."

Chapter Eight

Richard tilted his head as he slid from a murderous rage, where any lingering doubts concerning her innocence vanished into fury for the father who had no doubt beaten her into submission.

It was one more sin for which the man must pay.

Though he had used the threat of divorce against her father, he had never expected to hear the words coming from his wife.

"I beg your pardon?"

"I want a divorce." Her voice trembled, but her gaze never wavered from his. She moved to the grate, standing much too close to the fire as if a chill had seeped under her skin.

The amber flecks within her luscious green eyes gleamed in the firelight, with sincerity, with honesty, with rigid determination. She gripped her hands to her waist.

"Do you not see? It is the perfect solution. I know you did not want to marry me." The odd hum of soft silk gloves scraping together rose above the crackling flames. "I know my father forced you into this match."

The urge to cross the room, to take her trembling hands between his and ease her fears became strong, but he locked his knees in place. Warning bells were ringing. His pulse was pounding, his breath burning in his chest.

Or perhaps it was guilt clawing at his throat.

He was unprepared for this moment. For the admiration swelling within his breast. To save his honor, she was willing to take on the scandal of a divorce?

She deserved the truth, but he could not give it to her.

"That is not true, Leah. I needed your dowry. I've told you that already. Your father and I came to an amicable arrangement—"

"An amicable arrangement? Hah! I do not believe that for a moment." She started to pace before the fire, bringing Richard's gaze to the gentle sway of her hips. Backlit by the flames, the length of her legs were clearly visible beneath the shimmering silk. "Your eyes were flinging daggers at him this evening. I've no doubt if a man of the cloth had not been present, you would have throttled him."

As she moved, her gown billowed out, then circled back around her legs, caressing her curves in a sensual dance.

"Not that I am saying you would not have been justified," she said, oblivious to the desire stirring within him, the need he felt to touch his hands to her breasts.

He swallowed thickly, wanting nothing more than to press his mouth to her throat, to skim his fingers over her hips and below her dress.

"You have honored your obligations to my father by marrying me." She held out one trembling hand. "Now we can both regain our freedom through a divorce. It is the perfect solution and he will not be able to stop us."

Richard tried to attend to her words, but his thoughts were diverted by the soft turn of her neck, by the tender white flesh of her shoulders and back . . . and breasts, what little of those glorious curves were visible above her modest neckline.

"Divorce is not easily obtained," he managed to say, his voice heavy and raw. "On what grounds would we seek it?"

She was breathing rapidly, and he was losing his mind.

"What grounds are acceptable?"

He contemplated the row of buttons securing the back of her gown and how quickly he could remove it. "I am not entirely certain. But I believe adultery on anyone's part would be one. Have you committed adultery?"

Her glare told him she did not find him amusing.

Little wonder. His brain was dead, his tongue too thick to form rational words. "There is only one other reason that I know of, and I would rather not mention it."

"That is it?"

He nodded. Giving in to temptation, he crossed the room, drew her shaking hands between his. "And none of them apply to us. Even if they did, it takes years."

"Years?" The breathless pitch in her voice brought a smile to his lips. Her gaze dropped to his mouth, her green eyes darkening with a desire she did not yet understand. She might be speaking divorce, but she wanted him, as much as he wanted her.

She was his wife, with a lifetime stretched out before them. They had no choice but to build a future together.

Still, the future did not seem as onerous at this moment, knowing now, without doubt, that she was not involved in her father's schemes. Not only that, she was determined to right the wrong her father had wrought. She was a remarkable woman, determined to live her life with courage, dignity and honor, admirable traits indeed. And now she was his wife.

"Yes. Years," he said, stroking his fingers over her wrists, gliding his hands to her elbows where her gloves met her flesh. "To go through the courts. And then before Parliament."

His wife. The thought brought an odd, twisting knot to his throat as he slid her gloves down the length of her arms. His fingers stroked the soft flesh on the underside of her wrists.

"And one must also consider the scandal," he said, his last coherent thought as his mind started to undress her.

"What about an annulment?" she gasped, trying to concentrate on the moment at hand and not on the swishing silk as he stripped off her gloves. Of course, she knew the risk she was running.

She had finally remembered the neighborhood gossip, the outrage when Lord Greydon had sought to divorce his young wife. His son had died and he was wild with grief, but that had held no sway in society's eyes. The condemnation was vicious. Even the vicar had joined in, preaching on the evils of mortal sin.

The scandal would haunt her for the rest of her life, but Leah would hold her head high. In her heart, she would know she had done the right thing, the honorable thing.

But it was growing increasingly difficult to think with his fingertips tracing over her wrists, her thoughts scattering like pebbles tossed into the ocean.

"Where have you heard of these things?" His grin was decidedly wicked, as was the gleam in his smoky black eyes, which did not appear quite so black at this moment.

No, streaks of silver, quick flashes of lightning, were hidden in the devil's black eyes.

"We are married," he said, softly, gently, as if he cared about her feelings, as if he cared about her. "For better, for worse. We must accept it and move onward from here."

Though his eyes lingered on her lips, he made no move to kiss her, or to draw her into his arms. The only touch was his hands upon hers, fingers stroking over her palms.

"There must be something you want from this marriage."

I want your love, she thought.

"I want freedom," she said, and he laughed.

The sound was harsh, brimming with anguish, with hidden despair. What secrets did this man harbor?

What pain haunted his past?

"There is not a man—or woman—alive who is free."

He said it with such venom, a sudden rush of shame burned her skin. While she had worried and bemoaned her fate, never once had she thought of this man, of how *his* life had changed, of what sacrifices he had made to take a wife he did not want.

But she could no longer think. Not of divorce or annulments or blame. He was standing altogether too close to her person, holding on to her hands, his large, warm thumbs circling over her palms, the slight catch of his fingernails sending shivers up her arms. She swiped her tongue across her lips, which felt as parched as if she were wandering lost in the desert.

His gaze followed the course of her tongue.

"Do you grant me leave to kiss you?" His voice was a gruff whisper ripped from his chest.

Her words in the carriage must have hurt him, she realized, when she told him never to kiss her again. He would not demand his husbandly rights. He would not take her if she were not willing to give. He was making her choose.

Do you grant me leave to kiss you?

Her mind said no, but her heart said yes. He was her husband. For better, for worse. He was right. Despite the inauspicious beginning of their marriage, they had to build a future together, and she loved him. She did not understand the how or when or where or why of it. She only knew it was true.

Perhaps from the first moment she'd met him, or perhaps from the moment of their first kiss, when she had felt all his needs and his loneliness that matched her own desperate yearnings.

Do you grant me leave to kiss you?

"Yes." Before the word even left her lips, his mouth

covered hers, and all thoughts of divorce and annulments dissolved, along with her fears. All that mattered was this man and this moment, his lips moving fiercely over her mouth.

She clung to his shoulders, breasts crushed to his chest, as he dragged her against him, one large hand wrapped round the back of her neck, the other pressing low on her spine. Her thoughts swept away, lost in sensation, the heady heat of his skin, the spicy scent of his hair, her pulse pounding madly.

This man, her husband, with his fathomless eyes and his hungry kisses, his tongue teasing and tasting, his breath warm on her skin. A moan slipped from her throat. The sound seemed to inflame him, sent his hands around her back, his fingers tugging loose the ribbons and buttons securing her dress. As it slipped from her shoulders, soft silk pooling at her feet, she shivered, not from cold, but unbearable need.

Her stays followed her dress, until only her thin shift remained. He swung her into his arms, mouth clinging to hers as he brought her to bed. She should be afraid, but she felt surprisingly safe, even as his long legs slid down her shins, pressing her into the blankets. Firelight played over the harsh lines of his face, the dark depths of his eyes.

Lifting her hand, she traced his cheeks, learning the shape of his beard-roughened jaw. And then he was gone. Mesmerized, she watched as he drew off his coat, untangled his cravat in slow, aching motions. By the time his waistcoat dropped to the floor, she could not breathe, the air having disappeared from the room, then his shirt came undone and he was lifting it over his head. She closed her eyes.

Panic tried to claim her, urged her to leap from the bed, run from the room, from the house, from this man, from the danger beckoning her toward him. *He does not love you,* her mind screamed. *But he will,* her heart told her.

He came down beside her, slid his hand along her jaw, his thumb stroking and teasing, his skin rough and soft at the same time. He was not unaffected, his breath rushing in and out of his chest, same as hers. "Leah," he said, her name rolling from his tongue. Then, as if needing to say it again, "Leah."

Good heavens, how she liked the sound of her name spoken in his resonant voice, dark and seductive, that shook with the same need burning within her. "I do not understand," she whispered.

"You must trust me in this. This is as it should be between us," he said, but there was a startled look in his eyes that confused her, a fierceness to his hands as he gripped her arms before sliding his fingers into her hair, angling her head to better fit his lips to her mouth.

Then he clasped her shift in his fists, drew it up past her knees, and panic sent her hands to his wrists, gripping them. He did not laugh at her maidenly fears. He withdrew his right hand, stroked his fingers along her jaw until her eyes met his.

"Leah, you have no need to fear anything that will happen between us, here in our bed. This I promise you, on my honor."

She wished she could speak, but her voice was trapped, overcome with emotion. Covering his hand with hers, she kissed his palm, telling him without words that she wanted him, in her bed, in her body. This was right. This was love.

As he eased her shift past her shoulders, cold air shivered over her skin, but the heat of his hands soon banished the chill. His eyes darkened as his gaze roamed over her breasts, down the length of her stomach to the curls between her thighs.

His breathing was ragged, and her skin was afire.

"You are perfect," he said, before lowering his mouth to her throat, tracing a lazy path to her breasts. Licking, touching, tasting his way from her belly to her hips. Everywhere his tongue roamed he left shivering, burning flesh.

An uncomfortable yearning built in her belly, in her breasts, in the damp skin between her thighs. She slid her fingers though his hair, arched her back to better fit her breasts into his hands. Her breathing quickened until she was practically panting, sending her breath over his skin.

She had not known, could never have imagined, where he would touch her, the need he would arouse within her. His finger slipping deep inside her, rubbing her most sensitive flesh in slow, thrilling circles, stroking, teasing, seducing shudders and moans from low in her throat.

As shyness fled, desire urged her to move her hands over his shoulders, her mouth on his throat, learning the feel of him, the taste of his skin, his muscles firm, hard, stretching and straining beneath her palm. His dark gaze met hers, his smile slow and seductive, and she knew she had pleased him.

She grew bolder still, sliding her hands down his arms, spreading her fingers wide, running them over his chest, tracing the dark swirl of hair, lower and lower, but not so low as to touch his sex boldly pressing into her thigh. She was not quite brave enough yet.

When he finally moved over her, pushing his hips between her thighs, she was not afraid. His eyes were intense, dark and smoky, wanting her as much as she wanted him.

"Richard," she whispered. It was the first time she said his name, and a powerful shudder ripped through him. His fingers twining with hers, he moaned her name as he took possession of her body in one rapid thrust.

She gasped, though the pain was not nearly as shocking as she had expected, more of a searing ache, but he kissed her and soothed her, and soon even that burning disappeared, replaced by the most amazing sensations as he slowly withdrew, then slid deeper still. His mouth covered hers. His hands gripped her hair. His scent filled her lungs. Her body thrumming and aching, tension building, then she was shuddering, her mind floating away, as exquisite pleasure pulsed through her body. She cried out his name, the muscles of her passage convulsing.

He cradled her face between his palms, his eyes, dark and

relentless as he hovered above her. "You are my wife," he growled through clenched teeth. "There will be no more talk of divorce or annulments. Do you understand?"

She tried to nod, but he seized her lips in a furious kiss, as he thrust within her, as he shuddered above her, as he collapsed against her, as he gave her his seed.

His pulse racing swiftly, Richard rolled onto his side. Hands wrapped firmly round her back, he pulled her to him until they lay face to face, skin to skin, legs tangled beneath the sheets. She felt so small, so fragile in his arms, her skin still burning with the heat of their coupling, the sweet scent of roses clinging to her hair, the more arousing fragrance of their desire making him harden again, making him want her again, though he had yet to catch his breath. His tongue still held the taste of her mouth and her skin, but he wanted more. So much more.

He had wanted to go slow, to make it last, make it good, she was a virgin for pity's sake, but he had felt as if *he* were the virgin, hands shaking, fingers fumbling, ready to spill his seed just from kissing her. What was it about this woman that made him lose his mind? His senses? His control?

His earlier words came back to haunt him.

This is as it should be between us, he had told her, but it was not. He had lied. Sex was a bodily function. A meaningless joining of parts, a rush of release, then it was over.

It was *not* this perilous journey, fraught with emotion. Not this heat of possessive longing. This dangerous bent of his thoughts. His wife. His . . . wife. His.

His last coherent thought before drifting off to sleep, arms securely wrapped around Leah as she curled against his side, was that he should have heeded logic and reason.

He should have sent her to Cornwall.

Chapter Nine

When Leah awoke the next morning, it was all she could do not to pull the covers over her face and hide away in her rooms.

She recognized her longing for exactly what it was: a cowardly reaction, a fluttering embarrassment at the thought of seeing her husband again. Mumbling something about a morning ride, he'd left over an hour ago, but not before he'd pulled her close and kissed her to the point of breathless exhaustion.

Good heavens, what must he think of her?

She had certainly not followed her father's advice to lie still and do her duty. No, she had behaved like a wanton, moaning when his hands swept over her breasts, shivering as his fingers slipped between her thighs. Just the memory of his mouth on her throat, his tongue tasting and teasing, brought the heat of longing to her belly, the burn of desire to her skin.

Still, she was not a coward. She would not hide.

Nor would she feel shame at having responded to her husband.

She loved him. She could admit it now, even if only to herself. She didn't understand it any better today than she had yesterday, but she didn't care anymore. She loved him.

And he would come to love her, too. Perhaps not today or tomorrow, but soon, he would love her as much as she loved him.

But she would not win his love by cowering in her rooms.

She flung back her blankets, donned her wrapper, rang for her maid. As she waited, she made a slow sweep of her rooms.

What had seemed hideous in the firelight was even more so with the morning sun blazing on the yellow walls. The odd assortment of tables and chairs brought to mind a Chinese pagoda, Turkish temple and Egyptian tomb all at the same time.

A young girl about the same age as Leah arrived, a bundle of freshly ironed gowns draped over her arms. She bobbed a curtsy. "Good morning, Your Grace. I'm Marielle. I've unpacked most of your trunks and had water brought up."

Your Grace. Leah shivered. She would never get used to it. "Thank you, Marielle. A bath sounds heavenly."

She washed and dressed with excruciating care in a sprigged muslin frock, the swirling gold woven within the fabric a perfect match to her hair. It was a foolish vanity, but she wanted Richard to see her as an elegant lady and not the raggedly dressed hoyden he'd seen on more than one occasion.

Thank goodness he hadn't listened to her gibberish about a divorce. It was an ill-conceived plan, she realized that now, but she had been so frightened, nearly desperate, until he had shown her without words that she belonged to him.

A burning flush spread through her cheeks. She had to stop thinking about him or she would never get anything done.

She scribbled a note to her aunt, and another to Mrs. Bristoll with her new direction, then handed the missives to the maid.

"Marielle, please see that these are delivered."

A quick pat of her hair, a few deep breaths to steady her swirling stomach, then she opened the door and proceeded down the stairs. Once she reached the bottom, she froze.

One look around the massive hall with its gilding and marble reminded her that she had no idea where she was or where she was going. Richard had said he would introduce her to the servants and give her a tour of the house when he returned.

Perhaps she should have remained in her rooms after all.

Luckily, Geoffrey came down the steps behind her. He was dressed for riding, his brown eyes gleaming at her as he grinned. "Good morning, sister. You look confused. Could you, perhaps, be searching for breakfast?"

Leah laughed. "You save me again, Geoffrey. I begin to think you my knight-errant."

"At your service," he said with a regal bow and a flourishing sweep of his hands.

Chatting happily about the fine day and beautiful weather, he linked his arm through hers and led her down the corridor.

As they strolled past the library that looked as if it housed ten thousand books, Leah found herself gaping like a traveler in a foreign land. Each room they passed was more elegant and exquisitely furnished than the one before.

Her stomach grew queasy, her hands cold. While her childhood home was lovely enough as a tribute to her father's wealth, it could not compare with this grand palace masquerading as a house. The frightened child inside Leah wanted to run back to her rooms and hide, but she refused to give in to her insecurities. She was mistress of this home now.

"And this is the dining room," he said, then turned to leave.

"Wait! Aren't you eating?"

"Can't. I am engaged to meet with friends, and I am late."

Leah squeezed her hands for a moment, her fingernails digging into her palms. She breathed slowly and deeply, then stepped inside the room. It was empty.

She choked back a nervous giggle.

Good heavens, what was wrong with her? She needed to

gain control over her wayward emotions before she saw Richard again.

Leah had thought this room, at least, would be small and cozy, but it was huge, and paneled with the richest waxed mahogany she had ever seen. Still, it was a cheery room, lit by mullioned windows hung with gold-fringed crimson draperies.

Drawn by the enticing scent of roasted meats, she walked to the sideboard.

"Good morning," Rachel said as she breezed across the room and sat at the table. A footman appeared at her side.

"Just tea." She glanced at the plate in Leah's hands. Her lips pursed ever-so-slightly, her brows lifting in a dainty look of surprised disapproval.

Leah sighed. At home, breakfast was a casual affair, a serve yourself whenever you wanted. Everything here was rigid and formal, from eating to dressing for breakfast. Rachel's frock, a delicate, sarcenet silk the color of butter, seemed better suited for a grand ball than a morning meal, leaving Leah feeling frumpy and underdressed. But Rachel was smiling, her blue eyes soft and inviting. Here at least was a welcoming face.

"I know this might all seem a bit overwhelming," Rachel said before sipping her tea. "But I do not want you to be distressed. I will be right beside you during the days and weeks to come to lend you my advice and support. We will begin today by touring the house and meeting the staff. Tuesday is our at home day. That is when we receive visitors. We won't have to worry about that until next week. By the way, dear, that is Geoffrey's seat. You should sit one seat over, or at the head of the table. I hesitate to say anything. But if I do not, you will never learn our ways. Don't you agree?"

Leah glanced down the length of the gleaming mahogany table, which could comfortably seat fifty people. She looked back at Rachel, who sent her a vacuous smile.

"I wonder why I have never met your family," Rachel said.

In truth, Rachel had taken the seat that should have been Leah's, at Richard's right hand, but Leah kept her silence. She did not want to alienate her new sister the first time they spoke. "My father rarely comes to Town."

"Are you related to Major Jamison of the King's Guard?"

"No," Leah said, unfolding her napkin.

Rachel frowned. "Do not be so mysterious, Leah. We are sisters now. Tell me about your family, dear. Who are your relations? Where are you from?"

"I have only one aunt, my mother's sister, Emma Burton, who came to live with us after my mother died—"

"Oh, how sad that your mother is gone. But tell me more about your father, dear. How does he know St. Austin? Where are his estates? What is his title?"

And now the point of Rachel's curiosity became clear. Gone was the illusion that Leah had found a friend in her new sister.

"My father has no title," she said bluntly, refusing to cower beneath the intensity of Rachel's gaze. "He owns cotton mills. In Lancashire."

"Your father is in trade?" Her eyes were wide, lips pulled back, an expression of horror one might expect if a rat had just crawled across the table.

Leah would have laughed if she did not realize Rachel's reaction would soon be repeated in every drawing room in the *ton*.

"Never mind," Rachel said when Leah didn't respond. "Tell me about you and St. Austin. Where did you meet?"

"My father and Richard arranged everything," Leah said. She had no intention of discussing her marriage with Rachel. She might be smiling prettily, but her questions seemed more an interrogation than an interest in becoming better acquainted.

"That is as it should be, dear, but I am more interested in you and St. Austin." Leaning forward, Rachel dropped her voice to a conspiratorial whisper. "Surely you must realize legions of women have tried for years to bring St. Austin up to scratch, without success. That is, until you."

Visions of Lady Margaret Montague rose unbidden in Leah's mind. The proprietary air with which she'd clung to Richard's arm. Her silk skirts swaying flirtatiously around his legs.

Had he loved her? Had he thought to marry her?

It does not matter, she told herself, ruthlessly cutting off her thoughts. Just as it did not matter that she had once thought to marry another. They were wed. They had to build a future together, as Richard had told her, and then, shown her.

"Naturally, I'm curious about the woman who finally managed to snag him in the parson's mousetrap. Was it love at first sight, or a slow wooing? I'm on tenterhooks to know."

Richard striding into the room saved Leah from having to reply. When he glanced at Leah, his eyes appeared startled, as if he had forgotten he even had a wife, much less expected to find her at his table. A sudden nervousness brought her hands to her stomach, a breathless ache to her chest. She didn't know what to do or say. She peeked at him from beneath her lashes.

The perfect cut of his riding clothes drew her gaze to his broad back and tapered waist. Had she truly run her hands over the chiseled muscles hidden beneath the bottle green coat and buff pantaloons? Buried her fingers within the silken strands of his hair? Clung to his powerful hips as he'd entered her body?

She laced her fingers together on her lap. Heat spread over her skin, as if she had developed a sudden fever.

Rachel laughed. "Richard, your blushing bride looks as if she might faint dead away at any moment."

Leah grabbed her fork, attacked her eggs with a vengeance.

Silently, she cursed her fair skin that reddened when she felt the least discomfort or embarrassment. She needn't have worried about her clothing or the artful arrangement of her hair, she realized as he turned to greet her.

After a politely stated, "madam," he bowed, all stiff formality and polite indifference. Gone was the flesh-and-blood man who had touched her so tenderly in the night, replaced by the cold and arrogant Duke of St. Austin, his exquisite civility chipping off pieces of her suddenly aching heart.

Her thoughts grew foggy, her hands cold.

For a brief moment, she felt as if she were back in her father's house, back when she first met this man and his obsidian gaze had raked over her with his unrelenting stare.

She had not expected him to fawn all over her like some moon-struck calf, especially in front of Rachel, but she had expected some warmth, some sign that what had passed between them was as special to him as it was to her.

Somehow she managed to smile and nod and pretend to listen as Rachel continued her less-than-subtle probing, all conducted through a pleasant smile and gleaming eyes.

"I had asked Leah how the two of you met," Rachel said to Richard. "Perhaps you would care to tell the tale, St. Austin? Naturally I'm curious about the child you took to wife."

She turned innocent blue eyes on Leah. "By the way, dear, how old are you? Or should I say, how young?"

The butler walked over to the table and stood beside Leah. "Pardon me, Your Grace?"

She pushed her eggs to the side of her plate, mashed her toast with her fork. The unbearable churning in her belly sent a wave of nausea up her throat. The dreaded sting of tears touched her eyes. She did not know why she felt the urge to cry. It was silly, really. He was all that was polite and civil.

"Leah," Richard said. His voice was the same deep baritone rumble that had trembled over her skin in the darkness, only now it was filled with cold indifference.

She folded her hands on her lap and smiled at her husband as if she were happy. Then she saw it. The brief flare of sensual heat in his eyes. The sweep of his gaze moving over her lips, making her shiver as surely as if he stroked his fingertips over her mouth. Try as he might to maintain his indifference, he was not unaffected. It was a start. "Yes?"

"I believe Harris is speaking to you."

"Oh, yes, of course. What is it, Harris?"

"You have a visitor, Your Grace."

"Oh, for heaven's sake," Rachel said. "Who is it, Harris, and what do they want?"

"A Mr. Alexander Prescott, Your Grace," the butler said to Leah, his voice slightly hesitant. "Shall I ask him to return this afternoon?"

Alexander? Leah pressed her hand to her stomach, a burning flush once again creeping up her neck. He had said such hateful things to her last night, what more could he possibly have to say? "No, thank you, Harris. I would like to see him now."

"Very well, Your Grace," he bowed and strode away.

Rachel's brows shot up, her vapid blue eyes wide and perplexed. "A gentleman calling at this time of day? On a newly married lady? And without your husband's permission to call? Not quite the thing, Leah. Not the thing, at all."

A flash of anger swung her gaze to Richard. Her jaw tightened. "Do I need your permission to see my friends?"

Richard could see the fire burning in her eyes, as if she dared him to deny her. He was half-tempted to tease her, but he was anxious to get her out of the room before he did something foolish, such as behave like a jealous lout and forbid her to see her friend. Such as drag her onto his lap, bury his hands beneath her fetching, frothy confection of a dress, and have his wicked way with her with Rachel sitting not two chairs away.

"Of course you do not," he murmured, trying to ignore the

sudden leap of his pulse, the tightening muscles in his arms that if he didn't know better, he would swear was jealousy. "As long as you adhere to propriety."

Good God, he sounded like a prig and her cheeks were blushing with furious color. Her jaw tightened and her eyes narrowed on him as if she would wound him with her glare.

She gave a stiff nod, then turned and strode away, her foolish skirts swishing flirtatiously over her backside, and it was all he could do not to follow her. He recognized the name of her caller from his conversation with Pierce. The boy was calf ears in love with Leah, and now he was here.

It bothered Richard and he could not even begin to say why.

How had he managed polite indifference, when he'd wanted nothing more than to drag her into his arms?

He'd thought he had himself under control, the foolish thoughts from the evening before banished to the darkest corners of his mind, where they belonged. Then, caught up in his worry over whether or not his brother was drinking again, Leah appeared before him when he had not yet schooled himself for her presence.

Now the blood rushing through his veins straight to his groin told him his rigid control was a lie. Warning bells were once again clamoring, but his lust studiously ignored them.

He did not recognize himself. It must come from some primitive, primal instincts blazing to life within him.

Male satisfaction at having been her first lover.

It certainly wasn't love. That foolish notion was best saved for poets and schoolgirls and green youths lost in their first carnal stirrings. Before the truth came crashing down around them. Love did not exist, but passion did.

No, this wasn't love. But what it was, he did not know.

She certainly wasn't important to him, or necessary for his happiness. That road led straight to hell and he had no intention of traveling it. But she was his wife. He would treat her with the respect and consideration she deserved.

Polite civility, those were the key words.

And wanton abandon, too, he thought with a rueful sigh, images of the previous night making him sweat.

He stifled a groan as he realized he was gaping after his wife like a feeble-minded fool and Rachel was watching him, her blue eyes narrowed in shrewd calculation.

Damn, he had forgotten she was in the room. "What plots are you hatching in that devious brain of yours?"

"Richard, you are a brute. Do you not know you hurt me when you speak to me in such a manner?"

He returned his attention to his paper.

"Are you not the least curious what the gentleman wants? Did you know he was at the ball last night?"

That grabbed his notice, and with it came a flare of unwelcome tension, a tightening in his chest. It was anger at Rachel, he told himself, disgust at her machinations.

It was *not* jealousy directed at his new wife.

"I understand they are friends," he said.

"Friends," Rachel said, running her thumb over her fingernails, her eyes wide in feigned innocence. "Yes. I suppose one could call it that. I saw them together on the terrace. They were having quite an intense conversation."

Richard slapped his newspaper on the table. "You were spying again? How many times do I have to tell you to tend to your own concerns?"

"Anything that happens in this house is my concern." Rachel ran her index finger around the rim of her teacup. "Do you want to know what I saw?"

Richard pushed to his feet. He had to get away before he said something he would regret. Or else he would throttle her.

"I saw him grab her arms and pull her close," she called after him. "Then he—"

Richard slammed the door and headed for the library.

If, on his way, he happened past the receiving room where Leah and her young buck were talking, well . . . that wasn't exactly spying . . . was it?

He rubbed his hands over his face.

Good God, now he sounded just like Geoffrey.

Chapter Ten

"Mr. Prescott," Harris announced from the salon door.

Before Leah had time to rise from her chair, Alexander rushed across the room, his frock coat and breeches wrinkled and stained, as if he had slept in them. His hair was damp and clung to his brow. He dropped to his knees at her feet.

He grabbed her hands. His warm breath fluttered over her fingertips, wet with his tears. "Leah, forgive me. I know I do not deserve it. My words were wicked and spiteful and cruel, but I hurt so much, I wanted to hurt you, too."

She could not stand to see his beloved face twisted in so much pain. She closed her eyes, her throat swelling, burning as she dragged in her breath. "Oh, Alexander. There is nothing to forgive." She tugged on his hands, helped him to his feet. "Ours would be a sad friendship, indeed, if it could not survive a few harsh words. Please, sit beside me and we will talk."

No fire burned in the grate, it was too lovely a day, but her skin felt hot, damp with sweat.

He collapsed on the settee. Elbows on knees, he propped his forehead against his hands. "I could not sleep. All I could hear were my vengeful words, over and over, until I thought I would go insane. I had to see you. I had to set things right."

"There is no need to say anything more. I would rather we forgot it ever happened."

A cloud must have passed over the sun, for the light shining in through the windows suddenly dimmed. Then it brightened again, hurting her eyes. She wrapped her arms around her waist, when all she wanted was to take his hand in hers and offer him the same comfort she had needed so desperately.

But she could not. She was married to another man.

He dragged his hand through his hair. "I have to say this, Leah. I cannot live with myself knowing I hurt you. I know you never lied to me, or fed me false words of love."

His shoulders shook as he dragged in his breath. He pulled a handkerchief from his frock coat pocket. "I should have told you how I felt, but I thought twenty-two too young to marry. I never dreamed anyone would steal you away from me. But when you came to Town, I knew as soon as the men got a look at you, they would want you as much as I did. But still, I waited too long."

To give him time and privacy to compose himself, Leah rose and walked to the hearth, her gaze tracing the gold streaks swirling within the white marble. Twin vases filled with roses sweetened the air with the scent of summer.

She plucked off a few faded blooms, tossed them into the grate. If only she could as easily ease Alexander's pain, soothe her aching heart, punish her father for his treachery.

"I truly wish you would stop apologizing," she said, tracing her shaking hand over the mantel. "All is forgiven. I understood your pain last night. I understand your grief today. I have felt them, too. When I thought I had lost your friendship and respect, it hurt unbearably."

He crushed the heels of his hands against his eyes, drew a deep shuddering breath. "Well, then, are you happy with this match?"

"It is too soon to tell," she said softly, trying not to cause him any more pain. "But the duke has been kind to me, his family cordial. I believe I shall be happy here."

He surged from his chair. "Leah, I love you. I cannot bear the thought of you with another man. Come away with me, please. We'll flee to Scotland."

"Oh, you do not know what you are saying." She raised her hands to stop his approach. "I am married to another man."

"He doesn't love you as I do."

"I am sure he doesn't love me at all. But that matters not. I am his wife."

"It doesn't matter." His voice dropped to a pleading whisper. "Come away with me, Leah. I'd gladly suffer the scandal if it meant we'd be together."

It happened so swiftly. One moment he was staring at her through red, hazy eyes. The next he was grabbing her arms, pulling her against his chest, kissing her with all the force of his passion and the depths of his despair.

She twisted out of his arms. Legs trembling, tears rising, she yanked the nearest chair until it stood between them. "Alex, please, stop this madness. I love you, yes. I always have. I always will. But I know, now, it is the love of a sister for a brother, a friend for a friend." She held out one shaking hand. "It is my turn to beg, Alex. Please, be my friend. Do not do this to me."

He stared at her hand. "Do you love him, then?"

"He needs me, Alex. I cannot explain it, but I feel it in the depths of my soul. We were meant to be together."

The steady tick of the mantel clock seemed hideously loud in the silence. His shoulders heaved as he blew out his breath. He tilted his lips in a wry, self-deprecating smile. "It seems I must ask your forgiveness once again. In my madness, my wits have gone begging. If they come knocking on your door, would you please send them back to me?"

As he had intended, his quip teased a watery giggle from Leah, despite her threatening tears and his attempt to ease himself back from madness, even as they both realized their friendship would never, could never, be the same.

Through the lingering silence, Leah heard a sound very much like footsteps out in the passage. A feeling of numbness crept over her skin. An odd sense of time standing still, her thoughts scattered and dazed, as she glanced over her shoulder at the shadows moving beyond the door.

Lady Montague scooped tea leaves from a wooden caddy, then tapped them into a Wedgwood pot. "I must say, I am surprised, no—I am shocked at your visit here today."

No more shocked than Rachel. Never would she have dreamed she would enter this house to call upon this woman.

She perched on the edge of her seat, her spine rigidly straight and away from the back of her chair, as her mother had taught her and as she had perfected through years of practice. No one entering the room would ever guess her pulse was beating as wildly as Alison's feet during a fit of temper.

Her gloved hands folded one atop the other on her lap, she adopted a serene expression, calm, poised, regal. Everything a duchess should be. Everything that girl was not.

"When my butler announced the Duchess of St. Austin, I assumed he meant Richard's wife." Margaret added boiling water to the teapot from a silver urn, then closed the cover to let it steep. "Although I could not imagine why she would call on me. Aren't you styled the dowager duchess now that he has wed?"

"Do not be catty, dear Margaret," Rachel said with a practiced smile, bland, indifferent, supremely confident. "I am here to offer you my assistance."

Using a strainer to catch the sopping leaves, Margaret poured out two cups, then held one out to Rachel. "I cannot imagine what sort of assistance you believe I need."

"Why, securing St. Austin's affections, of course."

Margaret laughed, a sound as irritating as the clanging horse hooves hitting the cobblestones outside the windows. "I hardly think I need your help to lure him back to my bed."

"If you are willing to settle for that, then we truly have nothing further to discuss." Rachel placed her teacup on a small, claw-footed table to her right. With graceful dignity, she rose, her silk skirts snagging on the worn crimson brocade upholstery.

The carpets were faded. The paper peeling back from the walls. The house might be shabby, but Margaret's gown, spring green and trimmed with flounces and buttons, was the first stare of fashion. In the hunt for a husband, the woman obviously knew where to spend her funds. Inwardly, Rachel shivered.

Outwardly, she donned a smile. "I simply thought you more interested in the position of wife over mistress. Would you be so kind as to ring for my carriage?"

Margaret sipped her tea. "St. Austin has already taken a wife—and tossed her amongst the *ton*, quite theatrically. Though she did handle herself rather well. More pity that."

"Do not play the naïve henwit with me." Rachel resumed her seat, spreading her skirts around her seat. "Marriages can be dissolved and well you know it, given the right . . . evidence."

"But the scandal—"

"Is more damaging for the woman than for the man." Rachel let a moment pass, as if she found the topic distressing.

She was not worried about the scandal. Richard had power and position to ease the sting, and, as the wounded party, he would have everyone's sympathy. Especially the men, who all feared a bastard snuck in to inherit their precious lands.

As the women all wanted Richard in their beds, they, too, would be willing to look the other way. "And I have no doubt, he, himself, will be supremely grateful, after the fact, to have escaped such a degrading *mésalliance*."

Margaret's steady gaze held an intensity that would have made a lesser woman shift on her seat. Rachel simply lifted her chin and sipped her tea. Why had Richard found this woman attractive? Her hair was the color of weathered bricks, and she had freckles scattered across her cheeks.

No doubt it was her rather large bosom, accentuated by her overly tight stays. Men, such slaves to their passions.

Rachel thanked God every day that He had gifted her with luscious, gilt-colored hair and eyes so blue they shamed the summer sky. Not many women could compare with her beauty.

And not many men could resist her.

She pushed away her memories, lest they upset her carefully composed demeanor. For the first time in her life, she greatly feared she might lose everything, and years of scheming and maneuvering would have been for naught.

She could not let that happen.

Margaret stood and walked to the windows. "You have never considered me a suitable candidate for Richard's wife in the past. What has changed your position?"

"Nothing at all," Rachel said, following her across the room. "It is simply the lesser of two evils. Given the choice between you and that girl, I would greatly prefer you."

Margaret laughed again, squeaky wheels shuddering over the cobbles. "If that is supposed to be a compliment, it went wide of the mark."

"Do not be a goose." Rachel hid her grimace beneath a smile, though it was growing more difficult with each passing second. "We do not like each other, and we never will, but we could be allies in this." And Margaret would bear all the blame while Rachel reaped all the benefits. It was a deliciously wicked scheme. She nearly laughed aloud at her own cleverness.

Margaret pursed her lips. "What is wrong with the girl?"

"There is nothing wrong with her," Rachel said, pretending an inordinate interest in the pianoforte. She tapped on the keys. Grossly out of tune. "As far as I can tell, she is a sweet little thing. She simply is not one of us."

She leaned forward to whisper her confidence. "Her father is in trade. Cotton mills, of all things. Spinning, weaving and the like." She gave a delicate shudder. "What can St. Austin be thinking to bring such a girl into my home? That he should expect me to associate with one of the lower classes is beyond all bounds. Not to mention, expose my daughter to all her bourgeois ways. Why, it is unspeakable."

"Still," Margaret said, staring out at the street, as if mesmerized by the carriages rattling by. "The man must be quite wealthy. Is it possible Richard married her for her dowry? Is he having financial difficulties? If he truly needs her fortune, he will not appreciate any interference on our part."

"Hardly," Rachel said, flicking the notion away with a twist of her hand. "St. Austin has more money than he could possibly spend in a dozen lifetimes. No, it is more likely that he compromised the chit and her father found out."

The room was stuffy, cloyingly thick with the smell of Margaret's perfume. A slow heat spread across Rachel's skin. Anger? Jealousy? Disgust? She did not know. She did not care.

Nothing would keep her from her dreams.

She pulled her fan from her reticule, waved it before her face. "He is so damn honorable, he would even wed someone of her station just to make amends. But I ask you, should the rest of us suffer her presence for life because of some minor indiscretion on his part?"

"Absolutely not," Margaret said, her broad smile making her appear almost pretty, her eyes alight with delicious, malicious glee. "And I want to be Richard's wife more than I've ever wanted anything in my life."

You and a thousand others, Rachel thought, but she smiled and looped her arm through Margaret's, as if they were the best of friends, as they strolled toward the settee. "I have a plan. You see, there is this young man."

* * *

Leah walked along the garden path, the gravel crunching beneath her shoes a grim reminder of the footsteps she'd heard echoing in the corridor outside the gold salon. Had someone stood there, listening to her conversation with Alexander?

Watching as he—oh, God, she could hardly bring herself to even think it—as he had kissed her? Or had she imagined it?

She wrapped her arms around her waist.

Oh, how she prayed that were true. The entire conversation had been insane and so easy to misconstrue. And that kiss!

Even as an unwilling participant, to kiss a man who was not her husband was unthinkable. A sheen of sweat spread over her skin, from the sun or her turbulent emotions, she did not know.

She trailed her fingers through the fountain, rubbed the cool liquid over the back of her neck. Poor, sweet Alexander.

The depth of his grief had stunned her. Through all the years that she had cherished a tender regard for him, he had never indicated by word or deed that he thought of her as anything more than a friend. Had he really asked her to flee the country? Or could she have misconstrued his meaning?

No, the idea was too outrageous, too preposterous, for her to have misunderstood. He had joked that his wits had gone begging, but Leah was inclined to agree with him. He was definitely not himself, and he wasn't thinking clearly.

He was too good a man to suffer so cruelly.

Her father had spawned the misery Alex now endured, but was there a blessing hidden within his cruelty? Had he not intervened so despicably, would she and Alex have married?

How would they have built a life together, knowing, as she knew now, that she truly loved him, not as a wife should love a husband, but as a sister loved a brother?

He deserved so much more than that. He deserved a woman who loved him with depth. With passion. Without reservation.

As she loved Richard. Which brought her thoughts back to her nightmare. Who had stood listening at the door?

Richard? No, she could not conceive it.

He had too much honor. Too much dignity.

The more likely suspect was Rachel. This morning at breakfast, she had offered her friendship, while quietly ripping Leah apart in an oh-so-civilized fashion. Friend or enemy?

The answer seemed obvious, but Leah could not understand it. Why would Rachel hate her? Or did she? Was it all in her imagination? The last few days were a strain on her nerves, she would readily admit it. Everything had happened so swiftly.

Was she overwrought? Had she misinterpreted Rachel's questioning? Had anyone stood in the hall at all?

The warm breeze swirling around her carried the scent of roses, the whir of bees hunting through the blossoms—and the high-pitched squeal of childish laughter? She tilted her head as she listened. It was coming from somewhere off to the right.

Drawn by the sound, she followed the path around a bend, past the formal gardens with their geometrical flower beds to a summerhouse cut into the garden wall. It was covered in ivy, surrounded by roses. A tall oak tree guarded the entrance.

As she approached the door, she saw a blur of motion as someone jumped out of the shadows and shouted, "Boo!"

When her heart stopped pounding and she recovered her wits, Leah found herself staring at a chubby-cheeked cherub about four years old, though her mischievous smile was anything but angelic.

She wore a simple muslin frock with lace trimming high on the neck. She stared back at Leah through unusual eyes, as intense as a field of bluebells, a startling contrast against her fluffy black curls. "Did I frighten you?"

"Indeed you did," Leah said, shivering in not-quite-mock

surprise. She knelt to meet the girl eye to eye. She held out her hand, pointed at her palm, as if she were a gypsy woman reading a fortune. "See here. I've lost several inches off my life line."

The urchin traced the line Leah was pointing at with her dirt-streaked fingers, her eyes swiftly filling with huge silver tears. "I'm sorry. I was only playing."

"Oh, dearest, don't cry." Leah wrapped the child's hand in hers. "I was only playing, too. What is your name?"

The child swiped her hands over her cheeks, her tears disappearing as swiftly as they arrived. "I am Lady Alison Wexton," she said, tilting her head at a haughty angle that bore a startling resemblance to Rachel's demeanor, but her giggle was all little-girl softness. "I'm five years old. Well, almost."

"Almost five. My, what a big girl you are," Leah said, a familiar ache rising in her throat.

Her sister's child would be much the same age.

"There you are, Lady Alison." A gray-haired woman with a round face came puffing into the summerhouse. "You gave me quite a fright, running off like that. Do forgive her for disturbing you, madam. She is an impetuous child."

"Think nothing of it," Leah said to the nurse, then turned her attention back to the child.

"I know who you are," Alison said, curling a strand of Leah's golden hair around her finger. "You're my Uncle Richard's new wife. My mama told me all about you."

Leah could well imagine what Rachel had told the child.

"Not only am I your uncle's new wife, but I am your new aunt as well," Leah said, astonished her voice came out so steady, but she'd had too many years to learn how to hide this particular pain, never being allowed to so much as breathe Catherine's name, let alone mention the child. "Would you like to call me Aunt Leah?"

Rachel would most likely object to such an informal address, but it seemed absurd for a child to call her Aunt St. Austin.

"Will you be my friend?" Alison asked, chattering merrily. "I'm to take tea *alfresco*. That means outside. Will you join me?"

"That is the most wonderful invitation I have received today." Leah laughed, all her troubles momentarily slipping away in the face of this beautiful child.

She took Alison by the hand. "Perhaps afterward, we could play some games and pick some flowers to brighten up your uncle's library."

Chapter Eleven

Richard had important estate business that needed his attention, but instead of poring over ledgers and contracts, he was prowling his library, haunted by visions of Leah and her mincing young fop sitting cozily on the settee together.

His hands curled at the memory, his arms tightening with rigid tension. He hadn't been able to hear their words, but the tender expression of concern on her face had fired a rage within Richard that could only be described as irrational jealousy.

He could think of no other excuse for the vicious thoughts that had swept through his mind. Was she no better than the rest of her sex? Had she thought to cuckold him in his own home?

Cold logic told him his thoughts were extreme. She had done nothing to warrant this suspicion. The boy had only just learned that the woman he loved had married another. Of course, he would be upset. Of course, she would try to comfort him and break it to him gently, but cold logic hadn't stopped Richard from wanting to stomp in there and tear the pup apart.

Only the knowledge that he'd had no excuse for spying on his new wife had finally forced him to walk away.

He wasn't spying, he told himself. The door had been open. He had turned his head as he'd strode down the passage. He couldn't help it if he had seen them together. He rubbed his hands over his face to stifle his groan.

He truly was insane for now he was thinking just like Geoffrey. He needed fresh air to clear his head.

As he opened the window, he caught a flash of movement on the terrace. He brushed aside the sheer muslin under-curtain and craned his neck for a better view.

Leah and Alison strolled hand-in-hand toward the house, each clutching a bouquet of flowers in their free hands. Alison's looked more like a bunch of strangled stalks and broken blooms than anything remotely resembling a flower. Still, she waved it proudly through the air. They grew close enough for him to their voices. Alison talked without pause. Leah ruffled her hair.

They both laughed. Leah's delicately feminine voice mingling with childish giggles caught Richard unprepared, stealing his breath, tempting dangerous thoughts out of their dungeon. And that was before Leah knelt and drew the child into her arms, Alison clinging so tightly, her flowers fell from her hands and lay forgotten on the ground.

Richard's breath froze, the maternal scene spawning a wave of desire unlike anything he had ever known before. Not a physical desire, but a longing to join that happy group.

Mother, father, child . . . family.

Foolish, foolish thoughts.

Happy families did not exist, except in the make-believe tales Richard spun out for Alison before tucking her in to sleep.

Reality saddled a child with a mother like Rachel.

Still, how different would Alison's life be if she had Leah for a mother. He saw the genuine affection Leah lavished on Alison, saw it in that hug, saw it reflected in her smile as the two resumed their journey toward the house.

In that moment, Richard knew his children would be blessed with a rare and special gift: their mother's love. On the heels of that thought came a vision of Leah with her belly swollen huge with his child. The picture filled him with pure, male satisfaction and a raw, primal urge to go create that child—now!

Good Lord, the rush of desire took him off guard, leaving him sweating and aching and hard. This was bad, very bad. Married a mere twenty-four hours and already she was disturbing his thoughts, interfering with his work, and making him yearn for a future he knew he could never have because it did not exist.

Rational thought told him to keep his distance.

He had no desire to resurrect long-forgotten dreams.

What was dead was better left buried.

He stomped back to his desk, grabbed his ledger, tried to tally the figures. As the minutes ticked by and an hour passed, the urge to seek her out became unbearable. He wanted to—

Stop thinking about her! He needed to concentrate on these figures. He turned several pages, thumbed back to the beginning, then leapt to his feet and stalked straight to her room.

So much for resolutions about keeping his distance.

He wanted her. He needed her.

And by God, he was going to have her.

After returning Alison to the nursery, Leah headed for her rooms. As she turned the corner in the stairs, she saw Richard standing outside her door, his hand raised, the echo of his knock bouncing off the oak-paneled walls.

A furious rush of color spread over her cheeks as she approached him. She did not speak. Neither did he. The air around them seemed to grow still, silent, charged with tension as his dark gaze inched over her face.

He did not move. He did not so much as touch her, but she felt singed, as if she were standing too close to a fire.

When he lifted his hand and slid his knuckles along her jaw, a moan slipped from her throat. With an answering groan, he dragged her against him, strong hands gripping her hips, clinging fiercely, his mouth claiming hers as he fumbled for the knob.

She clung to him just as fiercely as he pulled her into her room, then kicked the door shut behind him. Trapped between his chest and the wall, his arms framing her face, she was surrounded, with his heat, with his scent, with his powerful presence. She slid her hands through his hair, then around his neck, his skin warm and solid against her fingertips.

Anxious to feel the heat of his body pressed against hers, she pushed his coat over his shoulders, tugged off his cravat. He smiled against her lips and she laughed, and then she shivered as he made quick work of her frock and stays. His hands slid down the length of her legs as he bent to remove her shoes. He was crouched before her, hand wrapped around her ankle. He didn't move for a long, terrible moment. Her breath wheezed in and out of her throat, waiting, needing, wanting him to touch her.

Clutching her shift in his hands, he pushed it up, his breath whispering over her skin as he ran his mouth along the tender flesh near her knee. She gasped, her legs trembling, damp heat building between her thighs. He angled one shoulder between her legs, nudging her knees apart, making room for his hands and his mouth and his tongue. Shuddering noises escaped her throat.

His hair was soft as a feather rubbing against her thighs. He moved ever upward, sending unbearable shivers down her legs. Throat clenching, need building inside her, she tugged on his shirt, urging him to take her into his arms.

A soothing murmur was his only reply, his breath whispering over the soft swirl of hair between her thighs. He continued his slow, torturous journey up the length of her body.

Finally he reached her breasts, tongue rubbing slow circles over her nipples before taking one deep in his mouth, torturing her with every pull of his lips, sending an answering tug through her belly and womb until he rose, dragging her shift over her head. His shirt disappeared as he pulled her toward the bed.

His stomach was taut and narrow, bronzed gold in the waning sun. Hair as dark as that on his head covered his chest, swirling ever downward toward his breeches.

When he fumbled with the buttons, she lifted her gaze, caught the wicked smile on his lips, the devilish gleam in his eyes, mere moments before he came down atop her on the bed.

Then there was no space for doubts or thoughts or fears.

There was only this man, moving above her, sliding within her, whispering sinfully wicked words in her ear.

This was hot, bold, desperately yearning.

A swift claiming, passionate heat. She clung to him fiercely, hands biting into his arms as her mouth moved over his shoulders, his throat. Stomach clenching, breasts aching, legs trembling as she wrapped them around his hips, as she pulled him into her body, as tension built toward its unbearable peak, as he shuddered and caught her close to his chest, as he buried his mouth in her hair.

"I love you," she cried against his throat.

He went rigid above her. Not even the rush of his breath reached her ears. The only sounds she could hear were the wild pounding of her blood in her ears and the echo of her words hanging in the sultry, heavy air.

When finally he pushed up on his arms and gazed at her though eyes brutally dark and as cold as granite, even the sound of her own heart beating faded away until nothing remained.

Tendons bulged on his neck. He held his jaw clenched so tightly, she thought it a miracle his teeth didn't crack.

"Never say that again. Do you hear me?"

Leah couldn't speak, lest her shaking voice reveal her growing distress. Her lips tingled.

She pressed them together. She would not cry. She would not disgrace herself more than she already had.

His dark eyes met hers. His features softened. "Leah, I am sorry. I do not want to hurt you." His voice sounded odd, distant, as if ripped from his chest. "I will try to be a good husband to you, but more than that I cannot offer."

His hands dug into her shoulders. "Dammit, do not look at me like that. You are young. You haven't yet learned. Love is a myth, a fantasy, spun out by poets for romantic young girls."

Leah found her voice could pass the knot in her throat, after all. "Please, do not belabor the point. You have made yourself excruciatingly clear. Now, as we have nothing further to say, would you please leave?"

Something flashed in his eyes, something wild and dangerous, like the eyes of a tiger trapped in a cage. "I find there is one other thing," he said, his voice low and dark, scraping over her skin. "You will not entertain gentlemen callers in this house again. Is that clear?"

He shoved himself off the bed. He did not wait for a reply. He did not collect his clothing. He did not look at her again as he stalked through the connecting door to his rooms.

Leah closed her eyes and curled up in a ball on her side.

So much for her dreams of love.

In the morning, he was gone. Called to Yorkshire on emergency estate business, according to a terse note propped on her bedside table. He had signed it simply St. Austin.

That was it. Nothing more.

Such a cold note, so impersonal.

When had he slipped it into her rooms? How had she not heard him? She would have sworn she'd slept not at all last night, as his vehement words swirled through her mind.

Amazingly, she had not wept. Too numb perhaps.

Too shocked. Too filled with grief.

She had even managed to go about her duties this morning, meeting with the housekeeper to review inventories of linen and plate, with cook to plan the week's menus, with Harris to arrange the refurbishing of her rooms. She'd arranged a delivery to Mrs. Bristoll's, taken tea out-of-doors with Alison, which seemed to be a daily treat, and now she was back in her rooms, writing a letter to her aunt. She longed for a visit, but she feared Emma would see past her façade, which would cause her aunt to worry.

The single candle on her writing table was not proof against the clouds swiftly gathering across the sun. A sudden gust of wind spattered rain across the windows and rattled the shutters. Harsh, wild, and unpredictable, just like Richard.

Leah was glad he was gone. She did not want to see him. She did not want to speak with him. And most of all, she did not want him to touch her. For if he were here right now, she very much doubted she'd be able to resist the powerful attraction that burned between them. Now she truly understood what desire was.

How it could make her sister give herself to the man she loved even without the bonds of matrimony. How it could make Leah love a man, want a man, need a man, who thought himself incapable of loving her back.

What had happened to make him so cynical? What had caused the grim twist of his mouth? The despair that had wracked his voice? The bleak starkness of his eyes that bespoke of so much pain? Had someone hurt him in the past? Hurt him so fiercely, he'd closed off his heart, buried his needs and his emotions, cast away hope, sworn never to love again?

At least, that's what he thought.

Leah thought differently. She loved him. She knew that as surely as her heart beat within her breast, but she would not burden him with the words. He was right. He hadn't really wanted her, hadn't asked for her love. Her despicable father had somehow gulled him into the match. Someday she would learn exactly how her father had managed that. But not now.

Now she had to discover the means to bring her husband back to life and heal his heart. She did not quite know how to go about it, but she had no intention of losing this battle.

Chapter Twelve

Richard slapped the road dust off his breeches as he headed for the house. The hot sun burning the back of his neck was nothing to the regret seizing his gut as a vision of Leah's soft green eyes, amber flecks barely visible beneath glistening tears, rose up yet again to haunt him as they had haunted him every hour of every day that he was away. Or was it guilt making his shoulders clench and his breathing hard and ineffective?

He had promised her civility, then he had trampled on her feelings like a rabid bull. How she must hate him now, but not nearly as much as he hated himself for hurting her so viciously.

As he reached for the handle, the door opened and Rachel stepped into his path. "Thank heavens, you are back."

She wore a sweet smile and a flowing blue gown that brought out the sparkle in her eyes. No one looking at this picture of pretty femininity would ever guess the evil lurking within.

Had she stood at the window every day for the past three weeks, awaiting his arrival? Plotting how best to antagonize him?

Richard brushed past her and headed for the stairs. He needed to seek out Leah. Not that he had any idea what he wanted to say, but he knew he needed to say something. Anything.

"I must speak with you," Rachel said, following at his heels. "You do not know what has happened here in your absence."

"I'm sure you will tell me all, and then some, but not now. I'm tired and I am dirty. All I want right now is a hot bath and a hot meal." *And Leah,* his treacherous mind added.

Rachel stepped into his path, her arms crossed over her chest. "I fear I must insist on speaking with you now. If you like, I could order your bath. Then we could have this conversation in your rooms."

Christ, next she'd be offering to strip off his breeches.

No doubt she would harangue him all the way up the stairs. Short of physically restraining her, Richard had no way to stop her. Nor could he trust himself to touch her. While he had never caused a woman bodily harm—and he had no intention of doing so now—he feared the temptation might prove too strong.

He turned and stalked to the library.

"You must do something about your wife," Rachel said as she followed him into the room, her cheeks reddening as she spoke. "She is turning the household upside down, wreaking havoc—"

"Stop." Richard raised his hand. "I see you are in the mood to play games, madam, but I am not. State your concerns, quickly and clearly. Now, if you please."

Rachel thrust her chin in the air. "Very well. I wanted to be as delicate as possible, but you leave me no choice. She does not know how to go about in society and she will not heed my advice."

"Perhaps she feels she does not need your advice." Richard grabbed a bottle of whisky from the sideboard. He was tempted to slug it straight from the bottle, just to shock Rachel into silence, but he poured a glass and took a civilized sip.

Rachel watched his every motion, as if she were memorizing the swing of his arm, the roll of his lips as he smoothed the remaining liquid from his mouth.

"She does not understand about calling cards and paying visits," she said, her voice slightly breathless, as if she'd just waltzed across the room. "She sees anyone and everyone who calls here. Especially that odious aunt of hers, and that young man, Andrew, Alex, oh, whatever he calls himself."

Richard schooled his features into a mask of indifference, but he could not quite hide the tension whitening his knuckles as he gripped his glass. Jealousy was a trait he had never admired.

When had it settled so firmly within his breast?

"Surely you are not suggesting her aunt is unwelcome?"

Rachel inched her chin higher. "She says whatever she thinks without regard to propriety."

"You make her sound like a Cheapside doxy."

"Must you be so crude? I like the child. Truly, I do. She is a sweet little thing, but she is also willful and stubborn. She brought a rodent into the house as a pet for Alison. A rodent, I tell you! I won't have it. I banished it from the nursery. Then I had to listen to Alison kick up a fuss."

Richard bit back his laughter, but said nothing.

It was far better to let the woman spend herself, like a thunderstorm. Then she would go away, at least for a few hours.

He was tired, his body aching from long hours in the saddle and his never-ending desire for his wife.

I love you. Her sweet words came back to taunt him as they had taunted him every moment of every day since she'd moaned them at the height of her pleasure. He could still see her eyes dark with desire, amber streaks gleaming in the firelight. He could still feel her body quivering beneath him, her hands clinging to his hips, her legs wrapped around his waist as her passage clutched his manhood, pulling him deeper and closer to danger.

As the longest, most emotionally devastating climax he had ever experienced shattered his senses, his reason, his control, his true danger had come crashing into his consciousness.

He cared for her deeply, too deeply. She was touching emotions he did not wish to feel, resurrecting hopes and dreams for a future for which he did not wish to yearn, nor did he even believe possible. She was a threat to the careful control upon which he'd rebuilt his life following Eric's death. To the distance he kept from the world around him.

To the security of his hardened heart.

He could not allow that to happen. So he'd denied her sweet words. In the most vicious manner imaginable. She was so young, so trusting, so giving and hopeful. It was only natural for her to imagine herself in love with her husband, but what did he do?

He'd chewed up her words and spit them back in her face.

God, he was such a bastard. How could he have been so cruel? Couldn't he have found a better time, a better place to destroy her dreams? The taste of shame did not sit well within his mouth and no amount of whisky was going to wash it away.

A spasm shot through his gut whenever he thought of her beautiful face, first aglow with passion and hope for a future he could never give her, then quickly transformed into shadows and pain as he'd disabused her sweet declaration.

I love you. How her words tormented him still.

Rachel planted her hands on her hips. "And she has undermined the staff, taken over the scheduling of servant duties and menu planning without so much as a by-your-leave."

"Why does she need your permission?" Richard said, thankful for the distraction from his torturous thoughts. He hitched his hip on the desk. "After all, she is the mistress of the house."

"But she doesn't understand the complexity of the task."

Rachel waved her hand through the air. "Oh, I know she says she has had tutors and such . . ."

Given all the trauma and heartache this woman had caused through the years, Richard had never seen her so agitated, not even when her husband had died, and over a domestic power struggle of all things. He would have laughed, were it not so predictably Rachel. "I begin to see the true problem. My wife is taking her rightful place as mistress of the house, and you do not like being relegated to the shelf."

"Oh, that is not it at all," she said, approaching him on soft, dainty footfalls. Ever the lady, even in the midst of a fit of pique. "I should have known you would somehow turn this around to me and my motives. That is fine. She is ruining your house, but since you do not care, who am I to say anything."

She drew so close, he could smell the stench of her lilac perfume, which threatened to make him retch.

He wanted to find Leah, to bury his nose in her rose-scented hair, to wash away the filth and stain of his past in her sweet, accepting innocence, to run his hands over the smooth caps of her shoulders, the lift of her breasts, and beg her forgiveness.

Good Lord, where had that thought come from?

He rubbed his throbbing temples. "What exactly do you mean by 'ruining the house'?"

"She is destroying the blue room. She is tearing down the wall and opening it up to the conservatory. She has decreed that from now on, all the family meals will be served there, as if we are servants for her to order about."

"I fail to see the problem—"

"Do you not understand what I am saying to you? She is tearing down walls and destroying rooms. She has totally demolished the duchess's bedchamber. After I spent so many years making it perfect. It was my last link to Eric."

She touched her fingertips to the corners of her eyes.

Richard curled his hands as potent fury pulsed through his veins. "How pretty you look with dainty tears clinging to your sooty lashes. Why, if I didn't know better, I might even believe your pretense of love."

"I did love Eric," she cried, raising her hands as if to clutch the lapels of his coat. His glare sent her hands back to her waist. "But I made a mistake. One terrible mistake. Will you punish me for the rest of my life?"

"For the rest of your life and beyond," Richard vowed, crossing to the windows. He looked out over the gardens, half expecting to see Leah and Alison strolling hand-in-hand, another image that had haunted his every waking hour while he was away.

Alison deserved a mother who loved her, a mother who would not use her daughter's life as a weapon to gain her way, a mother like Leah. "You will never know a moment's peace, even in death, as Eric never knew a moment's peace in life."

Rachel closed the distance between them, walking so close her skirts touched his shins. "You are a cruel man to hate me so, after all we meant to each other in the past."

"The past died eight years ago—"

"The past will never die."

"—on the day you married my brother."

"You know why I did that," Rachel said, her voice shrill, desperate. She clutched his arm. "My parents forced me."

Richard peeled her fingers off his sleeve. He twisted his lips in a thin, cruel smile. "My, what an accomplished liar you are. Why, I even begin to think you believe your own words. You married Eric for one reason only. You thought you could have your stud and your coronet, too. Unfortunately, you were wrong."

"That is not true. I loved you, then. I—"

"Do not say it." Richard towered over her, his breath harsh in his throat. "Or I swear, I will throttle you."

He turned toward the desk. He heard her walk up behind

him. He wished she would go away. But he knew it was impossible. He might haunt her through eternity, but she would haunt him, too.

They were partners in their misery.

"Although you don't believe me," she said, coming to stand beside him. "I did love you with all my heart. But I grew to love Eric after I wed him. He was such a kind and gentle man. Who could help but love him?"

Richard turned to face her. "Save your lies for your friends. The past is not the issue here. Your sensibilities are twisted about because my wife is taking her rightful position as mistress of this household. As you find your situation here so intolerable, I repeat my previous offers to provide you with an establishment of your own and a comfortable maintenance. You shall never want for anything."

"This is my home. Why would I want to leave it?"

"For one thing, you would be free of my presence. As I am so odious and cruel and disrespectful of your tender feelings, that should be reason enough."

"Hardly." Rachel crossed her arms over her chest. "I have learned to tolerate your animosity. I rarely, if ever, notice anymore that you are an ill-bred, ill-mannered lout."

"If you cannot accept your new status here, a move would be the best solution for all of us."

Her blue eyes narrowed as she contemplated his words. Then she smiled, a cold, calculated twisting of her lips. "Of course, I shall do what you think best. But if I leave, I take Alison."

Richard yanked a leather-bound volume off the nearest shelf. It was either that, or strangle the woman where she stood. He did not reply. It was an old argument, one he'd heard hundreds of times. He was ashamed to admit, even if only to himself, that he was finding it harder to fight the temptation to let the scandal fly, to let the resulting fragments fall where they may, but sanity always returned, along with the pain.

He would never allow a hint of scandal to swirl around Alison, or tarnish the memory of his brother's name.

Even if it meant he would never be free of Rachel.

"Were you to attempt to take her from me," Rachel was saying, "I would certainly weep to my dearest friends how abominable you were to deny me the comfort of my daughter's presence . . . not to mention *why* you felt obliged to do so. I know you do not want that to happen. How else could you explain taking her from her loving mother."

"Loving mother? The cruelest jest of the century." He dropped his book on the desk, the thud echoing through the chamber. "You do not care if Alison lives or dies."

Rachel shot her hand through the air.

Richard grabbed her wrist, twisted it away. He lowered his face until they were nose to nose. "Alison does not leave this house. If you ever attempt to remove her, I will hunt you down like the bitch you are. There is no place you could hide that would be safe from my vengeance."

Rachel slid her free hand along his stubbled jaw.

"You would never hurt me," she whispered, then pushed up on her toes, her eyes closing, her lips parting breathlessly.

"Do it," he said through his teeth, "and I *will* kill you."

Rachel hesitated a moment, her eyes meeting his, widening beneath the menace in his gaze. She dropped her hand, backed away, but she did not leave. She simply stared at him.

Her breathing grew shallow. Her chest rose and fell, as if she could not quite catch her breath.

Slowly, she flicked her tongue over her lips.

In his youthful ignorance, Richard would have found her display erotic, enticing. Now what clenched his jaw and hardened his hands into fists was the depths of folly that had caused him to fall so deeply under this woman's spell. He had been so young, so deeply *in love*. He sneered at the memory.

He could almost hear the water as it had bubbled over the rocks below the cliffs on the day he'd lost his idealistic innocence, when he'd learned love was nothing but lust wrapped in a pretty disguise.

The dizzying scent of wildflowers and heated skin had drugged his mind as he'd eased Rachel onto her back. The wild beating of her pulse beneath the softness of her skin had burned through his blood as he'd pushed her gown up her legs until her mound of honeysuckle hair gleamed against the darkness of the blanket, forbidden fruit, forbidden no more.

His first taste of passion. Through his years at university, he had never been able to casually bed another, not when his heart had been pledged to Rachel for years. Instinct had guided him to her entrance, or perhaps it was Rachel's grasping hand. Never once had he noticed her lack of pain, her lack of shock, her lack of innocence as he'd given himself to her. At the last possible moment, he had withdrawn. He would not leave her with a babe in her belly, not before they could wed. Three weeks later, she had married his brother and Richard went off to fight the French, all the while hoping to die.

He'd gone home only once, just after Waterloo, but he'd soon discovered there was a place worse than hell for sinners like him. Now he would never escape.

The memory of this particular betrayal had long since lost the power to hurt him. No, what galled him now was how easily and completely he had fallen for her lies.

His hands itched with the urge to smash his knuckles into the wall. Instead, he rubbed his fingers over his face as he paced to the windows. How artfully she had drawn him in, ensnared him more thoroughly than the fangs of a man trap, drawing him into her body with pledges of undying love and devotion.

Never could Richard have imagined such deceit.

He looked out over the gardens, but his mind dragged up an image of Rachel as she'd stood before him on the cliff face, backlit by a slate gray sky, mist blowing up from the churning sea. Hands raised, begging him to understand, her blue eyes as turbulent as the gathering clouds and brimming with tears, vowing her love, even as she confessed she was to marry Eric—his brother!—but nothing need change between them.

As if he would bed his brother's wife.

Rachel watched him silently, staring at him through seductively half-opened eyes, as if she thought passion would overwhelm him and he would drag her into his arms.

Did she honestly believe he would ever touch her again?

He stalked past her and out the door. He blamed his folly on youthful ignorance and indiscretion, lust run rampant with no control. He could not so easily excuse the lies and betrayals that came later, that destroyed everyone he loved.

As he passed the blue room, he decided to see what changes Leah had made. The last thing he expected to see was his wife hanging in the air on a ladder propped against the wall, fiddling with the draperies. "What are you doing up there?"

His bellow echoed off the windows. Leah shrieked. Her hands flew up in the air as she teetered on the edge of her step.

Heart pumping, Richard lunged and caught her in his arms.

She clutched his neck, her arms tangling around his shoulders, her fingers threading through his hair.

His body clenched and tightened. He fixed her with a stony stare. "What were you doing on that ladder?"

Her bewitching eyes met his, and he lost himself in their deep green depths, their dusting of gold mesmerizing him as swiftly as any sorcerer's spell.

"I missed you," she said, her voice a soft whisper, her warm breath fluttering over his cheeks. Her lips curved into a gentle smile. Her golden hair framed her face, her eyes reflecting the afternoon light, making them sparkle, a ray of sunshine in his desolate world. "I am happy you're home."

He searched her face for some trace of deceit. After the way he left, she should be hurling pottery at his head, but all he saw reflected in her smile was happiness and love shining in her eyes. He stomped on the tender emotions bubbling to life within him, forced a sternness into his voice that belied the desire and lust and need curling within his gut, tightening his muscles and tendons and groin. He would not fall for her spell.

Yet the dam around his heart cracked. Feelings he'd denied for years surged through his blood. Do not be a fool, the bitter man inside his mind screamed. Leave this house. Leave this woman. Grab Alison and Geoffrey and never look back.

But like a man possessed, he eased her down the length of his body, slid his arms around her waist. "Leah," he groaned, pushing his hands into her hair and covering her mouth with his.

Chapter Thirteen

Leah felt his desperation and clung to him just as fiercely, her fingers digging into the soft wool of his jacket.

Her breasts were crushed against his chest, but she couldn't get close enough. What demons tormented this man? What anguish drove his despair? If only he would let her into his heart, she would wash away his past. She supposed she could be churlish and childish and punish him for his harsh words, but she could not dredge up the energy. She hurt for the man he used to be, before betrayal caused him to close off his heart, leaving him emotionally dead, needing no one save himself. His was a lonely life, full of responsibility, to family, to tenants, to needy souls dependent upon his charity, but without tenderness or love.

Hers was a deceptively simple plan. She would show him her love with every breath, every touch, every deed, but she would not burden him with the words. Those she would keep wrapped within her heart. Only when he loved her as much as she loved him, would she say them again.

She ran her hands over his back, feeling the powerful muscles bunching beneath his shoulders, the desire curling up within her, tightening her belly, clenching her thighs, building an ache within her deepest, most intimate flesh.

The scent of leather and male and hot skin bronzed beneath the sun filled her senses as he pressed her back against the wall and slid one powerful leg between her thighs. The hard evidence of his desire ground against her hips. She pulled him closer, wanting to feel him, needing to feel him.

His clothing was wilted, his hair streaked with road dust, but never had he looked more handsome. He pressed her back against the wall, then dropped to his knees. His hot breath whooshed through her cotton gown. Desire licked through Leah, setting her senses afire, her body tingling and aching for his touch.

Air rushed in and out of her chest so swiftly, and still she felt breathless as his hands roamed down her sides, down her legs, under her dress. She tangled her fingers in his hair and closed her eyes, but she wanted to kiss him.

She cradled his face between her palms, drew him to his feet, and brought his lips back to hers. She moved her tongue along his teeth, his mouth, hot and greedy beneath her gentle probing, and it was as if her touch set off a terrible storm.

His hands roamed over her breasts, making them tingle and ache. His lips followed the path of his hands, mouthing a wet, hot, erotic path over the mounds of skin rising above her stays, his tongue delving between her cleavage, fingers slipping beneath the fabric, rubbing her nipples.

She moaned, or perhaps it was him, she did not know as she clutched fistfuls of his coat. He dragged the cradle of her hips into close contact with his swollen flesh, hard beneath his form-fitting breeches, letting her know he wanted her as much as she wanted him. It was enough. For now.

He might not love her, but in this they were equals.

This desperate need, this undeniable, unquenchable ache.

In some small part of her brain that still functioned, Leah heard Rachel's voice, somewhere in the distance, somewhere out in the hall, growing louder and closer. Richard dragged his lips from hers. He stared into her eyes, his own gaze, dark and stormy and filled with need, before possessing her lips once more in a demanding kiss that banished thought and reason.

They separated, then came back together, as if neither could bear to part from the other. Tongues touching and stroking. Delving and tasting. Legs tangling, fingers searching, until it was all she could do not to beg him to drag her to bed.

Finally, he propped one elbow on the wall behind her head, but he made no move to put a decorous distance between them.

His bottomless eyes searched her features, then he smiled, a devil-may-care grin. "So, you missed me? I thought perhaps you meant to use the hammer sitting atop that ladder on my head."

"No doubt you deserve it," she said. "But you seduced the notion right out of me, clever, wicked man that you are."

He laughed, the sound deep and resonant and tingling along her nerve endings like chocolate over her tongue. And there, the awkwardness of their last parting buried in humor and lightness.

Her throat ached with her pent-up emotions and the words she longed to say, but she would not regale him with her needs or demand from him that which he was not yet willing, or able, to give. At least not for the moment. She was patient. She would wait.

He stepped back, just as Alison charged through the door.

"It's my uncle, the duke," Alison said, leaping into his out-stretched arms.

He swung her around, clutched her against his chest, his features unguarded, his defenses down, as he smiled at the laughing child. The look in his eyes bespoke of deep affection, and something darker, a stark, desperate yearning.

His rumbling voice came out softly soothing as he carried Alison to the settee. "I have missed you. Have you missed me?"

"Ummhmm," Alison said, her black curls bouncing about her face. "But I went shopping with Aunt Leah."

"Did you? Did you buy anything for me?"

"No, silly. We bought fabric for dresses. Pink for me and green for Aunt Leah. Auntie gave me a dormouse, but Mama says it is dirty . . ."

Richard smiled at the child laughing in his arms. Tiny handprints appeared on his coat to mingle with the road dust.

When he looked up, his dark eyes meeting Leah's, the emotion blazing within was so stark, her breath caught in the back of her aching throat. Did he long for a child of his own?

She rubbed her hands over her belly. Thanks to her father's stilted explanation, she knew how children were conceived and where they grew. The one thing she did not yet know was how to tell if she were with child. Perhaps his babe already grew within her. Oh, how she prayed it was true.

For he would make the most wonderful father. And a child would help ease the pain of his past. She was desperate to know who had hurt him, what had happened to rip out his heart.

Several times, she'd nearly given in to the temptation to ask Rachel, but she always regained her senses.

She would wait to hear the truth from his lips, rather than the lies Rachel would no doubt throw out to hurt her.

As the minutes passed, she became excruciatingly aware of Rachel's eyes upon her. No doubt she had committed a faux pas of the most grievous sort by allowing her husband to kiss her outside of the bedroom, but she did not care.

Nor did she care if the flush on her cheeks proclaimed the extent of the passionate embrace upon which Rachel had intruded.

She refused to cower beneath her sister-in-law's silent scrutiny. She walked to the settee and sat beside Richard.

He brushed a curl from Alison's brow. "Would you like to

see what I have **brought for** you? And then an outing in the park? Perhaps an **ice for a treat**?"

"A present for me?" **Alison** bounced up and down on his lap. "Let me see, let me **see**."

"I should very **much like to** go along with you, St. Austin," Rachel said, her voice **a soft**, delicate purr that narrowed Leah's eyes. Richard did not seem to notice, as Alison chose that moment to squeal **in his e**ars.

"I would prefer **to spend tim**e alone with Alison," Richard retorted as he stood, **the child** clutched to his chest. Then he turned to Leah. "That is, **if you** have no objections, madam."

"Of course not," Leah said. She had chores of her own, not the least of which was a trip to Mrs. Bristoll's to check on Tommy. Yesterday, his fever had returned for the third time in as many weeks. It was a baffling illness that recurred with no precise interval, but left the youth feeling perfectly fine in between bouts of shivering and sweating. The doctor they'd consulted had prescribed purgatives and emetics, a cure which had left the boy much weaker than the illness that plagued him.

Alison buried her face in Richard's neck. He raised Leah's hand to his lips. The calloused pads of his fingertips sent a shiver up her arm, chased quickly by a flash of heat as his mouth moved over the inside corner of her wrist, his lips smooth and soft against her tender skin.

"Until later," he murmured, then turned and carried the child from the room

"My, my, my," Rachel said. "That was quite a tender scene we interrupted. Of course, you realize gently bred ladies do not go about conducting such passionate displays in public."

"I haven't seen my husband in three weeks," Leah said, rising from the settee. "I neither require nor request your approval to welcome him home in any manner I see fit."

* * *

Rachel curled her hands around the arms of her chair as she watched the foolish chit stride from the room. The girl might appear quiet and shy, but through their recent skirmishes, Rachel had learned she also possessed a strong-willed, stubborn streak as treacherous as the ebbing tide on the Thames.

It was not her softly stated rebuke that urged Rachel to follow her and push her down the stairs. No, it was the deplorable state of her frock, the bodice crushed, the skirts wrinkled and covered in road dust from Richard's bold caresses—in a public access room, no less. Rachel had even noticed a large, male handprint on her bodice, just above her right breast.

Impotent rage tightened Rachel's jaw. She didn't know why she was so surprised. She had assumed Richard would bed the chit. After all, he was a man of lusty appetites, as well she knew from experience. But knowing in theory, and seeing this visual, undeniable evidence of his lust for another woman was as painful as having a ram-rod shoved up her spine.

Not that he loved the girl, Rachel had no fear of that.

Richard would love but once in his lifetime, and she was the woman he loved. She had only to convince him that she was as much a victim of their tortured past as he was. Then all would be well. He had loved her once. He would love her again.

They were meant to be together.

No, he certainly didn't love his wife. She was nothing more than a willing body in the night. But it had to end. And soon.

The thought of Richard touching Leah, stroking her as he'd once stroked Rachel, pushed her out of her chair.

She had to meet with Margaret. There was no time to lose.

Rachel had firmly believed that Leah would want to flaunt herself before society as the Duchess of St. Austin, daughter of a merchant made good, but she couldn't have been more wrong.

Leah had refused to go about in society without her husband.

It hadn't helped that Richard had left so soon after the wedding. Now that he had finally returned, it was time to wage the war. The battle lines were clearly drawn, the enemy identified. Leah didn't stand a chance.

"Did Alison enjoy her outing in the park?" Leah asked, hoping mundane conversation would still her rapidly beating heart as Richard strolled around her newly decorated rooms.

His broad frame and powerful stride seemed as incongruous against the delicate Sheraton furnishings and mint green walls as would a panther prowling through Hyde Park. "Yes," he said. "Though she would have enjoyed it more were you with us."

He shot her a rueful grin. "You are quite accomplished at ducks and drakes, I understand, and can make your rock skip over the water at least five times before it sinks. I fear my own display came up sadly lacking."

Leah laughed. His unguarded expression as he swung his head around to meet her gaze caused her breath to catch in her throat. The dark depths of his eyes revealed no clue to the secrets he kept hidden away, but she did not ply him with questions. She would learn all she needed to know slowly, as he came to trust her, to love her, to need her as she needed him.

His hair had grown overlong while he was away and lay like black velvet against his blue superfine coat. The sun had bronzed his face, making him appear more Grecian god than underworld lord.

As he fingered the ivory counterpane, it was all she could do not to fling herself against his chest and beg him to stroke his fingers over *her* flesh, right now, upon that bed.

Good heavens, she wanted him to touch her everywhere.

"I do like what you have done to this room," he said, staring at the bed, his chest heaving slightly, making her wonder if he were experiencing the same stark desire that was building an uncomfortable tension beneath her skin.

Though spacious enough to sleep a dozen, the chamber suddenly seemed much too small, the air too thick to breathe.

"Do you?" she said. She bit her lip to hide her smile, or perhaps it was to trap her moan of desire in her throat. "I was afraid you might object, but you were gone so long and I simply could not spend one more night with that horrid yellow and garish red blazing in my eyes."

His low chuckle rumbled over her skin, deep like thunder and just as intriguing. "Garish red. An apt description, but it suited the previous duchess perfectly."

He moved to the satinwood writing table centered between the floor-to-ceiling windows. A gilded cage was positioned atop it. A dormouse crouched in one corner of the cage. "I take it this is the offending rodent?"

"I am afraid so." Leah sighed as she walked up beside him, so close, his scent of jasmine and amber filled her lungs. The heat of his skin burned through his coat and shivered over her arms. "I thought, perhaps, we could keep it in the conservatory. Then Alison could visit it whenever she wanted."

"Yes, that is fine." A bowl of chopped fruits sat on the table. Richard picked up an apple chunk, held it out. Big, black eyes stared at his fingers before the animal scampered forward and snatched it away. "I had one once, as a child."

"So did I," Leah said, trying to imagine him as a small boy, but failing miserably. He was so strong, so forceful, it was impossible for her to see him as anything but the magnificent man he was now. "Tell me of your childhood," she blurted out, despite her resolve to wait for him to discuss his past.

His features darkened, his eyes narrowed, and she regretted her hasty words. They had years to learn all they needed to know about one another. She did not want anguished memories intruding upon this night, their first together in so long.

The silence stretched out, the only sound was his rapid breathing and the breeze trembling against the window.

"There is not much to tell," he finally murmured, but the harsh tone of his voice said his words were a lie. "Eric was the eldest son, Geoffrey and I, the surety the title would continue should Eric . . ." He turned his gaze to the dormouse. "Should Eric perish before begetting a son of his own."

She slid her hand into his. "I am so sorry. I did not mean to—"

"Do not be concerned," he said, his fingers closing around hers. Good Lord, what was wrong with him?

His eyes burned and his throat tightened painfully. He would have preferred she fling crockery at his head, that she rant and rail at his callous disregard for her feelings.

Anything but this tender acceptance. This soft understanding for all he had suffered that threatened to unman him, and she knew not even the half of it. Nor could he ever tell her. Some secrets stained the soul too darkly.

Some secrets could never be revealed.

Shimmering tears darkened her eyes. "How did he die?"

"A riding accident." He swallowed against the thickening in his throat. "Just over a year ago."

He could not go there. His memories were still too bitter, still too raw. He turned his thoughts toward more pressing concerns. Since his return, he had yet to see Geoffrey and none of the servants seemed to know where he was. "When was the last time you saw Geoffrey?"

"Two days ago," she said, her soft smile showing no hint of concern, or that all was not as it should be. "He went to stay with friends. A house party in Edinburgh, he said."

Good Lord, he was a fool to think he could resist this woman, so quiet, yet so strong. Perhaps he should have remained in Yorkshire. "Did he mention with whom he was staying?"

"Lord Egglestone and Lord Isherwood." A note of panic crept into her voice. Her fingers tightened around his. "Is anything wrong? Should we be worried? I have no brothers to judge him by, but he does leave the house at all hours of the night and often stays away for days at a time. Rachel says that is perfectly normal for a gentleman of the *ton*, so I did not—"

"No, nothing is wrong," he said, or so he hoped. He kissed her fingertips, breathed the familiar scent of her skin, roses and lotion and soft, feminine flesh. "But I thank you for your concern."

The glare she sent him practically screamed, "Of course I'm concerned, I'm your wife, you idiot."

He ran his hand over his mouth to hide his grin. The tension gripping his neck eased. Egglestone and Isherwood were young and foolish, to be sure, but not as reckless as many of Geoffrey's friends. Not excessively given to drinking and gaming. Hardly likely to lead Geoffrey into too much mischief. Richard would dispatch his man of affairs in the morning to make certain all was well and Geoffrey was where he said he would be.

He could do no more this evening. His ability to think was quickly dissipating, his awareness overwhelmingly centered on his wife. She wore her golden hair loose and flowing over her shoulders. Her green eyes glowed in the candlelight.

Her frivolous dress bared just enough of the swells of her breasts to entice him, to dare him to delve beneath the bodice and explore the beauty hidden from view.

She sent him a shy smile. "I have made some other changes while you were away."

He smothered his grin. "So I have heard."

Her brows shot up. "I see. I suppose Rachel lost no time in complaining about me. I daresay I have vexed her sorely since I've been here."

"I daresay you have, but do not be concerned. Everyone and everything vexes Rachel."

"Why does she not have a home of her own?" She covered her mouth with her hands, as if she never meant to speak the words.

What could Richard say? That he would do anything in his power to be rid of Rachel, save the one thing that would guarantee heartbreak for them all?

He flexed his hands. "If Rachel left, she would want to take Alison with her." And Richard had no real reason to deny her, at least, none he could voice aloud. "She is so young. Too much has happened in her life. Her father . . ." His voice cracked. He dragged in a lungful of air, ran his hands through his hair, cleared his throat. "As her guardian, I want her here, with me, where I can see that her needs are properly met."

The intensity in Leah's gaze as she met his eyes made him uncomfortable, made him want to shift on his feet and glance away from her penetrating stare. It was as if she had just discovered he were some sort of hero, some sort of noble man, rather than a dastardly cur who had forced her into marriage to save his soul and keep his secrets. God, was he no better than her father?

"Alison," she said, true affection curling her lips and trembling in her voice. "What a love she is. Did she enjoy her present?"

"What do you think? Which reminds me . . ." Richard slid his hand into his pocket, closed his fist around the trinket he'd purchased on his travels. "I have something for you, too. Now, close your eyes."

"I am not good about surprises," she said, cupping her palms over her face to keep from peeking.

He drew her left hand into his. Her nervous giggle made him laugh, or perhaps it was his own nerves that had his hand shaking as he slid the bauble onto her third finger, until it rested against her gold wedding band. It meant nothing, or so he told himself, as she opened her eyes and peered at the ring, a large, square-cut emerald surrounded by shimmering topaz.

It was a conciliatory offering for the abominable way he had treated her before he left. Nothing more. Nothing less.

But she gazed at him through eyes ablaze with that deep emotion he'd glimpsed in the past, eyes that dared him to search his soul, to speak the truth.

Her sweet words rose up to torment him. *I love you.*

He rubbed his forefinger beneath the tight knot of his cravat, brushed away the sweat gathering on the back of his neck.

"A late betrothal ring," he whispered. He was not good with words. He could not say it had reminded him of her eyes, of the gold glimmering within their deep green depths, of the entrancing way she smiled at him, with the promise of forever in her gaze.

Too innocent and idealistic yet to realize forever was just a dream, but they had today.

God, she was so beautiful. He could not have spoken another word had his very life depended upon it. He cupped his hands around her neck, lowered his head as he drew her close.

He covered her mouth with his and felt the world explode. Every muscle, every tendon, tightened and clenched. Blood rushed to his groin until he was so hard, he couldn't breathe. It took all his strength of will not to shred her flimsy dress from her body, toss her upon the bed and bury himself inside her like a ravishing beast.

Instead, he forced his hands to slowly ease the ribbons fastening the gown at her nape, to bare her rounded shoulders to his touch with the slightest movement of his hand, trailing the path of his fingertips with his mouth. Exploring. Tasting.

The shape of her shoulders. The sweep of her neck. Her throaty moans threatened his fragile control. When her hands moved beneath his coat, fingers spread wide across his chest, he came undone. He tore off his waistcoat, buttons scattering over the floor. God help him, she laughed, albeit a quiet, shy, nervous laugh that touched a chord deep within him and made his breath burn in his throat. She reached for his shirt, dragged it out of his breeches, then up over his head. As her eyes ran over his chest, her lower lip disappeared between her teeth. Then she lifted her gaze to his and he thought he might drown in their deep green depths, filled with desire—for him. Only for him.

"I want you to touch me," she said, her voice quivering. Her face flushing the deep purple of the finest claret, she grasped her shift at her knees, then slowly, so torturously slowly, drew it up her legs, past her hips, past her breasts.

By the time she sent it sailing to the floor, he was shaking with the need to do just that. But she wasn't done torturing him yet. Her eyes locked with his, she reached for the waistband of his breeches and popped the buttons, her knuckles brushing against the tightly bunched muscles of his stomach.

So painfully aroused he thought he might come undone before he even touched her, he dragged her onto the bed. She was wet and hot and ready, her legs wrapping around him, her mouth moving over his neck, her scent surrounding him, her murmurs of want and need burning through his blood.

Perhaps later, he would think of all the reasons he should have kept his distance, why he should not have touched her, should not have wanted her—needed her—so desperately.

But not now, driven only by his reckless desire to run his hands through her hair, to breathe the rosewater bathing her skin, to taste the salt of her flesh, to reach for the future, rather than dwell in the past. He slid within her tight passage, plunging deeply, slowly, yet fiercely, until her inner muscles clenched around him, drawing him in with short, powerful pulses, her nails digging into his back.

I love you. Her sweet declaration tormented him, but she did not say the words. He only heard them in his mind.

He should be happy. It was what he wanted. Then why did he feel so cold when it was over, when he clutched her against his chest, when his frantic heartbeat eased and languid peace rolled through his body, when heavy silence hung in the room?

Rachel was already seated at the table when Leah entered the dining room the next morning. A sense of sadness brought a momentary pause to Leah's steps. She could only imagine how difficult it must be to lose one's husband.

Still, Rachel seemed to be handling the loss amazingly well. She never spoke of her husband, nor showed any grief at his passing. No, all she showed was animosity toward Leah and a strange sense of possessiveness toward Richard.

At least now Leah understood the woman's presence in this house. Richard's devotion and love for his niece were admirable traits Leah found irresistible. It gave her hope he would as easily accept Catherine's child into his home, if— no, not if, when—she finally found him, even with the taint of bastardry to his birth.

"Why are you hovering at my back?" Rachel tossed the challenge at Leah without bothering to glance up from her tea.

For three weeks, she had outwardly professed her friendship and support while quietly undermining Leah's authority with the staff. Oh, she always did it with a smile on her face, but the malice in her voice was unmistakable, as was the superior tilt of her chin and her patronizing smile.

In the past, Leah had bit her tongue, preferring not to quarrel with her sister-in-law, but no more.

It was time she took her rightful place in this household.

She drew a deep breath. "I am Richard's wife. As such, it is my place to sit at the head of his table during formal meals, and at his right hand on more informal occasions. Therefore, you are sitting in my seat and I am asking you politely to move."

It might sound churlish, perhaps even childish, but there

was more at stake than where each woman sat at the breakfast table, and Rachel's vicious glare said she knew it.

"No," Rachel said, lifting her brows. "You are ordering me to move, but I do not take orders from you, darling. This was my home long before you arrived. It will be my home long after you depart. Now be a dear and sit over there."

"I am not going anywhere," Leah said, fighting the urge to fidget with her dress beneath Rachel's unrelenting stare.

A long moment passed before Rachel finally turned her attention back to her tea. "Why are you making a fuss? The breakfast table is no place to indulge in a fit of childish hysterics."

"That is another thing," Leah said. "I am not a child, and I resent your referring to me as such at every possible moment."

Rachel widened vapid blue eyes. "My, aren't we in a snit this morning. What will you do if I do not move? Throw yourself to the floor kicking and screaming as Alison does?"

"I have never seen any such behavior from your daughter," was all Leah said.

They stared at one another until Rachel finally rose in a huff, her amethyst silk skirts flowing out behind her as she moved to the opposite side of the table. "You do realize, do you not, that you are behaving like the *enfant* you claim not to be."

"I do not know what I have done to offend you," Leah said quietly, "but I know you have taken me in dislike. I am sorry for that. I had hoped we could be as sisters. As we are not, could we, at least, strive for civility?"

Rachel puffed out her lower lip. "What is wrong, dear? Did you not get enough sleep last night? Or are you simply hungry from missing your evening meal? Oh, do forgive me, I must assume you were too busy feeding other hungers to bother attending the supper I arranged to welcome St. Austin home."

Leah wouldn't dignify that crude and utterly shocking remark with a response. Rachel's dignity was slipping, but Leah had no idea, truly could not understand, her animosity.

She placed her palm on the table as she took her seat, then nearly jerked her hand onto her lap as Rachel's gaze landed on the betrothal ring Richard had given her. The jewels shimmered like green and gold fire in the morning sun streaming in through the windows.

Rachel's eyes narrowed and her lips pursed in a surprisingly nasty glare, as Rachel was ever cautious to keep her features perfectly composed, with no trace of emotion.

Richard's arrival at the table damned whatever nasty comment the woman was about to make.

"I trust you missed me this morning," he whispered near Leah's ear, his breath warm against her throat.

He raised her hand to his lips, pressed a lingering kiss against her fingertips. His smile was as wicked as the devil's own and her breathing grew shallow. The man did the most amazing things to her insides, setting her senses aflutter with one heated glance from his obsidian eyes.

"Most desperately," she said.

"This is all very amusing," Rachel said, "But perhaps not quite table talk?"

Leah flushed. All sense of sanity and reason fled the moment Richard came near her. She was thoroughly ensnared, but she would not fight her feelings, or even try to hide them.

She walked to the sidebar, dished out two plates of poached eggs in a minced ham sauce, spiced bread with burnt butter, baconned herring, sausage and cheese. As she set the dish before Richard, he flashed her a scandalous wink, which brought a burning flush to her cheeks and earned a narrowed-eyed glare from Rachel. To hide her answering grin, Leah busied herself arranging her linen on her lap.

"I inspected the blue room this morning," he said, scooping up a forkful of eggs. "I admit I was a bit preoccupied yesterday and didn't see anything but you hanging on the top of that ladder. I must say, it is not quite what I expected, given Rachel's description."

Leah's bread turned to dust in her throat. "What did she say I had done?"

"Torn down the wall adjoining the conservatory."

Leah choked. "Rachel exaggerates. I would never!"

Rachel harrumphed, but Leah ignored her. "I met with an architect and had plans drawn up, pending your approval. I went ahead with my room because I did not think you would mind."

Richard nodded. "Tell me about your plans," he said. "And remember, I never want to see you up on a ladder again."

His ferocious glare made her smile. He did care. She knew it, even if he didn't yet realize it himself.

Not knowing what Rachel had told him but certain it boded ill for her, Leah described her plans to turn the blue room into an informal dining room and to open it up to the conservatory.

"I love that room," she concluded. "And it will be so nice for intimate family meals. And I should like to expand the rose garden—I do so love roses—but nothing else," she added swiftly lest he think she disliked his house. "Your home is lovely."

He covered her hand with his. "Our home, Leah."

"My, but you two are dripping treacle today," Rachel drawled. "Should I leave the room?"

Leah gripped the linen on her knee. She was beginning to think Rachel truly hated her, but she couldn't imagine why.

"Rachel tells me you have had quite a few callers while I was away," Richard said, staring at his plate. He moved his sausage around with the tip of his fork. "Have you met anyone interesting?"

His tone, low and almost slightly raspy, confused her, as did the thin slash of his lips. It was as if he had not meant to voice the question, but had been unable to rein it in.

"Rachel exaggerates. I have had none, save for my aunt—"

"What about that young man?" Rachel interrupted. "I do not remember his name, but did he not call?"

What mischief was this? Leah glared at Rachel, then looked at Richard. His lips were compressed into such a tight line, they appeared white in his sun-darkened face.

She touched his hand, then waited for him to meet her gaze before she said, "His name is Alexander Prescott, and I have not seen him. He has called here once, the morning after our wedding. He is a dear, childhood *friend*. A friend I have no wish to deny."

To her relief, he nodded, but his tense posture remained.

"My aunt has been my only caller," she continued. "But she has returned to Lancashire. It seems one of our neighbors has pestered her for years to marry him. Now that I am grown, she has finally accepted his suit. They have plans to travel on the continent, once they are wed."

Her aunt's departure from Town had been a sudden and devastating loss for Leah, leaving her alone in a city in which she had no true friends. But she was so pleased that Emma had found her own happiness, she could not selfishly mourn the loss of her company. Besides, she had both Alison and the children at the foundling home on whom she could lavish her affection.

Richard wrapped her hand in his. "Perhaps they could pay us an extended visit when we retire from the city."

"Honestly, Richard, what can you be thinking?" Rachel sneered. "Next you will invite the miller to move in."

"If you disapprove," he said, his voice curt, his features tight. "You are more than welcome to remain in Town."

"And breathe all that filthy sea-coal smoke? I think not. Alison would wither and die."

"Alison will go with me."

"And I will go with Alison. Our cozy little family."

"Tell me of your trip to Yorkshire," Leah said, anxious to

lighten the tension that was rapidly building in the room. "What was the emergency?"

"A grease fire started in the kitchens, then spread to stables and house—"

"There is nothing left?" Rachel shrieked, her tea cup clanging against the saucer as she plopped it down. "What of the furnishings? There was a fortune just in rugs in that house!"

Richard speared a herring. "Everything was lost, but thankfully, no lives."

"You mean," Rachel jeered. "That the servants were so cowardly, they didn't even try to save the furnishings."

Leah gasped. "You cannot possibly be suggesting they should have risked their lives to save a few trinkets?"

"Trinkets? Rubenses and Rembrandts are not trinkets—"

"That is enough," Richard said. "Let us be thankful there wasn't a loss of life, and that is the end of it."

A heavy silence filled the room, broken only by the sound of forks scraping plates until the butler appeared in the doorway. "Mr. Peterfield has arrived, Your Grace. I have shown him to the library, as you requested."

"Thank you, Harris." Richard slid back his chair. He bowed to Leah. "If you will excuse me, I must meet with my man of affairs."

"Wait!" Rachel shouted before he could walk away. "The Cunningham ball is tonight. You must attend."

"I do not want to go," Leah said, a sudden heaviness in her chest. One foray amongst the *ton* was enough to convince her she never wanted to endure that particular torture again.

"If you do not attend functions to which she has been invited," Rachel persisted, "people will assume you are ashamed of her, or worse, given the speed with which you were wed. Not to mention your sudden disappearance from Town so shortly after the wedding. Knowing the gossipmongers as you do, I am certain you can well imagine what the rumors might be."

Richard's black eyes grew darker still. The muscles in his jaw clenched. "You are right of course. We shall attend."

"But, Richard—"

"No, do not protest, Leah. In this, Rachel is right. We shall attend the Cunningham rout tonight." He dropped a quick kiss on her forehead. "Now, if you will excuse me, I have important matters of business to which I must attend."

Rachel smiled at Leah over her teacup. "I do hope you have something suitable to wear."

Chapter Fourteen

"Look at him," Rachel whispered to Margaret, who leaned in close to her side. "He is making a fool of himself over that girl."

She snapped open her fan. The stench of sweat from too many bodies crowded together in the Cunningham ballroom was enough to turn her stomach, but she swallowed back her revulsion as she watched Richard and Leah through the crowd.

Leah's hand rested on Richard's arm as they strolled around the room, their movements slowed by all the men vying to toady up to Richard. Whenever his attention was diverted, the women, Rachel noted with malicious glee, gave Leah the cut direct, or simply stared through her as if she wasn't present.

Rachel almost felt pity for the girl. She could not imagine how one would endure the social stigma of the cut direct. The dreadful thought was enough to send an indelicate, unladylike shudder across her skin.

The chit looked pretty enough, a sun-kissed glow on her cheeks that made Rachel want to scratch her fingernails across the flawless skin. It was amazing Leah appeared so well-rested, considering she'd not slept much the night before.

Rachel knew this because she'd stood in the chit's dressing

room and listened to the sounds of carnal relations emanating through the bedchamber door. Not that she had meant to spy.

Truly, the last thing she had wanted to see, or rather to hear, was the man she loved disporting himself between another woman's thighs. She'd only wanted to offer Leah help in choosing the right ensemble to wear this evening. The unexpected sounds of Richard's throaty groans mingling with Leah's breathless cries had left Rachel stunned, her feet frozen to the floor.

It was enough to make Rachel want to wreak physical violence upon her enemy, to take a whip to her hide, anything to cause her the same pain Rachel now endured. A slight sensation of panic made her blood pump faster, her heart beat erratically.

But she smiled, her outward appearance a complete contrast to her inner turmoil.

Unlike Leah, whose every emotion showed on her face.

The foolish twit had so much to learn.

Margaret frowned as she pushed a strand of auburn hair off her brow. "I do not know. Do you think he truly cares for her?"

"Do not be absurd," Rachel said. "His wick is pointing up and he is merely following, as any randy buck would."

Still, Richard seemed fascinated by the girl, too fascinated for Rachel to brush it off as mere lust.

Perhaps it was better this way. Once they drove Leah into the arms of another man, Richard would be devastated, and Rachel would move in to comfort him.

Margaret's startled laugh brought the attention of several couples toward them. Their widened eyes showed their surprise at Margaret and Rachel's tête-à-tête.

"Do try to control yourself," Rachel said through tightly gritted teeth, which kept her smile firmly in place. "We do not want to arouse St. Austin's suspicions. We may never get another chance. Do you know what to do?"

Margaret gave a surreptitious tug on her gown to pull her outrageous décolletage even lower. It was a wonder her nipples did not show above the Brussels lace. "That boy was so devastated by her marriage, he was quite the easiest conquest I have ever made. You may rest assured, if you get Richard's wife onto the terrace at the right moment, I will arrange everything else."

Rachel hid her grin behind her fan as she watched Margaret's manipulations with avid eyes. It was almost too easy.

Richard forced himself to smile as he made conversation with the supplicants crowding around him, each vying for his financial support or his political backing. As long as they welcomed Leah into their circle, he would endure their flattery and the come-hither glances cast his way by their debauched wives.

Leah's hand tightened on his arm. He sent her a reassuring smile, which she returned with a shaky curl of her lips.

She was so lovely, she made his hands ache and his heart swell. The flurry of golden curls framing her face brought out the amber flecks in her vivid green eyes. Her luscious eyes were wide, not with fright, but with an apprehensive wariness of her surroundings. He dropped his gaze to the neckline of her dress, a green gossamer silk which hid more than it revealed, and still, unbridled lust tightened his groin, made his blood grow hot and his neck sweat. He wanted to drag her into his arms. He wanted to run his fingers through her hair and over her hips.

He wanted to smash his fist into the face of each and every dandy drooling over her breasts.

The intensity of his feelings shuddered through him.

Reliving the betrayals of his youth had slashed open old wounds, revived old desires he'd thought long buried.

At the time Rachel had married his brother, the shock that

burned through Richard had seemed unbearable, but as that pain dissolved into supreme indifference, he had realized he had never really loved her at all. It was the youthful dream she had spun for him that he had loved.

Dreams of a family. Dreams of a home of his own.

His parents hadn't cared a whit about anyone but Eric, heir to the kingdom of St. Austin. While his parents had floated through society and traveled the world on their various adventures, it was Richard who had cared for Geoffrey.

He had comforted him when he was ill, soothed him when he was frightened, and laughed with him when he was happy.

But who had been there for him? He'd been just a boy himself. Bitterly, he thought how unfair it was to have more than one child if there wasn't enough love to spare.

He glanced at Leah. She was watching him with a trembling half-smile on her lips. He could well-imagine the darkness that clouded his features as he'd dragged himself yet again through the rubble of his past. He flashed her a reassuring grin.

Her answering smile lit her face with such joy, he wanted to pull her into his arms and bury himself in her sweetness. Did it matter how they came to be wed? Could they build a future on a foundation of deceit? Could he tell her the truth? The darkest secrets of his past? Could she possibly understand? Or would her eyes turn dark with disgust? Could he take that chance?

That she loved him, Richard had no doubt. He could see her love shining in her eyes, hear it in the soft cadence of her voice, feel it in the tenderness of her touch. He didn't know if he deserved it, but he was certain of three things.

He wanted her love. He needed her love.

And he was terrified, straight through to his soul, like a child shuddering in the night from a horrific dream.

He linked her arm through his. "Shall we dance?"

"I would love that above all things," she said, her breathless sigh caressing his lips like the softest kiss.

All he wanted was to sling her over his shoulder and drag her to bed. Instead, he pushed his way through the crush to the dance floor as the orchestra turned to a waltz.

"I thought of our last dance together many times while I was away," he said. As he wrapped her in his arms, he gave silent thanks to the man who invented this sensuous dance.

Color blossomed in her cheeks. How utterly charming she was. He pressed his hand into her spine, pulling her much closer than propriety allowed. To hell with decency, he thought savagely. She was his wife and he wanted to hold her.

"I dreamt of this often while I was away," he said in a voice gone husky and low. "Look at me, Leah."

When she lifted her luminous gaze to his, Richard was lost.

Smiling like a man enchanted, he twirled her about the ballroom, drowning in her glorious green eyes.

But for this moment, Leah would have been in misery. But for this dance, held close to her husband's chest, his hand wrapped around her back, burning heat into her spine.

The languid music, the sensual spell of his dark eyes meeting hers. If only she could demand he take her home and carry her to bed, but she was still too shy to be so bold.

"How much longer must we stay?" she said instead, hoping her eyes and her breathless voice conveyed the longing she felt.

He pulled her closer, scandalously so, until their chests were almost touching, until the merest whisper separated his cheek from hers. The shocked stares of the noble lords and ladies waiting to condemn her burned a hole in her back, but she did not care. So what if no one spoke to her, or looked at her except to sneer or send her nasty glares whenever Richard turned away. She would not let anyone see how much it hurt her.

This was his world, and if she wanted to be a part of his life, she would have to adjust.

"I will send for the carriage," he murmured as the music drew to an end. His eyes met hers and she could see his desire burning within them. It gave her a delicious sense of power to realize that he wanted her as much as she wanted him.

As he led her toward the door, Lady Margaret Montague stepped into their path. Margaret was shockingly draped in a deep blue dress, with an outrageously low neckline that barely covered her voluptuous curves. Her eyes fluttered demurely.

Insecurity swept through Leah. She gripped Richard's arm, but she couldn't bring herself to look at him for fear she would see desire for another woman burning in his eyes.

"Your Grace," Margaret murmured to Richard, her voice sultry and low.

"Lady Montague," he said, his tone polite, but not overly familiar, his arm warm and firm beneath Leah's hand. "I trust you remember my wife."

"Of course." Margaret gave a slight nod of her regal head in Leah's general direction. Then she turned toward her escort. "Might I introduce you to a friend of mine?"

As Leah glanced at the man who stood beside Margaret, the room receded, her thoughts grew foggy and the air seemed to shimmer, like the summer sun reflecting off a lake.

"Mr. Alexander Prescott," Margaret was saying. "The Duke and Duchess of St. Austin." Her eyes fairly sparkled with malicious amusement. "Mr. Prescott, I understand that you and the duchess originate from the same part of Lancashire. Perhaps you have met already . . ."

Her words hung in an awkward silence. Leah had not seen Alexander since the morning after her marriage. The day he had kissed her and begged her to run away with him. The day their old, comfortable friendship had withered and died, leaving a stiff formality in its place.

Still, the changes these few short weeks had wrought in him stunned Leah. Gone was his sunny smile, replaced by a grim twist of his lips. His eyes showed all of his pain, all of his heartache, all of his lost hopes and dreams.

That his attentions had turned to another should make Leah happy. She wanted him to find a woman who loved him, as he deserved, but what would Lady Margaret Montague want with an innocent, trusting soul like Alexander?

"Her Grace and I share a previous acquaintance," Alexander said stiffly. "Lady Montague, I believe they are starting another waltz. Shall we dance?"

"Why don't you and the duchess dance this set?" Margaret said, fluttering her fan before her face. Her sharp gaze turned to Leah's, a calculating challenge in her smile. "The two of you can renew your acquaintance . . ."

Leah could think of no reason to deny this dance, even if it was shockingly bold for Margaret to put forth the suggestion.

". . . and the duke and I shall contrive to amuse ourselves."

That is what I'm afraid of, Leah wanted to shout. The tension in the air was so thick, she could feel it pressing on her chest. She couldn't breathe. She had to get away.

She sent Richard a silent plea to take their leave.

Margaret's brows rose. "That is, if the duke does not object?"

No, Richard wanted to roar as an emotion he now clearly recognized as jealousy dimmed his vision and poisoned his thoughts. This was the young man Leah had wanted to marry.

Richard had never met him before, had caught only a glimpse of him from a distance on the day he had come to the house.

An ugly, insecure part of Richard he never realized he possessed had hoped the boy would be a gangly, awkward youth, with pustules and pimples ravaging his features, but the opposite was true. He was an Adonis, complete with spun gold hair, crystal blue eyes, and a past no doubt as spotless as the first snow of winter. The sort of man every woman dreamed of marrying, not some black-haired, black-eyed, brooding, beast of a man with a tortured past.

As if all this weren't bad enough, guilt bored a hole in his chest for his role in destroying Leah's dreams, a fact he had managed to avoid contemplating until this moment, presented with this vital young man she had once hoped to wed.

In truth, were it not for Richard and his sordid past, Leah would have married this man and given him beautiful, golden-haired babes—the thought twisted Richard into a murderous rage.

No doubt, this boy would have blessed her with a home full of laughter, not walls stained with silence, secrets, and sins.

Richard's hands clenched. His throat tightened as he told himself it did not matter. She was his wife. She was *his*.

But she had married him against her will.

To fulfill her father's dynastic dreams and to keep Alison safe from the gossip-mongers who would destroy her. Not that Leah knew any of that. And still she said she loved him.

How was it possible?

He felt physically sick, his skin hot, his stomach swirling, as eager ears all around them strained to hear his words.

Richard knew there was no way he could politely object to the dance unless he wanted to start a rumor as to his motives.

He choked back his refusal. "Why don't I fetch you a glass of champagne while you dance?"

He tried not to stare as Prescott took Leah into his arms.

After a few awkward moments of silence, the boy said something that made Leah laugh. The lad pulled her closer, too close, and gazed at her with a look of such naked long-ing that Richard felt savage, like a mad dog. He wanted to push his way through the crowd and tear the pup apart with his teeth.

Deprived of that pleasure, he turned his wrath on Margaret. "What is the meaning of this charade?"

She ran her fan over his arm. "Why, Richard, I do not know what you mean."

"Do not play coy with me," he said, brushing her hand away. "What game are you playing?"

"Lower your voice," Margaret whispered, turning her chin into her shoulder to hide the movement of her lips. "People are staring. And do stop murdering your wife with your eyes. Why, one might think you do not trust her. Is there more to their friendship than friendship?"

"What are you implying?" Richard said, his jaw so tight, he heard the joint pop.

"Nothing, Richard. Nothing at all. I simply wanted a few moments alone with you."

"I told you it is over between us."

"And I have accepted that. Truly I have. But I miss you still. Do you never think of me at all?" Margaret held up her hand. "No, do not answer that. I do not want to know."

She ran her fingertips along the edge of her fan, then waved it vigorously before her face. "My, it is hot in here. I feel a bit faint . . ." She swayed on her feet.

Richard swore as he grabbed her arm and propelled her toward the terrace doors. He had seen her faint many times in the past. The silly widgeon refused to eat during the day, then the oppressive heat and overwhelming crush combined with hunger sent her sailing for the floor at least once a night.

What a dreadful inconvenience and a dashed bore!

Why had he ever tolerated it in the first place?

The answer to that question was so obvious, it filled him

with self-disgust. "Will you never learn?" he muttered as he guided her through the French windows onto the terrace.

A breath of fresh air would clear her head, then he would be done with this charade. Thunder rumbled in the distance. Wind shrieked around the corner of the house. Her gown whipped against his legs. A soft moan escaped her lips as she slumped against his side. Damn. What a bother!

He swung her into his arms and carried her to a stone bench along the balustrade. He searched her reticule for a bottle of hartshorn. When he couldn't find one, he knelt beside her and patted her hand. Minutes passed and still she showed no signs of coming around. "Margaret. Wake up. It is raining."

The murky scent of wet grass and mud rose from the gardens below the railing. The spattering rain gathered intensity.

Finally, her eyelids fluttered open. "Where am I? Richard? Is that you? You've come back to me, darling. I knew you would."

Before he knew what she was about, she flung her arms around his neck and locked her lips on his. He grabbed her shoulders to push her away, but she tightened her hold, her hands clutching her wrists behind his head, her nails digging into his scalp.

As he slid his palms along her arms to disentangle her grip, he heard voices behind him, then a sharp gasp.

With a strange sense of doom, he knew it was Leah.

He ripped Margaret's arms from about his neck. He shot to his feet and spun around, the moments passing before his eyes in brief, indistinct flashes, like lighting followed by impenetrable darkness. His gaze swung past Rachel to Leah standing at her side, her golden hair shimmering in the torchlight, her cheeks the pale, ashen color of the moon. Her eyes wide with shocked betrayal as she met his gaze. Moisture that he hoped was rain and not tears dripping down her cheeks.

He took a step toward her, or, at least, he thought he did, but time was moving so slowly he couldn't be sure.

She grabbed her skirts and took a step back, as if she meant to run for the house or turn into the gardens beyond the terrace. But she was standing too close to the steps. As she moved, her foot came down with no solid support to hold her.

The last image Richard saw was of Rachel lifting her arms, then Leah was gone. A brief, startled cry carried on the wind to hit Richard mere moments before he heard the thud.

Chapter Fifteen

Richard flew down the short flight of steps, his heels skidding along the slippery stone. On the landing below, he found Leah sprawled upon her back, her hair spread out over the mud, her eyes closed, unaware of the rain beating upon her face.

His heart twisted hard and painfully within his breast. He dropped to his knees, turned his shoulders to shield her from the storm, brushed her soaked, muddy hair from her brow.

Her skin was as cold as the rain hitting his back. Blood poured from a gash across her temple, another to the back of her head, the wound there already swollen to the size of his fist. Several cuts and scrapes across her arms and elbows were her only other visible injuries. She was alive, but unconscious.

He yanked off his cravat, wrapped it around her head to stem the flow of blood, then gathered her in his arms and stumbled up the stairs and into the house. Panic tried to claim his thoughts as he listened to the too-shallow rasp of her breathing.

Margaret stood by the terrace doors. "Let me assist you."

"You bitch," Richard snarled as he brushed past her, heedless of whoever might overhear his words. "You wanted this to happen. You and Rachel. You planned this together."

"No," Margaret protested, but Richard ignored her.

He stalked through the ballroom. He was vaguely aware of the gaping stares and shocked gasps of those around him, but he didn't care. All of his thoughts, all of his senses, were centered on the frigid, motionless woman in his arms.

"Get blankets and a physician," he barked at a footman, who immediately ran to do his bidding.

Lady Cunningham rushed to his side. "What has happened?"

Before he could reply, Margaret said, "Her Grace was on the terrace when the storm hit. She slipped on the wet stairs."

"Oh, dear. This is terrible. This way, please."

Lady Cunningham led them to a bedchamber at the top of the stairs, then went to issue instructions and reassure her guests.

Richard gently set Leah on the center of the bed. His hands shook as he pushed the soggy hair from her cheeks. "Leah? Can you hear me? Open your eyes . . ."

Margaret came up behind him. "Please, let me help you—"

"Go away," Richard snarled, never taking his eyes from his wife's face, as pale as the crisp, white sheets beneath her head, save for the bright patch of red staining his cravat. "Haven't you done enough already? Are you proud of what you accomplished with your jealousy and spite?"

"You cannot think I planned this?" Margaret cried, reaching for his shoulder, pulling her hand away when he sent her an I-will-kill-you-if-you-touch-me glare. "Richard, truly, I didn't know where I was. In my confusion, I thought we were together again. I surely did not mean for your wife to see us like that, or for her to injure herself."

The sight of tears streaming down Margaret's cheeks jolted him from his blinding rage. Margaret might be lewd, crude, and more than a little rude, but Richard had never known her to be vindictive or purposely cruel. He sighed heavily. "I do believe you, Margaret. It's just that I am worried."

Margaret bit her lip and nodded. A moment later, he heard her footsteps retreat. It seemed as if an hour passed before Lady Cunningham returned with an armful of blankets, followed by a portly, bewigged man of about fifty who introduced himself as Doctor Somebody-or-other.

Richard didn't catch the man's name, nor did he care.

All he could think about was his wife.

The doctor stripped off his jacket and marched to Leah's side. "What happened?"

"My wife fell and struck her head."

The doctor clucked his tongue, but said nothing as he performed his examination.

Richard's gut twisted with each passing second until he could stand the silent torture no more. "There is so much blood . . ." The room seemed to swirl around him. It was absurd and sent a tingling chill over his skin. He should be immune to the sight of blood. He had seen enough of it during the war. But this was different. This was his wife.

"Head wounds tend to bleed profusely, even with very little damage," the doctor said matter-of-factly. "And she has quite a nasty cut to the back of her head, no doubt from striking a rock or the pavement during her fall. The gash across the temple is more superficial, a scraping off of skin as she twisted. No, it isn't blood loss that is a danger to her. It is the trauma to the head."

The doctor snipped away a chunk of Leah's glorious hair at the base of her neck. The bleeding had slowed to a trickle, but it sped up again as he washed the wounds. He smeared a thick paste over the gash, then wrapped a clean bandage around her head. Turning her onto her side, he examined her for injuries to her arms, back, thighs. She never opened her eyes.

An eerie sense of time grinding to a halt afflicted Richard. His heart seemed to stop. His skin, which only moments before was so frigidly cold, now seemed numb. "What can I do?"

The doctor frowned. "There isn't much anyone can do, except watch and wait. If she regains consciousness soon, I should hope for the best . . ."

He forced himself to ask, "And if she doesn't?"

"Let us wait and see, shall we? There is no use in dealing with uncertainties."

Richard ran his fingertips along her jaw. She was so still, so pale. What if he lost her when he'd only just found her?

"I would like to take her home," he said, his voice a shaky rasp that scraped his throat.

"I would advise against it, Your Grace. A jostling carriage ride is the last thing she needs right now."

Lady Cunningham came up beside Richard and placed her hand on his arm. "Leave her to me, Your Grace. My maid and I will get her out of her wet clothes."

"No! I will do it myself." He lifted his gaze to Lady Cunningham's. "Please, forgive my rudeness, madam, but I am worried. I would not leave her."

"I understand." Lady Cunningham gave his arm a reassuring squeeze, then ushered everyone from the room.

Richard unfastened the buttons of Leah's gown. He chafed her arms, her legs, her hands, then wrapped the blankets around her like a woolen cocoon. "Please, darling, open your eyes. I want to see your beautiful, green eyes."

Lady Cunningham returned, carrying on a tray a steaming bowl of broth, a pot of tea, and an assortment of medicine bottles.

A footman followed with extra blankets and a change of men's clothing in his arms.

"This is Robert," Lady Cunningham said, nodding at the servant as she set the tray on the bedside table. "He will be just outside the door should you need him. The doctor has agreed to stay the night. I dispatched a servant to your house to gather some clothing and such. These will have to do for now. I do hope they fit. They belonged to my husband when he was much younger, and much thinner."

Richard gave her a weak smile. "Thank you for your kindness, Lady Cunningham."

"Yes, well . . . if you should need me . . ."

Richard nodded. He waited for Lady Cunningham and the footman to leave before he stripped off his wet clothes and grabbed the borrowed garments. The shirt pulled across his shoulders. The breeches left his knees exposed. But at least they were dry, not that he cared.

Nothing mattered, save for his wife.

He pulled a chair next the bed, stroked Leah's cheeks with his fingertips. Her skin was so cold, despite the blankets and the blazing fire. Not knowing what else to do, he climbed onto the bed and gathered her into his arms.

"Oh, God, Leah, I don't want to lose you now."

Rachel smiled at Margaret as the two women stood beneath the portico waiting for their carriages. Nothing could depress her high spirits, not the soggy night air that would render her hair a tangled mess, nor her companion's grim face. "What is wrong with you, Margaret? Our plan worked perfectly, yet you stand there looking as if someone has stolen your favorite brooch."

Margaret leaned her hand against the nearest Doric column, as if she needed the smooth marble to help her stand. "I wanted to drive the girl into the arms of another man, not kill her."

"Do not be absurd. The child will be fine." A gust of wind spattered rain across the stone floor. Rachel pulled her cashmere shawl around her shoulders. "She has suffered a simple bump on the head. Why, Alison is forever tumbling here and there with nary a care. The chit will be up and about by tomorrow, with only a few scrapes and bruises to mark her injuries."

"I hope you are right," Margaret said, edging toward the steps leading into the carriage drive, as if to escape Rachel's presence. "Did you see his face? He loves her, even if he has yet to realize it."

"Nonsense!" Rachel would never consider it. Caught up in carnal lust, yes. But not love. Rachel was the woman he loved. Not some worthless slut pulled from the laboring masses. "She is a piece of fluff who has caught his fancy."

Margaret's dark-eyed stare held more than a hint of suspicion. Her lips moved, then she shook her head, as if she couldn't voice the accusation rolling around the tip of her tongue. Her voice dropped to a whisper. "But I do not want to hurt her. Not physically. That was not part of the plan."

"Of course not," Rachel said, shrugging her shoulders. "Neither do I. But we cannot let this inconvenient accident deter us from our course. We must march onward toward our goal."

Margaret gave a sulky nod. "What of Prescott? Once I left the ballroom with Richard, I never saw him again."

The torches along the wall flickered in the breeze. The flames danced golden over Rachel's skin. How much longer would she have to wait to feel Richard's hands running over her breasts, making her burn in her most secret places?

"Prescott left just after he and Leah danced. That boy is so green, he wore his heart on his sleeve all through their waltz. It was perfect." Rachel laughed aloud. "Mark my words, Margaret. The gossipmongers will have plenty to keep them busy tonight."

Leah heard voices floating in the darkness. She tried to open her eyes, but her lids felt swollen and wouldn't part, as if someone had sewn them together. She persevered and finally managed to drag them apart.

The room swam before her eyes in a misty haze.

Richard's face appeared above her, his mouth twisted in a fearsome frown. She should tell him not to scowl so fiercely—he was ever so handsome when he smiled—but she couldn't seem to find her voice. Her mouth was dry, her tongue felt thick. The only sound she could hear was a roaring in her ears, like ocean waves whipped up by a hurricane, the wind swirling through her head, the deafening pounding of the tide against a rocky shore.

The canopy above the bed caught up in the swirling storm spun rapid circles around her head. Her stomach heaved. Her heart beat faster, her throat convulsing until the nausea passed.

Richard disappeared. Another face appeared above her. A stranger this time. He spoke to her, but Leah couldn't attend to his words. A vision of Richard with another woman clutched in his arms swam before her eyes. Leah moaned and sank willingly into the sweet, painless void that hovered beyond the light.

The next time she opened her eyes, morning sunlight filled the room. An open window let in a humid breeze—and the clatter of horse hooves striking cobblestones on the street below her window? That wasn't right. Her room overlooked the gardens, not the street, and the Chinese wallpaper and crimson draperies confused her. This was not her room. Where was she?

Do not panic, she told herself as she drew a deep breath, her heart starting to race, her skin tingling with cold and fear. She lifted her head, but it set off a fearsome pounding, like a chisel striking her brain. The small movement threatened to send the contents of her stomach swishing up her aching throat.

She swallowed quickly to keep from retching.

Someone was clutching her hand. She turned her head by slow degrees, breathing deeply between each torturous inch until she saw Richard sitting on a chair pulled close to the side of the bed, his head resting on his arms, her hand clutched in his fist.

She wiggled her fingers, and even that small movement sent a spasm of pain up her arm. Bloodshot eyes popped open. A dark growth of hair bristled his cheeks. Shadows and lines etched the hollows of his cheeks and the creases of his lips.

Then he smiled. Slow. Soft. Tender.

One hand reached out to stroke her brow. "How do you feel?"

Some vague memory tugged at her awareness, reached through her confusion, but Leah couldn't seem to grasp it. She tried to return his smile, but her head hurt too much to risk moving even her lips. Her fear must have shown in her eyes.

He smoothed his knuckles over her cheek. His gaze shifted away for a moment. When he looked back at her, a grimness hardened the lines around his mouth and eyes. "You fell and bumped your head. Do you not remember?"

Another brief flash of memory, lost in the fog. Leah reached for it, but it dissolved before she could catch it.

A feeling of foreboding crawled over her skin. Perhaps she did not want to know. Perhaps it was better this way.

A soft knock sounded on the door before it opened.

Leah expected her aunt's cheerful smile to greet her, not the tall, stately woman who stood in the doorway with a breakfast tray in her hands. She looked vaguely familiar, but Leah could not remember where they might have met.

"How is our patient this morning?" the woman said.

"Finally awake," Richard replied. "And her belly is furiously grumbling for food, which is rather a good sign, do you not think, Lady Cunningham?"

Leah's cheeks burned, but she could not form a thought, much less speak a word.

Lady Cunningham smiled. "Well, then, I will leave this tray. I fear there is nothing too substantial on it. Clear broth and honeyed tea for today. If you are feeling up to company this afternoon, perhaps I could read to you?"

"That would be lovely," Leah managed, but she was too disoriented to truly understand the words.

"I shall see you then," she said, then walked from the room.

Richard took a napkin from the tray and tucked it beneath Leah's chin. He poured a glass of water, added a few drops of liquid from a bottle on the tray. He held the glass to her lips. "Drink it slowly. There is laudanum in it to ease your pain and help you rest. Rest is what you need most."

Leah gulped the soothing liquid. Mere moments passed before the soothing effects of the opiate dulled her senses. She felt herself drifting off. "How long have I been ill?"

Richard frowned. "We were at a ball. You slipped down the terrace steps. Do you not remember?"

Leah shook her head, a foolish mistake, she realized, as her vision blurred and her stomach clenched.

"Never mind." He kissed the back of her hand, then pressed her palm against his cheek. His morning beard felt soft and familiar against her skin. "Rest and get well. That is all I want you to concern yourself with."

By the end of the next week, Leah thought she might scream if Richard fussed over her for one more moment. As much as she enjoyed his ministrations and the proof that he cared about her well-being, she was tired of lounging around as if she were an invalid, incapable of so much as brushing her own hair.

The swelling at the back of her head had diminished. The scab covering the wound no longer itched. How she had injured her head remained a mystery. Vague images tortured her dreams, but she could not discern them. Richard told her she'd stumbled down the terrace steps, but why would she leave the ball in the middle of a storm? Why did his eyes shift away whenever she questioned him?

With a disgusted sigh, she pushed herself off the bed and paced to the cheval glass. A wave of dizziness nearly dropped her to her knees, but she breathed deeply until the spell passed.

She lifted her hair, which she wore down across her brow to cover the gash. The wound was starting to knit itself together, but the skin was still red and raw and would no doubt leave a scar.

Her simple, muslin frock, which Richard had helped her don before he'd left, rubbed against her aching ribs. She closed her eyes, shivered as she remembered his hands sliding along the curve of her back, his movements brisk, coldly clinical, while her thoughts had been anything but.

A quick knock on the door before it opened sent a guilty flush across her cheeks, but it was only Lady Cunningham, come for their morning visit.

"I take it St. Austin is away," she said, her brown eyes sparkling with shared mischief. "Or he would toss you back on that bed."

The only clues to her age, which Leah placed at about fifty, were the few streaks of silver highlighting her mahogany hair.

She laughed, then winced at the swift onslaught of pain. Perhaps she wasn't quite recovered, after all. "The doctor said I could return home, so he is off to fetch the carriage."

"There was no need." Lady Cunningham took a seat by the window. "I would have been more than happy to send you home in mine, though I must say, I am sad to see you leave. Since my daughter and her husband sailed for the Indies, I have been at odds and ends. I will miss our conversations, Your Grace."

"As will I. Please, call me Leah. I am not quite comfortable with that title yet."

"Leah. What a lovely name. And I am Abigail. Abby to my friends." She glanced around the room, as if expecting Richard to pop out of the shadows and scold her for letting her patient out of bed. "I wonder, each spring I host a subscription ball to raise funds for the Sunday schools in the poorer districts of the City, the Seven Dials, Covent Garden, and the like. Might I interest you in joining my committee? The work will not start for many months yet, but I thought, perhaps . . ."

"I should like that above all things," Leah said as she slid onto the seat across from Abby, her warm acceptance a balm to Leah's sorely bruised feelings. She did not remember much of the ball that ended with her injury, but she did recall the animosity of Richard's peers, the cold refusal to so much as include her in trivial conversation, much less the planning of a charitable event that was the perfect counterpart to her own philanthropic endeavors. They spent the next hour in pleasant conversation, Abby sharing the details of the last few balls, what went right, what ended in disaster. Leah making suggestions for the next.

Until Richard appeared at the door, all brooding dark eyes and disapproving frown as he glanced first at the bed, then swept his gaze around the room, his eyes finally finding Leah.

The same haunted look hung in his eyes that she had seen from the moment she'd first awakened following her injury.

What is wrong, she wanted to cry, but she forced herself to smile, albeit shakily, as she rose, careful not to let her dizziness show. His narrow-eyed gaze said she did not fool him.

He wanted to chastise her, Leah could tell, but he folded his hands behind his back and smiled. "Good morning, ladies."

"Your Grace." Abby swept her hands down the crisp folds of her muslin gown. "I was just telling your wife how much I have enjoyed her company, but if she does not get well soon, she will miss the remainder of the season. Leah, I shall leave you in your husband's capable hands."

"Thank you for everything, Abby," Leah said. "I will never forget your kindness to me."

Richard watched the door close, his smile thoughtful as he raised his brows. "Leah? Abby?"

"We have cried friends," she said, wishing he would take her in his arms, but he made no move to close the distance between them. With a boldness she didn't know she possessed, she crossed the room and slid her fingers through his hair.

"Kiss me," she said, and gently tugged on his neck until his lips touched hers. She longed to tell him of her love, but she spoke instead with her kiss, sliding her tongue along his lips, then deep inside his mouth.

"We'll have none of that," he growled, pulling her hands from about his neck, though his voice shook with the same desire heating her skin and curling in her belly. "Besides, I have a surprise. Wait here." He left the room, spoke to someone in the corridor, and returned with a giggling Alison on his hip.

Leah titled her head as she stared at them, cheek to cheek, matching smiles upon their lips, as if they had pulled off the greatest of intrigues. She could not even begin to name the emotion bubbling up within her as Richard used his free arm to pull her into his embrace. Nor could she explain the tears gathering in her eyes as they stood there, arms wrapped around each other, Alison's fingers playing with Leah's hair.

"We have come to take you home," Alison said, framing Leah's cheeks between her chubby palms.

Home. Never had a word sounded so sweet.

"Oh, I have missed you," Leah said, pressing her lips to the child's cheek, breathing the scent of her baby-soft skin.

Richard's smile held a tenderness Leah had never seen before, and the emotion blazing in his eyes was blinding, like staring into the summer sun. With Alison clutched tightly against his chest, he helped Leah down the stairs.

Once they were settled into the open carriage, he instructed the driver to take a turn through the park.

The sun was warm and pleasant on Leah's face. The breeze redolent of freshly cut grass and grazing sheep.

As the child nestling against her side drifted off to sleep, Leah slipped her hand into Richard's. His warm fingers closed around hers, his grip firm and tight. He sent her a smile, but the hard set of his jaw, the shadows haunting his eyes, sent a shiver of foreboding over her skin.

Chapter Sixteen

"Where is the duchess?" Richard demanded as he stomped into the butler's pantry, his voice bouncing off the oak-paneled walls.

Harris dropped a rag smeared with an ammonia-scented paste next to the candlesticks lined up on the table before him. He rose from his chair, his features schooled into impassivity, as if Richard's presence in the pantry were an everyday occurrence. "I do not know, Your Grace. Perhaps she went out?"

"I know she is out," Richard said, his jaw clenched, his voice tightly controlled to keep from bellowing at the man, who was not the object of his wrath. "I went to her room, only to find an empty bed when I should have found her resting. I have searched the house and the gardens, and there is no sign of her. So, I know she is out. What I want to know is, where is she?"

The butler winced. "As to that, I'm afraid I couldn't say."

"Pray, tell me please, is there anyone in this house who might know where she is?"

"Perhaps her maid," Harris offered. "Or the coachman."

Muttering a vicious stream of oaths, Richard strode from the room and marched to the stables. His breath hissed through his teeth as he breathed deeply to control his escalating tension.

There was a perfectly reasonable explanation for her disappearance, or so he told himself, even though he had tucked her into her bed and given her strict orders not to move until he returned from his meeting with his solicitors. A mere twenty-four hours since he had brought her home and already she was defying him. He would be damned if he let her sicken again.

Didn't she still suffer from spells of dizziness? Wasn't that proof she hadn't fully recovered from her ordeal?

She seemed to have no memory of the event that had precipitated her mad dash into the storm, and for that Richard was beyond grateful. How would she ever believe he was an unwilling participant in a seemingly passionate kiss with another woman when the evidence of her own eyes would say otherwise?

Hands planted on his hips, he strode into the stables and glared at the men mucking out the stalls. "Where is Her Grace?"

Four blank faces stared back at him.

"The Duchess?" he said, his temper flaring hotter with each passing moment. "Does anyone know where she is?"

One of the stable hands shuffled forward, his face the same pasty hue as the straw sticking out of his cap. "She went to Mrs. Bristoll's, Your Grace. I usually goes with her, but I hurt m'leg yesterday, so's Jack went with her today."

"Who is this Mrs. Bristoll and where does she live?"

"She's the one what runs that foundling home," the groom said, twisting his hands together. "The one o'er in St. Giles—"

"What?" he said, his voice soft, filled with chilling fury. "Who went with her? Never mind that. Saddle my horse. Immediately!"

What the bloody hell was she doing in St. Giles! It was the

worst rookery in the city, the streets crawling with vermin who would slit her throat for less than a farthing.

Heedless of the dust spewing into his eyes, Richard paced the stable yard. Sweat dripped down his back and soaked his shirt, even as an icy shiver numbed his skin.

God help him, when he got his hands on her, he was going to throttle her for the scare she was putting him through . . . that is, if she wasn't already dead.

One of the grooms led Kaddar from the stables.

Before he could jump on the horse, a landaulet pulled into the carriage drive. Dirt-streaked windows reflected the waning sun and obscured the occupant's features, but Richard could discern a mass of golden curls that could only belong to Leah.

He tossed the horse's reins to a stable boy, then stormed toward the vehicle and yanked open the door.

Her cheeks were sallow, her eyes red-rimmed from pain and lack of sleep, vivid proof that she still suffered from her injury. She opened her mouth, but he glared her into silence as he swung her into his arms and stalked toward the house. "If you value your life, madam, you will not say a word."

"But—"

"Not one word!"

His jaw tightened. His teeth scraped together. Her wide-eyed gaze held a hint of fear, which made him want to shove his fist into the wall. She should be afraid, but not of him.

Her reckless disregard for her safety could have cost them both her life and his sanity.

Once in the library, he lowered her onto a chair. She wore her hair down around her oval face, as if to hide the angry, red gash across her temple, a grim reminder of all she had suffered.

He leaned against his ebony desk, crossed his arms over his chest, and fixed her with his cold, dark stare. "Would you mind very much telling me why you aren't abed?"

She peered up at him from beneath her golden brows, the

setting sun catching the amber in her eyes. Tiny lines around her lips revealed her confusion. "Why should I be abed?"

His brows slashed up. He breathed deeply, a poor attempt to modulate the fear and fury shaking his voice. "Am I mistaken, or did you not suffer a serious head injury less than a week ago?"

She lifted her hands. "But I feel perfectly fine and the doctor said—"

"I do not care what the doctor said," Richard bit out through tightly clenched teeth. "*I* said I wanted you to rest."

He ran his hands through his hair and over his face. She looked lovely and innocent, dressed in a fetching sprigged muslin frock, a deep burgandy color that brought out the highlights in her hair. A perfect temptation to every randy buck and rotter prowling the filthy, over-crowded, crime-infested streets. "You went to St. Giles? I do not care what you were doing or why you were there. I forbid you to ever go there again."

"What did you say?" Her voice was low, quivering with an aching betrayal or perhaps it was rage.

He paced before the windows, aware with every step he took that panic had control of his tongue, but he could not stop his words. "I said, I forbid you to go there again!"

"You have no right," she said, jumping to her feet.

"I have every right," he said. "Before both God and the law." He leaned toward her until they stood nose to nose. Her enticing scent of rosewater wrapped around him, seemed to cloud his senses and burn away whatever rational thought he might still retain. He was worried for her life and she was looking at him as if he were Satan himself, come to steal her soul. "If you dare defy me in this, I will take whatever measures necessary, even if I have to tie you to your bed to force you to rest."

"The truth always comes out in the end, doesn't it?" she said, her voice low, trembling with icy indignation. Her hands balled into fists. Her cheeks flushed the same fiery red as the setting sun. "I have a sister, did you know that? No, I'm sure you didn't, because you know nothing about me."

Her bitter laugh rumbled through the room. "You are just like my father. To him, I was nothing more than a brood mare for sale to the highest title. To you, I am no more valuable than that chair over there. Well, let me tell you something—"

She jabbed her forefinger into his chest. "You can forbid me all you want, but you cannot stop me from doing as I see fit. Because no matter what you think, *Your Grace,* you do *not* own me."

Without another word, she turned and flounced from the room.

Leah rummaged through her correspondence, a small mountain of invitations and calling cards that had arrived during the week she'd spent at Abby Cunningham's. It was laughable, as not one of these women cared if she lived or died, but they dared not ignore her completely and risk the wrath of the mighty Duke of St. Austin. The arrogant, self-possessed, pompous blowfish!

Who did he think he was, to order her about like that?

His pretentious edict taunted her with its double-edged thrust. With one breath, he cried concern for her safety. With the next, he declared ownership of her body as if she were no more than a piece of furniture. He was just like Papa!

No, he was worse than Papa, who, at least, was honest in his vile intentions. Richard hid behind a mask of caring and concern. Throughout her illness, he had hovered by her side, refusing to allow anyone but himself to care for her. She had dared to hope that he had come to love her, if only a little.

Today, he had shattered those hopes with his callous commands and heartless words. Not that it mattered.

Nothing mattered at the moment but finding a competent

physician. Since her last visit to the foundling home before her injury, Tommy's condition had deteriorated so drastically, he appeared little more than a bundle of bones wrapped in his quilted counterpane. The shocking change heightened the pain still throbbing through Leah's head.

Unable to find the one card she needed, she shoved the papers aside. How could she send a footman to fetch the doctor who had treated her when she could not even remember the man's name, much less his direction? What was wrong with her?

Why could she not remember anything about her accident, either the moments before or the moments after? It was maddening.

She grabbed her cloak and headed for the door.

As much as it would embarrass her to admit her shocking lack of memory, Abby Cunningham would be able to give her the information she needed.

Richard threw his napkin on the table and picked up his brandy while Rachel kept up a constant stream of chatter, as if her escapades amongst the shops of Bond Street held even the slightest interest. He scowled at Leah's empty chair.

That she had failed to appear for their evening meal did not surprise him, given the force of her righteous fury. Richard had thought to join her in her rooms, but he had not wished to provoke another scene, which would hardly allow her to obtain the rest she needed. Self-disgust burned through him, more potent than the fiery brandy spreading heat through his veins.

How could he explain the throat-clenching panic that had caused him to behave so abominably this afternoon? Or the fear that had blurred his senses during the days she'd hovered between life and death? She was his wife. Of course he was concerned for her safety. Of course, he wanted her to rest and regain her health. Why couldn't she understand that? And what did that cryptic remark about her sister have to do with anything?

He stared into his brandy as if the answers to his questions lay hidden in its murky depths. He wanted nothing more than to take her in his arms and hold her through the night, but he refused to be accused of using her.

Didn't she know how much she meant to him?

How much he cared?

The door crashed open and a stable boy burst into the room.

Rachel's shocked gasp and muttered protest followed Richard as he lunged to his feet. Heart pounding with sudden, awful premonition, he strode toward the lad. "What is it, boy?"

"Your Grace. The coachman sent me to fetch you. Quick."

Chapter Seventeen

"Thank you for coming so swiftly, Dr. Ashcroft," Leah said, barely able to restrain her growing agitation. Tommy was so weak, he couldn't open his eyes for more than a few seconds at a time. She didn't think he would survive one more bout of fever.

"Your Grace," the doctor said, giving a stiff bow. "I trust you suffer no ill effects from your injury?"

"I am well." She nodded toward the trestle bed nestled amongst the pots and pans and preserves in the pantry. "It is this young man who needs your attention. You are the third medical man we have consulted since his illness began. As the last suggested spider webs and amulets, you find us rather desperate."

"I see." The doctor pulled his spectacles down to the tip of his nose, then looked up at her over the rims. "Would you please describe his symptoms?"

Mrs. Bristoll could not speak past her tears. She dabbed her eyes with a handkerchief clutched in her fist.

Using the back of her hand, Leah brushed the damp hair off her brow. "His first attack occurred four weeks ago." On the day she first met Richard and learned of her father's perfidy.

Good heavens, how much her life had changed in these few

short weeks. "At first, it seemed a bout of influenza with accompanying aches and pains, followed by many days of perfect health. Over the last week, Mrs. Bristoll said the fevers have come with increasing frequency. I, myself, was too ill to attend him in his duress."

"He shivers with cold," Mrs. Bristoll finally managed, her voice hoarse from smothering her sobs. "Then he burns, for long hours. Finally, he sweats through his bedding. Then he wakes, cool as can be. Next day, it all starts again."

"He has been purged from top to bottom," Leah added, "as per the first doctor's direction, but that treatment has had no effect, save to leave the boy weaker than the fever it was meant to fight."

The doctor nodded. "Tertian fever, from the sounds. It is often thought a common grippe, even by the most experienced of physicians, as the patient seems fine in between recurrences."

Leah wrapped her arm around Mrs. Bristoll's shoulders and gave her a reassuring squeeze. She hoped the woman took some comfort from the doctor's words, as Mrs. Bristoll was nearly overcome, blaming herself for failing to recognize the seriousness of the situation sooner than she had.

"Until the intermissions become more perfect," the doctor said, "more predictable, one can never be quite certain. Even then, only time and his response to treatment will tell the tale. Would you be so kind as to show me to my patient?"

"Certainly." Leah gestured toward the pantry.

The house was eerily silent, save for the squeaking floorboards above them as Mrs. Bristoll climbed the stairs and tucked the other children into their beds.

While the doctor pushed his fingers into Tommy's stomach, Leah stroked her hand over the boy's brow. It was cool and soft, no sign of the fever that was eating away his will to survive. In a few hours, did he not gain relief, he would be soaked with sweat and shivering as if he slept atop a bed of snow.

"I will need warm water," the doctor finally said.

Leah retrieved a bowl from the shelf, then shuffled into the kitchen to fill it from the kettle hanging over the hearth. She added enough cold water from the ewer on the wooden table to cool the liquid to a tepid base.

The doctor took off his spectacles, rubbed them with the ends of his cravat, before putting them back on. "He needs bleeding for the excess fluids in his lungs."

"Bleeding?" Leah clutched her hand to her throat. "But he is so weak."

Dr. Ashcroft offered her a gentle smile. "I would treat him no differently, were he your own child, Your Grace. As you can see, he is laboring to breathe. Bleeding will balance the humors and ease his distress. The cinchona bark will treat the fever. He will need several doses over the next few days. Though I must inform you, this substance brings no guarantees, save the cost. It is *very* dear."

"You need not worry about your fee," Leah said, sitting on a stool beside the bed.

The doctor pulled three phials from his valise. He spooned a powder into a cup, then added two different liquids. Slipping his arm beneath Tommy's shoulders, he dripped the decoction into the boy's mouth. "Now, I do not want you to worry when he does not awaken. Cinchona bark is quite bitter, so I have mixed in several drops of laudanum to keep his stomach from convulsing."

She closed her eyes. "How will we know if it is working?"

"If he remains cool when the time comes round for his next fever, then we will know." The doctor made a tiny nick between the first two knuckles of the boy's left hand, then submerged his fingers into the bowl to let the warm water draw off the blood.

Leah took Tommy's right hand in hers. It felt so small, so lifeless, her vision blurred beneath her tears. She had told herself not to get too attached. The chances that any of these children would live a year, two at the most, were never very good, better now that they dwelled under Mrs. Bristoll's roof, but still not good. When they arrived, they were under-fed. Under-grown. Under-loved. Withered stalks, never likely to bloom.

Of course, it was easier to tell oneself not to care, than it was to turn off one's heart. She tried not to think of her sister's child, but once unleashed, the thoughts made a never-ending circle through her mind. Was he fed? Was he clothed?

Did someone hold his hand as his blood filled a bowl?

Pile blankets atop him? Soothe his brow?

She closed her eyes as the room swirled around her. Someone called her name. It sounded like Richard, but that couldn't be. He belonged in another world, another place, where life was clean and tidy, and little children didn't die from hunger and neglect.

Through the buzzing in her ears, she heard the distant sound of boot heels scraping over the wooden floorboards in the kitchen. She turned her gaze to the door. It *was* Richard.

He pulled up another stool. His dark eyes held no hint of his earlier wrath, nor condemnation or disgust for the wretched soul huddling in the tiny bed. He did not speak. He simply stroked her hand as he sat beside her.

She turned her palm up, seeking the warmth of his skin to ease the chill in her heart. He laced his fingers through hers, and side-by-side, they waited through the night.

When the first feeble rays of dawn spilled gray light through the kitchen window, the doctor smiled. "I believe we can safely assume the boy is out of danger now."

As if she did not believe his words, Leah ran her fingers over Tommy's brow. He still drew breath, his skin did not burn.

She buried her face in her hands. Her thoughts seemed strangely detached, slightly disoriented, as if she were moving through a dream. She heard Richard speak, felt his resonant voice tremble over her skin, but she could not discern his words.

When he swung her into his arms, she wrapped her hands around his neck, pulled herself closer to his solid chest and the strength he offered. She was vaguely aware of Mrs. Bristoll tucking her cloak beneath her chin, of whispered words that made no sense, then Richard carried her to the carriage awaiting them.

He cradled her across his lap through the seemingly endless ride through the streets, his warm hands stroking gentle circles on her back, his murmured words, soft and soothing near her ear.

When they arrived home, he carried her to her room, swiftly stripped off her clothing, slipped her nightgown over her head, then wrapped her in his arms as he sat in a chair by the windows.

The morning sun burned against her skin and still, violent shivers wracked her body. She burrowed against his chest, seeking his warmth, his strength, his silent reassurance. He kissed her brow, rubbed his hands over her back and held her secure in his arms as her tears soaked his shirt.

She could not say what made her weep, the joy that Tommy still drew breath, or the grief for her lost sister, once unleashed, now trembling through her with penetrating horror.

When her tears dwindled to a final sob, the urge to hide from her shameful lack of control set her legs to trembling, but she tilted her head to meet his gaze. His midnight eyes peered back at her, their smoky depths filled with an emotion she dared not contemplate in her unsteady state.

He offered her a grim smile. "How do you feel?"

"About the same as the day I crashed into the rock." She did not recognize her own throaty voice.

His lips twitched, but his smile did not hide the concern in his eyes. "I daresay you looked better when you bashed your head." The rhythmic beat of his heart beneath her ear soothed her with its soft cadence. "Talk to me."

His deep voice rumbled in his chest. It was a comforting sound. Leah drew a shaky breath. "I have a sister. Her name is Catherine. She is sweet and kind and beautiful, and I haven't seen her in nearly five years."

Richard stroked her arm. "What happened to her?"

"The usual, sad tale . . ." Her throat tightened. A clenching pain burned within her breast. She closed her eyes. "A dashing rogue seduced her, promised her love and fidelity, then abandoned her when she found herself with child. My father banished her from our lives and forbade the mention of her name."

Richard clamped his arms around her, protective bands of steel to keep her safe as she waded through the pain of her past and her father's treachery. She smoothed her hand over his cravat, wrinkled now beyond repair. "I do not know where she is. I do not know if I have a niece or a nephew. Or they could both be dead and I would never know."

"How old were you at the time?"

"Fourteen." She curled into his shoulder, seeking his heat to banish the cold seeping through her bones. The chirping of birds nesting in the trees outside her window seemed an incongruous sound to the turmoil swirling within her mind.

"Catherine was seventeen. I do not understand. Why did she never contact me? Didn't she know that I would worry? That I loved her? That I would never condemn her? I would have found some way to help her, if only I had known where she was."

"I understand your anger at her—"

"I'm not angry at her. I am angry at my father."

"Of course you are." Framing her face with his hands, Richard stroked his thumbs over her cheeks in a soothing caress. His morning beard covered his chiseled jaw. He smiled tenderly, his eyes dark and mesmerizing in their intensity. "She abandoned you to wonder and worry about her fate. You have every right to feel angry. And hurt. But you have no reason to feel any guilt. There was nothing you could have done."

Leah started to protest, then collapsed in his arms. "Perhaps you're right. Perhaps I am angry at her. I do not know any more. Everything is such a muddle."

"Tell me about the foundling home."

"When I think of Catherine and her child, I cannot help but wonder, are they treated well? Or is her child scorned because he is a bastard?" Leah twisted her hands in his shirt. "Bastard! What a vicious word. As if a babe has any choice in when or where he comes into the world, or who his parents are."

Some dark emotion flared in his eyes before he pulled her tightly against his chest until no space was left between them. His familiar scent of jasmine and amber soothed her as surely as his warm breath fluttering over her brow.

"So many children in this world suffer for their birth," she said, her lips touching his neck, tasting the salt of his skin. "Especially amongst the poor. Back home, I thought their lives were bleak, but nothing compares to the wretchedness of this city. The filth, the squalor. It is bad for the adults, worse for the children because no one loves them, and they do not understand. Every child should have someone who loves him."

Her unspoken words hung in the air. Did someone love her sister's child? Care for him when he was ill? Comfort and hold him when he wept? What was his name? What color were his eyes?

Had her sister ever married? Did she have enough to eat? *Does she ever think of me?*

Leah shuddered, as if from a sudden fever.

She forced her thoughts back into the darkness where they could not cause her pain. "Mrs. Bristoll is a kind soul. She spends her money on food and housing, but what about clothing? A visit from the doctor is very dear. Who pays for that?"

"How did you choose this particular establishment?"

"Mrs. Bristoll is sister to the vicar in my home parish. When he learned I was travelling to Town, he asked me to deliver a parcel for him. Once I met her and learned of her good work, how could I not support her?"

"I understand your desire to help, but can you not confine your charitable deeds to a better part of Town?"

Leah almost laughed, but the ache in her chest was still too tight. "Oh, I don't know. Do you suppose Mayfair has many homeless children who need my help?"

He chuckled grimly. "I suppose not. But what about the Foundling Hospital? They would welcome your support."

Leah shook her head. "Do not misunderstand me. The Foundling Hospital is a wonderful institution, but those children have numerous people attending to their needs. There are thousands more with nowhere to turn. Those are the children who need my help. Those are the children—"

Richard pressed his fingertips to her lips. "Enough. I am convinced and converted. At least now I understand why it is so important to you. You may continue your visits provided you always take the Town coach and travel with four outriders of *my* choosing." Her sulky nod made him grin, as if he did not quite expect her to give in so easily. "I find it hard to fathom your father allowed you traipse around St. Giles."

Leah shrugged. "He did not know. He did not care, as long as I did not mention Catherine or her child or the poor or anything else he found disagreeable." She fingered the collar of his shirt, peeked at him from beneath her lashes. "Richard, I . . . I am dreadfully sorry for the hideous things I said to you yesterday. It seems I have a bit of a temper."

He laughed. "So I noticed. Unlike me, of course, who is possessed of the most even temperament. And that, my dear, is the closest to an apology you will ever wring from me. We men have rules, you see. Never apologize. Never admit defeat. And never discuss anything when we can issue orders instead."

"We shall have to see about that."

He laughed again, his smile soft and tender. Never had he looked so handsome, his hair unruly from his hands sliding through it, his clothing wrinkled, his shirt stained with her tears. The words she longed to say burned her throat.

"I did not set out to deceive you," she said instead. "I have simply kept my own counsel for so long, it never occurred to me to mention my visits to the foundling home. I just assumed you would not care."

"I care," he said vehemently. "I care about your safety."

But he did not love her.

It does not matter, she told herself as she pressed her lips to his neck, as he groaned and covered her mouth with his, hot tongue sliding between her teeth, as he shifted her in his arms and carried her to bed, as she shuddered in his embrace, first with unbearable need, then with unbearable pleasure, she told herself it did not matter. He was her husband, and he was all that was kind and caring. Perfectly polite. Exquisitely civil. Honorable to his core. It should be enough.

But the empty ache in her chest gave truth to the lies she told herself. As much as she chided her foolish notions, she wanted him to love her as she loved him. But she could no longer think. He was doing such wondrous things to her body. Hands sliding over her skin and between her legs, lips trailing fire over her breasts, drawing moans and whimpers from her throat.

She clung to his hips, legs wrapped round his waist, pulling him closer, holding him tighter, until his release sent his seed deep inside her womb, until she crushed her fist against her mouth to keep the words locked behind her teeth. *I love you.*

"Do it again," Alison said, her giggles echoing through the cavernous hall, the sound sweeter to Leah's ears than Handel's sonatas, especially when joined by Richard's rumbling laugh.

The scandalous wink he sent Leah brought a flush to her cheeks, but Alison didn't seem to notice. She was too busy hopping from one foot to the other while pulling on their hands until finally they swung their arms and her feet left the floor.

Alison let out a raucous shriek. Unfortunately, her joyous shout lured Rachel from the gold salon. Blue eyes narrowed, lips pursed, she glared at Leah. Even her palpable dislike, which seemed to grow more intense with each new day, could not ruin the contentment Leah felt from her afternoons spent with Richard and Alison, their routine these two weeks past.

He spent every morning out of the house or sequestered in his office while Leah divided her time between Alison, the foundling home, as well as other charitable foundations seeking her support, and the running of her household.

Promptly at two, Richard would arrive from wherever he was to escort Leah and Alison on an outing about Town. Each day brought some new destination, Hyde Park, the Tower, Vauxhall Gardens. They laughed and ate and grew so close, Leah thought her heart would burst with the love she felt for this man and this child. Only one event could complete her current happiness.

To hear some word from her sister, to know with certainty that Catherine and her child were safe.

How strange it felt to discuss, openly and without fear of her father's recrimination, all that had happened in her past. Her sister's downfall. Her mother's demise. The hopes and dreams she'd had as a child.

Slowly, Richard began sharing his life, too, though most of his past remained a secret, locked away. His eldest brother's death had hurt him deeply, as did Geoffrey's continued absence from Town. Railing against "Geoffrey's lack of consideration for his family's piece of mind," Richard vowed to strip the skin from his backside when the wastrel bothered to return. But behind his words lurked a deeper fear, something darker Leah could not name, but she heard it in his voice, saw it in the hard set of his jaw and the shadows darkening his eyes.

He swung Alison into his arms. "What say you, precious, tomorrow we shall explore the Menagerie, but now it is time for bed. Shall I tell you a story before tucking you in?"

"I do not want to sleep," Alison said, tapping her fingers against Richard's cheeks, a tragic pout on her lips. "I want to go with you and Aunt Leah."

Rachel ran her fingers along Alison's arm, her fingertips brushing against Richard's hand. "There, there, dear. Do not fret. Mama will accompany you and Uncle to your rooms."

The maternal tenderness in her voice was so incongruous to her usual distance, Leah frowned. Not that she thought Rachel a terrible mother. Just that Leah had never, before this moment, witnessed anything remotely resembling affection.

More a dignified tolerance of her offspring. A cold conviction that children belonged in the nursery, tucked away with the servants and other sundry items one might need for the future, but did not necessarily want in the present.

Alison shook her head. A strand of black hair caught on her eyelashes. "I want Auntie Leah. Her stories are funny."

"Funnier than mine?" Richard's brows lifted in mock horror. "I shall have to punish you for that precious piece of betrayal."

He tickled her waist. Alison shrieked until her giggles made him close his eyes, made his head lean back, made a spasm of emotion cross over his features that Leah could not identify.

The dark look Rachel threw at Leah was clear. Alison was Rachel's daughter and Leah best not interfere.

She was right, of course. As much as Leah enjoyed the moments spent with Richard as he lulled Alison off to sleep, she could not come between Rachel and her child.

"I shall tell you a story in the morning." She kissed Alison's cheek, then excused herself and returned to her rooms, where a steaming bath awaited her. Her maid helped her from her clothes and into the slipper bath. Oil of roses scented the water and soothed her to the brink of sleep.

She thought of Tommy, of the rapid rate with which he had returned from sickly child to boisterous boy. It was astounding, as was Richard's generosity. Not only had he accompanied her to the foundling home several times, he had even conducted a thorough evaluation of the building and made financial arrangements for its repairs and improvements.

Only a single dark cloud hung over Leah's happiness: Rachel's continued animosity, underscored by the neverending social obligations—the balls, the routs, the dinners—Leah hated them all. But it was a necessary part of Richard's life, so she kept her own counsel.

With a sigh, she climbed from the tub, donned a simple muslin frock trimmed with delicate lace, then sat at her dressing table to brush her hair. She leaned forward to inspect the scar across her temple, now faded to a thin, white line.

In time, she hoped it would vanish completely. Just as she hoped to banish the demons haunting Richard's past so he would be free to love again, free to love her.

Leah thought she was making progress in that regard. Yet, sometimes, she would catch him watching her, a dark, brooding stare that sent shivers of fear and doubt coursing over her skin.

And he was not sleeping at all well. She lost count of how many nights he had awakened, drenched in sweat. Haunted eyes seeking hers through the darkness.

Nightmares, he said, as he dragged her against his chest. But the desperation with which he clung to her, his heart thundering beneath her ear, told her it was something more.

Still, she refused to give in to her insecurities, not when the future before her suddenly seemed so bright. Richard's unwavering support and understanding had given her the strength to face her past, to come to terms not only with her father's betrayal, but her sister's disappearance as well.

While she still ached to find her sister, she no longer felt the fear that had burdened her for so long, the hidden shame that somehow she was to blame for her sister's fate. Richard was right. She was just a child. There was nothing she could have done.

The connecting door snapped open. The object of her thoughts strode into the room and stood behind her chair. He looked sinfully handsome in his evening dress, crisp white shirt and linen neck cloth the only relief from his black coat and matching trousers. The beguiling scent of jasmine and another scent, decidedly male and uniquely his, washed over her as he met her gaze in the looking glass.

His smile was soft and seductive and stirred the desire she felt for this man. She would be afraid of the power he held over her, if not for her confidence that he felt the same need, the same hungry desire that brought his hands to her neck, fingertips gliding over her sensitive skin. "Why aren't you dressed? We are due at the Elliots in less than an hour."

"I am not going," she said, wishing just once she could remain aloof, coldly detached, the prim and proper aristocratic wife she'd heard so much about from Rachel, a woman of breeding who did not melt from one heated touch, one whispered word.

"Why not?" His teeth grazed her ear.

Her lips pressed tightly together to stifle her moan. She shrugged and closed her eyes.

He came around the chair and knelt at her feet, his large hands resting suggestively on the outer curves of her thighs. "Answer me."

How could she describe the torture of mixing with his so-called friends? "I am tired, that is all."

He jumped to his feet. "I will send for the doctor."

"I am not ill," she said, grabbing his hand.

He crouched on his heels. "Then what is it?"

She gazed at his beloved face, his brows drawn together in a tight line, his dark eyes narrowed and intent upon her face. She couldn't tell him everything, but she didn't want him to worry, so she settled on a half-truth.

"We have had engagements six of the past ten nights," she said. "And these affairs last until dawn. I am still not used to this life you lead. I suppose I'm rather a dull sort, but I would much prefer to stay home and read . . . or something . . ."

His hands slipped beneath her frock, his fingers brushing over her ankles. Her shiver brought a smile to his lips and a dangerous glint to his eyes.

"Something?" he murmured. His deep voice seemed to slow the movement of time, sent a languid heat over her cheeks, a tingling heaviness to her breasts, a deep ache between her thighs.

She was aware of the rise and fall of his chest, of his appealing scent and the heat of his fingers stroking the soft skin behind her knees.

"Does that something have anything to do with me?"

This was seduction, this sweep of his hands as he dragged her frock up past her knees, his fingers trailing a slow path over her thighs. She sighed. "I'm afraid that it very much does."

His laugh trembled over the sensitive flesh of her inner thighs where his lips touched her skin, his hands moving ever upward, his mouth following the trail.

"You are so sweet, Leah. I can't get enough of you."

His fingers found her nether curls. With exquisite tenderness, he stroked her hot, swollen flesh. "I should very much like to stay home with you, too."

She dropped her head back against the chair and shut her eyes. One long finger slid inside her passage, stroked her and teased her until she could no longer contain her moans.

He rubbed his thumb over a particularly sensitive spot beneath her curls that tightened and bloomed beneath his masterful touch. "But we must attend this evening . . ."

Each slow circle sent a shattering ache through her belly and breasts. She couldn't comprehend his words. She bit her lips. Her breathing came in short, panting gasps.

A second finger joined the first. Stretching her. Filling her. But she wanted more. She clutched his shoulders in her fists, tried to drag him up the length of her body.

His throaty laugh matched her moan. "There is someone I want you to meet." His hot breath burned over her sensitive flesh as he gathered her chemise in his fist. He pushed it up to her waist. "He writes that he will be there tonight."

"Richard. Please—" She was naked to his gaze. She tried to clamp her legs together, but he wedged his shoulders between her knees.

"Hush," he commanded. "You are so beautiful . . ."

He removed his fingers, then slowly dipped his head.

Leah gasped, "Richard! What are you doing?"

She closed her eyes, her breath trapped in her throat as his mouth touched her most feminine flesh, as his tongue flicked out to lick her and stroke her and taste her desire. She tossed her head from side to side. It was so shocking, so bold.

It must be a sin because it felt so good. Each tug of his lips, each stroke of his tongue, sent flashes of heat and pleasure and need coursing over her skin, through her breasts and her womb. She whimpered and moaned until she could stand it no more. "Richard, I need to feel you inside of me."

He pushed to his knees, wrenched open his breeches. He grabbed her hips, dragged her bottom to the edge of her chair. The heat of his tongue as he captured her lips, the taste of his breath, and his hot, hard length pumping inside her sent wave after wave of unbearable pleasure rushing through her. Tension spiraled like a vortex in her belly, spinning ever tighter and tauter, drawing her deeper and down, until her world shattered.

She clung to his shoulders, clenched her teeth against the words she longed to say, though it was growing harder to contain them with each passing day. The love she felt for this man consumed her. The future stretched out before her, and it filled her with inexplicable fear.

Chapter Eighteen

"Do you see him?"

"No." Richard scanned the lords and ladies, huddled together in the Elliots' ballroom, their indistinguishable faces blurring beneath the blazing chandeliers. Too many people crammed into too small a space left the room airless and hot. The sound of swishing satins and silks and voices all talking at once only added to the stifling atmosphere. "Perhaps he has yet to arrive. Shall we have another dance, my dear?"

Leah shook her head. "You need not stay by my side. Go. Find your friend. Or play a hand or two of cards."

A hand or two of cards? He laced his fingers behind his back to keep from pulling her into his arms, with no regard to the eager eyes all around them. She was so blissfully ignorant in the ways of society rakes, who drank, gambled, hunted and whored twenty-four hours a day. A hand or two of cards?

The look he sent her was so blatantly sensual, she snapped open her fan and waved it before her face.

"It is unbearably hot in here," she said, her voice breathless, her eyes glimmering in the candlelight. "Perhaps you could find your friend and meet me on the terrace?"

Her cheeks *were* flushed an enticing shade of pink. And once he got her onto the terrace, he could, perhaps, slip her away into the gardens, where he might find a secluded grotto. . . .

Richard held up his hands. "All right, madam, you win. But do not promise your dances to anyone but me."

"How terribly gauche of you, St. Austin. Rachel tells me it is malapropos to dance only with one's husband."

"Rachel is an addle-pated, buffle-headed harridan with apartments to let. Her opinions—"

Leah laughed and walked away, the flowing gold silk of her gown skimming like a lover's hands along her hips. She cast a glance over her shoulder, innocent and beguiling, her green eyes beckoning Richard to come hither, to surrender his soul, to confess all his sins. But he could not.

His sins were too dark, too dirty, ever to be revealed.

Need and desire pulled him toward her, but he forced himself to walk away. He prowled the ballroom, stalked the gaming rooms, searched the smoking rooms. Pierce was nowhere to be found, damn his eyes. If it weren't for his missive saying he would be here tonight, Richard would be home making love to his wife.

Not surrounded by sycophants and ne'er do wells.

God, how he hated these affairs. Ignoring everyone, he went in search of Leah. So what if *le beau monde* thought he was living under the cat's paw? He did not care. She was his wife and he wanted her. He admired her. Her honor, her courage, her devotion to her sister. A pain they had in common, each tortured by the loss of a sibling, but Richard had hopes of easing Leah's grief. A goodly number of men in his employ were now searching for Catherine Jamison, but he would not tell Leah. He would not raise her hopes, or her fears, not until he had undeniable proof of her sister's fate.

He tried not to probe too deeply into the desire, the need, he felt for his wife. Or the danger she brought to his heart. Or the fear haunting his nights until he awakened soaked in sweat, heart pounding, muscles clenching. And even that fear, that constant, aching tension, did not stop him from wanting her, needing her, as he'd never needed anyone before.

And therein lurked his danger. He wanted her too badly, cared for her too deeply, needed her too much.

"Have you lost your wife?" the voice he hated above all others hissed as she stepped into his path. Rachel arched her brows as she waited for his response. Her royal blue gown intensified the clear blue of her eyes. Her wheat-colored hair framed her face in an artful arrangement of cascading curls.

As much as it disgusted Richard to admit it, she was beautiful, but hers was an illusion of beauty. Inside, where it truly mattered, she was as ugly as a garden slug, and just as slippery. His reminder of all that was wrong in his world, and everything he stood to lose.

Appearance and propriety must be maintained, he told himself as he schooled a bland smile for the crowd. "Leave me be, Rachel. I am not in the mood to fence words with you."

"Are you in the mood for your wife?" Rachel taunted. "That is too bad, as she is dancing with that young man again. My, but they do manage to find each other simply everywhere."

Richard's jaw clenched as a now-familiar miasma of jealousy swept away reason. He studied the couples waltzing by until he finally spotted Leah and her young fop.

Of course it was Prescott. It was always Prescott.

Everywhere they went, he arrived, dressed in elegantly fitted evening clothes, his hair flopping over his brow as if he were Byron or Shelley. The melancholy air of broken-hearted despair haunting his smile only added appeal to the quivering masses of eligible misses twittering behind their fans.

Richard felt his gut clench, but he was careful not to raise his brows or fist his hands or tighten a muscle as he watched Leah and Prescott dance. The boy was holding her too closely, smiling too fondly, his blue eyes darkened by the heat of the dance, or the burn of desire.

The last strains of music faded away. Leah's mouth curved in a tender smile as she spoke to Alexander.

When she turned and walked toward the terrace doors, Prescott stared after her with the same besotted look Richard knew adorned his own face.

A few moments later, Prescott followed her into the night.

Leah walked with chin held high toward the terrace doors. Ladies all around watched her approach, then turned their heads when she came close enough to greet them.

Because of her less than noble birth, Leah knew she would never be accepted by the *haut ton*. While the notion stung her pride, she would not let them see her pain. She kept her chin high, her back straight, and her smile as regal as might the queen herself.

She blew a sigh as she stepped through the French windows and strolled to the balustrade. The night air was cool, scented with roses and honeysuckle, and soothed her overheated cheeks. If only Richard would find his friend. Then they could leave.

"Wishing on the stars again?"

"Alexander," she said, sending him a shaky smile. Though shadows still haunted his eyes, they had fallen into friendship again, if a bit more stiff and formal than their previous association. Neither ever referred to the madness of his desperate kiss, or to his proposal that she elope with him.

"Isn't it a lovely night?" she said, settling on the weather as a safe topic. "I cannot understand why anyone would prefer to be squeezed alive in a stuffy ballroom, when so much beauty awaits them here."

"Yes, it is beautiful."

His voice lingered on the word *beautiful,* and Leah had to look away, out over the gardens lit by paper lanterns.

Footsteps and giggling voices approaching the terrace doors shattered Leah's hopes for a moment of peace.

She rubbed a shaking hand across her brow. "I cannot bear one more disapproving glance cast my way."

"Who disapproves of you?" Alex said. "Tell me now."

Leah had not meant to speak the words aloud. She grabbed his arm. "I should not have said that, Alex. They do not disapprove of me. They simply think me an unsuitable wife for a duke. Please, I do not want any trouble. I just want fresh air and some peace."

With a stiff nod, Alexander grabbed her hand and pulled her into the shadows around the corner of the house. A few moments later, four women walked into the purple glow of moonlight bathing the terrace. Leah recognized the voices of the Ladies Montague, Elliot, Richmond, and Cunningham.

According to Rachel, who delighted in telling Leah all the sordid details of the *ton,* each of them, save Abby Cunningham, had tried to bring Richard up to scratch.

She glanced around her. There was no staircase on this end of the terrace, no means of escape without being seen. Not only would she have to listen to whatever these women had followed her out here to say, she was trapped in the shadows with a man who was not her husband. The impropriety of her situation choked her. Perfect. Simply perfect.

She leaned against the mansion, the cold bricks cutting into her back, and gave a silent prayer they wouldn't linger long.

"What a dreadful girl," Lady Elliot said.

"I think she is charming," Abby Cunningham countered.

"Charming? Have you been tippling the Regent's punch?"

"What else can one expect from one of the lower classes?" Lady Richmond sneered. "They may dress in the first stare of fashion, but they cannot buy good breeding and manners. She is a contamination to us all."

"She bought him with her money," Lady Elliot said. "My lord told me her dowry was large enough to buy the King himself."

"Do not be absurd," Lady Richmond scoffed. "St. Austin is the richest man in England. No, she is *enceinte* and her father forced St. Austin to the church with a gun."

Lady Elliot laughed. "Oh, that is too delicious. Do you think she is having an *affaire de coeur* with that young man? He is always casting sheep eyes at her . . ."

Leah seized Alexander's arm. The rigid tension of his muscles warned her he wanted nothing more than to fling their gossip in their faces, but she held him fast. To reveal their presence would only add fresh coals to an already raging fire.

At least now she knew the rumors whispered behind her back. Though it hurt, she was careful not to make a sound.

"You are way off the mark," Abby broke in. "She spent a week in my home following her injury. She is a lovely girl and St. Austin's devotion was admirable. He never left her side until she was out of danger, and even then, only to fetch a carriage to take her home. I tell you, he loves her."

"Poppycock!" This from Lady Margaret Montague.

Leah felt her skin grow cold. Her stomach lurched. She did not want to hear whatever it was Margaret was about to say.

"Poor, dear Lady Montague," Lady Elliot crooned. "How perfectly odious of us not to consider your tender feelings."

"Yes," Lady Richmond added. "How hard it must be for you to see St. Austin and his wife together when you came closer than any of us did to wearing that title yourself."

"How it must hurt to know he deserted your bed for another's," Lady Elliot said.

Leah held her breath as she waited for Margaret's response.

The only sound came from the music floating through the terrace doors and the chirping insects in the shrubbery.

Lady Elliot broke the silence. "Surely you aren't suggesting St. Austin still shares your bed?"

"I never said anything of the sort."

"That is the problem," Lady Richmond retorted. "You haven't said a word. Tell us everything. We're on tenterhooks to know."

"St. Austin is the soul of discretion," Margaret said. "You must promise never to repeat a word."

Her heart squeezing painfully, her blood roaring through her ears, Leah peered around the corner, watched as three heads adorned with feathers and jewels bobbed up and down.

Margaret looked at each lady in turn.

"He never left my bed," she said.

Everyone gasped. Leah's stomach clenched, her thoughts shattered. Only the certain knowledge she would be discovered huddled in the shadows with Alex kept her silent. That, and the painful knot building in her throat. A familiar sensation teased her, a fleeting image, lost before it became clear.

She rubbed her hand over the back of her neck.

Margaret nodded. "It is true. He married her for the money, make no mistake about it. Eric ran amuck with the estates, as did his father before him. St. Austin inherited a tremendous debt. I knew he was going to wed."

The women gazed at Margaret with wide-eyed stares.

"We discussed it several times," she said. "I wanted to wed him, of course, but I didn't have the capital he required. It was I who suggested he look to the nouveau riche for his heiress, as she would be less likely to interfere in our lives—"

"You are lying," Abby declared and stormed away.

"How dare she insult me like that," Margaret said. "You may believe what you like. It does not matter to me in the least."

Margaret marched into the ballroom, her footsteps tapping furiously on the stone floor. Lady Elliot and Lady Richmond followed at a more sedate pace, their heads close together in clandestine conversation.

Leah walked to the balustrade. She gripped the railing, the

rough stone cutting into her palm, as Margaret's words echoed in her mind. *He never left my bed . . . never left my bed . . . my bed . . .*

The throbbing in her head intensified, clarified the blurred images haunting her dreams. In the darkness of her mind, she saw another night, another balcony.

Rain beginning to fall. Richard kneeling at Margaret's feet as she lay upon a stone bench, her arms twined about his neck. His hands clutching her wrists. His mouth pressed against her lips, locked in a passionate embrace.

The ground swirled beneath Leah's feet. She shoved her fists against her eyes, but the vision remained.

Alexander grabbed her shoulders, tugged her hands away from her face, pulled her against his chest.

"Hush, hush," he said as she sobbed against his waistcoat, her hands clutching the lace of his shirt. "Pay them no heed. They are spiteful biddies, not worth the price of your tears—"

"Unhand my wife," Richard's voice roared from behind them. He grabbed Alexander's shoulder and shoved Leah out of the way.

"Do not touch him," she cried as his fist connected with Alexander's jaw. Alex flew to the pavement.

Leah fell to her knees, cradled Alexander's face in her hands. He wasn't bleeding, but his eyes appeared vacant, slightly stunned. She helped him to his feet, then glared at Richard. Her skin shivered as an icy fury curled her hands into fists. "How dare you! What has he ever done to you?"

"He dared touch what is mine," Richard snarled, his jaw clenched. His nostrils flared. His arms and legs were rigid, as if he were struggling to restrain himself from further violence. "Step away from him. Now, madam, so I can teach him not to dally with another man's wife."

Of all the nerve! Leah sucked in her breath, marched over to Richard, and slapped him with all the strength she possessed.

His eyes glittered dangerously in the low light.

She wasn't afraid, though. Even as her fingers went numb and a stinging pain shot up her arm, she squared her shoulders and lifted her chin. "I am going home now," she said evenly. "If you so-much-as-touch one hair on his golden head, I will carve out your philandering heart with your own hunting knife!"

Chapter Nineteen

Philandering heart?

Richard rubbed his palm over his stinging cheek as he watched his wife disappear around the side of the house. Her words stabbed through the furious haze still clouding his reason.

What had she meant by that? And why was she crying?

It made no sense when she was the one dallying with another man, her face buried against another man's neck.

Not just any man, but a man she had once thought to marry, his hands moving circles over her back, his mouth touching her ear as he murmured seduction.

Richard flexed his fists as he advanced on Alexander. His muscles grew rigid. His skin tight. "Name your seconds."

"With pleasure," Alexander snarled, his too-handsome face twisted in a ferocious scowl. Hands on hips, he squared his shoulders as he glared at Richard. "I've wanted a chance at you for weeks now. But Leah wanted you. She wants you, still, though God knows you do not deserve that precious gift."

No doubt the boy was right, but that mattered not. She was his wife, and he'd be damned if he let another man touch her. "And you believe you stand a chance against me?"

"I may be a few years younger than you, but let me reassure you, my lord Duke. I know my way around a brace of dueling pistols, and I am eager for the deed."

Richard couldn't believe he was planning to shoot a young man, *murder* a young man, barely twenty-two. A vision of Leah's anguished face, her expressive eyes glistening with unshed tears rose up to haunt him. Her tortured voice echoed through his mind. *If you harm one hair on his golden head* . . .

How would he ever tell her he'd murdered her best friend?

He rubbed his hands over his face. "She will never forgive me."

"Nor me," Alexander said, the torchlight playing over the hard angles of his clenched jaw. "But I will take that chance. She deserves better than you."

"No doubt you are right, but she is mine."

Alexander's lips curled in a vicious sneer. "She is a possession to you. Nothing more. You drag her around Town, then throw her to the vultures and let them feast on her flesh!"

Richard narrowed his eyes. "What do you mean? If anyone has so much as spoken an unkind word to her, they will answer to me!"

"Unkind word? That is rich. Truly rich. Would that be the case, she could defend herself, but the fancy have much more subtle ways to inflict their wounds."

"What do you mean?" Richard ground out through his teeth.

"They never say anything to her. They look right at her—and right through her. She doesn't exist. Oh, they wait for you to turn your back, of course. They cannot be honest in their campaign against her."

The cut direct. Richard should have known. She hadn't wanted to come here tonight, but she wouldn't tell him why. She didn't want him to know how unhappy she was. The cold taste of self-loathing burned like bitter bile in his throat.

"And of course," Alexander was saying, his voice scathing,

his words more lethal than any dueling pistol with their cold precision. "When all else fails, there are always the rumors. But rumors only work if you follow her onto the terrace so she overhears your lies."

Richard swore viciously. He walked to the balustrade, dug his knuckles into the stone. "What are these rumors?"

"Hmm, there is the one about her buying you with her money. No, you don't like that one? Let's try this one. She was pregnant and her father dragged you to the altar with a gun. But that might not damage her reputation enough, so let's say she is having an affair with me. And if that doesn't hurt her enough, let us inform her that her husband keeps a ladybird. Oh, but that is just not bad enough, so let's add the juicy tidbit that the husband and slut plot together against her."

"Enough!" Richard said, holding up his hand. How could he have been so blind not to have seen? So stupid, not to have guessed? He knew only too well the cruelty of the *ton*. Tension clawed at his gut, tightened his fists, clenched his teeth. No one would hurt her again. "Who is responsible for these lies?"

"This last tableau was played out by Lady Montague and her friends, Lady Elliot, Lady Richmond and Lady Cunningham. Of course, they heard it from their lords."

"Lady Cunningham?" Richard could almost understand the malice of the other three, but not Abby Cunningham.

"I will admit, Lady Cunningham was the only one to rise to Leah's defense." Alexander's voice lost its biting edge. He sucked in a deep breath, then pushed it out in an audible gust. "You care about her, don't you?"

In the ballroom, the musicians struck up a lively country dance. Richard shifted his gaze to the flambeaux lighting the garden path, the glimmering gold flickering in the darkness reminding him of Leah's eyes, fury glistening with tears.

"It seems I owe you an apology. You have been a good friend to my wife while I have been blind—"

"Don't wait too long to tell her you love her," Alexander said, the bleakness in his voice as cold as gale winds raging across the Cornish coast. "I made that mistake, and I shall regret it for the rest of my life."

Richard met the boy's gaze and saw a reflection of his own lost youth, his own lost innocence. Prescott was struggling to understand why the woman he loved had married another. Through no fault of his own, the boy was suffering.

Any anger or jealousy Richard had felt paled beneath a sudden, unwanted sympathy. He held out his hand. "For Leah's sake, I would beg your pardon and ask for your friendship."

Alexander stared at Richard's outstretched hand for a long, tense moment. Then he sighed, his shoulders sagged. He looked like a man utterly beaten, but his grip was firm and strong as he grasped Richard's hand. "What will you do about this?"

"I have a few ideas. Care to lend your support?"

"Absolutely." Alexander grinned, then winced and grabbed his chin. "You know, for a duke, you have a powerful punch."

Richard rubbed his cheek. "So does the duchess."

Alex laughed, though the shadows never left his eyes. "I have never seen her quite so angry. I would not be surprised if she threw a few more at you when you return home."

"Neither would I," Richard said with a grin. But his amusement quickly died, replaced by shame as he remembered his reckless words and the outrage that had flashed in her tear-stained eyes. He needed to find her, but first, he needed to seek his revenge.

The two men entered the ballroom. With Alexander by his side, Richard schooled his features into a controlled mask of indifference, pushed a cold clarity into his gaze that belied the brutal fury pulsing through his veins.

At his approach, Margaret stepped forward, her lips curved in her most seductive smile. "Your Grace," she murmured.

Richard walked up to her, so close, his pumps touched her satin slippers. He held her gaze long enough for all around them to realize he was staring into her eyes, then he turned his back to her without saying a word.

Everyone around them gasped, then an eerie silence swept over the room as if four hundred people drew a single breath and held it, straining to hear Richard's next words.

He ignored them all and raised Abby Cunningham's hand to his lips. His smile was warm and familiar, as was the gleam in his eyes. "As always, Lady Cunningham, the pleasure of your company was the one bright spot in an otherwise dreadful evening."

With a slight lift of her brows and a nod of her head, she returned his smile. "Your Grace. And my compliments to your lovely wife."

He turned to the men. "My lords Elliot, Richmond, I am forced to withdraw my support from your proposed steamship manufactory." His voice was calm, his words clipped.

"What?" Lord Richmond blustered, his jowly cheeks flapping. "Without your support, there won't be a manufactory."

"Surely you realize steam-powered engines are the future of shipping," Lord Elliot said, clutching his chest, pulling at his cravat as if it were choking off his breath. "The *Savannah* proved that two years ago when she crossed the Atlantic in twenty-nine days. Think, St. Austin! This is the chance of a lifetime!"

"Yes, it is," Richard said, the echo of his voice bouncing off the walls. "More's the pity. Nevertheless, I cannot align myself with two spineless toads who cannot control their wives or their wagging tongues. Now, if you will excuse me, my *dear friend* Prescott and I have more enjoyable entertainments to attend."

"What did he mean by that, Alice?" Lord Elliot hissed. "If you have caused trouble for me with the duke . . ."

Richard smiled as he walked away. He'd let them suffer through their present misery for a few days. Then he would graciously offer to reconsider his decision, provided the men brought their wives to heel and offered very loud, very public support for Leah's position in society.

For the benefit of the gossipmongers, Richard laughed and joked with Prescott as he stalked toward the door. Anyone observing the two men would have no doubt that they were boon companions and any rumors of an assignation between the boy and Leah would be denied.

How could it be true if Richard befriended him?

His smile died as he reached the pavement. Leah had taken the carriage, so he sent a footman to hire a hack. He paced beneath the street lamps as he waited, all the while haunted by Prescott's anguished words and his probing questions.

Do you love her?

Leah stomped across her room to the connecting door. She grabbed the key and gave it a vicious twist.

Of all the nerve! To accuse her of dallying with another man when all along he was the one who kept a mistress on the side.

Pain gripped her chest until she could scarce draw breath. Each tick of the mantel clock marked the tortuous beat of her heart. She collapsed against the wall, crushed the heels of her hands against her eyes, but she couldn't stop the vision of Richard clutching Margaret in his arms, his mouth devouring hers in a passionate kiss.

Now she understood the haunted look in Richard's eyes following her injury and every time she'd questioned him about how she had fallen. He had feared discovery, feared she would remember his fondling and kissing another woman.

Oh, God. Her skin grew cold, even as fury burned in her belly. She raised a shaking hand to her lips, felt his mouth upon hers as surely as if he were kissing her now, the sultry sweep of his tongue as he tasted and teased her, the crush of his hands upon her breasts. The physical side of marriage was so special, so intimate, so personal!

How could he give to another what should only be hers?

As if her thoughts weren't painful enough, her mind's eye tortured her with images of Margaret in bed with Richard, stroking her hands over his naked body, clinging to his powerful hips, swallowing his groan as he shuddered his release.

Never had she imagined he would be unfaithful to her. She had never even considered it. How could she have been so stupid? So naïve? She had thought he was beginning to care for her, but she was wrong. She was no more to him than a body in the night!

Well, she would see about that. She was his wife. He was hers. And she was not going to share him with anyone.

His chamber door crashed open and she jumped. Her heart pounded as she listened to his footsteps stomp across his room.

The handle on the connecting door jiggled. Then he pounded on the wood. "Leah, I want to talk to you."

She did not reply. She thought perhaps she should wait until morning when she might be calmer, slightly more rational.

Or perhaps he was right. Perhaps it was better to face his treachery now while she had anger to sustain her.

She twisted the key, ripped open the door, then paced to the far wall, putting the length of the room between them. She couldn't bear the thought of his hands upon her, not after they had touched another. But he would not let her retreat. He strode toward her, sleek as a panther stalking his prey.

When she turned to run, he wrapped his arms around her waist. She opened her mouth to argue, but he shifted her into his left arm, covered her lips with his right hand.

"I know what you heard at the Elliots' tonight," he said, his voice tender and low, his thumb stroking over her cheek, his eyes as impenetrable as the midnight sky. "And I am heartily sorry. I have been stupid. Blind in my arrogance. I thought simply because you are my wife, you would receive the respect you deserve. I should have known better. Polite society. The word is a joke. But I've put a stop to the rumors."

She breathed his scent of jasmine and amber and a stabbing pain sliced through her gut. Did Margaret enjoy the scent of his cologne as much as Leah did? Did he kiss her hair and stroke her skin, whisper seductive words in her ear?

"I know the truth," she said, her voice quivering. "I know about you and Lady Montague."

"Leah, I cannot change the past."

Her weakness made her furious. Desperate to escape, she clawed at his hands. "I saw you together. The night of my injury. I saw you. Holding her. Kissing her!"

"It is not what you think." He turned her in his embrace, forced her to meet his gaze. "Leah, I understand your anger, but you are wrong. Margaret is not my mistress."

"I saw you together, at Lady Cunningham's ball."

She wanted him to deny it. Oh God, how she wanted him to deny it. But she saw the truth in his eyes. She shoved her hands against his shoulders, but he would not let her go.

No, he tightened his grip, smoothed his hands over her back.

"It is not what you think," he whispered against her ear, his breath feathering over her neck. "Margaret is not my mistress, but not for lack of trying. She lured me onto the terrace by pretending dizziness. I have seen her faint any number of times. I had no way of knowing she was not truly ill, not until she kissed me."

Leah tried to laugh, but a sob caught in her throat. "You expect me to believe that Banbury tale?"

"Why not? It is the truth. I cannot deny she once shared my

bed." He cradled her cheeks in his palms. His smile was so tender, his gaze so intense, she could almost believe him. "But I've not had any other women, not since the day we wed. What need have I of another, when all that I want is here in my arms?"

She leaned into his hand, forced a smile to her lips even though she felt as if she were dying inside.

"And when you tire of me, my lord?" she whispered through her tears. "Will another grace your bed, then?"

"Oh, Leah, I shall never tire of you."

Chapter Twenty

Leah wanted to believe him, but she was afraid.

"Part your lips for me, darling," he murmured against her mouth, his fingers fanning through her hair, sifting her tangle of curls over her shoulders and down her back.

She could almost believe he cared for her when he was with her like this. When he moved his mouth over her lips, fiercely, boldly, savagely demanding a response, his hands shaking as he stripped off her frock. When he shrugged out of his clothing, his dark eyes meeting hers, his sultry, dark eyes that glimmered with some deep, nameless emotion, she could almost believe . . .

"I will not share you," she said, pushing him toward the bed, pushing him onto his back. Straddling his hips, she framed his face, his beard-roughened jaw scraping her hands. "I throw your own words back at you. You are my husband, I am your wife, and even if you never come to love me, I will not share you."

"I am yours, Leah, and I surrender willingly."

His voice, low and raspy with need, lit a tingling ache in her belly, a yearning deep within her womb.

He wrapped his arms around her back, but she was having none of that. For weeks she had longed to explore his body, but had never dared, too afraid he would think her wanton and lewd. Not tonight. Tonight, he was hers to do with as she pleased. Tonight, she would learn the secrets only this man could share.

She grabbed his hands, pushed them high over his head. "Hold on to the bedstead. And do not move."

"I do not think I can survive such sweet torture," he groaned but he gripped the heavy oak panel, tight cords of muscle and tendon stretching from shoulder to wrist.

She flicked her tongue along the parted seam of his lips, tasted his sigh, as she explored the sultry depths of his mouth with shocking boldness. Her fingernails scraping over his shoulders brought forth a low chuckle from deep within his chest, a dark, earthy rumble that sent a delicious shiver down her skin. She moved her mouth over his throat, along his jaw, her breasts rubbing against his chest, the soft scrape ripening her nipples into hard, aching peaks.

"I love the way you taste," she murmured against the curve of his neck, then gasped at her wanton words. She felt his laugh against her skin, hot, bold, an intimate, sensual caress, a shiver rippling down her neck. Never had she felt so alive.

So powerful. She loved the feel of his skin. The burning heat of his flesh. The muscles that flexed and tightened beneath her fingertips. She feathered her knuckles down his sides, smiled against his stomach as his abdomen clenched.

He was all rigid, hard planes and burgeoning muscle, hot skin tightening with need. The room was in shadows, the only light sweeping in from the moon and the waning fire in the hearth. Mingling red and silvery light played over his strong, chiseled jaw, the broad sweep of his chest.

Good Lord, what a beautiful man.

Her need was growing, her skin burning, her thighs aching, and deep between her legs, a hot, sultry need to feel him inside her. Slowly, she traced a path ever downward until she wrapped her hand around his straining sex.

His body jerked, in shock or pleasure, Leah did not know until he moaned. She trailed her mouth along the same path, wanting to know him, every part of him, wanting to give him some measure of the same pleasure he always gave her.

"No—don't," he groaned, but she ignored his words and took the tip of his swollen flesh in her mouth.

His protests died in a gasp as he speared his fingers through her hair. She savored his response, his salty-sweet taste, his musky male essence that invaded her senses, swept away fear. This man was her husband and she loved him so much she thought she might weep. She was awkward and clumsy and a little bit shy, but he didn't seem to notice.

"Leah, Leah . . ." He writhed upon the bed. With a shattered groan, he grabbed her arms and dragged her across his chest. She gasped in surprise, then in pleasure as he raised her up and slid himself between her thighs.

What power she felt, riding astride him, setting the rhythm, the pace, the angle that drew urgent moans from his throat and built gathering pleasure within her passage, the hot, slick slide of skin upon skin. Leaning forward ever so slowly, her legs shaking, she threw back her head.

He surged up, hands coming round her back, gripping her hair, his mouth latching onto her breasts, suckling one aching nipple, then the other, each bold thrust of his tongue pulsing through her belly, each upward thrust of his sex touching her womb, until she was quivering, aching, shattering around him.

"Richard, I love you," she cried, the words torn from her throat as a wild, nearly unbearable climax swept her away. She collapsed against his chest.

Mere moments passed before she heard the echo of her words.

Afraid to look at him, she nuzzled his neck.

The words had risen unbidden to her lips. Yet she would not deny them. She would not deny her love for him.

He rolled her onto her back. His midnight eyes burned with

an intensity she could not identify. Time stretched into eternity as he stared into her eyes. Then he lowered his lips to hers, and slowly, reverently, drew her against his body, his heart pounding wildly beneath her palm.

A loud thud startled Leah awake.

She clutched the coverlet to her chin. Her eyes wide, she stared into the darkness, listening for the noise that had awakened her. Her imagination tortured her with images of footpads and murderers skulking through the house, searching for their next victims. She heard nothing but silence and her husband's even breathing. It must have been a dream.

She sat up, glanced at Richard. He lay sprawled on his back, the covers tangled low on his hips. Moonlight played across his chest, sun-bronzed and naked to her gaze. She ran her fingers through the dark hair covering his flesh. *I love you.*

Her words came back to haunt her. She'd not meant to say them, but her emotions were strained, her senses shattered. His eyes had gleamed stark and dangerous in the candlelight, his jaw, rigid and tense, but he had not denied her declaration. No, he had kissed her and stroked her and made love to her so tenderly, she almost believed that he loved her as much as she loved him.

Even if he were incapable of speaking the words.

It might be an illusion, but it was sweet, just the same.

As she sank back onto her pillow, a sudden onslaught of nausea brought her hands to her lips. She swallowed as her throat convulsed and the bed seemed to swirl about her head.

She needed a drink, something stronger than water to settle her stomach, a few sips of brandy, or perhaps a claret.

Or a loaf of bread, she decided as her stomach gave one more violent twist. She thought of waking Richard, but she did not wish to disturb him when he seemed so peacefully asleep, with no night horrors to decimate his dreams.

She poked her head out her door. The wall sconces still burned in the passage, their feeble light marking the direction toward the stairs. As she rounded the curve to the hall, her foot struck a shadowy object draped across the landing.

A male voice groaned. Long fingers grabbed her ankle, pulled her to the floor. She landed on her hands and knees, her palms scraping across the hard wood surface. Her skin grew cold, her heartbeat racing, she sucked air into her lungs, but before she could scream, a familiar voice called out, "Leah?"

"Geoffrey?" She crawled over to him, cradled his head on her lap, hands searching for any hint of injury. "Are you hurt?"

His brown hair was damp with sweat and reeked of smoke. He opened his mouth, as if to speak, but belched long and loud instead. He giggled. "Ooops. Beg pardon."

Only once before, at a village fair, had she seen a man so inebriated he could not walk, but she recognized the signs, the crooked smile, the red-glazed eyes, the stench of brandy rising from his clothes like haze from paving stones on a summer day.

"Love you, you know," he said in what she imagined he thought was a whisper, the bellow pounding through her already aching head. "Best thing that ever happened to this family."

"Thank you, my lord. I love you, too." She slipped her hands beneath his arms, but he was too heavy for her to move. "Can you stand on your own? Or should I fetch a footman?"

"I can do it." He rolled to his stomach, pushed onto his knees. "Not a crook shanks, you know."

"I know," Leah said, rising from her own ignoble position on the floor. "There is nothing wrong with your legs a little coffee and some rest won't cure. Come. Let us get you to bed."

Draping one of his arms around her shoulders, she leaned

into his side. He was so heavy and his legs were so wobbly, Leah greatly feared they might tumble backward down the stairs, but he lunged forward instead. Together, they stumbled down the hall, bounced off the walls, stepped on each other's toes.

By the time they reached his rooms, they were laughing.

"Now, lean against the wall whilst I open . . . the . . . door."

"Shouldn't," he murmured, slouching toward the floor. "Unseemly, don't you know."

"Nonsense." Grabbing his arm before he collapsed, she guided him across the room, dark save for the moonlight shining in through the windows and the shadowed lamplight flickering beyond the open door. "There is no harm in a sister helping her brother to bed when he is incapable of getting there on his own."

She yanked back the quilted coverlet, eased him onto the mattress. His eyes drifted shut as she tugged off his boots, then pulled the coverlet up to his neck. She adjusted the pillows beneath his head, brushed his sweaty hair from his brow. "Sweet dreams, my lord. I shall see you tomorrow."

He grabbed her wrist. Tears dripped down his cheeks and onto his neck. "Don't go . . . please . . . don't leave me alone."

"Good heavens, what is wrong?" She needed to fetch Richard, but she couldn't leave Geoffrey. Not like this. She laced her fingers through his. "What has happened? Please, tell me."

He gazed up at her through bleary eyes. "I'm in a muddle, Duchess. I can't explain. Richard should thank me, but nooo . . . he rants and rails . . ."

His slurred words caught Leah unprepared. Her heart raced. Her neck grew slick with sweat, from worry or from the heat of the room, she could not say. A sick premonition twisted her already fragile stomach. She should leave. He had no notion of what he was saying, but she couldn't. "What do you mean? Why should Richard thank you?"

"Because he loves you," Geoffrey said, nodding. "Alison, too. Not Rachel. She's evil. Killed Eric, don't you know . . ."

With a sigh, Leah dismissed his wild words. She didn't know if she were relieved or more afraid of what truth might lurk beneath his drunken ramblings. "Please, go to sleep, my lord."

"I'm in the suds, Leah. Ruined."

"You are merely illuminated," she said gently, stroking his damp brow. "The world will seem much brighter in the morning."

He shook his head, eyes clenched shut. "No. Richard will kill me. I'm ten in the hundred."

"Nonsense. Richard will help you—"

"It's too late." He rocked his head back and forth. "There is no hope. I will never come about."

Richard was vaguely aware that he was dreaming. He willed himself to awaken, but it was no use. He was too deep in his nightmare. A horde of feasting scavengers crowded around a table smothered with food, whisky dripping onto the floor, an eerie echo of his life's blood leaking from his heart.

Endless toasts to welcome home the weary soldier. Eric at the head of the table, Rachel playing dutiful wife by his side.

Richard drained his glass as Eric lavished passionate kisses on his wife. Mingling tongues. Roaming hands. Why not take her here on the table for all of us to enjoy, he screamed as he grabbed a bottle, then floated away on the puffy white cloud of euphoria that only accompanied blessed numbness.

White cotton transformed into angry black thunder. Richard tossed about, deafened by the rumble of endless explosions, blinded by the shafts of piercing white light, until the sky shattered and he landed with a sickening thud in the middle of his feather bed. Arms and legs mangled, surely broken, but no pain. Perhaps he was dead after all.

Eternal sleep. He closed his eyes and surrendered his spirit. Warm hands stroked. A tongue, barbed like a serpent's, licked him up and down, brought his withered flesh back to life.

He was in bed with a she-devil, but his drink-clouded mind didn't care. He wanted release. He plunged between her parted thighs. The demon beneath him moaned his name.

Please . . . no . . . please . . . no . . . please . . . no . . .

The door creaked. Boot heels clanked.

A brother's voice, now long dead, howled his name.

A hand reached up, malevolent eyes gleaming red in the darkness. "Rachel."

Drenched in sweat, heart pounding, Richard bolted upright on the bed. Cool night air hitting his damp skin shuddered down his back. Through the sluggishness of his lingering dream, he heard Leah's voice. He swung his gaze around until he found her, standing beside the bed, a candlestick clutched in one hand. The other hand, she held wrapped around the base of her throat.

"I-I tried to wake you," she said. Her eyes were wide, her hair spilling wildly about her face, shadowed in the dim light. "But I couldn't. You were thrashing about and calling for—"

"It was a nightmare," he said bleakly. He ran his hands through his hair and over his face. "Nothing for you to worry about. Come back to bed."

She nodded, but looked unconvinced. Then she grabbed his hands and tugged. "Geoffrey's home and he is so foxed. You should have heard the wild things he was saying . . ."

Her words struck home like a volley of well-aimed arrows, hitting Richard's deepest fears. His heartbeat skidded to a painful halt, but he willed himself to remain calm as he rose and shrugged into his shirt and breeches. "What exactly did he say?"

She waved her hand through the air. "Nothing specific. Incoherent words, mostly, then he started weeping and spoke of things I did not understand. About how angry you would be when you learned the truth. I sat with him until he fell asleep, but I am truly worried. He said something about being ten in the hundred. What does that mean?"

Usurers charging ten percent interest. Outrageous!

If Geoffrey were that desperate—

Richard shoved Leah aside and bolted from the room. She called after him, but he couldn't answer for the panic swelling in his throat. His legs were too heavy, his steps too slow as he raced down the passage. *Please, don't let me be too late.*

He flung open his brother's door—just in time to see Geoffrey raise a pistol to his temple.

Chapter Twenty-One

A moment of terrible silence passed, the seconds punctuated by the thunderous beat of Richard's heart. He recognized the gun as one of a matched set of dueling pistols. It belonged in a case locked in the gun room, not in Geoffrey's hand, poised to blow his brains against the wall.

Richard's thoughts grew sluggish, his skin cold, yet dripping with sweat as panic tried to overwhelm him, as guilt and recrimination choked him, as he stared at Geoffrey, so far gone on drink he could scarce stand upright without swaying as if tossed about by hurricane winds. A loaded pistol in his hand.

Muscles clenching, legs trembling, Richard shuffled forward. There would be time for recriminations later.

Now, he needed his wits clear and his senses sharp.

"Put the gun down," he said in a tightly controlled voice that betrayed not a hint of the icy fear shredding his guts.

The image of his brother's beautiful face, tears streaming down his cheeks, his eyes hollowed by despair, burned itself into Richard's brain. He took another slow, measured step.

"Do not move!" Geoffrey said, his voice shrill, desperate.

Richard held up his hands. "Let us talk, Geoffrey."

"It is too late. Do you not understand?"

Richard inched one foot forward. "I understand you are hurt. And I want to help you. But you must put down the gun."

"I've done it up right this time, Richard. But I won't let you pay the price. Not like before." A spasm twisted Geoffrey's lips, compressed his swollen lids until his features resembled a gruesome death mask. "I did not mean to tell, you know. He tricked it from me."

"I know," Richard said, sliding another step closer, his skin tingling in the suddenly frigid air. "It does not matter. It never mattered. All I care about is you."

Geoffrey waved his hand, the pistol teetering wildly beside his head. "I cause you nothing but grief. How you must hate me."

"No! I love you. I need you. You are my brother."

"Go away. I do not want you to see this."

"Will you shoot yourself in front of me?" Leah said from the doorway, her voice soothingly low and soft as a lullaby. She took two steps into the room. "I thought you were my friend, my brother. You told me tonight that you love me. But I have to wonder if you spoke the truth. Do you love me so little you would make me watch while you kill yourself?"

Geoffrey dragged his tortured gaze to Leah. "You do not understand. I won't hurt Richard anymore!"

"You must be jesting. You are hurting him now. Or do you truly believe he will be happier when you are dead? Will you make him bury yet another brother? And what of Alison? Do you truly think she will be happier without her uncle? Do you think . . ."

Richard didn't attend to her words. He prayed Leah would keep Geoffrey's attention fixed on her while he shuffled forward on legs that felt as if they were fashioned from a blacksmith's anvil. His breath burned like acid in his throat. He was almost close enough. Ten more paces and all would be well.

Geoffrey's gaze swung back to him. "I never meant to hurt you, Richard." His finger tightened on the trigger.

"No," Richard screamed as he hurtled through the air, as he heard the gun explode, as the din deafened his hearing and the smell of blood made him gag. He landed on his hands and knees.

He crawled across the floor. Somewhere in the distance, he heard an anguished scream. An ever-widening puddle of blood seeped through Geoffrey's shirt, but Richard could not see the wound, his vision blurred by smoke and tears and grief so great, he thought it would consume him. Yet again he had failed.

"Get a doctor," he screamed, but Leah had already run from the room. He could hear her shouting orders as her voice receded down the hall. He dragged the counterpane off the bed, jammed it against his brother's chest. Geoffrey's lashes fluttered open.

"Why, damn you?" Richard demanded, hot tears burning his eyes. "Don't you know how much I love you?"

"Not worth your love—"

"Shut up, you stupid, bloody fool. I will not let you die. Do you hear me? Goddamn your everlasting hide. You will live. And then I will thrash you for putting me through this."

The choking rasp of his voice belied his angry words. How much anguish was one family to suffer? How much pain to atone for one man's sins? A child's future shrouded by secrets and lies was not enough? Eric's death was not enough? Now this?

Geoffrey gave a watery laugh, wheezing as he sucked in a breath. "Can't do nothing right. Not even this."

Two footmen rushed in with Leah close behind them. Her cheeks were pale, but she issued orders as clearly and calmly as Wellington wading through a smoke-covered battlefield. "Help the duke get him on the bed. Be careful of his head. Bring the doctor the moment he arrives, and bring clean linens for bandages."

A chamber maid carried in a basin of fresh water.

Leah soaked a cloth in it, stroked it across Geoffrey's fore-head and cheeks, but he had succumbed to the pain and the alcohol and was unaware of her presence.

"He will be all right," she said, gripping Richard's arm.

The warmth of her skin seemed to flow through her finger-tips and diffuse through his body. Her reassuring presence was the only calm in the whirlpool of pain and fear swirling around him.

He felt oddly detached from the moment, as if he were watching the events from a very great distance, through a spy glass or a telescope, his vision blurred by darkness and fog.

His skin was cold, his mind numb. He had no awareness of the passage of time. It seemed like hours, but it could have been minutes before the doctor who had treated Leah follow-ing her injury rushed into the room. His periwig sat crooked on his head. His waistcoat was mis-buttoned, as if he'd dressed hurriedly and in the dark, but he hustled across the floor with an air of barely suppressed energy that belied his bulky frame.

He set to work removing Geoffrey's shirt. "You might wish to leave," he said to Leah. "This is likely to be distressing."

She shook her head. "No, I will stay and assist you."

Richard would have been shocked had she answered oth-erwise. If there was one thing he had learned about his wife, she had a core of steel hidden inside her soft, feminine body.

The doctor gave a curt nod. He peeled Geoffrey's shirt from the wound. "The ball ripped through the fleshy part of his left shoulder," he said, probing the gaping hole with an in-strument that looked as if it were designed for torturing inno-cent souls during the Spanish Inquisition. "Tore away a chunk of skin, a bite of muscle, but doesn't seem to have hit any bone."

Richard's stomach rolled, but Leah didn't appear disturbed. She took the bloody probe when the doctor held it out to her, then handed him the next instrument he called for.

The doctor squinted, his spectacles slipping down his nose as he picked out bits of cloth from the mangled flesh. "Provided the infection doesn't settle in, he should be right as rain when he heals, though he will have a great deal of pain, and perhaps a decreased range of motion. All and all, a very lucky young man."

After washing the wound, the doctor stitched it closed, then spread a poultice over the battered skin and bandaged the whole in strips of linen. "The secret is keeping the wound clean and properly bandaged. Give him laudanum for the pain and contact me at the first sign of distress."

"Thank you so much for coming," Leah said as she guided the doctor to the door. "Let me see you out."

Richard pulled a chair close to the bed. He clutched his brother's hand in his fist. Geoffrey lay as still as death, his face the same bleached white as the pillow covers beneath his head. If it weren't for the rhythmic motion of his chest, Richard would believe him already dead.

The door creaked open. Richard knew it was Leah, knew it without her saying a word. He listened to her soft footsteps pad across the floor, felt her arm encircle his shoulders as she came up beside him. He pulled her close, seeking her warmth, seeking her strength and her sanity in a world gone suddenly insane.

She took his hand in hers, and together they sat in silent vigil through the night.

Eight hours later, Geoffrey lay unconscious still, his body trembling from top to toe as if he had an ague. His breathing was shallow, his arms and legs restlessly twitching.

Richard peeled back the linen to examine the wound. It showed no signs of putrefaction, no increasing redness or heat. Nothing to explain the moisture on his flushed cheeks.

"He is not feverish," Leah said, smoothing her palm over Geoffrey's brow. "Do you think he has taken an infection?"

"No," Richard said. He closed his eyes, rubbed his finger-tips over his temples. "It is the drink. Not only is he fighting the infection, he is fighting his addiction to the drink."

"Have you seen this before?"

"Several times, my love. In the army."

Self-disgust clawed his gut, but he closed his mind to what should have been. He needed his thoughts centered on the here and now. He drew her into his arms. Her eyes were clear and bright as she gazed at him, though shadows darkened the skin beneath her lashes and lines of fatigue framed her lips, another spike of guilt to shred his already decimated soul.

Still he did not release her.

His only comfort through this nightmare came from her quiet strength, her unwavering support, and the certain knowl-edge that Alison was safely tucked away in her rooms.

"Water," Geoffrey croaked.

Richard lifted his brother's shoulders while Leah held a glass to his mouth. His lips and tongue trembled so fiercely, the liquid dribbled down his chin. Leah grabbed a spoon from the bedside table and trickled the water into Geoffrey's mouth.

With painstaking patience, she waited for him to swallow, then repeated the process until he pinched his lips together.

Richard ran his hands over his face. His night growth of beard scratched his palms. Hours passed. Day melted into night.

Then day again. Time blended and blurred as Geoffrey drifted in and out of awareness. At times he seemed almost lucid, then frantic and incoherent. He ranted and raved.

He demanded a drink, then he begged and he pleaded.

They dosed him with laudanum to ease his distress.

"If he doesn't stop thrashing about like that," Richard fi-nally said on what he thought was the third day, "he will damage his injured shoulder. We have to tie him down."

Leah shredded a cotton bed sheet into strips, then handed them to Richard to lash Geoffrey's arms and legs to the bed-posts.

She slipped her arms around Richard's waist, leaned her forehead into his shoulder. Legs trembling nearly as violently as Geoffrey's, Richard pulled her so firmly against his chest, he could feel her heart beating through her skin, warm and strong and alive. He buried his lips against her neck, his eyes burning with what he suspected were tears, but he blamed on fatigue.

"Let me go," Geoffrey screamed. "Untie me, you filthy savages, or my brother will kill you."

"Where does he think he is?"

Richard rubbed his fingers over his aching eyes. "As a young man, my grandfather traveled extensively in the colonies. On the rare occasions that he bothered with us at all, he used to fill our heads with stories of bloodthirsty savages. As a child, Geof-frey's favorite game was to playact those stories."

"I see." Leah stroked the back of her hand over Geoffrey's cheek. "You are merely dreaming, my lord. Richard and I are here with you."

"My legs!" Geoffrey screamed. He heaved against the re-straints. "My legs are afire. Richard, help me . . ."

Richard forced his brother to swallow some tea laced with laudanum. After a few minutes, the drug took effect and Geof-frey slipped into a fitful slumber. Richard turned to Leah. She had yet to leave Geoffrey's side, save to eat or bathe or check on Alison. Her skin was ashen, her eyes pale hollows in her cheeks, and still, she was so beautiful, she made his heart ache, made his throat clench. "You need sleep."

She shook her head. "I would not leave—"

"I insist, Leah. You look ragged and weary unto death. I will not have you sicken again. You must rest."

"What a dreadful fright I must be," she said, a weary grin on her lips, a teasing sparkle creeping into her green eyes.

She smoothed her hands over her hair, clenched in a tight knot at the base of her neck. "We both need rest if we are to be of use to your brother. Perhaps we could sleep in shifts?"

"Good idea. You take the first sleep."

She stared at Geoffrey for such a long moment, Richard thought she would argue. But when she turned to him, she simply nodded. With a gentle reminder to call her if Geoffrey awakened, she went up on tiptoe and kissed him. As she stepped back, he seized her wrist, hauled her against his chest, buried his face in her neck. The warmth of her body seeped through his bones, a soothing balm to the raw agony slowly destroying him.

"I love you," she said, leaning back to look in his eyes.

He covered her lips with his. He devoured her words, tasted her breath. He needed her, now more than ever, but she needed to rest. He forced himself to release her. "Go. Sleep. I will call you should he awaken." He turned his head, kissed her palm.

She hesitated a moment, then nodded and left the room.

Richard dropped onto the chair beside the bed. He wanted to murmur soothing reassurances, but his throat was so tight, he could scarcely breathe, let alone speak.

Instead, he clutched his brother's hand in his fist, holding him fast against the demons torturing him.

Geoffrey opened his eyes and stared straight at him.

For a moment, his gaze appeared clear, as if he were lucid, then his mind's aimless ramblings began. "Eric, take care . . . never meant to tell . . . Richard, where are you . . ."

He rocked his head on the pillow. His cheeks were warm and flushed. "Told Jamison and look what happened. Richard, I'm sorry, so sorry . . ."

From the moment Geoffrey had started raving, Richard had feared what his brother might say, what Leah might hear. He tried to reassure himself that it wouldn't matter if she heard Geoffrey's words. They were disjointed. Disconnected.

Without context, she would not understand their meaning. But he didn't believe it, and it filled him with dread.

"Richard, where are you?"

"I'm here, Geoffrey. I am here." He draped a cloth soaked in extract of henbane over his brother's forehead. He was so steeped in regret and self-reproach, he didn't hear her approach. He had no idea she was in the room until the scent of lavender water attacked his nose and she placed her palm on his shoulder.

He pushed her hand away, then stood so she would not be tempted to touch him again. "What do you want, Rachel?"

"To see how my dear brother is faring, of course."

As if she cared. No, she was here to see how she could best twist this tragedy to her advantage.

She wore a delicate peach morning gown that brought out the natural blush in her cheeks. Her eyes were clear and bright and free of fatigue. Obviously she wasn't losing any sleep.

"I do not understand your anger toward me, Richard. Truly, I don't. If, as you say, the past is dead and buried, why can you not at least be civil to me? Or can it be . . ." She placed her hand over his, stroked her fingertips up and down his arm. "That you are lying. That you love me still, as I love you."

Richard grunted. "Hardly, madam. The sight of you sickens me until I must search for a chamber pot or cast up my accounts where I stand. The sound of your voice leaves me praying for deafness, and your touch makes my skin crawl. Now, remove your hand from my arm or I will remove it for you."

"Is it crawling with distaste? Or are those shivers of desire you would try to deny?"

He glared at her until she lifted her hand. "This is hardly the time or place for this discussion. I do not want Geoffrey distressed any more than he needs be from his illness."

"Are you suggesting my presence might distress him? I have never been anything but kindness itself to Geoffrey."

Richard snorted. "Do you honestly believe everyone

around you sees you as an angel come to delight us with your ethereal presence? Geoffrey saw the way you treated Eric, with your taunts and your torments. He blames you for Eric's death. As do I."

Her eyes flashed with anger and something else, something darker that Richard could not discern.

"You are both wrong," she said. "I did not force that bottle to his lips. Nor did I heave him atop his horse and send him racing pell-mell into the night."

"You made his life unbearable. He drank to escape you!"

"And what of you, oh-holier-than-thou! Do you think yourself blameless in all this?"

"I know the role I played." Richard strode to the windows. He glanced out at the horizon, at the clouds dotting the night sky, at the carriages crowding the distant street as society rushed from one soiree to the next. "And I live with the guilt of it every day of my life."

"I heard Geoffrey's words when I came in," Rachel said, coming to stand before him, gazing up at him with a malicious gleam in her eyes. "I know why you married the chit. You did it to protect Alison. How admirable! How noble! How supremely fitting! I only wonder, what your wife will say when she learns the truth? Will her eyes still shine with love and adoration as they do now? Or will hatred burn in her gaze?"

"If you tell her," Richard said through his teeth, his back tightening, icy fury turning his skin cold, his hair damp. "I swear on everything holy, I will kill you!"

She smiled up at him from beneath her lashes, a demure, seductive smile, as if she had not heard the deadly menace in his voice. "Now, Richard, is that any way to talk to the mother of your only child?"

Chapter Twenty-Two

Leah hadn't meant to sleep, had meant only to rest for a few moments, but the next time she opened her eyes, twelve hours had passed. Silently cursing her weakness, she threw on her clothes and scurried down the hall. By the time she returned to Geoffrey's room, he appeared to be resting peacefully.

She wished she could say the same for Richard, whose long legs were curled up over the arms of his chair, his black hair a stark contrast to the red brocade upholstery and the afternoon sun lighting the room. Though covered with a soft growth of beard, his cheekbones appeared more pronounced and his jaw was rigid and clenched. His head hung to the side at such an odd angle, she thought surely he would awaken with a stiff neck.

Still, for the first time since this nightmare began, he was sleeping, and she would not disturb him, even though all she wanted was to draw him into her arms and offer him the comfort he would never seek. He was so strong, so brave for everyone around him, yet he seemed to think he should suffer alone.

Never had she witnessed such depth of emotion, the love of a brother for a brother. Her father's example of familial devotion had always been sadly lacking. She dabbed at the corner of her eyes, surprised when her fingertips came away damp.

Sometime during the night, Richard had released the bindings securing Geoffrey's arms and legs. She placed her hand against Geoffrey's cheek. His skin was cool and dry. His eyes, as they opened and met her gaze, appeared clear, free of confusion and pain. She smiled. "Would you like some water?"

He tried to speak, but only a rasping grunt emerged. He nodded, the motion making him wince and his lips curl, as if his stomach were churning.

She held a glass to his mouth. "Drink it slowly. And do not mind the taste. It has laudanum in it to ease your pain."

"Enough," he sputtered. "What happened? Have I been ill?"

Her hand trembled as she returned the glass to the bedside table. She chewed on her lower lip. How much should she tell him? "Well . . . you returned home several days ago, quite late at night. Do you remember any of this?"

The muscles in his throat tightened. "Vaguely. Go on."

"You were . . . distressed. It seems you lost quite a bit of money and—"

"I remember," he said, his voice a breathless whisper. His right hand crept up his chest, traced the bandage wrapped round his left shoulder. His gaze searched the room until he found Richard. He let out a strangled moan. His eyes closed, his lips tightened. "God, he will never forgive me."

"Do not talk nonsense," Leah chided gently, her own breath raw in her throat. She drew his hand away from his wound, tucked the bedding up to his neck. "You have given us all a tremendous fright, but Richard most of all. He is consumed with guilt that you did not trust him enough to confide in him. Do not hurt him further by distrusting his love for you."

Geoffrey pressed his knuckles against his eyes, but it did not stop the tears from leaking down his cheeks. "I know you are right, but the world seemed so bleak. It seems bleaker still."

"Hush," Leah said, her throat growing tighter with each breath she drew. "There will be time enough for worries when you are strong again. But first, you must rest and heal."

"Geoffrey," Richard said as he surged from his chair. His smile was a rigid clenching of his teeth and his eyes blinked rapidly. He fell to his knees beside the bed, seized his brother's hand in a grip so tight, Geoffrey winced.

Leah rose and tip-toed from the room, leaving the two brothers alone to shed their tears.

Richard rubbed his hands over his eyes. A mountain of paperwork covered his desk. Bank books and deeds. Contracts and mortgages. Ledgers and other statements of his personal wealth.

He shuffled through the documents, trying to decide what to keep and what to liquidate to cover Geoffrey's monstrous debt.

The entailed properties couldn't be touched, nor could he alter the provisions of his marriage contract or funds in trust for Alison's dowry. Rachel's jointure also remained untouchable.

With a sigh of disgust, he shoved the papers away.

How was he supposed to concentrate on finances when all he could think of was Leah? Restless energy sent him prowling the room. He rubbed one palm over the back of his neck, the muscles stiff and aching from barely suppressed tension.

Over the last seven days, Geoffrey's condition had continued to improve. His wound showed no signs of infection and his body was slowly adjusting to the lack of alcohol.

Still, Richard had hovered by his side.

When he had left the sickroom, he'd secluded himself with

Alison, easing the child's fears over her uncle's illness. Or he had pleaded fatigue and retired to his chambers. Alone.

Like the worst of cowards running from a battlefield, he was avoiding his wife, and he knew it, but he could not face her.

Not with his emotions so raw and revealed.

All through Geoffrey's delirium, Richard had feared what his brother might say, what Leah might hear. The only time Geoffrey had ranted about the past, Leah had been absent from the room. It had seemed as if God had finally answered his prayers.

But Rachel had learned the true basis behind Richard's hasty wedding. That woman was so perverse, she truly believed Richard would one day forgive her and welcome her back into his bed.

Now it was only a matter of time before she found some means to destroy him, to destroy Leah, even as she destroyed her own daughter, a child Richard loved more than he loved his own life.

A child sired upon his brother's wife.

Good Lord, it sounded ugly, even to him. He could only imagine the malicious glee with which society would feast upon the scandal. At the moment, Alison was too young to understand, but one day soon, his beautiful child would learn the truth.

As would his wife. His sweet, trusting, innocent wife.

A greater fear than he had ever known sucked the breath from his lungs, turned his skin cold, made his arms shake.

Too late he had recognized his peril.

He was falling in love with his wife.

No, he thought savagely. He had recognized his danger early enough, but he had failed to heed his own warnings.

How had she become so important to him so fast? Why had he allowed her into his heart when he had vowed never to love again?

He should have guarded against her. He'd meant to, but

he'd failed. He had admired her courage from the start when she had stormed his home and threw his marriage offer in his face. Again when she braved the hatred of the *ton* for his sake, and when she refused to cower under his edict forbidding her to go to the foundling home. Although she grieved for her lost sister, she refused to allow her despair to overwhelm her. Instead, she launched a one-woman mission to save the children of England.

Now it was only a matter of time until she learned the vile truth, only a matter of time until the admiration that burned in her gaze turned to disgust, then from disgust to hate.

Not that Richard could blame her.

How could she possibly understand that he slept with his brother's wife—sired a child upon his brother's wife—when he couldn't understand it himself? How could she ever forgive him when he could never forgive himself?

Richard knew that he would lose her, and he didn't think he would survive. He had to protect himself. He had to put some distance between them. Now. Before he came to depend upon her love. Then it wouldn't hurt so much when she turned away from him in disgust. It wasn't too late to save himself.

He ran his hand through his hair and stiffened his resolve. He had no choice! He had to defend himself.

A rap sounded on the library door. Harris appeared in the entry, started to speak, but a loud voice interrupted him.

"No need to announce me, old man. I know my way in."

Pierce, Viscount Greydon, strode into the room. He tossed his riding crop and gloves onto the nearest chair, then stripped off his beaver hat, releasing a riot of sandy hair lightened by the sun. "Heigh-ho, Richard. Why are you toiling away on such a fine day?"

Richard managed a smile, even though his lips felt numb and his ribs ached, as if his heart were being carved from his chest. "It is about time you showed your face in Town. I began to think you preferred the rusticating life."

"Me?" Pierce said, a rakish smile lifting one corner of his lips. His teeth gleamed against the deep bronze of his face. "Never! I was delayed for a few days at the White Hart by a lame horse and a buxom blonde. You know me, Richard. Never one to turn a blind eye to a damsel with overripe melons, fit for the feasting and willing to share."

Richard laughed, his friend's good humor a welcome balm for his overheated mind. "Pierce, I hope you never change. It would be a sad day for all the lonesome wenches of the world. Have a seat, man."

"What of you?" Pierce said, his brown eyes sparkling as he flopped onto a wing chair across from Richard's desk. "The *on dit* is that you are so smitten by your new wife, the Cyprians and Impures have given up all hope of your ever gracing their beds again. I have heard from those in authority that you hover over her at all the routs and balls, growling and snorting at any man who so much as even glances at her."

The all-too-accurate picture Pierce was painting of Richard's behavior made him wince. He had acted like a love-sick fool because he *was* a love-sick fool, his thoughts consumed by Leah, by the scent of her skin, the taste of her lips, the heat of her passion, his body thrumming to life, just from the sight of her smile.

"Pure exaggeration," he said, his throat tightening on the lie. "I've had disasters aplenty these few weeks past, and with you gone from Town, I've lacked a companion wicked enough to accompany me in my debaucheries. Care to free me from my domestic chains this evening?"

"Absolutely," Pierce agreed cheerfully. Then his smile waned, his brows drew together, the sparkle of merriment vanished from his eyes. He circled the brim of his top hat through his fingers. "So, how fares your brother?"

"You've heard, then?" Richard pinched the bridge of his nose. "What is the gossip?"

"That he tried to pop himself off."

"And he nearly succeeded, too, the half-wit."

"So he recovers?"

"Thanks to God and my wife." Richard ran a shaking hand over his face, his mind conjuring images of his brother with a gun pointed at his head, an image likely to haunt Richard all the days of his life. He could still smell the smoke, the blood, the acrid sweat of his own fear. "He has seen the light, or so he says, and vows he will mend his wicked ways. And as he was tied to his bed for over a week, he couldn't get at the liquor cabinet, so his body is free, too, which is why I cannot offer you a brandy. I've ordered it all packed away. When he starts to get around, I want no temptations glaring him in the face."

"Sounds as if the boy is ready to grow up," Pierce said quietly, his gaze meeting Richard's. "For your sake, I hope it is true. You look haggard as Hamlet lost in his madness."

"Thank you for sharing that," Richard drawled, scrubbing his hand over his jaw, the bristle reminding him he hadn't shaved in days. "But enough of my troubles. Tell me the news from Greydon Hall. What are your plans for the estate?"

Pierce studied the toe of his black Wellington boots. "'Tis very bad news, I'm afraid. The coffers are empty. The estate bled dry. I am forced to raise the ready the hard way. The contracts are signed. The announcement will soon be made. I'm to marry an heiress."

Richard's eyes widened in shock. Then mirth replaced shock. He snorted and laughed until he was laughing so hard his sides ached. Pierce's features remained grave, as if he were perched atop a horse with a noose wrapped around his neck, waiting for the animal to be yanked from beneath him.

"'Twasn't a jest, then?" Richard said, still laughing. "Who is the lucky lass?"

"Lady Julia Houghton."

Richard shuddered. "A haughty beauty and cold as ice. Out with it, man. I want all the gruesome details."

"The Houghton estate marches with mine," Pierce said bitterly. "The marquess has only the one child, a daughter to his ever-lasting disgust, who, for some unfathomable reason, has decided it is I she wishes to wed. After three seasons out, with no prospect of a match in sight, her father finds himself so desperate, he is even willing to settle her on a mere viscount, a newly titled and lascivious lord, no less. The letters patent, it seems, allow the properties to pass through the female line. You behold before you, Richard, a prime stud."

"I know how you feel," Richard said quietly, sliding his pen and standish to the right hand corner of his desk, before sliding them to the center again. "I was bought and paid for myself."

Pierce grunted. "I believe your circumstances differed greatly from my own. You sacrificed yourself on the altar of paternal devotion. I, on the other hand, am selling myself for money as any other bawdy basket would."

"You are in good company, then," Richard said, wishing he could slam his fist into the wall, anything to drive away the guilt and pain gnawing his gut, the visions of Leah haunting his dreams, the aching need he felt for his wife. "Half the husbands of the *ton* were bought and paid for by their wives. What say you. Let us retire to the Stag and drown ourselves in whisky."

"Lead on," Pierce agreed, rallying his usual good cheer.

A soft knock sounded on the door.

Until that moment, Richard had never known he had a yellow streak as wide as the Thames running down his spine. His hands shook, his breath burned. The room suddenly seemed much too small, the walls pushing in on him, with no means of escape. He wanted to lock the door, bar the entry. Anything but face her.

Instead, he shoved his hands into the waistband of his breeches and gave the call to enter. He held his breath.

First the door opened a crack. Then her dainty hand

appeared. Then Leah peeked around the corner, all golden hair and shining eyes. Her smile lit her face like a sunburst on a cloudy day, blinding in its intensity.

"Forgive me," she said, her gaze meeting Richard's, her lips curved in a tentative smile, as if unsure of her welcome. "I did not realize you had company."

Her melodious voice, soft and enticing, wrapped around Richard, drawing him closer, his feet moving of their own accord. He forgot about resolutions and defenses and Pierce as he gawked like a schoolboy at his wife, tension running from his fingers to toes, clenching the muscles along the base of his spine, not understanding her words until the door started to close.

"No, wait," he shouted, and even to his own ears, his voice sounded desperate, as if once the door closed, he would never see her again. Stupid, foolish dreams.

She stepped into the room. Her golden hair flowed over her shoulders in luminous, cascading waves. Her simple frock of pomona green paled beneath her clear green eyes, their dusting of amber catching the light shining in through the bay windows, her bewitching green eyes that had enslaved him.

Richard's throat clenched, his mouth so dry, he needed a bucket of water to ease his thirst. He locked his knees against the overwhelming urge to drag her into his arms, to ravish her lips, to take her here on the library floor. He was insane.

A gasping sound brought Richard's attention back to his friend. Pierce stood as stiff as a day-old corpse, his face stark, his eyes wide and fixed on Leah's face. His lips moved, but no sound escaped, then a name carried on a whisper.

Richard shot his gaze to Leah, but she didn't appear to have heard. A concerned frown narrowed her eyes.

"Perhaps you should send for a doctor," she said.

The sound of her voice seemed to snap Pierce out of whatever spell had possessed him. His breath escaped in a furious gush. His cheeks turned as crimson as his waistcoat.

He bowed. "Forgive me for frightening you, Your Grace. I am travel weary. Nothing more, I assure you."

With stiff formality, Richard performed the introductions. He had to get her out of the room before he gave in to temptation and dragged her into his arms, with no regard to propriety or sanity or Pierce's presence in the room.

Leah smiled. "I am happy to meet you, at last, Lord Greydon. I have heard many bad things about you, you know."

"All true, I fear." Pierce gripped her hand, raised it to his lips. His gaze studied her face with relentless intensity. "I understand you come from Lancashire. Near Preston?"

"That is correct," Leah said. "And you are the new Lord Greydon. My aunt wrote that the old lord had died. She hinted at dark scandals and ancient secrets. My aunt has a flair for the melodramatic. Much as I do, I'm afraid," she added with a soft sigh.

"By any chance, would you be related to the Burtons of Heallfrith Manor?"

"Burton was my mother's family name," Leah said. "But my mother passed away and only my mother's sister remains—"

"There is no one else?" Pierce said sharply, making her brows lift and her eyes widen.

"What did you want, madam?" Richard interrupted, anxious to sweep her from the room before Pierce blurted out suspicions that would only cause her pain.

His rudeness made her blink. She tilted her head as she turned to him, a warm flush spreading over her cheeks. "Alison and I wished to invite you to join us for supper in the gardens. Or will you take a tray with Geoffrey?"

"I shall dine out with Greydon this evening," he said, taking her arm and leading her toward the door, then wishing he had never touched her as the heat of her skin, the scent of roses clinging to her hair, made his blood burn, his body harden, his heart break. "Was there anything else?"

Leah shook her head.

"Then I shall bid you adieu."

Confusion at his curt tone narrowed her eyes. "Yes, of course," she said. "Forgive me for disturbing you. It was a pleasure to meet you, Lord Greydon."

She dipped a speedy curtsy, then walked with quiet dignity through the door. The room turned bleak without her. He rubbed his hand over his chest, as if he could rub away the hollow gorge where his heart used to be. He had to distance himself from her, and he had to do it fast, because he wanted her as he had never wanted anyone in his life, and it was killing him.

He drew a steadying breath, then turned to Pierce.

"Although I think I know the answer, would you mind very much telling me what just happened here?"

"Richard," he said, his voice choked, his face as white as his cravat. "You are never going to believe this. Your wife looks just like her. The resemblance is amazing. They could have been sisters."

Chapter Twenty-Three

Through eyes clouded by whisky, Richard leaned his back against the door as he stared at the naked whore on the bed.

Never had he seen such massive breasts. While he watched, she lifted and squeezed and played with herself. One hand slipped between her thighs, dipped into her wetness, an erotic display that failed to entice him. The stench of ale and sweat was thick and heavy in the room. It clung to the bedding, to the walls, to the very air. Bile rose in his throat.

What was he doing in this rancid, rat-infested sewer when he could be home with his wife, the only breath of fresh air in his stinking, miserable life?

Leah . . . just the thought of her name sent the heat of longing through his veins. But it wasn't a mere physical desire, though, of course, there was always that, the burning need, the desperate, hungry ache to possess her. But this was different. Something he had never experienced before. The sheer desire to cradle her against his chest, to breathe the scent of her hair and skin as she lay in his arms, her soothing voice relating the mundane details of her day, which children at the foundling home needed what articles of clothing, which charity was soliciting her support, what meals she had planned for the week.

He wanted her worries and her joys. Her sorrows and her pain. He wanted her, dammit. Only her.

His gut clenched, once again sending the threatening taste of bile up the back of his throat. He pulled a sovereign from his pocket, tossed it on the bed, then stumbled from the room to the next chamber along the passage.

He pounded on the door. "I am leaving," he shouted through the wood. "I will send the carriage back for you."

The door snapped open to reveal the naked, smiling viscount.

"Done so soon?" Pierce chided in a drunken slur. "Do not bother with the carriage 'til morning. This bawdy wench and I should be done by then."

With a dismissive wave of his hand, Richard strode down the stairs and through the taproom, filled with drunken sots and sailors and whores, their boisterous laughter following him onto the streets. Once inside the carriage, he extinguished the lamps and let the darkness surround him. The wheels rattling over the uneven paving stones jostled his already aching head.

Most people wondered why he bothered with a reprobate like Pierce who seemed hell-bent on his own destruction. Only Richard knew the man behind the mask of devil-may-care depravity. They were kindred spirits, each haunted by the sins of their pasts.

On rare occasions, the gentle heart of the man Pierce used to be would shine through. Like the time he had offered those insightful words to Richard on how horrible it must be to watch one's children die. But for one cruel twist of fate, Pierce's life would have turned out very differently.

If Richard's suspicions proved true, Pierce was the father of Catherine Jamison's child. There was no doubt that the two of them could have met. Pierce spent many a month throughout the years at his uncle's estate, situated not many miles from Leah's childhood home, but Pierce was not a man who would seduce an innocent maiden, then abandon her to the streets. He confined his illicit relations to bawdy wenches and courtesans, women to whom he paid good coin to service his needs.

No, if it were true, something more sinister had to have happened. Richard would wager a thousand pounds that Leah's father set the whole sordid story in motion. It was one more piece of the puzzle he was working to solve, though at this point, his solicitors had turned up nothing. The lack of clues was not surprising, given how many years had passed.

The carriage lurched to a halt. Richard trudged up the stairs, entered his room, then stalked straight to Leah's door.

His blood roared in his ears, pounded through his veins, the whisky muddling his brain until his need turned savage. He curled his hands into fists, dragged them down the door.

With eyes clenched tight, he choked on a moan.

How long would it take to purge her from his heart?

To purge her from his soul?

An insidious voice inside his mind taunted him. *Open the door. Or are you afraid?* He grasped the knob, turned the handle. Just one look, he promised himself.

He wanted just one look. What harm could it do? He wrenched open the door. She was asleep on the chaise, her golden hair curling over the cushions, gold fire against plush green velvet. An open book lay on the table beside her. A candle burned low on its base.

His knees wobbled as he approached her, which he blamed on the whisky and not her perfume, a blend of rosewater and her own enticing essence, more powerful than the most potent of opiates.

His fingers shook as he brushed the soft curls from her brow, traced the fragile line of her jaw. Heat shot up his arm, burned through his bones. His head was throbbing.

This was madness. He knew what he stood to lose.

Careful not to awaken her, he gathered her into his arms

and carried her to bed. But when he should have released her, he didn't. He couldn't. He pressed a tender kiss upon her brow, but not her lips. He knew if he kissed her lips, he would never let her go. He dragged his gaze up the length of her body, memorizing her shape, her form. Her long, lean legs outlined by the silk of her dress. The gentle flare of her hips. The sweet curve of her neck. He wanted to wrap her in his arms, to hold her against his chest. He wanted to love her.

His mind churned with the words, to love her.

With a supreme effort of will, he dragged his gaze to her face, burned her image into his brain. Her sun-swept hair. Her oval face. Her cheeks that glowed with a natural joy that couldn't be dampened, not even in sleep. Her lips that had so often parted for his kiss curled into a smile, and he hoped she was dreaming of him. Then he cursed himself for a fool.

He pulled the coverlet over her shoulders, turned and stalked to his door. Before he crossed the threshold, he paused.

One more look. He wanted one more look.

He knew he would never see her like this again.

Rachel suppressed her smile as she strode into the blue room and found Leah and Richard already seated at the table. Neither spoke nor raised their gazes from their plates. The only sound was the clank and clatter of silver scraping china.

A bubble of delicious laughter threatened to choke Rachel, but she pressed her lips into a sober line and took her seat with all the grace and dignity of her station. She had to take care not to let her feelings show, but it was so hard. Too hard.

Every time she looked at Richard, she felt her stomach curl and her breasts swell, aching for his touch. She longed to trace the hard slope of his jaw, to kiss his brooding lips, to run her fingers over his sex, to draw him into her body.

Good heavens, her pulse was beating frantically, and an unladylike sensation of wetness covered her skin.

She pushed her gaze to the wall.

For weeks, she had been forced to watch Richard and his foolish wife grow closer while all her attempts to drive them apart had failed. Absurd as it had seemed, Rachel had even begun to fear that Richard was falling in love with the girl.

The thought had driven Rachel to the edge of reason, until she could scarce think for the jealousy and the fear that this time, she had truly lost him. But all that was over now.

Richard had spent every night of the past two weeks at his clubs or carousing with his scurrilous friend, Greydon, while Leah remained at home with Alison and Geoffrey.

Though Leah tried to hide her growing agitation, her expressive eyes showed all of her pain, all of her confusion while her face was as stark as the moon in winter.

And to think, Rachel owed it all to the fiasco of Geoffrey's botched attempt to take his own life and the delirious ramblings of that drunken fool. The truth behind Richard's hasty wedding had surprised her. Yet it made such perfect sense.

He was so damned honorable, he would sacrifice his life for those he loved, and he loved Alison above all others.

She was his flesh, his blood, and Rachel's only real weapon in her fight to win him back. How stupid of her not to have realized it sooner. Now she knew what she had to do.

"Tonight is the Houghtons' ball," Rachel said into the silence. "You are promised to attend."

"I'm afraid I cannot," Leah said, her voice quiet, almost hoarse, as if rubbed raw from smothered sobs.

Richard's hand tightened on his fork until the long bones running from wrist to knuckles strained against his skin.

So, Rachel thought, he still harbored feelings for the chit. She would have to act fast, before he cast caution to the wind and confessed all to his young bride. Rachel could not let that happen. She greatly feared that Leah might forgive him anything.

"Nonsense," she said, as if instructing a wayward child. "You must attend. It is an engagement ball for Richard's dearest friend and his betrothed. If you do not go, everyone will assume you disapprove of Lady Julia. I know you do not want that to happen. All you need to do is dance once or twice, and then you can leave. That shouldn't be so difficult, should it?"

His jaw as rigid as a chiseled slab of granite, Richard shoved back his chair. He stood and bowed in Leah's general direction. "I shall return in time to escort you to the ball. Now, if you will excuse me, I have business to which I must attend." He turned on his heel and stalked from the room.

Leah stared at her plate.

"You do look a trifle peaked," Rachel murmured, before sipping her tea. "Are you unwell? Should we fetch the doctor?"

"Do not trouble yourself on my account." Leah pressed her linen to her lips, then folded the cloth and placed it on the table, as if she were preparing to leave.

But Rachel wasn't through with her yet. "I cannot help but notice that you look upset. 'Tis a pity. Somehow I thought it was different this time. I thought he truly cared for you. But I can see I was mistaken. It seems St. Austin is incapable of lasting affection, after all." She paused, as if she were reluctant to continue, relishing the pain that closed Leah's eyes and turned her cheeks a ghastly shade of gray. Then she leaned forward and whispered, "He was in love once. Very deeply."

Leah's brows lifted, but she did not reply. She turned her gaze toward the conservatory beyond the door, the towering palms and ornamental trees, silvery green in the morning sunlight.

The silence lengthened until Leah finally blurted out, "What happened?"

Rachel sighed mournfully. "Such a sad story. Worthy of a Shakespearean tragedy. Two star crossed lovers separated by their parents and the circumstances of their birth. She was the daughter of a marquess, you see. Too high for a mere second son. Her parents forced her to wed another. Richard has never recovered. I fear he will never love anyone but her."

Leah placed her hands on the table, then slowly pushed from her chair. Her face went as white as the tablecloth beneath her palms and she swayed on her feet.

For a moment, Rachel thought the girl might faint, but she took a steadying breath. "Please, forgive me," she said, pulling her shoulders back and meeting Rachel's gaze. "I find I am a trifle unwell after all. But never fear, I shall rally."

Rachel smiled into her teacup. She almost pitied the girl.

Chapter Twenty-Four

This was the last ball she would ever attend, Leah decided as she made her way toward the door, intent upon finding the carriage and returning to the house. Her progress slowed as every woman she passed seemed determined to greet her, and every man, to ask her to dance. Where before she was a pariah, tonight she was the reigning toast. Never had she felt more alone.

No doubt she owed her new-found popularity to the great hulking beast walking at her side, the arrogant Duke of St. Austin, daring meager mortals to offer his wife some slanderous look or misguided word. As much as she willed herself to remain unaffected, she breathed the intoxicating scent of his skin, felt the heat of his fingers brushing over her arm as he touched his hand to her elbow. It was all she could do not to fling her arms around his neck and beg him to love her. But she would not degrade herself with such a pathetic display of neediness.

She wished he would leave her alone, join his friends in the gaming parlours, anything but slip his hand from her elbow to her spine, warm fingers splaying wide to guide her past the couples rushing to join the first country dance.

He had not so much as looked at her since they arrived,

save for a scathing glance at the neckline of her gown when she'd first removed her cloak. Though modest in comparison to the ladies around her, it was more daring than anything she had worn before. Her tightly laced stay, while making it nearly impossible for her to breathe, pushed her breasts together and thrust them upward. If she had hoped to elicit some response from Richard, she had failed miserably, but she kept her smile on her face and laughed at the witty banter of her companions.

From across the room, she could feel the intensity of Lord Greydon's stare upon her face, the same searching look with which he had graced her when first she had met him in her husband's library, and again as she had made her way through the receiving line to meet his affianced bride. It made her uncomfortable, and Leah couldn't begin to say why. It was not as if it were a predatory gaze meant to seduce her. Rather, it was as if he were trying to solve some mystery, or as if he were trying to see inside her soul. What he hoped to find, Leah could not imagine.

His bride-to-be did not seem to notice. Lady Julia Houghton tilted her head, the candlelight reflecting off the diamond tiara resting atop her chestnut curls, her equally dark eyes gleaming as she smiled at Pierce. Murmured voices around Leah called Lady Julia cold, arrogant, distant. Leah saw a charming young lady of wealth and beauty, innocence besotted with a man destined to hurt her, though she had yet to know it.

Once, Leah had been just as trusting, just as innocent.

Now she was the greatest fool. In love with a man who did not love her, nor could he even bear to sleep in the same room.

At first, Leah had not noticed anything amiss. It was only natural that he would stay by Geoffrey's side until the crisis had passed. But when Geoffrey had started to recover, when the danger was over and life should have returned to normal, Richard had grown more aloof, more distant, avoiding her, avoiding her bed, far from the flesh-and-blood man who haunted her dreams.

Oh, whenever their paths happened to cross, he was all that was polite and civil, as if they were strangers, as if they just met, as if he had not kissed and stroked every inch of her body, his body pulsing with need. Jealousy and suspicion churned through her belly, clouding her thoughts, ensnaring her reason.

What had happened to make him so distant? Why would he not look at her? Speak to her? What had she done?

"Shall we dance?" The husky timbre of his voice curled heat within her belly. His lips were so close to the curve of her neck, she could feel his words vibrate over her skin.

A momentary urge to beg his forgiveness for whatever crime she had committed threatened her composure before pride surfaced and anger surged. She would not belittle herself for anyone.

The first sweet strains of a waltz floated over the deafening babble of voices. She willed herself to remain aloof, indifferent to his touch, but when she placed her gloved hand in his, when he circled his arm around her waist, her heart beat wildly within her breast. The air in the room grew unbearably hot, sucking the breath from her lungs. Or perhaps it was his dark gaze lingering on her lips, his black-as-night curls slanting roguishly over his brow, his bland smile, all that was polite, all that was civil, a sham for the gossiping crowd.

She sought to distance herself from the devastating effects of his touch. "So kind of you to ask me to dance, but you needn't have troubled yourself on my account."

"Do I detect a hint of sarcasm in your voice, my love?"

My love. A meaningless endearment that, uttered in his seductively deep voice, brought a tingling ache to the back of her throat. "Not at all. It is simply that I have more dance partners than there are dances—"

His fingers tightened on her hand. "You play a dangerous game if you strive to make me jealous."

"I would not dream of it," Leah said, staring over his shoulder at the blur of faces along the walls, at the torches and Grecian statuary placed strategically about the glittering room. Anywhere but at the man pulling her altogether too close to his person. His scent invading her senses. The threat of tears stinging her eyes. "After all, jealousy is nothing more than the fear of losing the one you love to another. As all you feel for me is supreme indifference, what have you to fear?"

"If you tempt my wrath, madam, be prepared to reap the consequences."

"I do not take your meaning. Of what are you accusing me?"

"If you have offered your favors to one of those foolish fribbles panting over your breasts, you will soon regret it."

Polite civility dropped its mask, replaced by a crudeness that shocked her. She tried to pull her hand from his grasp, but he tightened his grip.

"You may find this hard to believe," she said, forcing a smile. "But there are some women who do not live in the gutter. Now, release me. I have no desire to finish this farce."

"Ah, but I desire you to." He swept his leering gaze over the swells of her breasts. His eyes darkened, his lips tightened. By the time he returned his gaze to her eyes, his jaw had hardened, as if he were chewing on rocks. "You shall smile at me and bat your lashes and throw back your head as you laugh so that I may feast upon the sight of your creamy flesh, your pink-tinged nipples beneath your transparent dress, just as all the other randy bucks have enjoyed the sight all evening. You have left them fairly foaming at the mouth and itching to wrap their hands around your breasts . . ."

She glared him into silence. She wished she had spurs on her delicate slippers. She would dig them into his shins. She wished she had a dueling pistol. She would put a bullet through his black heart. She wished the dance would end and he would release her. What had she done to deserve such ill treatment?

Such vicious words and vile accusations?

Nothing! She had done nothing, except offer him her love, more fool she. Well, that was over. He didn't want her love, had never wanted her love. He had said that most emphatically right from the start. She was finished playing the fool. She would not, could not, compete with the demons from his past.

If he did not want her love, it was his loss, not hers.

Then why did she feel so desolate? So empty and alone?

They finished the dance in silence. When the music ended, she yanked her hand from his grasp and left him standing in the middle of the dance floor. She saw Alexander standing with her new-found friends. She fixed her smile in place and hoped he wouldn't see past her facade.

She half-expected Rachel to step into her path and offer more unsolicited, yet excruciatingly painful information about Richard's past, or some other insult whispered through a smile.

Tonight Rachel seemed content to watch from across the room as Leah's life fell apart. As much as she told herself she didn't care, questions plagued her. Who was the woman Richard had loved? Was she in this room at this moment?

Did she love Richard still? Having provided her husband with the requisite heir, was she now gracing his bed?

She felt half-wild, as if her heart were ripped from her chest, leaving an aching empty shell, but no one around her seemed to notice that her laugh was a sob in disguise.

She willed the muscles of her face to form a smile.

All thoughts of leaving thrust aside, Leah linked her arm through Alexander's. "I believe you have promised this dance to me, Mr. Prescott."

It was terribly forward of her, an act worthy of Lady Margaret Montague, but she did not care. She would not allow

Richard to see how much he had hurt her. She would salvage her pride. Tonight she would dance with Alexander and Lord Derrington and any other lord or mister who asked.

Tonight she would have fun. Even if it killed her.

The room was dark, the fire burning low in the grate.

Shadows swirled around him as Richard stood at the door connecting his room with Leah's, his forehead propped against the smooth oak panel, his neck covered in sweat. His head throbbed, as did his heart. It should be getting easier, but, God help him, it was getting harder with each passing day.

"She is not there," his brother's voice rumbled through the darkness.

Richard stifled a curse. He swung his gaze toward the shadows, where Geoffrey sat in a chair near the windows, bathed in ghostly yellow moonlight. "Why are you here? Should you not be abed?"

"You are a fool," Geoffrey said, his features showing no signs of pain or discomfort. His banyan of crimson brocade hung loose about his shoulders, covering his wound. "You know that, do you not?"

Richard grunted. "You are not the first to remark it."

Geoffrey made a sound of disgust. "I know what you are doing. I see you trying to drive her away. I see the fear in your eyes. And the love, too. You are a fool."

"I am a bigger fool for standing here listening to you."

Richard strode across the room, stooped on his heels to peer into his brother's eyes. "How do you feel?"

Geoffrey shrugged, his gaze drifting over to the windows. "I have felt better, but I have never felt worse."

"I'm proud of you," Richard said, his eyes hot, his throat a dry, burning ache. "I know you have the strength to beat this thing."

Geoffrey shuddered. "Good God, I hope you're right. It has to get easier because it could not possibly get any harder."

"I do not know what I would have done had you succeeded in planting that bullet in your brain." Richard pushed to his feet, prowled around the room. He lit the candles on the tables, briefly thought of stoking the fire, but the room was warm, the air thick and heavy. He rubbed his hands over his face, as if he could banish the haunting image. "Were it not for Leah, I would have been too late, and you would be dead."

Geoffrey stared at his hands, clasped on his lap to still their shaking. "I will never forgive myself for scaring either of you like that. Poor Leah. She deserves better, after all she's been through. Not to mention your boorish moods."

Richard dragged his hands down his face. Leah. Just the mention of her name sent a stabbing ache through his chest.

With savage determination, he yanked his thoughts away from Leah and back to Geoffrey. "What about the gaming?"

"That madness is gone," Geoffrey said, leaning his head on the back of his chair. "Or perhaps I haven't noticed it because I still crave the drink too much. But I do not mean to put it to the test. I will never put you through that again. I only hope, someday, I will be able to repay you for all you've suffered."

"Forget it," Richard said, then shook his head. "No—never forget it. But learn from it, Geoffrey. And never doubt me again. Come to me when you are in need."

Geoffrey surged from his chair. "What of your needs? What of your madness? I know what drives you and I know what haunts you, but you may be destroying your only real chance at happiness in this lifetime. Tell her everything, Richard. She loves you. She will understand."

Richard laughed bitterly, but said nothing.

"You blind, stupid idiot. Do you know what I think? I think you are punishing yourself by driving her away. Do you think this is what Eric would have for you? That he blamed you—"

"Of course he blamed me," Richard exploded. Arms flung

wide, he stalked to the other side of the room. "He found me in bed with his wife. I assure you, it is a moment I am never likely to forget. The pain. The betrayal on his face—"

"He hated her," Geoffrey said, following on Richard's heels, refusing him a moment's peace, badgering him with relentless intensity. "Richard, you have convinced yourself that he was in love with her, but that is not true. I lived there. I know. He hated her, and she him. He was never good enough for her because he was not you."

"Eric came to me before he died," Richard said quietly, rubbing the back of his neck. "Did you know that?"

"What did he say?"

Richard shook his head as he strolled to the windows. A heavy mist hung over the gardens, shimmering eerily in the silver light of the pre-dawn sky. The betrayals of his past, the agony of his future, collided in one brief flash before his eyes.

"I already knew Alison was mine," he finally said, pulling the words past the knot in his throat. "Rachel could not wait to share that news. In vivid detail, she described her intimate relations, or rather, her lack of relations, with Eric. As if she thought it would make a difference, as if I would ever take her back."

"Richard—"

He held up his hand. "Please, do not try to excuse my behavior. Eric already did that. It was the last time I saw him alive, the first time I had seen him since that awful night." He stripped off his neck cloth, tossed it onto the bed.

Leaning one hand on the mantel, he stared at the coals, mere embers in the hearth. His skin grew as cold as the dirt covering Eric's grave. Perhaps he should stoke the fire, after all. "He said that he knew Alison was mine. That he would protect her. That if I needed his forgiveness, it was mine, but he placed no blame on my actions."

Richard glanced over his shoulder. "Do you not see? He loved me so much he would forgive the unforgivable just to save my worthless hide. Should I shame his memory by declaring him a cuckold before the world? Even worse, that the man who put the horns on him was his own brother? Should I expose Alison to gossip and ridicule for the rest of her life? Do you honestly expect me to do these things simply to save my own soul?"

His right hand cradling his wound, Geoffrey slumped on the edge of the bed. "Can you not simply accept his words? That he knew the villainy of which Rachel was capable? That she betrayed you both? That he did not blame you?"

"I blame myself. I should never have gone back there."

But then Alison would not exist and Richard would not trade her life, even to regain his honor.

It was a vicious circle with no way out.

"Suffering Christ, Richard, it was your home."

"Never mind. I do not wish to discuss this."

"How can I make you understand—"

"Enough, I said." Richard could not discuss it. Not with his heart aching so badly, he thought he might weep like a babe.

Geoffrey walked to the door. Before he opened it, he turned back. "You are making the greatest mistake of your life. You underestimate your wife, and you belittle her love for you. Tell her the truth. Now. Before it is too late."

He shoved open the door, then slammed it shut behind him. The sound rattled through the quiet room.

Richard sank onto a chair near the fire, stared into the smoking ash. Could Geoffrey be right? Could he bare his soul?

Could he tell Leah the sordid truth about Eric and Rachel and Alison and the role he had played in the destruction of their lives?

Could she somehow understand? Forgive this most grievous of sins? Not that he thought she would blame the child. He knew she loved Alison as if she were her own. But it was more complicated than that. Much more complicated, and so sordid. So dirty.

Not fit for Leah's innocent soul.

Had he asked Rachel to sneak into his bed when he was too drunk to deny her? Had he asked to betray his brother with his brother's wife? Hadn't God already punished him with a vengeance by giving him a child he could never claim?

Did he have to pay for the rest of his life?

Intermittent light as the clouds moved over the rising sun shone through the windows. The night shadows slowly receded along the walls, revealing the deep crimson flock paper, the gold and crimson draperies, the family device carved into the plasterwork above the marble chimneypiece.

And still no sound arose from Leah's room.

Richard buried his face against his hands.

Tonight her eyes had sparkled with something akin to hate while his arms had burned with the agony of holding her through the dance. Her sweet scent had clouded his reason, while his vile words had stung and wounded.

Her gown, a luscious gold silk that highlighted her hair and brought out the gold dust in her eyes, had made her shine like a sunbeam in the middle of a rainstorm, with a neckline that had revealed a satiny sweep of sloping curves that left Richard hard and aching, shaking with desire. It was no wonder the rakes had swarmed around her, their eyes never rising above her chest.

Every tick of the mantel clock gave birth to some new, lurid vision to feed the rapacious monster snarling in his brain.

Minutes dragged by. An hour passed before he finally heard her enter her chambers. With jealousy running rampant through his veins, he flung open the door and stalked into her room.

Chapter Twenty-Five

Rational thought warned Richard he was making a dreadful mistake. He should return to his rooms, but one glance at the slope of her breasts rising above her outrageous neckline pushed all rational thought away. She stood before her dressing table, her hands sliding her long gloves down her arms. The slow, sensual swish of silk slipping over her wrists brought memories of their wedding night, of his hands fluttering over her skin.

She was so achingly beautiful, he shook with the need to sweep her into his arms, to touch her, to hold her, to taste her sweet flesh. His groin tightened. His hands curled into fists.

He shoved them against his thighs to keep from yanking her into his arms. "Have you any idea what time it is, madam?"

She pulled the pins from her hair, ran her fingers along her scalp until the curls tumbled down her back, soft, sensuous silk he longed to feel spilling over his chest. The scent of her perfume seeped into his lungs.

He breathed deeply. "Where have you been?"

Her lips pressed into a tight line, she finally turned to confront him. Her eyes appeared huge, shimmering liquid pools, the gold flecks hidden within the green catching the morning sun.

He leaned toward her, drawn without conscious thought,

until his glance moved over her shoulders. The provocative cut of her gown, the flimsiness of the fabric, the memory of all the men at the ball who had drooled over her barely concealed breasts, sent him into a seething rage. He was irrational, and he knew it, but he could not seem to stop himself. Jealousy had control of his brain. "I asked you a question, madam. Where have you been? And with whom?"

She crossed to the far side of the room before turning to face him. He let her go because he was afraid he might give in to temptation, toss her upon the bed, and bury himself within her sweet body. But he could not touch her. Certainly not in anger. Definitely not in the fog of jealousy. Nor even in passion.

Where was all his rigid control? The utmost respect and kindness with which he had pledged to treat her? He rubbed his fingers across his brow, then down the back of his rigid neck.

She wrapped her arms around her waist, her head held high as she faced him. Finally, she spoke, her voice soft, low, as if reasoning with a tantruming child. "I do not understand your question, Richard. The Houghton ball lasted until dawn, as these events often do, as you well know. You must be more specific in your choice of words. I gather what you really want to know is if I've betrayed my wedding vows?"

The muscle beneath his jaw clenched. "Have you?"

The frigid blast of her smile made him shiver.

Her lips quivered, but she thrust her chin high in the air. "As long as we are questioning marital fidelity," she said, "perhaps you won't mind my asking whose bed are you gracing these days?"

Her voice was as cold as his blood ran hot. Clever girl, turning his words back on him.

"It certainly is not mine," she said. "Or are you even limiting yourself to one? There are so many for you to choose from, or so Rachel informs me, when one considers the opera singers and dancers, Cyprians and Demireps, not to mention the noble ladies who would betray their wedding vows gladly if you would cast them so much as a come-hither glance with your ebony eyes."

"What I do is not the issue here."

She crossed her arms over her chest. "Of course. How silly of me. You are free to do as you will while I must remain the devoted, faithful wife, eager to gobble up the crumbs of your affection if and when you see fit to toss some my way. That hardly seems fair, my lord."

"If anyone has touched you," he said, his voice low and filled with menace. He leaned toward her, lowering his head until they stood eye to eye, "He is a dead man."

She did not back down. Instead, she curled her fists in the lapels of his frock coat, whether to pull him closer or to push him away, he did not know. "You are insane."

"You are right. I am insane. With jealousy! An altogether unpleasant emotion, eating me alive from the inside out, but I can't seem to control it. Tonight, I watched the men ogling your breasts . . ." He dropped his gaze to her heaving chest. "And the desire to kill was so strong, unlike anything I have ever felt before. So, tell me, madam. Do I have any reason to kill Prescott, or any of the other wolves in men's clothing?"

She rolled her lips between her teeth, but did not reply.

Eyes locked on her mouth, he wrapped his hands around her upper arms, then wished he hadn't as the heat of her skin burned his palms. "Answer me!"

"No."

His brows lifted. "No? I have no reason to kill anyone? Or no, you will not answer me?"

Her eyes widened, her face paled. A shiver trembled over her skin. That he had caused her trembling fear made him flush with shame, with self-loathing, with utter despair.

He turned on his heel and fled from the room. She was right. He was insane. But she was the madness in his brain.

* * *

Leah pressed a cool, damp cloth against her swollen eyes. Her throat was raw and her sides ached, but she did not cry.

Nor did she open her eyes when she heard her door creak. It could only be Richard and she did not want to speak with him. Perhaps, if he thought she was asleep, he would leave her alone.

It was a cowardly reaction, but she was too weary for one more confrontation, one more angry demand for explanations, as if she had done something wrong, as if she were the one who had changed, when it was he who had changed.

Leah could almost point to the moment her marriage fell apart. It was the third day of Geoffrey's recovery, when fatigue had finally forced her to seek her own bed. What had happened during her absence from the sickroom? What had caused Richard to turn away from her? Why was he pushing her out of his life?

It was almost as if he were afraid, but that made no sense.

What a fool she was. Last night, she had vowed she was through with him. But it was a lie. She loved him still.

She always would. He was etched into her soul from the moment they met, when his obsidian eyes had entranced her.

The Persian carpet muffled the heavy thud of his boots as he crossed the room. He lifted the cloth away from her face.

So much for pretending she was asleep.

He dipped the linen into the basin on her bedside table, twisted out the excess water, then draped it over her forehead. "Why did you not tell me you have been ill?"

"It is nothing," she said. She did not want his pity or his pretense of concern. "I am fine. I just need to rest."

"The doctor should be here in a moment. Leah, I . . ." He trailed off, raised his eyes to stare through the windows at the darkening sky. The first spatter of rain tapped on the glass.

Dark shadows sharpened the hollows beneath his eyes. Deep grooves creased his forehead and the corners of his lips.

This proud, arrogant man looked up at the ceiling, as if unsure what he wanted to say. Leah found herself fascinated, unable to look away, until his eyes swept down to meet her gaze.

He cleared his throat. "I fear my behavior toward you, both last evening and earlier this morning, was . . ."

"Reprehensible? Unconscionable? Unpardonable?"

"Quite." His gaze never wavered from hers, his dark eyes intensely disturbing. "I find myself in the extremely awkward position of having to . . . beg your pardon."

The last words came out on a rush, and startled a laugh from Leah, despite her throbbing head. He tilted his head, his eyes widening, the affronted look of a youth who had declared his love to a maid, only to have it tossed back in his face.

"I imagine that caused you a prodigious amount of pain," she said, her voice scraping over the raw ache in her throat. "You do not use that word often, I am sure."

He gave a brief nod. "I believe this was the first time."

"I do not doubt it," she said, touching her fingers to her lips to hide her smile. His gaze followed the motion.

The longing she read in his eyes set her heart to racing and her skin to burning. His warm, familiar scent beckoned her closer, tempted her to lean her hand against his cheek and claim his mouth with her kiss. The strain of their relations stood in stark contrast to their playful bantering and brought the dreaded tears to her eyes.

His smile faded. "Truly, there was no excuse for my outlandish attack on you and I am heartily ashamed. Much to my surprise, I find I am a jealous man, an ugly emotion I never experienced before I met you. But I promise you, this will never happen again. I only hope you will forgive me."

His confession should have made her happy, for it meant

he must care, despite his recent distance—if he didn't, why would he be jealous? But her head hurt too much to worry about it and, this time, she truly thought she might weep.

She must have dozed off, for when she next opened her eyes, Richard was talking with Dr. Ashcroft. The portly doctor tugged on his periwig as he listened to Richard, their voices too low for Leah to discern their words.

After Richard left, the doctor pulled up a chair beside the bed. "His Grace tells me you are not feeling quite up to snuff. Let's see if we can't determine what is wrong with you, shall we? It appears you have been crying. Does this happen quite often?"

Leah nodded. Truly, she hardly ever cried, but over the last few weeks, it seemed as if every new day brought a reason to weep. Usually, she managed to choke back her tears.

Then there were days like this one.

"And the sight of food makes you ill?"

"Yes," Leah said, a sticky sheen of perspiration rising on her brow, fueled by her growing agitation. She fingered the edge of her coverlet. "Do you know what is wrong with me?"

"Two more questions should confirm my diagnosis. You have been married for how long? Two, three months?"

"Almost three."

"And when was your last monthly flow? Sometime before your wedding, I suspect. Is that right?"

The intimate question brought a burning heat to her cheeks.

"There is no need for modesty with me, Your Grace. You must tell me everything if I am to make my diagnosis."

Leah had to think back in her mind. He was right. She hadn't had her woman's time in months. She hadn't even noticed.

Good heavens. She placed her palm against the flat of her stomach as she glanced up at the doctor. Dared she hope?

Her breath caught in her throat. The furious beat of her heart sent blood rushing through her limbs. Her fingers tingled and her feet grew numb. She glanced up at the doctor.

He nodded, and his glasses slipped down to the tip of his

nose. "Felicitations, Your Grace. I believe your child should make his appearance in about seven months."

Leah pressed the back of her hands to her lips. Her eyes drifted shut, her thoughts racing ahead of her breath. She imagined a black-haired boy who looked just like his father. Then the image of a raven-haired daughter with charcoal eyes rose in her mind. How surprising life was. Just when the world seemed so bleak, God granted His most precious gift.

A baby. She vowed she would be the most wonderful mother. She knew without doubt that Richard would be an amazing father.

"Now, you must remember to eat," the doctor was saying. "Even though food might not sit well at first. That will pass. And get plenty of rest." He stood, dragged his waistcoat into place, then turned to leave. "The duke will be most pleased."

Leah grabbed his hand. "Wait. You cannot tell him."

"Why ever not? His Grace is dreadfully worried. I must reassure him that nothing is wrong."

"But I want to tell him myself. You must understand?"

He patted her hand. "Of course. I will simply inform him there is no need to worry. You can give him the good news."

"Thank you," she said, her voice trembling. She watched him until the door closed behind him. Then she laughed.

A babe! She jumped out of bed, and threw on her clothes. Perhaps now the ghosts of Richard's past would be banished from their future.

Richard stood in the conservatory, staring at the dormouse as it huddled in the corner of its cage. It stared back at him through wide, solemn brown eyes. It was surrounded by beauty, by roses and orchids and oriental camellias, a beautiful flower with the sweetest perfume, but still it was an animal trapped in a cage. Much as Richard was trapped. By his past. By his sins.

By a fear so great, it weakened his knees and made his

hands shake. Hot shame burned in his throat. He had no excuse for his vicious behavior, save for his sanity slowly ebbing away.

Rain hitting the glass rooftop thundered through the conservatory, its roaring din deafening in its intensity. A wild gust of wind rattled the frame. Richard closed his eyes, his mind calling forth a vision of Leah, all golden-haired innocence, her limbs trembling as he brought her pleasure to a peak.

His desire was so strong, he started to shake, but it was more than a physical ache. He wanted to hold her in his arms when she slept, comfort her when she wept. He wanted to love her. Damn, but he loved her.

A pain hit the center of his chest, a burning sensation that intensified with every breath he drew. His long, lonely life stretched out before him. He could not bear the image without her in it. He had only two choices.

He could remain trapped in present misery, or he could risk all for a chance at happiness with his wife.

It seemed a simple enough decision, but Richard greatly feared it would be easier by far to chop off his own hand than to put words to his deepest shame.

Soft footsteps pattered the stone floor behind him. The scent of lavender water filled the air. He crushed a fistful of orchid petals as Rachel moved around the table, stopping only when her shoes touched the tip of his boots. He would never know a moment's peace. Not with this she-devil living under his roof. The instrument of God's vengeance. The price of his sins.

He cursed violently under his breath. He had to get away before he succumbed to his baser instincts and murdered her where she stood.

Leah went to the library first, where Richard spent many an hour poring over ledgers and documents. The room was empty, so she went to his study, the steward's room, the estate offices, and even the stables, where she got caught in a sudden gust of wind and rain. All the while, she rehearsed the words she would use. *Richard, we are going to have a babe. Richard, I am with child. Richard, you are going to be a father.*

None seemed adequate to express the thrill of the moment. How would he react? Would he whoop with joy? Take her into his arms with infinite tenderness? Stare at her in shocked silence?

Once back in the great hall, she met the butler, standing sentry at the door. "Have you seen the duke?"

The servant gave a stiff bow. "I believe he is in the conservatory, Your Grace."

"Thank you, Harris," Leah said, her smile so wide, she no doubt appeared a bit demented, especially with her damp hair curling wildly about her flushed cheeks. She did not care. She was too happy. As she set off down the corridor, she buried the niggling fear that Richard might not be pleased. After all, every man wanted a child to carry on his name. And a man like Richard most of all, with houses and titles and estates.

At the conservatory door, she paused to calm her rattled nerves. Through the shrubbery she could see Richard's coat, green kerseymere hugging his broad back, black pantaloons sheathing his legs. Standing before him was Rachel, her gown a peach gossamer silk elegant enough to appear before the king. Rachel's eyes were wide, luminous blue, and shining on Richard's face with a look of utter adoration.

Leah's breath coalesced in her throat until she felt as if she were choking. The rain pounding on the roof drowned out any words they were saying, but there was no mistaking the charged tension shimmering between Richard and Rachel, the almost sexual energy hanging in the sultry, humid air.

Before she could approach them, Richard strode away and stalked through the door that led into the gardens. Rain swirled in through the entry, snapping over the stone floor until the howling wind slammed the door.

Leah stood motionless, frozen in place by the stunning suspicions forming in her mind. Then her feet were moving, drawing her closer to the woman who had made her life miserable from the moment she'd entered this house.

"You are in love with my husband," she said, amazed her voice sounded so steady, so calm and assured, when she was a quivering mess inside. She thought of her babe and she drew a deep breath to quiet her spiraling pulse.

Rachel's brows lifted, her lips pursed, not in puzzlement or surprise, but more a satisfied smirk. "Of course. And he is in love with me."

It was a lie and Leah would not respond to it. "I want you to leave my house. You may make your own arrangements or I will make them for you, but you will leave. Today."

"You poor, pathetic child." Rachel shook her head. "You do not understand. I suppose you have spun dreams of happily-ever-after and years to come. The problem with dream worlds, Leah, is that, sooner or later, they come tumbling down around one's ears. It is me he loves. You are simply a means to an end."

"You are the one spinning dreams," Leah said, with more conviction than she felt. "Richard loathes you."

Rachel laughed, a soft, delicate sound. Ever the lady, even when shredding her enemies. "Oh, did he tell you that?"

"He did not have to tell me. I can see it in his eyes every time he looks at you." Or was it all a sham?

The traitorous thought sucked the breath from Leah's lungs and she thrust it away.

"Is that hate you see . . . or desire?"

Leah fought to gain control over the tempest inside her mind. That something had happened to cause Richard's recent desertion from her bed, she could not deny, but it was not this.

At least now she understood Rachel's animosity. All her sweetly worded insults, her whispered innuendoes meant to raise friction between Leah and Richard. Rachel would say anything, do anything, to hurt Leah and think her gullible enough to believe it. "I will not listen to any more of your spite. I will make preparations for your departure. You *will* leave. Tonight."

Head high, back straight, Leah walked toward the door.

Rachel scooted around her, swift as an eel, and blocked the path. "If it weren't for you and your despicable father, Richard and I would be married now."

Leah gasped. "I do not believe you. Even if he had wanted to marry you, he couldn't. You are his brother's widow. His sister! In the eyes of both God and the law."

"It matters not. He would have damned the proprieties. Or we would have fled the country. Do you not see? He has always loved me. And I him. We were the best of friends as children. We would have wed, too, if not for my parents. They betrothed me to Eric against my will. Richard was devastated. He joined the army, supposedly to fight the French, but he was really running from the pain of seeing me with his brother."

"Your love is cheap. Not worth the words used to utter it." Leah ached for the devastation Richard had endured from such a cold-hearted betrayal. No wonder he had closed himself off, denied his needs and his emotions. Why would he ever risk love again when he'd offered his heart to this shrew, only to have it trampled upon as if it were an unwanted frippery. "Had you truly loved him, you would have defied your family to wed him."

"It isn't that simple, as well you know," Rachel said, giving a delicate shrug. "A woman has precious little power over her destiny. There was nothing I could do. But Richard couldn't understand. He was hurt. And you are right. For a time, he hated me. But all that changed when Eric died. I was free. Richard was free. And we were reunited. Then your treacherous father came along with his blackmail scheme."

Rachel was a liar. Not a word coming out of her mouth

could be trusted, but it did not stop the vicious, ugly words from looping through Leah's mind, *Blackmail scheme, blackmail scheme, blackmail scheme.*

She willed herself to walk away, nay, run from the poisonous miasma building around her, but her feet would not move, as if they were lashed to the floor by the creeping ivy. "What do you mean?"

Rachel shrugged. "I cannot believe you haven't guessed. But it isn't for me to tell. Let's just say, Richard has a secret, and he is terrified of society learning the truth. Honor and pride and all that. Your father learned his secret, from Geoffrey, of all people, and he forced Richard to marry you."

Leah wanted to flee, to hide from the awful words that attacked her deepest fears, but it was as if she had turned to stone and couldn't move. She tried to shut out Rachel's hideous words, but they hacked through her defenses, lashed her with their insidious implications.

"Why do you think he wed you?" Rachel was saying. "You cannot possibly believe he wanted to marry you? It was to protect someone he holds dearer than he holds his own life. It is me he loves. Never forget it. Why do you think he nearly ravished you in the salon the day he returned from Yorkshire?"

Leah shook her head. Her skin grew cold, despite the heat of the plants and the furnace forcing tropical weather in the midst of London. Her thoughts were as foggy as the steamy mist.

And all the while, Rachel continued her torturous assault. "It was me he wanted. We were together in the library, but I told him I could not sleep with him, not with his wife in the house. Because of your father, he cannot send you away. So I sent him to slake his lust on you. How does it feel to know when he closes his eyes as he beds you, it is me he sees beneath him?"

With a look of bored detachment on her face, Rachel studied the orchid to her right. "Do you want to know the basis of your marriage? Richard weds you and beds you and your father guarantees his silence after the first male child is born. Once he gets his heir on you, he will leave you. Never doubt that."

Leah's hand crept to her belly. "No, I don't believe you."

Rachel walked up behind Leah, her invidious words hot against Leah's neck. "Think of how it must be for him. Forced to bed a woman thrust upon him by the vilest of treacheries. But he gritted his teeth, closed his eyes, and did his duty. You are only useful until you bear his babe. Then his secrets will be safe. Then he will cast you aside. And if you do not believe me, ask him. Go on," Rachel taunted in her ear. "Ask him to send me away. Make him choose between us. Or are you afraid?"

Chapter Twenty-Six

Rachel's laughter followed Leah from the conservatory, but she kept her back straight, her head high, and forced her shaking legs to carry her from the room. Her stomach was churning, her blood rushing too swiftly through her veins.

She forced a serenity to her expression as she progressed down the corridor. She would not let the servants see her distress. If only her thoughts would turn as numb as her skin, but they tortured her with each step she took as she went in search of Richard. That her father would stoop so low as to blackmail a peer of the realm, Leah did not doubt.

But what could he know? What secret could a man have that was so dark, so dirty, he would do anything to protect it, even marry a woman he must hate? And what of Richard? What of all the tender words and passionate moments in his arms?

Had they all been a lark? Designed to keep her complacent until he sired a child upon her?

No, she would not believe it. It could not be true.

He might not have wished to marry her, and he might not love her, but he had come to care for her over the course of their marriage. Of this, she was certain. To believe otherwise, she would have to believe every kiss, every touch, every moment in his arms was a pretense and she could not do that. He was too noble, too honorable, to commit such a heinous act of deception.

But what of his recent desertion from her bed? Did he already know that she carried his child? That his seed had taken? His mission accomplished? Could he truly love Rachel?

Leah clenched her eyes against the memory she had tried so hard to deny. The night of Geoffrey's suicide attempt, when she had gone to fetch Richard, he had been dreaming, thrashing about on the bed. Richard had blamed his distress on a nightmare.

Afraid to think otherwise, Leah had accepted his words.

But she could no longer pretend. He had called out a name. *Rachel, Rachel, Rachel,* over and over she heard his low-pitched voice groan the hated name. The same seductive voice that had so often whispered Leah's name as he drove himself within her body, deep within her body until he touched her womb.

That he loved Rachel once, Leah could understand. But not now. She saw the hatred that flashed in his eyes every time he looked at Rachel. She heard the contempt in his voice every time he spoke the woman's name. Whatever he may have felt for her, it was in the past. But Rachel still loved Richard, so she had spit her venom at Leah to hurt her and wound her and drive her away.

Leah would not let Rachel win. She would not allow Rachel to poison her mind against her husband, the father of her unborn child. The thought of her child flamed **her** anger into rage.

Never would she allow her babe to be used as a pawn in a battle between her husband and her father.

She retraced her earlier steps until she found Richard in the library. He stood before the windows, looking out over the gardens. His hair, wet from the storm, glistened in the slate-gray light beyond the glass. He had removed his coat and waistcoat, slung them over a chair, along with his neck cloth.

He rolled his shoulders. His damp shirt pulled over every ridged muscle in his back. She must have made a sound, perhaps a choked gasp as she remembered the heat of those muscles beneath her palms. He swung around, met her gaze, his eyes dark, shadowed by fatigue, by pain, by some emotion she could not name.

She wanted to run, to flee to the safety of her room, but she forced herself to approach him. She tried to speak, but the words tangled up in her throat. She drew a deep breath, started again, but still, no sound came out. Her courage fled along with her voice and she swayed on her feet.

Afraid she might faint, she staggered toward the nearest chair. He caught her elbow in his hand, the heat of his palm soothing against her frigid skin as he guided her to the settee near the hearth. A small fire burned to ward off the chill of the storm. He knelt before her, his beloved face sun-bronzed and rugged, his eyes narrowed in concern. "The doctor said there was nothing wrong with you. I shall have that quack's head."

"No," she said. A sob rippled up her throat, but she choked it back down. "I am well. I assure you."

"You do not look well. Your skin is as gray as day-old ashes and your eyes are black smudges in your face."

She managed a weak smile, a faltering laugh to cover her sobs. "What a dreadful fright I must be."

He held her hand in his, rubbed circles over her palm. The motion, soft and seductive and oh, so, familiar, brought a watery mist to her eyes. She rolled her lips between her teeth. She would not cry. Nor would she listen to Rachel's words, the hideous refrain circling through her mind.

She longed to rest her palm against his jaw, to rub her cheek against his neck, to press her lips to his.

Instead, she gathered her courage and her dignity.

It was time to face the truth.

"I know why you married me," she said. "I know my father blackmailed you."

She watched the lump in his throat move up and down as he swallowed. His eyes closed. His lips tightened. His jaw grew hard, an unforgiving slope of granite.

For a moment, Leah thought he might deny it. Then he opened his eyes, their dark centers turbulent as the storm outside the window and just as bleak. Was that pity or regret she saw in his eyes?

"Yes, it is true," he said, his voice rough, his hand tightening on her fingers. "How did you find out?"

She pushed herself from her chair. He approached her slowly, warily, as if he feared she would bolt from the room, or leap from the windows. Did she appear as wild as she felt, like the wind rattling the shutters, like the rain beating the glass? "How you must hate me."

"No," he said quietly. "I wanted to hate you. I tried, but it took only moments in your presence to realize you were an innocent victim in your father's grand scheme. You are too sweet, too innocent to partake of such a deception."

Unable to bear the compassion in his eyes, she turned away. Her life was a sham, her marriage not truly a marriage. What it was, she did not know. Her skin burned with shame, with despair, with bone-crushing fatigue.

She raised a shaking hand to her brow.

He came up behind her, gripped her shoulders. "Who told you?" When she did not respond, he dug his fingers into her skin. "Was it Rachel? What did she say?"

Leah shook her head. She stepped out of his grasp, then turned to face him. "Tell me of my father's trickery."

She saw a flicker of emotion in his obsidian gaze, a flash of relief, perhaps, or rage, before he closed his eyes. It happened so swiftly, Leah almost thought she had imagined it, for when he looked at her again, his gaze was clear and hard.

He folded his hands behind his back. "It matters not."

"It matters to me," she said. "I have a right to know. Do you not see? My life is based on a lie, my marriage on treachery. How am I to live with that?"

He sliced his hand through the air. "You are not to blame for your father's misdeeds. It has naught to do with you."

"It has everything to do with me. I tried to set you free. I offered you a divorce, but you refused."

No words. He simply nodded.

"And now? If I offered now, would you agree?"

"Never," he said, grabbing her arms. He dragged her close until she was crushed against his chest, until his hot breath caressed her face, until his sensual scent seared her lungs.

"Why? For my father?"

"No. For you. Because you are my wife. It has nothing to do with your father, and everything to do with you."

To her shame, silent tears slid down her cheeks. "Then what has happened to change you so? Why have you become so distant, so cold?"

"Because I am a fool, as more than one person has tried to tell me. My love," he whispered, then touched his lips to hers.

Oh, God, she could almost believe all would be well when he kissed her like this, hot and demanding. His tongue ravishing her mouth as she wanted his hands to ravish her body. Reason fought with desperate need unfurling within her as he dragged her against his chest, her breasts tingling as the dampness of his shirt seeped through her dress, his mouth trailing a fiery path along her jaw, then down the sensitive curve of her neck.

It had been so long, too long, since he had touched her in passion, but she wanted more than passion. She wanted his love.

As the serpent taunted Eve in the garden of Eden, Rachel's words taunted Leah. *It is me he loves . . . and if you do not believe me, make him choose . . .*

Leah shook her head. "Not yet. We need to talk."

He ignored her words, slanting his mouth once more against her lips, his tongue thrusting within, the slow, delicious sweep drawing a moan from her throat and dampening the flesh between her thighs. She wanted nothing more than to tumble to the floor with him atop her, his hands scraping against her thighs as he shoved her dress up to her waist and drove his straining sex deep within her body. But she had to face the truth.

She pushed against his chest, broke from his embrace. She stumbled to the window, her vision blurred by the rain as she stared out over the gardens. He walked up behind her.

Afraid he might touch her, she wrapped her arms around her waist. Her heart and soul cried out in fear, *do not do this*.

But Rachel's hideous words chanted, *make him choose, make him choose, make him choose*.

Leah knew she was making a dreadful mistake by paying any heed to Rachel's vicious lies, but she could not seem to stop herself. As if from a very great distance, she heard herself say, "I want you to find Rachel a home of her own. I cannot live with her another day."

His face blanched. "And what of Alison? I am her guardian. I want her here where I can see to her needs."

Leah stared at the floor. While Rachel's words had tossed about in the turbulent storm in her mind, she had never once considered Alison. Leah loved that little girl so much, it hurt her heart, but she could not stand the mother. She could not live in the same house with Rachel any longer, not with her vindictiveness and her coveting of Leah's husband.

"Perhaps she would agree to leave Alison with us?"

Richard laughed, a bleak sound with no humor. "No. She would never agree, and I have no reason to keep her from her mother, at least, no reason that would not ignite a blaze of gossip. And I will not do that."

"Even if she took Alison with her, we could still see her

every day. We could still see to her needs. Not every child lives under the same roof with their guardian."

"I thought you loved her."

"Of course I love her," Leah said. "I could not love her any more than if she were my own daughter. But she is not my daughter. Nor is she yours. She is Rachel's."

He stared at her through eyes devoid of emotion. Neither spoke. The mantel clock ticked off the passing seconds. Every stroke brought a new pain to Leah's already aching heart.

His chest heaved as he sucked in his breath. "You have seen the kind of mother she is and still you would ask this?"

"I have never seen her ill-treat Alison. Are you saying she abuses her?"

"No, she does not abuse her. Not physically. She simply does not know the child is alive. And believe me, that hurts more than a physical slap to the face." Richard clenched his fists at his side. "Damn it! Why are you doing this to me?"

"Twice I offered to set you free. Twice you refused. I cannot live with that woman—" Leah bit her lip to stop the tumble of words, but it was no use. She was far beyond rational thought, tossed about by the turbulent emotions controlling her tongue. "I am your wife," she said. "Either she goes, or I go."

His eyes flashed with chilling fury. "Do you dare to offer me an ultimatum?"

"It is your choice," she said, lifting her chin. It was far too late to turn back now.

"You do not know what you are asking."

She gazed out the window. An impenetrable fog hung over the gardens, a silvery ghostly presence, undulating in the rain.

"Do you love her so much, then?" Her voice came out a choked whisper.

He grabbed her arms, forced her to meet his gaze. "Of course I love her. She is my niece."

"I meant Rachel."

Richard thrust her away. "Do you think I care a whit about Rachel? It is Alison—"

"You whisper her name when you sleep. Did you know that?" She had tried to deny it, tried to tell herself over and over again that it was meaningless, that he was having a nightmare, as he had said. She laughed a brittle laugh. "I've heard you. In the night. You whisper her name. Have you nothing to say?"

His features hardened, as if turned to stone. "As you have already tried and convicted me, madam, there seems little enough to say."

Leah shook her head while her dreams wilted like the last roses of summer. She gathered the remains of her shredded dignity and walked to the door. She opened it, but turned back for a moment. "You know, Rachel said you would never let her leave. It seems she was right."

Richard shouted her name, demanded she stop, but Leah ran until she reached the safety of her bedchamber.

She twisted the key in the lock, then ran to the connecting door and locked it, too. His chamber door crashed open.

His booted feet stomped across his room.

With her hands twisting in the folds of her gown, Leah stared at the door. The handle jiggled.

A vile oath floated through the wood.

A heartbeat later, the door crashed against the wall and Richard stood before her, a raging Ares, savage god of war.

Leah refused to cower before him, even though she was trembling so fiercely, she had to lock her knees to keep from collapsing on the floor. She had created this horrible situation. She would not hide from her own foolishness.

"Never lock that door against me, madam," he said, his calm voice an understatement to the rigid tension in his arms and legs. "Do I make myself perfectly clear?"

Leah didn't even try to raise her voice above the lump in her throat. Her eyes wide, she simply nodded.

"Excellent. Now that we understand one another, you may see to the packing of your bags. As living with me makes you so unhappy, you may retire to my Cornish estate."

Leah lifted her chin. Her lower lip quivered. She needed to end this interview before she disgraced herself more than she already had. Good Lord, what had she done?

He glared at her. "Have you nothing further to say?"

"What is there to say?" she managed, pushing the words past the knot in her throat. "You have issued your commands. I am to go into exile—"

"How so? Is this not what you wanted? Is this not what you asked for? Was this not the purpose of the scene in the library? To force me to send you away? To gain the precious *freedom* you demanded on our wedding day? You simply latched on to Rachel to force my hand."

Leah clamped her lips together. Of all the arrogant, ignorant, sanctimonious nerve! To assume to make judgments on her motives! If only he had heard Rachel's terrible words.

He rubbed his hand down the center of his chest. His gaze shifted away, as if he could not bear to look at her. "Leah . . ."

"If you do not mind," she said, surprised her voice came out so soft and reasonably controlled. Her skin was so cold, she started to shake. "I would like to prepare for my journey."

He took a single step toward her, as if pulled by an invisible hand, then he gave a curt bow before striding from the room.

Leah dropped to her knees, buried her face in her hands.

Oh God, what had she done?

Richard stood outside the nursery door, hidden in the shadows, as he watched Leah kneel before Alison.

Her hands shook as she drew the child into her arms. Her voice quivered as she said good-bye, each word spoken in her soft, melodious voice a whiplash stripping the flesh from his back. He sucked in his breath, drawing air deep into his lungs in a desperate attempt to flush the pain from his chest.

He was glad he could not see her eyes.

Alison pushed out of Leah's grasp, backed away until her shoulders bumped into her nurse's knees. The tears drenching her cheeks gave the lie to the belligerent set of her mouth.

He should walk away. He should leave while he still had control over his emotions, but he was no more capable of moving his feet as he was of dragging his gaze from his wife.

"I have a favor to ask of you," Leah said, lifting a rag doll in her hand and offering it to Alison. "Could you look after my friend while I am away? Her name is Mary and she is very special to me. My mother gave her to me when I was not much older than you."

Alison puffed out her lower lip. "You lied to me. You said you would be my friend. You said you would never go away and you're leaving me. I hate you," she shouted, then turned to flee. She stopped, grabbed the doll out of Leah's hands, then ran into the adjoining room, her weeping drifting back through the door.

Leah buried her face in her hands. Her shoulders heaved, but no sound emerged from her silent, smothered sobs.

Richard bolted for the stairs. He could not allow himself to think, or worse, to feel, for fear his black heart would shatter, the fragments scattering over the floor until nothing remained. Rachel stepped into his path. The malignant gleam in her eyes, the gloating triumph in her smile, left no doubt that she'd enjoyed every heart-wrenching word she'd just heard.

"If you open your mouth, if you dare say a word," he snarled as he pushed past her. "I will kill you."

Geoffrey stood at the bottom of the stairs, casually dressed in a loose banyan tossed over his shirt to hide his wound. He glared at Richard. "I understand congratulations are in order. You have finally managed to push her away."

"Geoffrey, for the love you bear me, do not. Not now. Not today." Richard stalked the perimeter of the hall, through the arched columns to the door, then back again. The echo of his boots beating the parquet floor filled the void between them.

Soft footsteps approaching the bend in the stairs caught his breath in his throat. A moment later, Leah appeared.

The hall grew silent, the air, musty and damp against his sweating skin. The only sound he could hear was the thumping of his heart. He was amazed it was still beating, for he thought surely he was dead. He wanted to drag her into his arms, to bury his lips within her hair, to beg her to stay, but pride and anger smothered with despair kept the words locked within his throat.

Geoffrey dragged her into his arms. Kissing. Hugging. Whispered words. Richard wanted to plant his fist between his brother's eyes. After a last evil glare cast his way, Geoffrey stomped off, leaving Richard alone with his wife.

She raised her gaze to his. Oh God, her eyes, usually so alive with her inner joy, were deep green pools of emptiness, no emotion, no life, in their dark depths. The crushing weight of a thousand bricks bore down on his chest.

He'd stolen the laughter, the joy, from her eyes.

"Richard, I . . ." Her voice faltered as she drew several missives from her reticule. Her hand shook as she held out the letters, careful not to let her fingers brush against his.

To keep his mind occupied and off the drugging scent of her perfume, he sorted though the letters, one to her aunt, one to Mrs. Bristoll, and one to him outlining detailed instructions regarding the foundling home as well as several other charities she had chosen to support.

Even in her misery she thought of others above herself.He could not breathe, nor could he stop himself from taking her hand in his, her skin soft against his calloused grip.

A shudder coursed through her. She tugged on her hand, but he couldn't let her go. He linked her arm through his and led her through the door and down the steps where two elegant traveling carriages stood lined up on the street.

The butler, the housekeeper, and Leah's maid stood beside the second coach waiting to board. The master of the horse, the coachman, and the grooms, all handsomely attired in the formal burgundy and gold livery of the Dukes of St. Austin, stood alongside a dozen outriders ready to give escort.

It was an entourage fit for royalty, a meager gesture because she did not understand. It was a symbol of his love for her. Don't think! Just move!

He led her to the carriage, helped her up the steps.

She kept her gaze pinned on the floor as she settled back against the velvet-covered squabs. He gripped the door as he memorized the delicate curve of her chin, the slight tilt of her nose, the dark shadows beneath her eyes, the lines of pain etched into her cheeks.

He'd etched that pain there.

He slammed the door. "Drive on!"

The carriage rolled away, a misty blur through the moisture in his eyes. He wanted to run after it, to drag her out and into his arms. He wanted to kiss her and hold her and beg her to stay, but the coach and six picked up speed and disappeared into the morning fog. It was too late. She was gone.

Chapter Twenty-Seven

Richard sprawled face-down across his bed. His chamber door opening and closing rattled through his drink-dulled mind.

For a moment, his heart lifted, his blood surged.

Then he remembered, she was gone and he was in hell.

He needed another drink, a potent brandy to scrape the skin from his throat, a highland whisky to burn all thought from his brain. Too bad he'd packed it all away.

Damn Geoffrey and his recklessness.

If it weren't for that bounder, Richard could stalk to his own library and drink himself into the oblivion eluding him.

Rough hands seized his legs, shoved him onto his back.

He pulled his eyes open to see his wretched brother standing beside the bed, his two heads swimming in and out of clarity.

"Now I know how I looked after a night's debauchery, and it is not a pretty sight," Geoffrey said, yanking off Richard's boots. He tossed them onto the floor with a loud thud that rattled through Richard's brain.

He pulled his goose-down pillow over his head. "Begone, Geoffrey. I do not feel well."

"That is hardly surprising. It isn't bad enough you've been

silent as a stone for nigh onto four months—and now this? Drinking and carousing with that no account reprobate?"

Had it only been four months? It seemed more like a thousand years since last he'd seen her. His throat clenched. His eyes grew hot, swollen, stinging from the sweat dripping down his brow. "If that ain't the tosspot calling the kettle black."

"But *I* have reformed my ways. More so since you slid into the stews. Now I know how you felt when I stumbled home, steeped to my nose in gin and debts. I am worried about you."

"No need to worry," Richard murmured, closing his eyes. "Just had a bit too much tonight."

"Tonight and every night for the last fortnight. It is not like you, Richard, and you have to stop. Before you end up like I did, with a pistol pointed at your brain."

How could he explain that he was drinking to drive away his demons? Not that it worked. Nothing worked. They were always there, lurking at the edge of his awareness, waiting for him to sober up. For weeks, he had tried burying himself in estate business, but thoughts of Leah haunted his every waking moment.

What was she doing right now? At this moment? With whom was she speaking? Did she think about him? Miss him as much as he missed her? Love him as much as he loved her? Or had he killed any tender affection she might have felt for him?

Just when Richard thought he truly might run mad, Pierce had returned to Town. His penchant for drinking, his unfailing wit, and his ability to mind his own business made him the perfect companion for a man in misery. In drunken oblivion, Richard had finally found the respite he desperately needed. And even then, only for the moment, only until the drink dissipated, leaving him aching and alone, with only his demons to destroy him.

"Why don't you go to her," Geoffrey was saying. "Tell her everything. She will understand."

"She already knows and she hates me."

"That is absurd. She loves you so much." Geoffrey waved his hand. "She only knows part of the story, and Rachel's version at that. You must go to her."

"You don't understand. I cannot!"

"Then you deserve your empty bed."

Geoffrey looked as if he wanted to say more, but Richard closed his eyes and started to snore. He waited for his door to slam shut before he swerved his way across the room and entered Leah's bedchamber. He almost expected to see her pacing before the fire, as she had on their wedding night, her sensuous gown of silver silk swaying around her hips in a flirtatious dance that had driven him mad. Her golden hair shining in the firelight. The taste of her breath upon his lips, the heat of her skin, her arms holding him close, pulling him in.

He collapsed on her bed, buried his face in her pillow. He dragged in a breath, tried to convince his drink-dulled mind that he could still smell her rosewater perfume, though months had passed since she'd last entered these rooms.

He thought of going to her. Every minute of every day, he thought about going to her, but he always vetoed the idea.

Why should he? She would only reject him, now that she knew his darkest secrets. But she didn't know everything, he told himself. She didn't know the truth about Alison.

He could still hear her voice echoing her words. *I couldn't love Alison any more than if she were my own daughter. But she isn't my daughter, nor is she yours. . . .*

Why had Rachel decided to keep that bit of truth to herself? To spare Leah's feelings? Richard very much doubted that.

To protect Alison's name? Possibly, but not very likely.

So she could spring it at a later date, if and when Richard should ever reconcile with his wife?

Definitely. Rachel would stop at nothing to hurt him, even if she had to ruin Alison's life in the process.

* * *

Rachel paced the gallery that circled the central stairs. When she heard Richard's door open, she pushed herself against the wall in hopes the shadows would hide her.

Her heart thumping, her skin tingling, she dared a peek over the banister. She watched Geoffrey slam Richard's door, then stalk to his room and slam that door, as well, the noise shattering the silence in the vaulted hall.

Little bubbles of laughter tickled up the back of her throat until she felt nearly giddy. She closed her eyes and breathed deeply to steady her nerves. While she knew her marriage to Eric had devastated Richard, she had never dreamed his anger would last a lifetime. Now she realized she had badly under-estimated his loyalty and devotion to his brother.

Why couldn't he understand that she had only married Eric for the title? That she had acted for Richard as much as for herself? Hadn't she resolved matters nicely?

Wasn't the title his just the way she had planned?

She had been so close. All she had needed was a little more time. Once Richard's grief had passed, he would have turned to her for comfort, as he always had in the past, before Eric, before Alison, before that cur, Jamison, and his despicable daughter walked into his life. But Rachel had triumphed over that stupid girl, too. A few whispered words here. A few in-nuendoes there. But her greatest maneuver had been simply to state the blatant truth behind the basis of Leah's marriage.

Leah was too innocent, too trusting a soul, not to fall into Rachel's trap. Running to Richard and demanding the truth. Demanding he choose between a wife he hadn't wanted and the woman he had loved all of his life.

As Rachel had watched Leah's departure from the salon window, it was all she could do not to shout in triumph.

Never had she expected that Richard would withdraw into silence, into icy civility that chilled Rachel's heart. It was almost as if he cared for his wife, as if he missed her.

But how could that be?

She was nothing more than an inconvenience thrust upon him to protect his daughter. Sometimes Rachel forgot that most powerful weapon she held in her arsenal. But no more.

She finally had a plan she was certain would work.

It was a simple enough plan. She didn't know why she hadn't thought of it before tonight. She was so excited, she could scarcely breathe. With shaking hands, she smoothed the wrinkles from her wrapper, adjusted the lace ruffling the neckline.

The candle in the wall sconce to her left sputtered and popped, the sound startling Rachel through the silence. She pushed away from the wall and peeked around the corner.

The corridor was empty.

She took a deep breath, then headed for his room.

It might have been minutes, or it could have been hours before Richard finally drifted off to sleep. Even then, he hovered on the edge of awareness, his thoughts of Leah teasing his senses, bringing a shiver to his skin, as if her soft hands were pulling his shirt from his breeches, as if her palms were smoothing over his shoulders, touching his back, as if the bed were dipping and she were pushing her body up close against his.

But something was dreadfully wrong.

These hands were cold, and the scent attacking his nose was not roses but . . . lavender water?

This was not a dream.

This was his nightmare, come back to haunt him.

He opened his eyes. "Rachel."

Chapter Twenty-Eight

She smiled up at him, a sensuous lifting of her lips, a languorous flutter of her lashes, a sultry whisper as she murmured, "Richard, it has been so long. Kiss me, my darling."

Perhaps he had imbibed too much. Perhaps he had finally slid into madness. Or perhaps he was simply weary of fighting his baser instincts, weary of her torments and lies.

Whatever the reason, he slid his hand up the length of her arm, then over her shoulder. She moaned and lifted her chin, her palm cupping the back of his neck, urging him to kiss her.

He fanned his fingers wide, wrapped them around her throat, then slowly, oh, so exquisitely slowly, he started to squeeze.

She stared at him through wide, defiant eyes, as if daring him to do it. It would be so easy. In a matter of minutes, he could be free of her forever. He wanted it so badly, had wanted it for so long. She was the plague of his life and he was sick unto death of her and her torments. If it weren't for her trickery, he would never have betrayed Eric. If it weren't for her maliciousness, he would never have lost Leah.

His skin grew cold, his breathing harsh. As he stared into the eyes of the woman who had made his life a misery for so long, a stunning revelation hit Richard with ruthless brutality, as if a wall crumbled, revealing a part of himself he had never seen.

Rachel was evil, there was no doubt about that, but it was not her fault that he had lost Leah. It was his own fear that had driven Leah away. Fear that she would reject him once she learned his secrets. Fear that he would come to love her.

Love made a man vulnerable. Love hurt.

So he had pushed her away, but it hadn't stopped the pain, because it was too late. He already loved her.

With a growl, he shoved Rachel off the bed before he added murder to the litany of his sins. "Get out of here—and never think to try this again. Or next time, I *will* kill you."

She grabbed her dressing gown from the floor.

As she flew from the room, Richard stumbled to his feet, collapsed onto a chair near the hearth. He buried his face in his hands. Good God, how he loved her. With every breath he drew, with every beat of his heart, he ached for the comfort only Leah could give. She was everything that was good and decent in his life and out of fear, he had sent her away.

His breathing grew ragged, his chest ached, as his fears lashed out at him, stripping his will, urging him back into the darkness, but he thrust them away. So what if Rachel told the world that Alison was his daughter? He loved Alison more than life itself and longed to claim her for his own. Yes, it would cause a scandal, but they would survive. Life would go on, perhaps even better than before, once the truth came out.

And he had not betrayed his brother. Never in a conscious word or deed had he betrayed his brother.

His guilt and shame had nearly destroyed him, but now he could see the truth. Eric had understood that, had loved him until the end. Never had he blamed Richard, nor condemned him in any way. He'd even taken Alison into his heart and claimed her as his own to protect her from the world.

A vision of Leah's lovely face rose before his eyes and Richard saw the truth with stunning clarity. He could tell her everything. About Eric. About Rachel. Even about Alison, and she would understand. Because she loved him.

And she loved Alison. She would never condemn the child, nor love her any less because she was Richard's natural daughter.

Why had it taken him so long to understand? Why had he made their lives so miserable? Wasted so much time?

He rose from the chair, staggered into his room, rang for his valet. New fears struck out at him, weakened his will, warned him it was too late, but he would not listen.

Only one thing remained to be done.

To go to Cornwall and reclaim his wife.

"Those clouds look sure to rain, Your Grace. Perhaps we should return to the house."

"In a moment, Marielle," Leah said, watching a falcon fly against the wind, its high-pitched kaw frightening the smaller birds from their nests amongst the cliffs.

The violent churning of the waves crashing into the rocks below sent a foamy spray high over the ledge. The salt-spiced air tasted tangy in her mouth.

The rising wind whipped her hair from its pins, and she laughed. She slipped her hands inside her cloak, rubbed her palms over her belly, and smiled as she felt the rolling movement of her babe beneath her skin. She had no clear memories of her journey into Cornwall, only vague impressions of long, tedious days, followed by long, tedious nights. The scenery along the route should have entranced her, but she passed it by without notice, a nondescript blur in her misery.

At first, she had felt as if she'd died inside while her body continued to live. Left with no choice, she rose every day, donned her dress, combed her hair, and went through the motions of her day. But as one month melted into two, and two dissolved into three, a miracle happened. Her child moved within her.

At first, it felt as wispy as effervescent bubbles lightly tickling her skin, but with each passing day, the movement grew stronger as she grew bigger, filling her with joy and hope for the future. Now she had grown too big and bulky to hazard the most treacherous heights of the cliffs, but she loved to sit on this lower ledge and watch the sea batter the shore.

The dark, churning water was so drugging, so intense, it was like staring into Richard's eyes.

Her skin grew warm despite the brisk November wind as shame swept in along with her memories of their last confrontation.

She could not comprehend what had possessed her to give in to Rachel's malicious taunting, to issue her husband an ultimatum he was bound to reject. She truly hadn't believed any of Rachel's words. She knew Richard despised his sister-in-law with a passion she was only now beginning to understand.

But he was a proud and forceful man. His response had stemmed from wounded pride and male ego. No one was going to tell him how to live his life, including his wife. So she'd found herself banished to the furthermost recesses of Cornwall.

God, how she missed him, but she had her pride, too.

Her stubborn will refused to allow her to write to him, to plead for forgiveness, to beg to come home. But stubborn will and stupid pride made for cold and lonely company when she was alone in her bed with only her memories to sustain her.

Perhaps he was right. Perhaps she had merely latched on to Rachel as a convenient excuse when what she'd really wanted, truly wanted, was his total surrender. His avowal of love.

Whatever the reason, she knew she had to write Richard soon.

He had a right to know he was about to become a father, but every time she picked up her pen, fear stayed her hand, convinced her she could wait until tomorrow, and for the to-morrow after that, and so her letter remained unwritten.

She tried not to think of where he was, of what he was doing, of with whom he was passing his time. Such torturous thoughts only made her pulse race, her heart beat madly, and she needed to remain calm for her babe.

Rachel's insidious words rose unbidden to Leah's mind.

Once Richard gets his heir on you, his secrets will be safe . . . he will cast you aside . . . he will leave you. . . .

As much as her common sense told Leah that Rachel was a liar who had bent the truth to fit her own designs, her vicious words preyed on Leah's deepest insecurities. While fear of losing Richard tormented Leah day and night, she could not allow her child to be used to satisfy her father's evil schemes.

With a sigh, she pulled her fur-lined cloak tighter about her neck. Either way, she had to write to Richard soon.

She had to tell him about the babe.

Leah pushed herself up from her seat upon the rocks, then linked her arm through her maid's. They followed the winding path back to the house, their pace slowed by damp patches of slippery moss growing atop the rocks.

The butler met them at the door. "You have a visitor, Your Grace."

Leah smiled. "A visitor? How mysterious, Harris. Is it the vicar? I thought we weren't meeting until tomorrow."

"Leah." A voice, low and deep and achingly familiar, coming from the shadows in the crimson drawing room.

A form materialized in the doorway, slowly took the shape of a man. Broad shoulders encased in burgundy wool. Long legs wrapped in buff pantaloons, cut so exquisitely, every muscle from shin to thigh was outlined in precise detail. He leaned one hand against the jamb. The other, he held stiff by his side.

"Richard." She was not sure if she said the word, or if she even breathed. She clutched her cloak at the neck.

The thick, fur-lined wool covered her body from shoulder to toe and provided some protection from the chill shivering through her bones. Her feet felt frozen to the marble floor while her stunned brain registered the fact that he was well and truly here, and by the hard line of his jaw and the rigid slant of his eyes, he was none too pleased about it.

She had often fantasized about seeing him again. She had imagined herself on her knees, begging his forgiveness for her rash words. She had imagined him on his knees, begging *her* forgiveness for sending her away. But never had she imagined he would still be angry.

What if he wanted to put an end to their marriage?

For the sake of her babe, Leah knew she had to control her wild emotions, but her racing heart sent her blood rushing through her veins. A spasm clenched her belly, wrapped around her spine until she nearly doubled over from the pain, but she drew a deep breath, gathered the skirts of her cloak and dress into her hands and walked up the stairs with as much dignity as she could manage. She knew he followed because she could hear his boot heels on the marble steps.

She could not let him see how vulnerable she was. She could not let him see how much she still loved him.

With the wet weather and rutted roads, the journey from London had taken Richard over a sennight. He'd had time aplenty to rehearse what he wanted to say, what he *needed* to say.

Now that the moment was here, he could not remember a word.

She walked to the windows, as if needing to put distance between them. He stood by the fire, hands clutched behind his back to keep from pulling her into his arms.

Her cheeks were flushed, her hair windswept and curling

wildly around her face. Never had she appeared more beautiful, or more vulnerable. He wanted to drag her into his arms and shout out his love, but his tongue felt thick and swollen and wouldn't form the words. Her eyes, which had gleamed as she'd greeted Harris, had turned dull and flat when she realized Richard had arrived. The crushing sensation in the center of his chest grew heavier still.

"You look . . . well," he said, then silently cursed the sudden nervousness that had him stammering like a child.

Her eyes were wide, her gaze shifting away, then coming back to meet his, as if she were afraid. She clutched her hands to her throat, her cheeks suddenly pale against the dark fur of her cloak. "Why are you here?" she asked, her voice soft, choked.

He took a step toward her, as if pulled by an invisible hand. He shook with his need to touch her, to draw her into his arms, to bury his lips against her hair.

"I have come here for you," he said, though the words held no hint of the emotions clenching his gut.

Her chin titled down, her brows drew together, as she tried to discern his meaning. Her eyes brimming with moisture, she opened her mouth, as if to speak, but he held up his hand.

"Please, do not." He pushed his fingers through his hair, an awkward, stumbling clod out to win his lady's heart, a lady who must surely hate him now. "Please, listen to what I have come here to say."

He crossed the room, took her hand in his. Her skin felt cold, fragile against his palm. He heard her sharp gasp, watched confusion and fear cloud her expression.

She pulled her hand from his grasp, laced her fingers at her waist, as if to keep him from reaching for her again, as if his touch caused her pain.

A fist-sized knot formed at the base of his throat, choking him. He pulled off his cravat, dropped it to the floor.

"I know I have wronged you," he finally managed. "I know

I have hurt you, but I have come here to ask—no, to plead your forgiveness. And to beg you, please, take me back. Flawed that I am, it is all I can offer you."

He watched her eyes fill with shimmering tears.

Desperately, he searched for the words. He knew he could hold nothing back, even if it meant baring his soul before her until he stood naked beneath her gaze. The time for half-truths was past. "You are God's gift to this sinner, and even though I do not deserve you, I will never give you up. I have lived in darkness for so long, it took me time to understand. I need you, Leah. I want you beside me every day for the rest of my life. But most of all . . ."

He raised his hand, palm up. "Leah, I love you."

Eyes shut, breath locked in his throat, he waited, the silence in the room agonizing in its intensity.

A heartbeat passed. Then another. Each painful thump sent a trembling through his hand as he waited. He was aware of her wispy, uneven breathing, her shuddering sigh, then the soft, tingling slide of her palm covering his.

He groaned as he dragged her into his arms. His thoughts scattered, his breath hitched. He dropped to his knees, flung open the folds of her mantle.

"Oh . . . my . . . God."

Chapter Twenty-Nine

"Oh, my, God," he said again, because he could think of nothing else to say. His brain had stopped working as he knelt before her and stared at her belly thrusting against her paisley frock, her big, round belly, heavy with his child.

His breath rushed from his lungs, and he realized he had forgotten to breathe. No wonder she'd seemed so afraid.

He surged to his feet, nearly lost his balance as his blood rushed from his head. "Why did you not tell me?"

She pressed her fist to her lips, her hand shaking as badly as his legs.

The swelling in his throat grew larger until he thought he might choke. "You should have told me."

"I wanted to tell you. I tried—" She choked on a sob, but she lifted her chin, faced him with her unwavering gaze, wet with her tears. "I searched the house for you. You were in the conservatory with Rachel. After you left, Rachel told me of my father's perfidy. I couldn't tell you, then. I could not let my babe be used as a weapon between you and my father . . ."

Her voice dropped so low he had to strain to hear her words. "I could not ask you to let me stay, knowing how you must despise me."

"I did not bed you because of my bargain with your father,"

he ground out through his teeth, his guilt and his anguish churning a hole in his stomach. "If you believe nothing else I tell you, please believe this. From the first moment I met you. You were a beacon of light in my black world, and I wanted you."

Like an opium eater, he could not get enough.

He would never get enough. He shook from the power she held over him, a power he'd never thought to yield to another, but he knew he was safe in her hands. Still, he had to make her understand. "I have never despised you, never wanted you to leave. Leah, I love you."

"Then why did you send me away?"

He brushed his knuckles over her cheeks, stroked her tears with his thumbs. "What did Rachel tell you?"

"That you love her. That you have always loved her. That you would have wed her if not for my father. And you admitted my father forced you to marry me. I knew it from the start, you know. Oh, not exactly what he had done, but that he had done something. Why else would a man like you ever think to wed someone like me? Please tell me, Richard. I have a right to know. What weapon did my father use?"

He knew a greater fear, then, than he had ever known in his life. He wanted to lie, but he would have no more secrets between them. Their entire future rested on this moment.

The moment he had dreaded. The moment of truth.

"Alison is not my niece," he said. "She is my daughter."

My daughter. It was the first time he'd spoken the words aloud. Such sweet words that caused him so much pain.

Leah buried her face in her hands. Her shoulders shook from suppressing her tears. His chest grew tight, and tighter still, as if steel bands were wrapped round his ribs.

Then she lowered her hands, lifted her gaze to Richard's, the amber streaks glimmering within her tears. "How can you say that you love me? That my father used that precious little girl to gain his own ends is despicable. It is unspeakable. How you must hate me," she sobbed and spun away.

The pale light from the gathering storm cast harsh angles over her face, the lines of pain streaking away from her eyes. The disgust trembling in her voice, aimed not at him, but at her father? Dare he hope?

He walked up behind her, so close he could feel the rise and fall of her breathing. When she didn't object, he slid his arms around her waist, cradled her back against his chest, rested his cheek against her hair, inhaled the sweet familiar scent of roses that had haunted his dreams.

"I have never blamed you," he said against her ear. "Or held you responsible for your father's misdeeds. I told you once, I wanted to hate you. I admitted it. But I could not. You were a breath of fresh air in my rank life, and I was afraid. Because I knew, right from the start, I knew I could love you. God knows, I tried not to." He smoothed her hair from her brow. "Leah, I love you."

She turned her head until her cheek rested against his shoulder, until he could not see her features, save for her reflection in the windows. "How can that be true? After what my father did to you, how can that be true?"

"You don't seem shocked that Alison is my daughter. Did Rachel tell you?"

She shook her head. "There is a lovely portrait of your brother in the long gallery in this house. The moment I saw it, I knew she could not be his. I do not know why it took me so long. After all, she looks just like you."

"Do you not want to know how I came to have a child by my brother's wife?"

"Did you love her very much?"

He released his grip on her, stalked to the hearth, ground his fist against the marble chimney piece. "No. I thought I did. When we were young. But I have since come to realize that I loved the dream she spun for me. I had planned to make her my wife. Of course, that was before she married my brother."

The fire was dying. He knelt and tossed a log on the flames, sending a flurry of sparks up the flue. "So I joined the army. After Waterloo, they had a celebration to welcome me home. Feasting, drinking, and the like. I did a *lot* of drinking. So much so that I found myself naked upon my bed. I don't even know how I got there. The next thing I knew, there was a woman beneath me. I thought I was dreaming."

He sucked in a searing breath. "I thought it was a dream. Until she whispered my name. Then I knew. But my nightmare had just begun." He pressed the heels of his hands against his eyes, but nothing could stop the anguish that wracked his body. Nothing could stop the vision that pounded his brain.

"I heard my door open. I heard Eric's voice. And I saw his face when he realized the woman beneath me was his wife. I will never forget the look on his face."

"What happened?" Leah whispered.

"Nine months later my daughter was born. Eric never denied her. Geoffrey says he treated her as if she were his own. I should have been grateful for that, but I was living in hell. Knowing I had betrayed my brother. Knowing I had a daughter I couldn't see, couldn't touch, couldn't hold."

Richard met Leah's gaze, shimmering with unshed tears. He wanted to lay his head against her breast, but he was afraid to touch her, afraid he would lose the weak grip he had on his control. "I never even saw her until she was four years old. Oh, sometimes I would watch her from a distance, when her nurse took her to the park. But I couldn't go home. I couldn't face my brother, knowing I had betrayed him. Then Eric died."

Christ, his eyes felt hot and wet, as if he might weep. He rubbed his hands over his face. "My daughter—my sweet, beautiful, innocent daughter—lives with me, in my house, and I can never claim her for my own."

His breathing grew harsh, his skin too tight from the tension hardening his muscles. He prowled the room. "As if all that weren't bad enough, I robbed you of your innocence, kept you from marrying the man—" God, he could not even put it into words. He ground his teeth. ". . . the man you loved, merely to cover my sins. And then I sent you to have my child, alone and unprotected. I am as villainous as your father."

He closed his eyes, dragged his hands down his face. He knew she approached. He could hear her soft footsteps pattering across the rug, but he could not bring himself to meet her gaze. He felt exposed, vulnerable, his deepest sins revealed.

"I have loved you for the longest time," she said, fluttering her fingertips along his cheek.

His fears must have shown in his eyes as he met her gaze, for she nodded. She stroked her hands over his shoulders, gave a soft, self-deprecating laugh. "And I wanted to wed you. Truly, I did. How could I not, when you swept into my life with your demon-dark eyes and your too-hungry kisses that swept all thoughts of any other man out of my mind?"

Her tone was teasing, but her smile faltered. "I think, at first, it was infatuation. I was drawn to you from the moment we met. You are so handsome, so forceful, so strong. How could I resist falling in love with you? Then I convinced myself that I must love you because of the intimacies of our marriage bed. But those are callow reasons, and I am ashamed. Now I know the man you are, the sacrifices you have made . . . and I am the one not worthy of your love."

She dammed his protests with her fingertips. "Yet you say you love me, and I thank God for the gift He's granted me. I thank God for the gift of your love."

Richard dragged her into his arms. Her tears splashed

against his cheeks, mingled with his own, while his tongue mingled with hers. He dragged his mouth along her jaw.

"I love you," he groaned, the words made all the sweeter by the taste of her breath upon his lips, then her whispered response, "And I love you."

He slid her mantle from her shoulders, slowly worked the ribbons that secured her gown beneath her breasts.

She captured his hand, but her gaze shifted to the wall behind his back. "I have grown so large. I will displease you."

He placed two fingers against her lips. "I thought you understood, but I guess I haven't made myself perfectly clear. I have always thought you beautiful, but I do not love you for your face, or your body, or your hair. I love the person you are, the beauty inside you. You carry my child in your womb. And I want to see you. All of you."

Holding her gaze with his, he returned his hands to the ribbons of her gown. His fingers trembled as he lifted the frock away from her shoulders and let it slide to the floor, sending her soft cotton shift along with it. He had never seen a pregnant woman before. He held his breath, swallowed past the knot in his throat, then dropped his gaze.

Her stomach was round and high beneath her breasts. Her breasts were swollen, her nipples huge. A ripple rolled across her skin. His gaze shot to hers and she smiled, took his hand, and placed his palm flat against her skin, until he felt it.

A firm, swift kick. He laughed as he dropped to his knees, reverently ran his hands over her belly.

"Our child," he whispered as he worshipped her with his hands and mouth.

She wrapped her fingers in his hair as he met her gaze.

"Thank you, for the gift you bear me, here in your womb." He kissed her belly, then pushed to his feet, brought his lips within a whisper of hers. "Thank you for loving me."

He swept her into his arms, surprised at her lightness

despite the burden of his child nestled within her. He gently placed her on the bed. She leaned up on her elbows.

Her gaze never left his hands as he removed his cravat, shrugged out of his waistcoat, peeled away his shirt. He groaned and shoved his breeches to the floor. Her eyes darkening, she stared at his rigid shaft as he came down on the bed beside her. Her drew her hand to his chest. "Touch me. Please, touch me."

He sucked in his breath as she ran her fingers through the thick mat of black hair covering his chest, her touch tantalizingly soft and more erotic than anything that had come before. All the barriers were down. All the secrets told.

A lifetime of love beckoned him home.

He pushed her back against the pillows, moved his mouth to her throat, drank the sweet taste of her skin. She gripped his shoulders, her moan of pleasure bringing him too close to the edge. It had been so long, too damn long since he had touched her. He wanted to make it last, but he was nearly undone.

He trailed a lazy path to her breasts, drew one dusky peak into his mouth as his hands wrapped around her flesh, amazed at the changes in her body. She was always beautiful, but now she was lush and glowing, radiant in her pleasure.

He gazed up at her flushed face and he smiled. "Soon our child will suckle at your breast."

"You are a wonderful father to Alison," she said. She ran her fingers through his hair, pushing the fringe back from his eyes. Her voice came out low, trembling with emotion, with admiration, with need. "I know our child will be blessed."

A father. The idea had yet to fully penetrate his senses. He was going to be a father again, only this time, there was no shame in the knowledge. No aching betrayal. No desperate longing for a child he could never claim.

There was only love. Only joy.

Then he thrust all thoughts of the child from his mind, brought his mouth to her thighs. He licked and nibbled his way down the length of her leg, pausing at the underside of her knee, laughing when she shivered as he slid her silk stockings down to her ankles, as he journeyed ever lower.

He could feel his pulse pounding, his heart racing, his sex straining, as he retraced his path along her other leg.

Swift, hot, urgent need sent his shoulders between her knees, his lips searching through her soft curls, his tongue tasting her arousal, his fingers joining his tongue, stroking, laving, until she convulsed against him, until she cried out her sweet words, "I love you."

He pulled her into his arms, cradled her against his chest, breathed deeply to ease his thundering heart.

"I want to please you," she said, her voice sultry and low, her eyes glazed, her hair spilling erotically over his chest.

Her breath fluttered over his still burning skin. "You cannot please me any more than you already have—"

Her hand circled his erection, fingertips lightly stroking over the sensitive tip, then down to the base. His skin coiled tightly with each tentative stroke. All hope of protest slipped from his mind. She did not need him to teach her the tempo, the rhythm, the tension, she learned by his grunts and moans.

She destroyed his control. He wanted to spread her legs wide, lift her thighs over his hips, and drive himself deep inside her body, wanted her sheathing him when he came, but he feared hurting the babe. Lost to sensation, to want, to need, to love, he shoved his fingers through her soft hair, waiting until his climax was nearly upon him before dragging her lips to his. "I love you."

Chapter Thirty

Rachel was travel weary, covered with dust, her arms and legs aching from long days spent in a jostling carriage. The last thing she wanted was to see the man she loved fondling his wife in the breakfast room of Wexton Manor. The sound of lip-sucking kisses seemed incongruous amidst the scents of scones and clotted cream. He must be out of his mind!

She wished she had a whip. She would strip the skin from his backside until he came to his senses—and that was before he stepped away from his wife. Leah's loosely flowing woolen frock could not hide the advanced state of her swollen belly.

The bile rising in Rachel's throat nearly choked her. The air around her grew so cold, as if the windows were thrown open to the wind. Even the breath within her lungs seemed frozen.

She started to shake, but she needed time to think.

So she gritted her teeth, whipped on a smile, and walked with quiet dignity into the room. "We have found you at last."

The color drained from Leah's face until her cheeks were as pale as the frost dusting the windows. She was afraid, and well she should be. Richard wasn't afraid, though. His narrow-eyed glare could melt the frozen ground.

"Come make your curtsy to your uncle," Rachel called over

her shoulder as she untied her bonnet, which she handed to a footman, along with her fur muff and wrinkled blue cloak.

Clattering footsteps echoed out in the entry before Alison came charging into the room, her nurse racing to keep up with her. Richard caught Alison against his chest. Her gay laughter mingled with his as he swung her high in the air, her wool cloak swinging out around her feet.

He set the child down in front of his wife. "Say good morning to your Aunt Leah."

Rachel waited in breathless anticipation for Alison to toss hate-filled words at Leah, as she had back at the house. When her daughter rushed into Leah's arms, exchanged whispered words of love and apology, Rachel bit back a scream.

Not only was that harlot scheming to steal her man, she was scheming to steal her daughter too. Rachel would not let her win, but she needed a plan. Her last attempt had been a disaster. She had believed all she needed was to remind Richard of the passion that had raged between them, so she had slipped into his bed. She should never have done that, she could see that now. Not until he was ready to accept her love, to admit that he loved her still. But the temptation had been too hard to resist. She had wanted him so badly and for so long. Before she could see him again, he had fled Town to escape her. Now this!

What could she do? He was far too noble to abandon his wife while she was heavy with his child. Even after the birth, the child's presence would connect them for life.

If all that weren't bad enough, they were stuck on the coast of Cornwall, with its windswept cliffs, its slate gray sky, its distance from London, with nothing to distract him, no society worth mentioning, no business to take him away from his wife.

"Richard, this child is hot," Leah said, her lips pressed up against Alison's brow.

He touched the back of his hand to Alison's cheek. "Mrs. Parrish, Lady Alison is ill. Did you fail to notice?"

"No, sir. I told Her Grace we ought not to travel."

"See that the physician is sent for, at once." He waited until the servant carried Alison from the room before approaching Rachel. She had to lock her knees to keep from retreating.

"I shall have your explanation for this stupidity."

She peeled off her gloves, forced a nonchalance into her tone. "It is a cold, Richard. Nothing more, nothing less. The child constantly has a cold. I cannot possibly wait for her to feel well every time I wish to travel."

"Then you should have left her in London with Geoffrey."

"Nonsense," Rachel sniffed. "Alison goes wherever I go and she always will."

"Only at *my* discretion," he said, his voice, a low, dangerous growl as he leaned toward her. "If you ever do anything this foolish again, I will remove her from your care. And lest you think me less than serious, let me reassure you. I will start a scandal that will rock the *ton* for years to come, and *you* will never recover."

When he was standing this close, she could smell his skin and yearning churned within her stomach, made her legs weaken and her pulse beat a frantic rhythm in her ears. How long would he keep up this pretense? How long would he pretend not to care?

"You would not dare," she said, longing to lay her palm against his cheek, to lick her tongue over his lips, to stroke his manly flesh. She swallowed. "What of your precious Alison?"

"Nothing would give me greater pleasure than to shout to the world that she is mine. Then I would reap a double benefit, for I would be free of you as well."

Rachel glanced at Leah to see if she had heard his words, but the stupid chit had moved to the far end of the room, no doubt to give them privacy for their conversation.

She breathed deeply, uncertain how to reply, how far to

push him. She was saved from having to answer when Harris entered the room and strode to Richard's side. She moved a little closer, studied the warm sienna silk paper hanging the walls as if she'd never seen it before.

"Mr. Enderson of Bow Street has arrived, Your Grace. He awaits you in your office," the butler said.

"Excellent. I will join him shortly."

Though her heart was racing and her breathing shallow, Rachel drew upon years of training to maintain her serene countenance and even tone of voice. "Why do you need a runner?"

"A business matter," he said, but she could see the lie in his eyes. Why had he hired a Bow Street Runner? Had she made a mistake? Did he suspect? How could he? Too much time had passed.

No proof would exist at this late date.

He murmured something to his wife before leaving the room.

Rachel listened to his footsteps recede down the hall before approaching Leah, who was watching Rachel through placid eyes, seemingly unaware of her danger.

She folded her arms across the shelf of her distended belly.

Rachel followed the movement, then dragged her gaze to the mullioned windows, to the view of the lawn sloping down toward the trees. Anything to keep her thoughts off the child. "So, you have reconciled with your husband, have you? Did he happen to mention—"

"Stop," Leah said, holding up one hand. "If you think to shock me by blurting out that Alison is Richard's daughter, save yourself the trouble. I know the sordid story, and you know, I pity you. So desperate for the man you threw away, you had to climb into his bed when he was insensible from drink just to have him. You ruined his life, and you shamed his brother."

She pities me? Rachel almost laughed, the stupid fool. "We have been together these few months past. Did he tell you that?"

Rachel leaned toward Leah, lowered her voice. "No, I see he did not. It was me he wanted and me he had. He was hot and heavy and huge. He took me and took me, in *your* bed in the London house." She looked pointedly at Leah's swollen belly. "If he hadn't learned of your conception, we would be together still. It seems he won his bargain with your father, after all."

Leah shook her head. "I honestly feel sorry for you."

"Save your pity for yourself," Rachel said. "It's me he loves and he always will. We share a past. We share a history."

Leah smiled. "Do you want to know the funny thing about the past, Rachel? It is over. Finished. Dead. It is the present and future that have yet to be written. You may share a history with Richard . . ." She ran her hand over her belly. "But we are his future."

The nerve of the insolent chit!

Rachel glanced at the sidebar, saw the carving knife resting on the breadboard. Her fingers itched to grab it, to plunge it over and over again in the middle of Leah's overgrown stomach.

She resisted the urge. She needed to think!

And then Richard was back. He ignored Rachel as he crossed to Leah's side, took her hands in his, pressed them to his lips.

"Something has come up," he said. "I must leave."

She clutched his fingers. "Is it Geoffrey? Is he well?"

He kissed the back of her hands, lingering over her knuckles. Rachel thought she might retch.

"It is nothing for you to worry about, my love. Merely a business matter. Still, I would rest easier if I could delay my departure until Alison recovers from her cold."

"Do not worry about Alison," Leah said. "I shall see she is cared for."

"You forget she has a mother to see to her needs," Rachel

said with dripping sweetness. "Do go on, Richard. You know I would never let anything happen to your daughter."

He did not respond to her taunt. Instead, he gathered his wife in his arms and gave her a kiss so fierce and so hot, Rachel wanted to dump the water pitcher over his head.

Unable to bear the sight of the man she loved in another woman's arms, but determined not to show it, Rachel turned and walked with icy dignity from the room.

"Uncle Richard is home," Alison said, running into the crimson drawing room.

Her cheeks were red from trotting down the stairs. Her hair springing free from her plaits, she grabbed the stitchery from Leah's hands and tugged until Leah stood and accompanied her to the windows. She pointed down the long tree-lined drive. A moment later, the coach came into view.

"See, there. I told you."

"Indeed, you did." Leah laughed as she slipped her arm around Alison's shoulders, but her smile quickly died as a spasm clenched her womb. She breathed deeply, careful not to let her discomfort show on her features. She wiped her hand across her brow, surprised to find it damp with perspiration.

She had thought she would have another month to prepare, but the midwife had told her this morning she didn't think this babe would wait that long, given the position of the child so low in the belly, and the sporadic pains plaguing Leah's back.

The woman had assured her there was nothing to fear, that many babes came a few weeks early, and many came a few weeks late. Leah didn't want to admit it, but she was afraid.

She was glad Richard was back. Two long weeks had passed since he had left and Leah had begun to fear he would miss the birthing. She wanted him with her when her time came.

Not that he could help her, but just knowing he was near would be a comfort to her. She understood him so well now. She ached for his lonely childhood with his cold and distant parents. She ached for the bitter betrayal he had suffered at the hands of the woman he had loved. But most of all, she ached for his anguish over his unwitting betrayal of his brother and the guilt with which he had tortured himself for years.

Rachel marched into the room. She cast a glare at Leah as she stalked to the window, but she said nothing.

What vicious attack was she planning now?

From this distance, Leah could hear no sound as the carriage rolled over the frozen ground and came to a stop. A footman jumped off the box and opened the door, then Richard stepped out, his features indistinguishable beneath his beaver hat and with the collar of his greatcoat turned up against the cold. Puffs of steam from his breath floated away on the wind.

"It is him," Alison shouted. "May I go out? Please?"

"Stop kicking up a fuss and go back to the nursery," Rachel said. "Why are you always running loose? Where is that wretched nurse?" She turned her shrewd gaze on Leah. "Where do you think he has been? Or, more importantly, with whom?"

Leah had discovered the best method of dealing with Rachel was simply to ignore her. She removed the plaits from Alison's tousled hair, ran her fingers through the soft strands, letting the curls flow over her shoulders. "Now you look all grown up for when you greet your Uncle Richard."

Once on the ground, Richard turned and held up his hand to aid someone inside the carriage. A slim, gloved hand appeared, followed by a daintily booted foot. The wind gusting around the house pushed the woman and she slipped, her foot skidding off the step. Richard grasped her waist to steady her,

then eased her to the ground. Her hood fell back, revealing a
stunning young lady with flaming red hair and ivory skin.

Rachel snickered. Before she could launch her venomous
attack, Leah took Alison's hand in hers and led her from the
room. By the time they reached the entry, Richard was standing in the hallway, speaking softly to the woman beside him.

Alison launched herself at his leg in her customary greeting. He laughed as he kissed her, then motioned Leah forward, a mysterious smile upon his lips.

From a distance, the young woman had appeared lovely,
but up close she was stunning. She had ivory skin and wide-
set eyes, blue as cornflowers with a deeper blue circling the
edges and silver streaks glinting like diamonds near the dark
centers, a startling contrast to her gingered hair.

A momentary twinge of jealousy caused Leah's steps to
falter, but she pushed aside the foolish thought. She had faith
in her husband. She did. She approached him at a slightly
more dignified pace than Alison's. "Welcome home."

He set Alison on her feet. His mouth tilted in a somber
smile. "Leah, there is someone I would like you to meet."

When she was a few paces away from him, he stepped
aside.

Next to the woman, gripping her hand, was a young boy.
He had sandy hair and dimpled cheeks, but it was his eyes
that stopped Leah's breath, that made her heart feel as if it had
ceased beating, the gray-green eyes of her sister.

She pressed her hand to her throat.

"Leah," Richard said softly. "May I present to you Matthew
Jamison, son of Catherine Jamison."

Chapter Thirty-One

Leah was vaguely aware of time moving forward, of movement around her, of Richard's hand on her elbow as she dropped to her knees. She heard words being spoken, though she understood naught of what was said. It was as if she were standing out on the cliffs, the gusting wind blocking all sound save for the deafening waves thrashing the rocks below.

All she could see was this child. Her sister's child, staring back at her through Catherine's eyes, his dusty hair covering his pallid brow. His skeleton suit clinging to his too-thin chest. He hid his face in the skirts of the woman beside him. After a few moments, he peeked at Leah from behind the cloth. "Why are you crying?"

"Am I?" She swiped her hands over her cheeks, amazed to find moisture clinging to her fingertips. She imagined she looked truly frightful. She was a stranger to him after all.

She took a deep breath to calm her emotions. "I am just so very happy to meet you. I have wanted to meet you for ever so long."

She crushed her fists against her thighs to keep from grabbing his arms and dragging him to her chest. She wanted to run her hands over his shoulders, to smooth his damp hair from his brow. Anything to prove he was well and truly here, and not a dream.

"You look like my mum."

Leah nodded. "I am your mother's sister. I am your aunt."

"My mum's dead," he said, twisting his hands in the nurse's skirts. The woman reached down, smoothed her hand over his back.

Leah closed her eyes. She had long suspected, but to finally hear her worst fears confirmed sent a stabbing pain through her chest. A tingling numbness spread over her fingers and toes. She was aware of Richard kneeling beside her, of his hand stroking soothing circles over her back.

"I did not know that," she said, stretching out her arms. She needed to touch this child. Her sister's child. "Do you think you give me a hug?"

She held her breath as he stared at her through somber, shadowed eyes. Then he took a step toward her and she yanked him into her arms. She kissed his cheek, stroked his brow, memorized his scent of rough-and-tumble boy, gingerbread he must have eaten for breakfast, and the crisp winter air clinging to his clothes. She could hear Richard speaking to her, but she was afraid that this was a dream, that if she opened her eyes this child would be gone.

"Leah," he said, his deep voice rumbling near her ear. "Why don't you let Harris show our guests to their rooms? It has been a long journey, and I think young Matthew might like a snack, then a rest. What say you, young man? Are you hungry?"

Leah felt his head nod against her shoulder.

She gave him one final squeeze, then leaned back on her heels. "Run along then, Matthew."

Alison ran up to them. "Do not worry, Aunt Leah. I will share my toys with him. Uncle Richard says he is my cousin. I have never had a cousin before." She took Matthew's hand in hers. Chattering all the while, they followed Harris and the nurse up the stairs.

Rachel opened her mouth, as if she were about to speak, then she spun on her heels and flounced down the hall.

In her shock, Leah had forgotten Rachel was even in the room. She turned her cheek into Richard's chest, fingers clawing his waistcoat. Richard pulled her into his arms. Her shoulders shook, her silent tears soaked his cravat, and he held her as she wept.

The house was silent, the children long since tucked into their beds. Richard listened to the fire snapping in the hearth while relishing the simple pleasure of holding the woman he loved in his arms, her cheek resting against his shoulder, her hair spilling enticingly over his chest. The swell of her belly pressed against his side, but the child lay quiet.

Light from a single candle on the bedside table caught the amber in her eyes as she leaned up and kissed his jaw. "You are so wonderful, Richard. You have given me the greatest gift. However did you find him?"

He brought her knuckles to his lips. Her fingers trembled beneath his palm. "After you told me of your sister, I hired Bow Street Runners to search for her."

"But you never said a word."

"I did not want to raise your hopes." He traced his fingertips along the curve of her arm. "I had no notion if they would succeed in finding her after all these years."

Her sigh sent her breath fluttering over his chest.

"Do you know what happened to her? How she . . . died?"

If only some means existed to spare her this pain, but she deserved the truth. "For a time, she wandered about from place to place. She finally settled in Holdhan where she worked in a spinning factory."

"Holdhan?" She pushed herself up on her elbows, her eyes

glittering green shards of stained glass reflecting the turmoil of her emotions. "It was one of my father's factories, was it not? Do not bother to deny it, I see the answer in your eyes. He knew where she was all along, and he did nothing to help her. I don't know why I am so surprised, but I am."

He brushed his knuckles against her cheek, wiping away her tears. If only he could as easily soothe her aching heart. "She seems to have had a great many friends there. It may comfort you to know that she spoke of you often."

Leah tilted her face into his hand. "If you can tell me, I would like to know. When did she . . . die? How?"

"A year ago," Richard said quietly, his throat tightening. "Of a lung infection. I am told it is a fairly common illness among the factory workers."

She collapsed in his arms, buried her face against his neck. Her tears scorched his skin, clenched his heart. He knew only too well the anguish of losing a sibling. If only he could spare her this pain, take it into himself.

"I should like to go there to visit her grave—oh, dear God, she does have a grave, does she not?"

"She had a proper burial," Richard hastened to reassure her. "She rests in the parish churchyard. I will take you there after you have recovered from your lying in."

She was quiet for such a long time, the only sound her softly flowing breath, Richard thought she had fallen asleep.

"Who cared for Matthew after she died?" she whispered, her anguish all too apparent in the huskiness of her voice.

He sighed. There was no easy way to say it. Better just to spit it out. "He was in the parish poorhouse."

"Oh, God," she cried. "He is lucky to be alive."

"He was safe," Richard said firmly. "It was a clean, decent establishment. The children well-fed and properly clothed. And now he is here with you."

"Oh, Richard, I never thought I would meet him, or . . ."

"Shhh," he whispered. "Sleep now, my love. It has been a

trying day. We will speak of this again tomorrow." He wrapped
her in his arms and murmured soothing words until she slept.

He didn't know how he was going to tell her the rest. It was
such a complicated tale. But he decided he could wait a day
or two. Perhaps he was acting the coward, but he didn't care.
It would break her heart.

Leah stood at the salon window the next morning, watching the children play. Supervised by their nurses, they chased
each other up and down the garden paths, oblivious to the
winter wind or the black, billowing clouds sweeping across
the sky.

"She is beautiful," Rachel said, coming to stand beside her.
"With all that red hair. Much too beautiful to be a nursemaid.
Much too refined. Mark my words, Leah, all is not as it seems."

Leah clenched her jaw, but said nothing. Her head was
throbbing from lack of sleep, her dreams haunted by memories of her sister. Of the fights they had indulged over the
most foolish of things, of the secrets they had shared, of their
mutual grief at their mother's passing.

Now Catherine was dead, and Leah was left to grieve alone.

As she watched Matthew turn a somersault on the hard,
packed earth, thoughts of all Catherine would miss in her
son's life looped through Leah's mind. Kissing his scraped
knees. Soothing him after a nightmare. Welcoming him as he
brought home his bride. She pressed her fist to her lips. She
had to take care not to show her grief for fear of frightening
Catherine's son.

The rising wind kicked up tiny whirlwinds of dust. The
children marched toward the terrace just as the first raindrops
hit the glass. With a quick prayer that Rachel would not
follow, Leah brushed her hands down her skirts and hurried
to greet them as swiftly as her overgrown girth would allow.

"Did you know Lord Greydon arrived this morning?"

Rachel called after her, her voice echoing off the stuccoed ceiling.

Leah did not stop walking or give any indication she heard Rachel's words, though her breath caught in her throat.

She told herself his presence here meant nothing, but she did not believe it. On the rare occasions she had met Lord Greydon, he had stared at Leah with such relentless intensity, prickling sensations had shuddered over her skin.

Her stomach churning with sick premonition, she marched to the library. Voices raised in heated debate drifted through the wood. A momentary fear urged her to turn away, but she gave the door a swift push.

The conversation stopped mid-sentence as both men turned to stare at her. She did not look at Lord Greydon. She did not want to see his reaction or the expression on his face.

She saw only Richard as he strode toward her.

His dark eyes narrowed on her face. His jaw, rigid and tense as he took her elbow in his hand, confirmed her fears.

"Why is he here?"

"I sent for Greydon because I needed to speak with him." The touch of his hand was warm and familiar, his voice aching and low. "Why don't you wait for me in your rooms?"

She shook her head. "No. I want to know."

He tightened his grip, exerting a gentle pressure as he led her toward the door. "I would prefer to speak with you in private, *after* I finish my interview with Greydon."

"No." She dug her heels into the rug, pulled her arm from his grasp. "I know it involves Matthew. I want to know."

She grasped his hand. "Please, Richard, I want to know. I can bear no more secrets popping up to hurt me."

The dark fringe of his hair fell into his eyes as he gave a stiff nod, then he led her to a chair near the hearth.

The room seemed inordinately quiet, even the fire seemed subdued, dying in the grate. Leah was intensely aware of the rain hitting the windows, but she could not hear it.

All she could hear was the pounding of her heart.

Lord Greydon collapsed into a seat across from hers. She could see his long legs, encased in buff pantaloons, his elbows, swathed in green wool, leaning on his knees, the top of his head as he buried his face in his palms.

When he finally raised his red-rimmed gaze to hers, Leah silently screamed she did not want to know, could not bear to hear what he had to say.

Perspiration clung to his forehead. He started to speak, but the words came out garbled. He cleared his throat and began again. "I thought you were her, you know. The first time I saw you, I thought you were Catherine."

He closed his eyes, and Leah knew he was seeing Catherine in his mind. Her vision dimmed. She could not seem to draw in enough air. Richard tightened his grip on her hand.

"I met Catherine when I was staying with my uncle at Greydon Hall," Pierce finally said, his voice shuddering. "I saw her walking across a field, carrying a basket. She was so beautiful." He rubbed his eyes with the heels of his hands. "I didn't want to startle her by charging across the field on my horse. So I tied him to a tree, then chased after her on foot. I think, at first, she was frightened. She wouldn't talk to me, or tell me her name. But I was enchanted. I persisted and pursued her until she told me her name was Catherine Burton."

He raised his gaze to Leah's, his eyes as red as the logs burning in the grate. "Why did she lie about her name?"

Leah stared into the fire. She did not want to feel anything for this man, this seducer of her sister.

"My father—" A sob choked off her voice. "My father would not have wanted her to know you."

Pierce said nothing, but his chest hitched as he drew in his breath. "I went to that same field every day for a week, hoping to catch a glimpse of her. Just when I had given up hope of ever meeting her again, she appeared. She smiled, and I knew she was happy to see me."

"She used to help the vicar deliver parcels of food to the poor," Leah said, but Pierce didn't seem to hear her.

He stared out the windows, as if fascinated by the rain. "We talked for hours. She agreed to meet me the next day. After that, we met every day." He fixed Leah with a hard, disconcerting stare. "I did not use her. I did not cast her aside. I loved her. I wanted to wed her. I received an urgent summons from my mother. My father was very ill, not expected to live through the week. I went to our usual meeting spot—I waited, but she never came! I delayed leaving as long as I could, but I had to return home before it was too late."

"Of course you did," Richard said with quiet sympathy.

Leah closed her eyes. How cruel fate was. If not for his father's illness, Catherine might have married this man she had loved. If she had married him, she might still be alive.

"As it was, I barely made it," Pierce whispered. "My father died mere hours after I arrived. Then I had to see to Mother and her affairs. It was nigh onto two months before I could return. I went to all the surrounding villages, searching for Catherine Burton. No one knew her." He laughed, a sound as harsh and bitter as the wind driving the rain in from the ocean. "At least now I know why. Finally, some old codger pointed up the road and told me Miss Burton lived at Heallfrith Manor. He must have meant your aunt, but at the time I thought he meant Catherine."

Pierce clenched his shaking hands into fists. "I pounded on the door. When the butler answered, I demanded to speak with his master. Over and over, I called the man Mr. Burton. How he must have laughed at me, never bothering to correct my mistake. He was not pleased to see me, although he didn't seem surprised . . ."

Leah closed her eyes against the picture Pierce was painting of her father's cold-hearted cruelty.

"I told him I was in love with his daughter, that I wanted to wed her," Pierce said, his voice, a raw, aching wound. "Your father merely laughed, said Catherine wanted nothing to do with me, that she'd never tie herself to a nobody like me. I didn't believe him. I demanded to see her, but he said she'd left to marry another. He produced a note saying as much. Of course, now I realize it must not have been written in her hand."

Pierce pushed his fists into his knees. "What choice did I have? I left. Over the years, I convinced myself that I hated her. In truth, I never stopped loving her." He rubbed his hands over his face, but his tears returned faster than he could swipe them away. "I never saw her again. I never knew she loved me still. I never knew about our child. If only I had known—"

"And all that time," Leah said, her voice scraping over the rawness in her throat. "My father knew where she was, and he never said a word, never offered to help her."

An unbidden, but deep compassion for this man who had loved her sister so well brought words of comfort to her lips. Before she could speak, he went down on his knees and seized her hand.

"Your Grace . . . Leah . . . I want my son."

Chapter Thirty-Two

Leah pushed him aside and struggled to her feet.

"No," she said as she paced to the window. She stared at the trees in the distance, bending beneath the wind, blurred by the rain. Richard came up beside her, lifted his hands as if to draw her into his arms, but she could not show any weakness.

She backed away, turned to face Pierce, hardened her heart to the anguish in his eyes. She would not lose her nephew.

"He is my son," Pierce said, standing before her, his jaw rigid, his arms tightly clenched by his sides.

"So you say, but how do we know it is the truth and not some elaborate story you have woven—"

"Do you honestly think me a fool?" he said, his voice vicious and cutting. "Do you think I would come here to claim another man's son? A bastard at that?"

"Do not say that word!" Leah clutched her hands to her ears. She knew she needed to conquer her fear lest this monster take advantage of her weakness, but she was helpless and lost, sinking in a swamp of muddy confusion.

Only one thing was clear. She would not lose her nephew.

Richard pried her hands away from her ears, pressed them to his chest. She wanted to crawl into his arms and pretend this was a horrible dream, that any minute she would awaken and all would be well. "How can we be sure he is Matthew's father?"

"I saw the parish register," Richard said gently, his hands stroking soothingly over her arms. "His name is recorded as Matthew Pierce Daimont Jamison. Although she never claimed Pierce as the father, I think that is proof enough."

She glared at Pierce, who had stood quietly through this exchange, then turned back to Richard. Her pounding heart and growing fear confused her thoughts, shortened her breath. She started to shake as ugly suspicion reared its head. She could scarce give voice to the accusation. "Is this a conspiracy? Are the two of you plotting the best way to take him from me?"

"Leah, stop this at once," Richard said, his voice harsh.

For a wild moment she wondered if he might slap her. Perhaps he should. Perhaps that would clear the hysteria from her brain. Did she look as wild as she felt? As wild as the Cornish winds whipping the breakers into a frenzy?

"I do not want you to overset yourself," Richard said, gently, soothingly. "Think of the babe."

Leah nodded. He was right, of course. She took a deep breath, turned to face Pierce.

The rigid slant of his jaw, his dark brown eyes that burned with ruthless determination told her he would never give up.

Well, neither would she. She searched for a logical argument to dissuade him from this course.

"You cannot possibly wish to claim him," she finally said. "What would your future wife think?"

Pierce rolled his shoulders, as if brushing away a distasteful throught. "This has nothing to do with Julia."

"Of course it does. You would be asking her to raise a child you had with another woman. One born outside the bonds of wedlock. Do you think she will welcome him with open arms?"

"She will do as I say," he said through his teeth.

"But will she accept him?" A violent trembling raced through Leah. Her tears rose in her throat. "Will she love him as her own? Or will she resent his presence in her household?"

"She will do as I say."

"She will hate you!"

"I do not care if she hates me," Pierce said, his jaw rigid. He planted his feet hip-width apart. "It is a marriage of convenience, for her as well as for me. You, of all people, must understand that."

Leah sucked in a searing breath. She glared at Richard.

A guilty flush stained his cheeks, and she knew he had told Pierce the circumstances behind their marriage. That he could have discussed such intimate details with anyone, especially this scapegrace, was insufferable. Like a rabbit caught in a snare, she felt hopelessly trapped, but she would not yield.

She gave a scornful laugh. "Your reputation precedes you, my lord. You live in the brothels and spend your days hopelessly drunk. How are you to raise a child?"

"I may have turned to the stews," Pierce said quietly, his gaze never wavering from hers. "But it was in desperation. I thought I had lost the woman I loved for the lack of a title. I did not know the truth. I was bitter and angry and I have wallowed in that anger for five long years. But that is over."

He raised a shaking hand to Leah. "I do not know how to explain it, but I feel . . . redeemed. As if Catherine has reached out from beyond the grave to give this gift to me—to save me."

Unable to bear the naked truth in his eyes, Leah turned away. Pressing her fingertips against her brow, she shook her head. "You look at me and you see Catherine. Well, he looks at me and he sees her, too. He has been hurt so much in his short life. He has a family here that loves him. You cannot say that. You cannot guarantee your lady will love him. Oh, God—"

She covered her face with her hands.

Richard dragged her into his arms. She could hear his heart beating, hear the air moving in and out of his chest.

She clutched his shoulders as if she were drowning and he were her lifeline to safety, to sanity.

"Pierce, wait for me here." His voice rumbled beneath her ear, a soothing sound that cut through her pain and confusion.

He helped her to her room, eased her onto her bed. He arranged some pillows behind her back to relieve the pressure of her heavy stomach, then poured her a glass of brandy.

She drank it desperately, seeking the warmth of the potent liquid. He brushed her hair away from her face. His eyes were shadowed, his lips tight with tension as he sat on the edge of the bed and gathered her into his arms. She leaned back to look into his eyes. "Why did you not tell me any of this?"

"I intended to, but I thought I would have a few more days." He sighed, his warm breath brushing her ear. He kissed her brow, stroked her back. "I sent a missive to Pierce before I left Holdhan, but I did not think he would arrive so quickly. I should have known better. I am sorry you had learn the truth like that. I'm so damned sorry you had to go through that. I wanted to tell you in private."

"It was not your fault. I insisted. How foolish of me. I should always listen to you."

Richard cracked a weary smile. "Yes, you should. But I know that you won't." He pushed her back against the pillows, arranged her hair about her face. "If it comforts you at all, I have known Pierce for many years. He is a good man. He told you the truth. He loved your sister. He turned to the drink in despair."

"I heard the truth in his words." Leah plucked at the blankets, her heart thundering as loudly as the rain against the windows. "But I do not want to lose my nephew. Do you think Matthew belongs with him?"

Her stomach twisted as she waited for his answer.

"It is not a matter of what I think," he said, tracing his knuckles along her jaw. "It is a matter of what is best for the child. Under the law, a father has absolute authority over his children." He raised a hand to stifle her protests. "I know you do not like that, but that is the law. In this case, where they were not wed, I am not sure what the legalities are. But I do know this. Pierce is a good man. He will make a good father."

"But—"

He placed two fingertips against her lips. "Hush, and listen to me. Pierce is the first to admit he has not lived an admirable life, but he means to change. For the child, I hope he succeeds." He laced his fingers through hers. "You see, I know how he feels. It was not so long ago that I was living in the stews myself, wracked by guilt and bitterness. If Eric had not died, I would probably be in my grave by now. But I had to sober up. For Alison."

Leah closed her eyes as swift, merciless, shame swept through her. "Oh, Richard, I am so sorry."

"Whatever for?"

"For my selfishness. For—"

His lips against hers stole whatever protest she was about to make. His tongue swept in, his kiss all that was tender, a gentle stroking, a silent offer of his love.

He cradled her cheeks between his palms. "You have done nothing but try to protect your nephew, as you should. The point I wanted to make is that Pierce can change, too. He can reform. When he does, he will make an exemplary father."

She tried to look away, but his palm on her cheek forced her to meet his gaze. "But not yet, and I believe he recognizes this truth. And in his heart he knows the best place for Matthew is here with us. I also believe we cannot deny him a place in Matthew's life. 'Twould be cruel to do so. Wouldn't you agree?"

Leah wanted to deny him, but she nodded her head.

"I love you," he said, bringing his lips to hers in a kiss that was as reverent as it was soothing.

When he broke the kiss, she moaned her protest, but he rose from the bed and tucked the coverlet beneath her chin.

He stroked the back of his hand along her jaw. She thought he might kiss her again, but he turned and strode from the room.

The emotional upheaval of the last hour had drained all of Leah's energy, but she could not sleep. Her thoughts consumed her, dragging over the confrontation with Pierce, every word, every nuance, every heartbreaking detail.

The room was dark, the afternoon sun covered in hazy black clouds. The rain had slowed to a dull drizzle, the moisture trickling down the glass. A fire burning low in the grate cast dull shadows across the room. She clutched her coverlet beneath her chin. Her eyes stung, but not from tears.

Her door opened. Leah expected Richard, but it was Rachel.

Draped in a heavy woolen cloak of royal blue, the hood pulled low over her face, a matching muff clutched in her hand, she rushed to stand beside the bed. "Leah, I do not want to upset you, but you must get up. It is Matthew. He's missing."

"What?" Leah struggled to a sitting position. Her frock twisting around her gaping belly made it difficult for her to swing her legs over the edge of the mattress. "What do you mean, he is missing?"

Rachel wrapped one hand around Leah's arm and hauled her to her feet. "He overheard you and Richard discussing his future with Lord Greydon. Everyone heard you. You were quite loud about it. But that is beside the point. He thought you didn't want him, thought you meant to send him away. Now he's run off. I tried to stop him, but he was too swift. Poor child. He was weeping so disconsolately. He ran toward the cliffs."

The cliffs? Heart pounding, Leah stepped into her half-boots, didn't bother to lace them. She couldn't reach her feet and she had no intention of asking Rachel for help.

She did not believe Rachel, nor could she dismiss her words as a lie. Not until she saw for herself that Matthew was tucked away in the nursery, where he belonged.

She lumbered for the door, but Rachel blocked the exit with her back against the wood, a lurid smile upon her lips, her muff pushed up her arm so it rested between elbow and wrist, and in her hand, aimed at Leah's midsection, was a pistol.

Chapter Thirty-Three

"I am sorry I upset your wife." Pierce hitched his hip on a table covered with books and maps. "I have been more than half-mad since I received your missive. Truly, I am sorry."

Richard stalked to the liquor cabinet and sorted through the bottles of brandy and claret until he found the whisky, hidden at the back. He would have to pack it all away before Geoffrey arrived, but for now, he was grateful to have it.

This situation was distressing for all involved, and he could see no easy way out. He shoved a glass into Pierce's hand. "Upset her again, and I vow, I will kill you."

Pierce slammed his glass on the table. Amber liquid sloshed over the rim and dripped onto the rug. "I said I was sorry, but how would you feel? To find out you have a son you never knew existed? And the woman you thought had betrayed you, never did? And now she is dead? I feel as if I've been horse kicked in the gut. I cannot breathe. I cannot eat."

Richard swallowed his whisky, the languid heat spreading through his veins nothing to the temper he held under rigid control. "I know only too well how you feel, as I have been there myself, and that is the *only* reason you are still breathing at this moment."

"Good God, I forgot." Pierce yanked his hands through his

hair. His eyes were hollowed by shadows, his cheeks sunken crevices framed by his hard, jutting jaw. "Everything seems to have slipped from my mind except the fact that I have a son and Catherine never stopped loving me . . ."

Richard stalked to the windows, his heart aching for Leah, for Pierce, for the child, and for all the suffering still to come. "I am happy for you, Pierce, but my wife raised valid issues which you need to address."

"Such as?"

"Your betrothed, for one. Lady Julia might be beautiful, but she is also an ice princess. I cannot see her welcoming your bastard into her home. And do not try to fob me off with platitudes about how no one will care because he is just a child. Julia is from a rich and powerful family who will not look kindly upon the situation. Not to mention that the child will offer visual evidence of the woman you once loved. The woman you love still, even though she is in the grave."

Pierce laughed bitterly. "Why should that matter to Julia? She cares naught for me."

"She might not care for you, but neither will she want it flaunted in her face that you once loved another, even if that other woman is dead." Pierce looked about to argue, but Richard cut him off. "You know as well as I, appearances—and discretion—must be maintained above all things. Bringing your bastard home to your wife is hardly discreet."

"I said I will explain," Pierce snarled, grabbing his whisky, slugging it down in one swallow. He swiped his hand across his lips. "She will understand. Even if she doesn't, the contracts are signed. It is too late for either of us to cry off."

"I know that," Richard said gently. "But will she blame the child? That is the question you need to consider. And what of your drinking? I never thought you would mend your ways for a wife, but if you think to raise a child—"

Pierce let out a growl, a low, animal sound of frustration. "I told you I mean to change. Why are you plaguing me?"

"But how do you know you will you succeed?" Richard said with brutal honesty, pushing from his chair. He paced to the windows. "Look at Geoffrey. The foolish lad nearly did himself in. As did I, before Eric died. I shudder to think what would have happened had Alison been in my care at that time."

"What are you saying?"

No matter how they proceeded from here, someone would get hurt. Richard sighed. "Until you gain control over your life and have settled matters with Julia, I believe the child should remain here with us."

"I do not know what to do," Pierce groaned. He rubbed his hands over his face, then looked at Richard through eyes as empty and desolate as the windswept moors. "At least let me see him, Richard. I don't even know what he looks like."

Leah clutched her cloak against her neck as she trudged along the twisting garden path. Rachel followed a few paces behind. Whenever Leah paused for breath, Rachel pushed the pistol's sharp point into her back to urge her along.

They passed beneath a stone arch covered with honeysuckle, which would bloom in the spring but stood now stark and bare beneath the winter sky. The heavy drizzle soaked through her hood and drenched her hair. Her skin grew numb as the wind slid up the gaping fabric at her wrists and shivered over her damp skin. If only her thoughts would grow as numb, but she could not let fear control her mind or she would have no hope of escape.

She leaned her hands against her knees and dragged in a heaving breath. "Rachel, I need to rest."

"Keep moving." Her voice was a soft purr, but the metal pressed against Leah's spine was hard.

The ease with which Rachel had abducted her from the house astounded Leah. As if they were two friends heading for an afternoon stroll through the gardens, Rachel had looped her arm through Leah's, pressed her muff, with pistol hidden inside, up against Leah's belly, and led her through the corridors.

Of course, no one had ever suspected Rachel was dangerous. Not even Leah. She had hoped to alert someone to her distress, but they passed no one. The servants were all busy about their duties in the service areas, the children with their nannies in the nursery, and Richard and Pierce secluded in the library on the far side of the house. With the pistol shoved up close to her babe, Leah had not dared to fight for control of the weapon.

She skidded over a patch of wet moss, her arms flailing as she fought to keep her balance. Every step brought them closer to the roaring crash of waves against sheer black rocks, the taste of salt, tangy and putrid in her mouth. She stopped and turned to face Rachel. She would be damned if she allowed Rachel to toss her over the cliffs.

"What did she say?"

"She was not in her rooms." Richard rubbed his hand over the knot at the base of his neck. Nor was she in the nursery with the children. He told himself there was no need to panic, but as he glanced at Pierce's expectant face, a shiver of apprehension brought sweat to his back. She was extremely upset, their child due at any moment, and now she appeared to be missing.

He strode to the entry hall, his footfalls matching the rapid beat of his heart. It was foolish, he told himself. There was no reason to fear. It was a large house, with any number of rooms, and she always had some project or other under way. Taking inventories. Refurbishing the upholstery.

If he didn't find her in one of the drawing rooms, he would assemble the servants and search the house. Then she would turn up, dusty from a foray into the attics, or some such place, and he would feel foolish. But at least he would know she was safe.

He found Harris in the entry hall, instructing a newly hired footman in his duties. "Have you seen the duchess?"

"Not since luncheon, Your Grace." Harris gave a slight lift of his brows, a silent query for further instructions.

A petite maid wearing a cap and dusting the foyer scurried over to him. She gave a quick cursty. "Beggin' your pardon, sir, but I saw Her Grace."

"Where did you see her?" His voice, laced with panic, came out louder and harsher than he'd intended.

"I was dusting in the gallery. I saw Her Grace and the dowager duchess leave the house by the garden door. They were moving fast, sir, like they were in a hurry."

Leah and Rachel? In the gardens? In the rain?

"Harris, fetch my coat."

"And mine, also," Pierce said.

"When did you see them?" Richard asked the maid.

"It must be nigh onto an hour ago, sir."

"Thank you. That will be all."

The maid bobbed another curtsy, then returned to her dusting. Harris brought their greatcoats, and within minutes the two men were in the gardens following the trail of footprints over the mud. The tracks led across the lawn and up the hill.

"I do not like this," Pierce said, pulling the brim of his hat to block the rain from his eyes. "Why would they take a stroll through the park, and in the rain, to boot? I honestly cannot see Rachel exposing her cheeks to the wind."

Richard shook his head while he scanned the tracks ahead of him. "There is nothing much in this direction except for—"

The cliffs. He took off at a run, shouting over his shoulder, "Get help."

A heartbeat later, he heard the faint, but unmistakable sound of a pistol retort carrying on the wind.

* * *

The bullet slammed into the ground mere inches from Leah's feet and made her legs feel like twin puddles of melted snow.

"This is an amazing weapon," Rachel purred, stroking the pistol. "It has six revolving barrels. That means six shots, Leah, and there are still five left. So I suggest you start moving before I shoot you where you stand."

"What difference does it make?" Leah said, her low voice lost in the wind. "You will kill me either way."

She had yet to start breathing again. Her heart was beating so swiftly, she thought surely she would collapse at any moment.

For the sake of her babe, she could not give up.

"Yes," Rachel agreed cheerfully. "But I would prefer not to shoot you. I have other plans for your death. And, of course, there is always the slim chance that you might escape." She jabbed the gun at Leah's belly. "Now do as I say."

Leah stumbled along the well-worn path. Mercifully, the rain had stopped, but the damage was done. Her clothing was soaked through to her skin. The wind was so frigid, even her bones felt frozen. But a new, greater fear was tormenting Leah.

The dull ache that had plagued her back for the past two weeks had grown stronger, more intense, and now spread to encompass her lower abdomen. A few moments ago, a gush of liquid had poured down her thighs, followed by a sticky substance Leah greatly feared might be blood.

Every few minutes, a vicious cramp seized the muscles in her belly and unbearable fire shot through her back, as if an invisible hand had fingers squeezed around her spine.

They walked on another hour, until the path became too steep and treacherous for Leah to maneuver. The bitter wind whipped the waves into a swirling frenzy and knocked Leah to her knees.

She crawled to a sheltered crevice dipping between two higher peaks, where the wind was less brutal. Using the solid surface for balance, she dragged herself to her feet.

A quick glance told her the tide was high. The waves crashing into the rocks below sprayed her face with brackish water. The nauseating stench of rotting fish clung to the rocks beneath her hands, the uneven surface littered with seashells and lichen. Dizziness made her consciousness swirl as wildly as the wind. Her stomach heaved. *Do not look down. Do not panic!*

"Richard must be searching for us by now," she shouted at Rachel. "You realize that, do you not? Even if you manage to kill me, Richard will discover the truth."

"You think he loves you," Rachel said in a bored, even voice, as if she were offering Leah tea. "But he does not. You are nothing but his whore, his slut. He has used you the way a dog ruts with a bitch in heat. The way a stallion mounts a mare. Did you honestly think I would let you have him? Did you think I would close my eyes and look away while you spread your thighs for the man I love . . ."

As Rachel ranted into the wind, Leah scanned the path ahead.

She could see the engine house from an abandoned tin mine hovering on the edge of the cliff. She could attempt to run, but her great bulk and the slippery stones would make a fast flight impossible. Or she could charge Rachel, wrestle her for the gun, but then they would both most likely tumble over the edge into the waves below. Neither option had much hope of success, but she could not stand there and wait to die.

Seizing the weapon seemed her best chance. She took a step toward Rachel as Rachel spewed her vile words. The wind whipped her hair across her cheeks, stung her eyes, but she kept moving.

Rachel supported the pistol with both hands. "I know you won't believe this, but I truly did not want to kill you. I simply wanted you to go away."

"I can do that." Leah held up her hands. "If you put the gun down, I will leave and you will never see me again."

"No! It is too late for that."

"Please, Rachel. Think of my babe. You are a mother. You know how precious a child's life is. How can you hurt my baby?"

Rachel's wild laughter carried on the breeze. "And that is the point that drove us here, is it not? Richard would never let you leave. Not now. Not with his seed growing in your belly. So you see? I have no choice. You must die."

Rachel's hands were starting to shake. The gun was too heavy and her fingers too cold. She had to end this now, then return to the house before anyone found them missing.

The treacherous path, littered with lichen and ice, slowed her steps as she stalked toward Leah. Crouched amid the rocks, Leah's gold hair streamed out behind her, carried by the wind. Her wide green eyes glared back at Rachel with a hint of defiance amidst the fear. Just looking at her made Rachel itch to put a ball through her heart, but she could not.

It had to appear an accident, or all hope was lost.

Everyone would bemoan her death, Rachel most of all.

What was she doing out on the cliffs, they would say, and with her belly so far gone with child? Foolish, stupid woman. To walk the paths in the midst of a storm.

With no evidence to point toward murder, no one would ever suspect. And Richard, in his grief, poor man, would turn to Rachel for comfort. She laughed aloud at her flawless plan.

But first, she had to push the foolish woman over the edge.

"Put the gun down, Rachel."

She spun around, her heart hammering, her blood rushing

through her ears. She squinted against the wind, but she saw nothing beyond the rocks. Then Richard appeared as if conjured up by the swirling mist, wrapped in a great coat from shoulder to shin, his hair tossed about by the wind, his features as harsh and jagged as the wild cliffs behind him. He appeared a great brooding beast of the night, a devil-dark man with magical hands that stirred a feral hunger within her heart.

"You must put the gun down," he said.

She kept the gun trained on Leah. Impotent fury shook her legs. She was trapped, discovered, but she would not suffer alone.

The deafening wind had masked the crunching pebbles and seashells beneath his boots as Richard crept forward, his knees trembling, his back soaked with sweat mixed with rain.

He surveyed the scene with quick efficiency, his mind closed to the panic threatening to overtake him. Leah hovered dangerously close to the edge of the cliffs while Rachel moved toward her, gun teetering wildly in her hand, her shrill keening echoing off the rocks.

In the dim light, Richard could make out the weapon, a revolver known as a pepperbox because its cylindrical cluster of barrels resembled the top of a pepper pot. The guns were heavy and awkward and extremely unreliable. More often than not, when one cartridge fired, the others would explode. He had bought it to add to his firearms collection. Never could he have imagined he would see it armed and aimed at his wife.

Rachel's frenzied gaze darted from Richard to Leah as if she couldn't decide whom to attack first.

Then she fixed Richard with a wild stare. "This is all your fault. You should never have married her."

"I know," Richard said, a savage rage unleashing the bloodlust, curling his hands, tensing his legs as he prepared to pounce. But he kept his voice calm, steady, as he crept forward. "You are right. I see that now. But you must put down the gun."

"I love you," she said. "I have always loved you, but everyone tried to separate us. My parents. Eric. Now her."

He had to keep her talking, keep her attention centered on him and away from Leah. "I understand, Rachel. You love me. You have always loved me. Let us go home. It is cold and drafty up here. And Alison needs you. I need you."

He nearly choked on the words. A quick glance at Leah assured him she was safe, at least for the moment.

Sheltered between two crags, she looked so small, so fragile, with her drenched cloak clinging to her belly, her hands clutching her throat. Her wide, frightened eyes gleamed silver in the stormy light. Her terror for his safety was etched into the grim lines around her lips.

Good God, a greater fear than he had ever known threatened to unman him, until he didn't know if it was rain or tears dripping down his cheeks. He would not let her die.

He would not lose Leah or their babe.

"I never wanted to marry Eric," Rachel said, her arm shaking from the strain of supporting the gun. "I did it for you. So you could have everything."

The implication of her words froze the blood in his veins, as surely as if it had turned to ice. "What are you saying?"

Rachel started to weep, a loud wailing that rivaled the wind, then she laughed through her tears. "I had to do it. You would not come back to me any other way. And now this."

"I do not understand what you are saying." Richard edged toward her, his eyes holding her gaze. "Eric died of an accident. A fall from his horse."

She merely laughed. "This would have appeared an accident, too. Out for an afternoon stroll, she lost her way in the mist and tumbled over the edge. But now there is no use. No hope."

Her gaze darted around the cliffs, the wild eyes of an animal run to ground, hopelessly trapped, desperate to escape.

A fantastical moment passed in which Richard felt as if he were a soul disembodied, floating between time and space, the individual seconds framed within the blink of his eyes. He saw Rachel raise the gun, point it at Leah. Saw the tendons of her hand tighten as her finger squeezed the trigger. He saw himself lunge, his arms stretching, reaching, but even that seemed to happen too slowly, as if the wind were pushing him back.

Then, as if realizing her danger, she spun around until the gun aimed at him. Braced for the impact, he gave silent thanks to a God who had so often deserted him.

Then a flash of movement, a swift silvery light cutting through the darkness, the reflection of moonlight on her hair, and he knew it was Leah, rushing forward, hands lifted.

"No," he screamed. He wanted to die, to take the bullet, to save her life. Instead, she shoved her hands into Rachel's back, pushing as they both plunged toward the edge of the cliff.

He saw a flash of light, blinding in his misery, as the gun discharged, then acrid, dark smoke suspended on the wind and the ground dissolving beneath Leah's feet.

Chapter Thirty-Four

Richard dove for the ledge.

He grabbed Leah by the waist. The momentum of her forward motion nearly tumbled them both over the edge, but he shoved the heels of his boots against the rocks, locked his knees, and leaned backward, pulling toward solid ground. He clung to her, his muscles trembling, arms aching, fingers frozen from the rain. The wind slammed into his back and still he clutched her to him until the bones in his back and legs ached from the exertion.

The furious breakers, whipped up by the storm, smashed into the cliffs below, shooting water high in the air. The salt stung his cheeks, and the frigid water burned like fire against his skin. Time crawled by, punctuated by the mad throbbing of his pulse. It seemed an eternity that they hovered on the edge. In reality, mere seconds passed before he fell backwards onto the ground, pulling Leah down atop him.

He rolled her over, knelt above her. She was unconscious, her face as white as a new-fallen snow and just as cold against the lips he pressed to her cheek. He searched her neck for a pulse. It was thin, thready, but it was there.

The rock beneath her was stained with blood but he refused

to contemplate the source. His mind centered on only one purpose. Get her safe. Get her home.

Someone was shouting, calling his name, but he felt disoriented, his thoughts frantic, swirling like the wind, the never-ending litany driving him mad—get her home, get her safe.

He pulled her into his arms and ran up the path, his muscles burning with every step he took.

Then Pierce was beside him. "You must be exhausted. Let me carry her for you."

Richard shook his head. He could not speak past the panic clenching his throat. Nor could he release her.

Further ahead, he saw footmen and grooms and, thank the Good Lord, horses. He forced his legs to keep moving, his blood to keep pumping, his heart not to lose hope.

"Help me get her on the horse," he shouted into the wind. "Send for the doctor. Meet me at the lodge. It is closer."

"And Rachel?" Pierce said.

"She went over the edge. No doubt she is dead, but have the men search for her anyway."

When they reached the horses, Richard shifted Leah into Pierce's outstretched arms just long enough to climb onto his mount. Then he gathered her against his chest and kicked the horse into motion, his mind devoid of all thought, save the haunting refrain, *Please don't die, please don't die, please don't die.*

"She has a few minor cuts and scratches on her hands, Your Grace, but our greatest threat to her life is the bleeding."

Richard clutched her hand to his chest. Her skin had yet to warm, though he had piled woolen blankets atop her. She never moved, never made a sound as the doctor poked and prodded, and all the while her blood streamed from her body.

"Can you not make it stop?" Richard said. His stomach lurched. The room tipped precariously onto its side.

The doctor, his forehead covered in sweat, ran his fingers over her wrist, feeling for a pulse. "I shall do everything within my power, but both the mother and child are in danger. Unless she is delivered, and soon, neither of them stands much of a chance. With your permission, I should like to give her a decoction to hasten the birth along."

"Do anything you must to save my wife." Her face was so pale, her breathing so shallow, he could not even hear it moving in and out of her lungs. His throat swelled, his eyes burned.

She lay as still as death, even as her body struggled to be free of their child. How could she survive such pain?

How would he live without her?

He closed his mind to the thought.

She would not die. He would not allow it.

Four hours later, their son came screaming into the world.

Richard did not even see him. All he saw was the river of red that gushed from her body along with the child.

"Do something!" he cried. "Jesus Christ, do something . . ."

The room swirled around him, as if he were back on the cliff, teetering on the edge, his wife clutched in his arms, only this time, he lost her. The air in the room seemed inordinately cold, though a fire poured heat from the grate.

He fell to his knees, grabbed her hand, crushed her cold, lifeless fingertips against his lips. Eyes clenched against the vision of her life's blood draining from her body, he stroked her hair from her brow.

The doctor blended a mixture of shepherd's purse and yarrow and forced it down her throat. "To clot the blood," he said.

He repeated the process with white willow bark dissolved in wine, then he bathed her privy parts with a decoction of feverfew. "To fight infection," he said.

So much blood, Richard thought. How could she live?

But as long as her heart continued to beat and she drew

breath, he would not lose hope. He pressed her hand to his lips.

In a never-ending litany, he uttered every prayer he had ever known, hoping, just this once, God might listen.

In the morning, the fever set in.

Leah moaned. "Richard, forgive me . . ."

Her words, like a whiplash, flayed his body, flayed his soul. "My love, there is nothing to forgive."

Never had Richard felt so helpless. All he could do was bathe her brow, hold her hand, and listen to the delirious ramblings of her fevered mind. She called for her sister, her aunt, her nephew. She called for Alison and Geoffrey. She pleaded with Rachel to spare her child's life.

But most of all, she cried for Richard. Over and over, she called his name, begged his forgiveness for killing their child.

Richard thought he would perish beneath the torture of her sweet voice so wracked with anguish and despair. How could she think he would ever blame her for anything?

It was himself he cursed and hated and blamed. If not for him and his sordid past, she would never have been in danger.

He should have protected her, but no, she had protected him.

It was his life she had saved out on the bluff. He would gladly give up his life so that she could live.

The doctor came up behind Richard. He hesitated a moment, then laid a hand on his shoulder.

"I fear there is nothing more I can do, Your Grace." His voice faltered. He cleared his throat. "The bleeding has slowed to a trickle. But she is very weak. Now, it is a matter of hoping and praying and her will to survive."

Richard rubbed his cheek against her hand. He heard the doctor's words, but they had no meaning. "I should like to be alone with my wife."

The doctor patted his shoulder. "I will be outside the door if you need me."

There was nothing left to be done but hope and pray. Richard's mind understood that, but his heart refused to listen.

He leaned over the bed and growled in her ear. "You will not die. Do you hear me? I will not allow it. I need you—" He could not stop his tears rolling down his cheeks. He did not even try. "I need you, Leah. Everyone needs you. Alison. Matthew. Geoffrey. Our little boy. You haven't even seen our little boy. I do not even know what you want to name him. We never decided. You must come back to him, to me. We cannot be a family without you."

He was sobbing now, his back heaving with the force of his grief. "Leah, my love. Please, open your eyes. I cannot face life without you. So you must come back to me. Without you, there is no me . . ."

She heard Richard's voice, choked with agony, wracked by hopeless despair, calling her through the darkness, dragging her back to the pain. Sobbing. Begging. Pleading.

Don't leave me. Don't go.

But she was tired. So very tired. She wanted to sleep.

He would not allow it. Every time she drifted away, he would squeeze her hand, bathe her brow, whisper words that she didn't understand, until finally she pulled open her eyes.

Her vision blurred. The room swirled about her head. He sat beside her, his cheek pressed against the palm of her hand, his shoulders shaking with his heart-wrenching tears.

"Richard," she said. Her voice dragging over her dry, aching throat was so low, he did not appear to hear her, but she had not the strength to try again. She was so cold, deep inside, she started to shake, yet her skin felt damp, sticky with sweat.

She squeezed his hand, seeking his warmth, seeking his

comfort. His shoulders tensed, his head swung up, his dark eyes met hers through his tears. His brows rose, his mouth inched open, a faint expression of uncertainty, as if he were lost in a dream, or perhaps she was dreaming, she was so confused. He gave a sigh, from deep within his chest, kissed the back of her hand.

"I love you," he whispered again and again, his voice trembling over her knuckles. His scent of jasmine and amber filled her with peace, eased her anxiety.

Then memories rushed through her mind.

Bright flashes of light. Rachel. The cliffs.

She moved the palm of her hand over her stomach.

It was empty and flat, and she moaned. Pain, intense and blinding, speared her back, spread down her legs. Her throat closed. He covered her hand with his, but she turned her eyes to the wall. Her heart shredding, her soul dying.

She had killed their child with her foolishness. She had murdered him out on the bluff as surely as if she had driven a stake through his heart.

How would she survive this pain?

He stroked her cheek with his fingertips. "Wouldn't you like to meet your son? He is most anxious to meet you."

Her lungs hurt. She couldn't drag in enough air. "We have a son? He is alive?"

Richard smiled, his devil-may-care grin that did not hide the trembling of his lips. "Yes, ma'am. Alive and screaming. A red, wrinkled, squalling bundle of baby boy. Would you like to see him?" He did not wait for a response. He ran from the room.

A heartbeat later, he sat beside her on the bed, a wrapped, wriggling bundle cradled in his arms. He moved his fingers to the swaddling blankets, peeled the edges away to reveal her beautiful baby boy. He was chubby and pink and screaming to wake the dead. Tears dripped from her cheeks onto her neck.

"Our son," she whispered, amazed by the thick tuft of

black hair covering his head. With a shaking hand, she traced the contours of his face, his arms, his hands. She marveled at his tiny toes, his miniature fingernails, his long, dark eyelashes. "He is perfect."

Richard gently placed the babe belly-down across her chest.

"Of course. Given who his mother is, I would expect nothing less." The gleam of moisture in his eyes belied the teasing tone of his voice. He leaned back, a mischievous twinkle in his eyes. "There is only one thing wrong with him, madam. He doesn't have a name."

"Eric," she said quietly, brushing her fingers over his downy soft hair. "I should like to name him Eric. If it would please you."

She looked up at him, then, and Richard thought he would drown in the clear depths of her eyes, deep green eyes dusted with amber that entranced him still, as they had from the first moment they met. And he had almost lost her.

"Nothing would please me more," he said, his voice breaking over the words. "But now you should rest." He cradled his wife and his son in his arms until they slept.

Chapter Thirty-Five

Leah sat on a bench in the gardens with her aunt by her side and her three-month-old son resting peacefully across her lap. Beyond the sloping lawns, golden streaks of gorse stretched out along the cliffs, a startling contrast to the endless blue sky.

"You must be tired of holding him, dear. Why don't you let me take him for you?"

Leah grinned as she gently shifted Eric into her aunt's out-stretched arms. "Do be careful of his head."

"Not to worry, dear. I know how precious he is." Emma kissed the baby's brow. A faint sigh escaped her lips.

She wiped her cheek against the sleeve of her dress, a soft cotton of forest green that made her appear so young, so pretty, or perhaps it was her love for the man she had married. "I am so sorry I was not here when you needed me."

Leah slipped her hand through the crook of her aunt's arm. She knew her aunt blamed herself for all Leah had suffered at Rachel's hands, as if Emma would have been able to stop her. "Please, do not."

"No, I must. I love you as if you were my own daughter. If only I had known you were in danger."

"How could you have known?"

Her aunt gave a sad shake of her head. Wisps of gray hair fluttered about her face. Her lips trembled.

"Truly, Emma, I love you. You are more than a mother to me. You are my dearest friend." Leah blew out her breath to relieve the ache growing in her throat. "Look at us. Two watering pots on such a fine day."

Emma brushed her hand over her eyes. "I know you are right, dear, but whenever I think of the danger you were in, I feel faint. And Matthew—who would have ever thought we would have Catherine's child here with us. If only our dear Catherine . . ." She crushed her shaking fist to her lips.

"I know," Leah said, wrapping her arm around her aunt's shoulder. Her gaze drifted to the children, hiding amongst the azaleas, their childish laughter carrying on the breeze as they waited for their fathers to seek them out.

Matthew darted from behind the hedges, a swift blur amidst the pink blooms, only to be scooped up by Pierce. Joyous shrieks escaped the boy as Pierce swung him around, hands clutched beneath his shoulders. Leah turned her gaze to the distant ocean. The sun glinting off the water stung her eyes.

"Matthew seems happy here," Emma said, "and Alison fairly dotes on him. She is such a lovely child. Has it been very hard for her?"

Alison had snuck up on Pierce and shoved her shoulders into his legs to help Matthew escape. The two children joined hands as they ran toward the fountains, their shrieks frightening the sparrows and starlings from the shrubbery.

"She is sad, of course," Leah said, a chill sweeping down her arms. She tried never to think of that night on the bluff, when Rachel had fallen, her body crushed on the rocks. "Rachel was not much of a mother, but Alison loved her."

"She is lucky to have you and the duke to care for her, not to mention this big brute. I vow he has gained five pounds just today."

Leah smoothed her knuckles over her son's silky cheek.

His mouth twitched into a smile before parting in a soft exhalation. Whenever she thought of how close she came to losing him, she shuddered, as if a violent wind whipped over her skin. Never could she have imagined the depth of love she would feel for this child. "He looks so much like his father."

"Do you think so? I should think he looks more like you."

Leah laughed. "With that black hair and those dark eyes?"

"Well, he is rather handsome, is he not?"

"Sinfully so," Leah said, thinking of his father with his wicked smile and his dark, good looks. His brooding eyes and his hard chiseled cheeks, his slanted jaw and his lips and his tongue and his hands, his wicked, wicked hands that knew just where to touch her . . . Good Lord, a burning flush spread over her cheeks.

Her gaze sought him out. He and Pierce were huddled together, their arms wrapped around the children, as if a serious conversation, or a conspiracy, were under way.

He looked up and caught her staring. From this distance she could not make out his expression, but she imagined his eyes went dark and sultry, and his gaze made a leisurely scan of her face, leaving her aching and tingling, as if he'd swept his fingers over her skin.

She could see his teeth gleaming in the sunlight, and she knew he was smiling, as if he had read her mind.

"Leah, your cheeks are crimson. Do you feel feverish?"

"Not at all," she said, unable to meet her aunt's too-knowing gaze.

"Well, you look tired, dear. Why don't you lie down?"

Leah smiled reassuringly. "Honestly, I feel fine."

"I insist. Go. Get some rest. There is no shame in admitting you're tired."

Leah narrowed her eyes on her aunt's face. "If I did not know you better, I would think you were trying to be rid of me."

"Nonsense! I am worried for your health. We all are. Especially that husband of yours. He bid me to make certain you rest today. He thinks you are doing far too much."

Leah started to protest. She was weary of being treated as if she were as fragile as old bones, easily broken. The wounded look on her aunt's face shamed her. "You are right," she conceded. "I think I shall lie down for an hour or two."

"And so you should," Emma said, her lips quirking into an I-don't-believe-you-for-a-moment grin. "Now, run along, dear. And do not worry about this precious angel. I will give him to his nurse when he awakens."

As she walked to her chambers, a heavy weight settled on Leah's chest. Not that she was unhappy. She wasn't. She thanked God every day for sparing her life and that of her child's, but she had a difficult decision to make.

Unable to sleep, she dragged her volume of Lord Byron's poetry from her dressing table. Stretched out on the window seat, she opened the book to her favorite verse, but the words blurred on the page. She leaned her cheek against the window, the glass cool and soothing against her heated cheek.

Her door opened. Richard strode into the room, all tousled black hair and smoldering eyes.

She studied her hands to shield her suddenly stinging eyes.

"Leah?" He sat beside her, pulled her into his arms, the beat of his heart strong and steady beneath her ear. "What is it? What is troubling you?"

She pushed herself out of his arms, rose and crossed to the hearth. She did not want her need for this man to distract her. "You were right about Pierce," she said, her voice scraping her throat like a wave dragging over the sand. "He is a fine man."

"I have always thought so." Richard walked up behind her, so close she could feel the heat of his thighs against the back of her legs. "Leah, please, share your worries with me."

She turned to face him. She wanted to lean against his chest, to let him take away the pain, but she forced herself to stand tall. "He has managed to piece his life together . . . I begin to see the man Catherine loved, and I think him a wonderful father to her son." She rushed through her words before she could change her mind. "I think Matthew belongs with him now."

He pulled her into his arms, cradled her cheek against his chest. She slid her hands around his neck, clung to him desperately as she accepted the truth of her words.

From the moment Pierce had discovered he had a son, he had practically lived with them. His love for the boy was obvious, as was his determination to rebuild his life. He had struggled to conquer his obsession with the drink, much the same as Geoffrey had, and he had succeeded. While he had a long way to go until all of his wounds were healed, he had made a steady start. Matthew belonged with his father. It was the right thing to do.

"Catherine would have wanted it that way," she said, and as soon as the words left her lips, Leah knew it was true.

"You are so wonderful," Richard murmured, kissing away her tears, running his lips over her jaw, then down the curve of her neck.

His scent of jasmine and amber seduced her senses, lit an unbearable yearning, a desperate love that left her shaking with need. She slid her fingers through his hair. A gentle tug brought his lips a mere whisper away but he would not close the distance between them. She pushed up on her toes, traced the seam of his lips with her tongue, licking and tasting until he finally opened his mouth. With a savage growl, he clung to her, hot hands roaming her back, down over her hips, cupping her bottom, until she fairly purred against his lips.

She smiled as he scooped her into his arms, his mouth clinging fiercely, furiously, his tongue delving inside.

When he strode past the bed and out her chamber door, Leah gasped. "What are you doing? Put me down."

He merely laughed as he continued down the stairs, past a line of giggling maids. His boot heels rapped on the hardwood floor with each determined step he took. "Do you know what day this is?"

Leah started to shake her head, then she smiled. "Our anniversary."

"Yes. A year ago today, we were wed." He strode down the steps and out the doors, his boot heels crunching the seashells on the gravel drive. "Cloaked in secrecy and shame."

Leah closed her eyes. She did not want to be reminded of the circumstances that had brought them together, her father's perfidy, the pain of Richard's past. He followed a narrow path past the conservatory and did not stop until he reached the stone chapel, built by some long-ago Wexton. Beneath the sun, the slate roof shimmered with a yellow glaze of lichen and moss.

His eyes were as dark as the midnight sky and just as mysterious as he opened the chapel door. Alison stood just inside the entry. Matthew fidgeted by her side.

Both children were dressed in formal attire as if they were on their way to an evening soirée. Garlands strung with hothouse roses hung from the pews.

Leah's senses scattered as she scanned the expectant faces filling the benches. Emma and Geoffrey and Lady Cunningham, Mrs. Bristoll and Tommy, and all the children of the foundling home.

Even Alexander was there. And the vicar?

She turned to Richard. "I do not understand."

He bent on his knee before her, clasped her hand against his lips. The love shining in his eyes burned so brightly, she thought surely she could see into the deepest part of his soul.

"Leah, I love you and I am not ashamed to say it. I love you, and I want to marry you, to give you myself and a lifetime of happiness."

She raised a shaking hand, wiped away the moisture gathering in her eyes. Her lips quivered as she stared at him in helpless wonder.

He smiled tenderly, his own eyes bright with unshed tears. "Leah . . . will you marry me? Will you promise me forever, here, now, before God and our friends?"

"Silly man," she said, smiling through her tears. She wrapped her arms around his neck and kissed him.

They were kissing still when he swung her into his arms and carried her down the aisle.